EVERYTHING
IN ALL THE
WRONG ORDER:
THE BEST OF CHAZ BRENCHLEY

EVERYTHING IN ALL THE WRONG ORDER:

THE BEST OF CHAZ BRENCHLEY

Subterranean Press 2021

First Edition

ISBN
978-1-64524-011-2

Subterranean Press
PO Box 190106
Burton, MI 48519

subterraneanpress.com

Manufactured in the United States of America

This book is for Karen.
Most of these stories I wrote before I knew her.
None of them would make any sense without her.

TABLE OF CONTENTS

INTRODUCTION

BY ELIZABETH BEAR

THE FIRST TIME I MET CHAZ Brenchley, I was at the only Eastercon I've ever managed to attend, in Glasgow, Scotland, sick as a dog from unfamiliar UK concrud microbes (they breed 'em mean on those islands), only managing to stay fed because Charlie Stross was sliding bacon butties under my nose at regular intervals. I was the comic relief on a charades panel, because it turns out that in the UK, charades has *rules*. And everybody knows them.

Chaz was the soul of kindness and guidance. He took me under his rather elongated wing (Chaz is a tall person) and taught me the rules in whispers.

Charades is a pretty good game for someone who has utterly lost their voice, it turns out. Until you're the person who is supposed to be shouting guesses.

Oh well; I lived.

The story I've just related may seem unrelated to the content of a short story collection, but I think that it illuminates elements of Chaz's personality that shine through in his work.

These stories are dense, chewy, complicated, nuanced, and full of grief. But they're also kind.

They're not kind in the expected way. They aren't the sort of kind that softens the edges of hard experience, flawed protagonists, ugly realities, self-destructive choices. They're kind because they *don't* flinch from these things, or from those consequences—but they always stand ready to forgive. They are surgical in their niceness—nice in the sense of a distinction, as well as in the sense of a kindness.

These are, by and large, stories about horror. About surviving liminal experiences. About the pain of being left behind when others go on where we cannot follow. They are about the horror of uncertainty, of not being able to help those we love. Or of living with the consequences of our own failures and cruelties, or our failure to intercede in the cruelty of someone else.

You may wish to take these stories slowly, a few at a time. They're mostly quite short, but they're dense, full of emotion and lyricism, rich with detail. Nobody bends a sentence like Chaz, and when you pause to look them over, you will likely find a few that take your breath away. I know I did.

These stories are replete with a quiet, meditative kind of heroism—the heroism of endurance rather than violent action. The strength to do what needs to be done—sit by the dying, pursue a loved one bent on self-destruction, let go of what is lost—or to face up to the failure to have done so and do better next time.

You won't find a lot of concrete answers here, a lot of capital-letters Good and Evil. You will find a lot of accommodation, a lot of people making the best of forced choices—exile, betrayal, impecuniousness. The prototypical Chaz Brenchley hero is skint, damaged, ostracized, and about to make a really wrenching decision.

You *will* find a lot of ghosts. You will find the community of the outsider. You will find a lot of farewells. You might find a little comfort for your own hard choices, ghosts, alienation, and goodbyes. You might, at least, find the sense of somebody who will sit with you in your grief.

That's not a small thing.

UNCANNY VALLEY

S O THIS IS HOW IT GOES. How it went. How it will have gone.
Something. Language is as slippery as meaning is as slippery as time; we
have nothing to hold on to but each other.

Will have.

It'll be a hard thing to look back on, when we must.

SO. You in the lead, me with my eyes fixed on your extraordinary cyclist's
calves, muscles like woven steel cables. You could suspend a bridge with those.

Not that you need them, hereabouts. Do cables slacken off, for lack of
traffic? Do bridges sag?

Probably not, but I worry even so. Of course I do.

Here's the only climb on this whole damn trail—and it's a ramp, not a
hill, doubling back on itself halfway, to lift us up over the freeway. Call it a
bridge, then, and call that ironic if you like.

There you go, released at last, rising in the saddle and pumping some wicked gear to test yourself, this brief chance you have. I follow more sedately, falling behind with every revolution, almost stalling out at the turn and needing to grab hold of the railing to keep myself vertical. I'd be embarrassed, but I know that you're not looking. You're way ahead, you've peaked.

I find you halfway over the bridge, you and your bike both just leaning on the rail, chilling while you wait. Watching the commute, almost static below, four lanes in both directions.

"I'm sorry," I say. Gasp, rather. It's a very new thing, this bike. My legs and lungs are burning, both.

"What? This is a ride, not a race. It's only fun if we do it together."

"Not that." You've been very good, honestly: sticking with me all the way, once you found a pace that I could stick to. I do stubbornness where you do grace; between them, I think they'll see us through. "I'm sorry it's so dull here."

"I'm not bored," you say. Your hands don't shift, but your eyes reach out to touch me, up and down and all over. Your mouth quirks a deliberate innuendo.

"Really? Because I am. I don't mean the bike trail," which is frankly as much as I can manage, and who knew I could even manage that? Don't claim that you did; all you had was confidence. Not the same. "And I don't mean you, damn you," which ditto ditto. "It's this place, this endless fucking suburb, from the city down to San Jose. Endlessly flat and endlessly repetitive, not a thing to see that's worth the looking at. High-rise office blocks in rectangles of glass and concrete, apartment complexes all the colours of beige, fifty miles of bloody bungalows cheek by jowl and so determined to look different from their neighbours they have no idea how very much they look alike. And everything stitched together with freeways and expressways and highways and boulevards and Christ." You're laughing at me now, but that's only fuel to the fire; if it amuses you to see me rant, then I can cheerfully rant for ever. You're as new as the bike, and you leave me just as breathless. "And they call it a valley, but that's only because there are mountains over there and mountains over there," with a nod to each horizon, east and west. "In between it's not a sodding valley, it's a sodding alluvial plain. Which come the flood, please God, for we deserve it."

"No one gets their just deserts," you say, which just about covers God for you too. Whatever I've done in all my life, nothing in it, not all of it together amounts to earning you. "Don't be angry," you say. "Look at me."

And I can do that, I can do that and do that, and of course you're right, it's a panacea. It's a way to stop looking at the rest of it, everything, the desolation of mediocrity. What need I the black tents of my tribe, when I have the red pavilion of your heart?

SO there you have it. I'm a besotted romantic, apparently. But this is Silicon Valley, where cynicism comes with the territory and maps itself as opportunity.

The trail is pretty much all I have to offer you, least and best. It takes us to the Bay, which is some kind of horizon, something to look at. Boats and birds, a better class of traffic. Coming home, though, as we are—well, it doesn't actually bring us home. It spits us out a couple of miles short, so that we have that much of traffic lights and trucks, of bike lanes that appear at one junction and vanish the next, of Bay Area drivers whose God-given right it is to cut us off or blast their horns at us for following the rules or somehow neglect to see us altogether.

And yet we make it home intact, and home is my house, just one more bland bungalow in a street and a neighbourhood of just the same, with two-car parking and a front lawn and a back yard with a six-foot fence all around. And I really shouldn't complain, because after five years it's worth twice the mortgage and that number won't be going down; and of course I do complain, because where's the impact, where's the history, where's the ambition? Our town centre believes itself and declares itself historic because one of its buildings—*one*—is a hundred years old. Every plank and every joist replaced again and again, but none the less: a centenarian by virtue of occupation. That's what history means, right? It's still Grandfather's axe.

Bikes under shelter at the back because you insist on it; you first in the shower because you're quicker than I am, both in and out. I'm pulling the cork on a bottle of Cab as you emerge, still damp but only metaphorically steaming, black of hair and lean of form and brown by courtesy but only in the way that twilight is brown, meaning not really, not at all. If I were an artist I'd need green and purple on my palette, to come anywhere near the shadows that your skin addresses.

No artist I, but I can look and look at you.

You hold your hand out, empty, asking. *Drink, or fuck?* It's the eternal question, in the drear of a valley Sunday afternoon. Later there will be Netflix and curry in cardboard containers, and we'll sit like kids on the floor with our backs to the sofa and food between us, arguing amicably and spilling rice on the rug, killing another bottle before we go to bed. Or go back to bed, because there is always this gap to bridge, this pause in the day, this hesitation between here and there.

This question, that this day I answer with a gesture towards where two glasses stand on the coffee-table. Olives and salami from the farmers' market. What can you do but smile, and shrug a little, and go pull some clothes on while I shower in my turn?

When I come out there won't be an offering here for me, as I am here for you. No artisanal aperitif, no alcohol, no you. But I know this going in. If I make space for you, you'll vacate it.

I shower and dry and dress at the best speed that I can, too slow for you; and here's my empty house, as expected. As foretold.

Nil desperandum, and *say not the struggle naught availeth,* and *keep calm and carry on.* I walk through the kitchen, through the mud-room, out into the yard.

I always think I should make more use, better use of the yard, but I never do. You apparently don't stop to think, you're just here. In the middle of the lawn, on the bench appropriated from departing neighbours up the street, drinks and nibbles beside you on the table cobbled together from a couple of plastic crates and a vagrant plank, no interest whatever in the actual patio table with its appropriate chairs and extremely shady umbrella back over there on the actual patio.

So I join you on the bench, you pass my wine and offer an olive, we spit stones companionably into the firepit and the only shade we have is what little the cherry tree can cast across us, *en passant*.

"You haven't been here in cherry season," I say, because you know this, and it's always best to start from common ground. "You'll enjoy that, you can laugh at us. My friends and I, we like to go full Japanese, sit under the tree and drink tea while the blossoms fall. Wear kimonos, if they've got 'em. I don't, I don't do dressing up, but…"

"But your friends are all pretty as a picture. I know, you showed me photos."

"Did I? Right."

"A lot of photos, actually. And you were in none of them."

"Well, no. Behind the camera, and all that."

"Other people have cameras. Also, other people take selfies."

"Yeah. Those would be other people, right enough. I'm still me. And camera-shy. That's the *point* of all that fancy equipment, something to hide behind. Not to have to be in front of it."

You smile, and reach out to stroke my hair. It's a pact we have: you won't tell me that I'm beautiful, and I won't tell you that you're wrong. It may be the most pointless pact in human creation, because of course we both break it all the time, just not in words. Subtext is instinctive, seemingly.

"It must have been a sight at cherry time," you say, "when all of this was orchards." That's not an exaggeration. We actually live on Orchard Row; I could take you to Almond Avenue and Peach Street and half a dozen others, but this whole neighbourhood is called Cherry Gardens, and many of the yards host a survivor. I like to think they whisper to each other in the night, or send messages by the bees. Hell, I know they send messages by the bees. Pollen is pillow-talk for trees.

"I have photos of that too." I'm halfway to my feet before you can pull me down again.

"I know, you showed me the book. But they weren't in colour, and the trees weren't in blossom."

"We could fix that," I say idly, settling back against your side. "We could fix both of those. Software goes where film-stock never trod."

"Or of course we could just go down to the library and ask to see their archive, because they're bound to have pictures of cherry-blossom time. Just because they're not in your book doesn't mean they don't exist. There were Japanese here a hundred years ago, weren't there? Even if not, it's still the same effect. A whole orchard of blossom drifting on the wind, someone must have photographed it."

"Still won't be in colour, mind."

"There were still orchards here fifty years ago. Hell, there are still pocket-orchards even now. There are going to be colour pictures. Just because you're obsessed with olden times…"

"I'm not really. Really I'm not. You have to admit, though, the houses were better-looking a hundred years ago."

"And the people were better dressed."

I don't care about the people, or what they were wearing. "You're right, though," I say. "It wouldn't be hard to marry the colours from later pix to the structures of the early ones. And the costumes, yeah yeah. We could do a whole technicolor pictorial tour of the town as she used to be. When's the next big-number anniversary? I know we missed the centennial, but…"

By the time we decide that there are no significant numbers between a hundred and one-twenty-five, and that neither of us is willing to wait that long nor likely to be hereabouts in any case, the idea has morphed in any case, that way ideas do.

Is it you who says it first or is it me, and does it matter? I think both of our minds are already turning the same way. Of course they are. Two geeks in Silicon Valley, of course we'll come up with tech implementations, what-ever the idea.

"It's an app. Isn't it?"

"Of course it's a bloody app. Use the GPS for location—"

"—and the acccelerometer and magnetometer for orientation—"

"—right, and then hack the camera so they don't see what's there now—"

"—they see what was there a hundred years ago. Right."

"The library can't have images of everything."

"Doesn't matter. It'll have enough. Most of the downtown, all the distinctive buildings, plenty of representative housing, miles of interchangeable orchards. We can cheat it, write an engine that extrapolates to fill in the gaps. Period housing and trees in serried ranks, it'll be fine."

"Cherried ranks."

"Oh, despair and die. Can we call it that, 'Cherried Ranks'? Probably not. This is going to be great…"

IT was always going to be hard work. Two of us to share all the coding, all the research, all the scanning and manipulation. Two of us at first, that is. Who ever thinks to ask for help, with their own bright difficult demanding baby?

Friends find out, though, by intent or happenstance or late-night drunk confession. They offer time, skills, contacts: for the laugh, for the company, for the sense of community, for something to do. Or for a consideration.

"Not money, I'm not asking you to pay me. How about stock?"

"We don't have stock. We can't monetise this, for crying out loud: what d'you want, advertisements marching across the view? Logos printed on cherry petals? What?"

"There'll be money in it somewhere, brother. When it takes off. You can sell the code, at least; every small town in America will need this. Take my advice, see a lawyer, set up a corporate structure now. And give me stock."

"WHAT about the people, though?"

"What say?"

"Half these pix have people in them. More than half."

"We can shop 'em out." Little distant figures, mostly, studding the fields and warehouses, occupying the streets. Lending human scale to an otherwise bare and unconvincing view. They tend to be more prominent in the portraits of private houses—pride of ownership, I suppose; we all see ourselves as larger and more meaningful in our own space—but still, it's no hard task to edit them out. People are more transient even than buildings, it turns out, in the timescape of a town.

"We can, yes. But should we? The whole point is to show the place as it used to be. Which was occupied, purposeful, intended. Take the people out, we lose the point."

"Hunh. But if we leave them in"—or hell, their vehicles, their horses, the horseshit in the gutters, everything that really shouldn't be a fixture—"then the picture's obviously static, it looks the same every time they come down that street, it's just a photo rendered into a kind of fake 3-D and we lose any sense that it's a living landscape."

"Same if it's an empty landscape," you say. Winningly in every sense, I guess. "It's still the same every time, and now it's uninhabited. Which is actually freakier than just being frozen in time. Think ghost towns, the *Marie Celeste,* any office building after the workers go home…"

"Okay, so what do you want to do? We can't animate 'em."

"Can't we?"

"No," emphatically. "We don't have the resources." I've stopped saying *or the skills,* because you just counter that with *we can hire the skills.*

"We could pursue the resources," you say instead.

"For this? To fill a virtual town with virtual people, coming and going, realistically? We'd need Disney."

"We can talk to Disney."

"You have ideas above your station."

"I know. Always did." And you smile and reach out and stroke my ankle, which is utterly unfair and disarming and an invitation to surrender, which I do.

"Even so," I say eventually, "that's an order of magnitude beyond where we are."

"I know it. That's 2.0, or 3.0 more likely. It's a promise for the future. Meantime, we've got to do something: more than an abandoned township, less than an active population. Can we have the engine shuffle figures about at random, so that no view's ever entirely empty, but it's never quite the same as last time? It'll still be static at any given moment, but randomly static. Differently static. Yes?"

"Oh, yes. And the trucks and the horses and the wagons. And the horse-shit. If it's transient, we can shift it. Market stalls there by daylight, gone at night. The town drunk, there all the time, day or night." I was getting into this. "What else?"

"Trains coming through. On a bloody schedule. We've got the timeta-bles, we can do that. And the population changes with every train. Did you have a model railway in your basement as a kid?"

"Yes, of course I did."

"Because that's what this is, really. It's just a bloody train set, with more scenery than we ever had before."

"On a scale of 1:1."

"Yeah, that."

ACTUAL funding comes from a small start-up comms company that wants to play with the big boys. It thinks this is a way to get its new tech noticed. Now we have actual offices, servers, employees. No day jobs any longer, only this. We can make up our own titles; you want to be Lord High Mukamuk. Of course you do. In the interests of not frightening the bank and the VCs and so forth, not giving hostages to fortune—or the Fortune 500—you're chairman and I'm CEO.

There's some piece of paper somewhere that officially refers to us as The Former CR Corporation. *Cherried Ranks,* still hanging in there.

"This is weird," you say, standing in the doorway of what will be our shared office: two desks, two chairs, a sofa for when we need to get comfy together. An actual filing cabinet, for actual paper files. We're still waiting on monitors, keyboards, connectivity. "Isn't this weird?"

"Come here," I say, "and let me make it weirder."

So you do, and so do I. I've been keeping this, just for this occasion, the way regular people would keep a bottle of champagne. I pull my phone from my belt and touch it on, and show you. Orienting it carefully north-west and holding it up at eye height and almost at arm's distance, like an artificial horizon.

"I've seen a thousand of these," you murmur, not really complaining, only waiting.

"I know, and it feels like a hundred thousand—but this one's ours." The photo on the screen is black and white, with a cryptic notation in one corner, a file number from the library written in white chinagraph pencil.

There's a lane, a fence, an orchard. That's all. The image doesn't move as I orient the phone, because nothing's up and running yet, it's only a photo on my phone—but still you smile, as your eyes move from the screen to the window and back.

"That live oak in the lane there, by the gate," you say. "That's the same tree, isn't it?"

"Yup. Taller, stouter, a hundred years wiser; still the same tree." Grandfather's axe hasn't come anywhere near it. It used to guard a gateway; now it oversees our car park. With our car parked directly in its shade. I decide to have that slot marked, "Reserved for Chairman and CEO," the two of us together. We'll probably bike in most days, but even so.

"I thought I'd get a blow-up print of this," I say, "and hang it on the wall there, between our desks."

"You're right," you say meditatively. "That is exactly where it should go." And then you step out into the corridor, and come back in with a framed print, two foot by three foot, that you'd hidden in the office next door, you sod.

"Two minds with but a single photo," you say, smug to the max.

OF course that's where we'd like to start, home ground, X marks the spot: we could take over the world from here, spreading outwards like a new religion. Every journey starts with a single step, and where better to begin?

But work like this is all about data overlap; the more pictures we have, the less we have to postulate, the better our work and the easier our task. We don't only have this single view of our future office space, and we're confident of finding more, but images of any given single orchard are always going to be thin on the ground. And if we're not that much like a religion, perhaps we're more like bacteria, infecting a Petri dish. It only makes sense to begin where the environment is richest.

We have more photographs of downtown than anywhere else. Of course we do, that's how people work. Everything regresses to the mean. More pictures mean more angles, more details, more data points. Grist to the mill. Our rude crude mill-engine just loves grist.

So we give it what we've got, it gives us all it has. It's like a first date, awkward and hesitant and oversharing, because once we've started we don't know when to stop.

Some day, no doubt, there'll be a VR iteration with goggles and gloves, the whole surroundsight experience, and you can waltz down the street with a lady of the town, if she's willing. I'm sure we'll be able to render willingness some day. And then argue about the meaning of consent with software objects. But we're building this for phones, for today, pushing one boundary at a time. I hope.

Ritually, you and I stand at the end of our one-street downtown. "Phones at twenty paces," I say, but in truth we're side by side, lining them up neatly adjacent, holding the same view and pointing nothing at each other. Yet.

The rest of the crew is grouped behind us, supposedly looking over our shoulders. It's the captain's privilege to be first over the top. In truth, of course, they've all got their own phones in their hands and chances are they're already ahead of us. We're being very careful not to look, not to look back. Only forward.

You say, "Ready?... Engage."

You're an iPhone, I'm an Android, because it's important to us that we're not two instances of the same person, really not; but we thumb our apps on in sync, and there we are. Looking in one direction, seeing two views. All around us Main Street as she is, full vibrant colour, action, noise; on our phones, Main Street as she used to be a hundred years ago. One recognisable building. Everything silent, static, still black and white because colour rendering lies ahead, in our estimable future. We might only be looking at a photograph, until we turn left and right respectively, stand back to back and the view turns with us. Servers far away are churning through data and spitting back images almost in real time, barely a detectable pause. Nothing I'm seeing now on the phone has survived to the present day, but the patterns make sense. Streets and buildings overlay the landscape then much as they overlie it now, because human needs and desires don't change much or quickly. Ingenuity takes leaps and bounds, perhaps, but even then it pauses, glances back, wants to lead us where we want to follow. Better faster brighter, still the same. We're creatures of the valley floor, evolved to suit.

We turn slowly southerly, as though we've practised this. Hell, of course we've practised this. We knew people would be watching. Some of them may even be recording us, the way we asked them to. This is archival, if it's not historic.

All the way around and our arms line up again, our hands, our phones. One view of how things used to be, orchards and farmhouses from here to the distant line of mountains.

"Toto," I say, "I don't think we're in Kansas any more."

"It's California," you say, "as it always was. As witness. And by the way?"

"Yes?"

"Don't call me Toto."

AFTER that, of course, everyone calls you Toto. To your face—sometimes—and also in print, in phosphors, all over. Images from the movie are everywhere: on our website, in people's cubes, in their emails. On our office door.

"They're not going to buy me a bloody puppy, are they?" you ask, seemingly genuinely anxious.

"I don't suppose so, no. You might get adoption papers for Chanukah," because that's the kind of people we employ: pushing a joke to its limit, in the most virtual way they can realise. "Some kid far away gets to take a rescue dog home, everything paid for, just so long as he pretends to call it Toto and sends you a card every year. Paw-prints and reports. SIT scores. You get to send checks in return."

"The gift that keeps on taking?"

"Yup. Exactly that. How's the Moveable Feast coming along?"

That's iteration 2.0, which of course we're working on before the first release goes live. It's going to be such a surprise. People will log on for what they're used to, for the view, for a glimpse of time gone by; and they'll find people going by. Someone they saw outside the hardware store glimpsed suddenly in profile in the livery stable, harnessing a carriage-and-pair. That grease-monkey in dungarees servicing a two-stroke dairy truck, wasn't he the messenger boy standing on the pedals to drive his bike through the muck of Main Street after what must have been an awesome storm? Could there possibly be two boys that willing, that adaptable, that dirty…?

And so on, and I'm so looking forward to it; and all you say is, "Look."

And you pick up a remote from your desk and work some thumb-magic, and the screen on the wall comes to life.

We've hung it opposite the print, because this is opposite to that: that's the frozen capture, where this is the live feed. If I turn it on, it's iteration 1.0 and I can drive it anywhere within our compass, look at any view the engine's rendered. You can take it further, look more inwardly, see where we hope to go.

Show me.

"Look," you say, and the screen comes to life. Here's a picnic under the cherry trees, because apparently the Japanese had nothing to teach our ancestors: chairs around a table, linen napery and dishes in profusion, it's really not my idea of a picnic but there they all are, picnicking away. One girl in white is standing at a little distance off. She draws my eye, but it's not—or not only—because she has made that little private space for herself, *not at the table, not eating, not one of you.*

She's also the only one looking at the camera, the only one apparently aware of it, of posterity, of us.

Not happy about it, perhaps. Camera-shy—or narrative-shy, perhaps, not wanting to be one of the happy family? She must actually be one of the family, she's that well-dressed. Certainly not a servant. The servants would be the ones who struggle to keep her dress that white, after she drags the hem of it all over the orchard.

"Look," you say again, and work the buttons on the remote, make the image zoom in. Did I even know we could do that?

There's her face, and here's our engine working, extrapolating, showing us more detail than the original could ever have retained. Picking out her face in painful detail: staring, accusatory, distressed.

"I've no idea what her story is," you say, "but there has to be one, doesn't there? She has to have a story."

"Everyone has a story," I say. "It's just that most of them are as dull as other people's dreams."

Not hers. You don't need to say it. That's where we are now, that we often don't need to say something aloud, we can just let it go for granted. It's a comfortable place to find ourselves, but sometimes I think it's lossy, that too. Sometimes I think those two go hand in hand.

I want to take your hand right here, right now, as you gaze at her, as you stare and stare.

"I wonder where else we can find her?" you say. "There has to be more than this."

"I'm sure." Photographs were all the vogue for wealthy families between the wars. People of property like to see themselves *in situ*. It's like a receipt from the moment, a guarantee through time, *I was here. Remember me.* Better than a tombstone.

ONE thing we've always known we'll need is awesome image search. We'll write our own in the end, but for now we're making do with the best on the market, bought-in expertise. You set that free to run, to rage through all our digitised stock. Dark-haired young women, women in white: soon we have her lined up in dozens of different shots. Walking and riding, in motor-cars and on horse-drawn wagons. In streets, in stores, in ballrooms. Alone or with companions, except that she's never truly with them, she's always stood apart.

And she's always, always the only one you really want to look at.

"Have you noticed a thing?"

Several things, yes, and not all of them in the images; but I was ever conformable. I say, "She's always looking at the camera," like she's preternaturally aware of it, even in the candid shots that should have caught her off guard, "and she's never smiling." Indeed, she always has that same haggard, hag-ridden expression, as though the act of photography is somehow a betrayal. Perhaps it is. "And she's on her own, always. Even in company."

"That, sure, all of those—but something else."

I hate guessing-games, and I can always wait you out. Not so conformable after all.

"What she wears," you say at last, complicit in my refusal, "those dresses—or that dress, maybe, it always seems to be the same one, though I suppose she might have a wardrobeful—is twenty, thirty years out of date, compared to what everyone else is wearing."

You're right, of course. These people dress in country fashions, provincial to the core—no flappers here, no short skirts and bobbed hair—but that white dress of hers is Edwardian, Victorian even, mutton sleeves buttoned to the wrist and the hem barely showing the heels of her sensible boots. She always has a hat, but it's clear that her hair is piled up beneath it, ready to tumble halfway down her back at the removal of a pin.

"What d'you think, then—country cousin who won't or can't fit in with the fast crowd?" To my mind they're all country cousins, but everything's comparative. "Maybe her isolation is down to them, not her. And she feels it deeply, and resents it deeply, and that's why she's always scowling."

"Or she was raised in a cult, and now she's being obliged to live with relatives who laugh at her strange dress and old-fashioned ways, and that's why she resents them."

"Did they have cults, backaways?"

"Oh hell yes," you assure me. "Weird Victorian sex-cults, everything we'd need. She wears white to mark her out as a Virgin of God, only God in this case is some seedy creep with just a pinch of charismatic fervour, and 'virgin' is a technical term that only means she only sleeps with him. Maybe he calls them Brides instead of Virgins, it's much the same. And they still get to wear white. And she only wants to get back to him, but she's not allowed. He's been run out of town on a rail, his house is closed and the only family she ever knew has been scattered to the four winds, never to meet again in this life."

"How come you know all the good stories?" I grumble, because of course I can't compete. I could almost believe every word of it, though I know you're making it up out of whole cloth.

You just smile, and pat my butt, and turn back to the monitor. The search engine's found another picture. This one shows her at the railway station, standing as ever apart from her party, looking as ever at us while they watch their train come in.

"That coalsmoke's going to play merry hell with her whites," I say, trying to sound cheerful against the mood that oozes from the screen, from her. "Pity whoever has to do her laundry."

"Maybe she has to do it herself," you say.

"Oh, surely not? Even the poor cousin taken in reluctantly, even then… This isn't Cinderella. Even the governess gets to enjoy the services of the household," I finish emphatically, not quite making that up. Sure that I'd read it somewhere.

"She might insist. Her clothes are that particular, maybe she wants to take care of them herself. Or maybe it's ritual, required. Cult. That would get right up the servants' noses, having a member of the family down in their quarters, interfering with their work. Maybe they hate her as much as the rest, as much as she hates them. Maybe that's why she never even has a maid with her."

Maybe it is, though hatred isn't normally a disqualifying factor. "Who is she, though?" I ask. "Her name's got to be in the metadata, for one of these pictures at least…"

What we call *metadata* these days, people used to call *scribbling in pencil on the back of the print*. Our scanners have been scrupulous about copying whatever information there was, front and back, and checking library files in case they knew anything more.

Nevertheless: we can put names to most of those we see around her, and not at all to her. There seems to be no record. Baffled, you take off on a mission: back to the source, to each of the original pictures, to double-check the prints and interrogate the archivists. Neither of us really believes that you'll get anywhere, but she's preying on your mind. You'll get no work done either, till you've either hunted her down or else admitted her lost to human ken, a face without a name. Pixels shorn of their metadata, a story no longer told or remembered.

Your obsessive nature is an old story hereabouts, but neither one of us is at all likely to be forgetting it. You go off with my weary blessing. Of course I can do the work of two, for however long it takes you to burrow through to victory or else admit defeat.

DEFEAT really doesn't suit you, as a concept. The good thing about your current state of baffled rage—the only good thing, because neither does bafflement suit you, and I find rage incredibly hard to live with—is that defeat can always be relabelled as victory deferred. There is an answer out there, you just haven't found it yet. There's always tomorrow, and you're very, very bad at giving up.

Much less bad at giving me grief about it. What's yours is mine, stress not excluded; a trouble shared is—yeah, just that. A trouble shared.

Still. There's always something I can give back. "Let's go for a walk, you. Toto."

"Hunh?"

"Test run. Something to show you."

"Oh, you shit. I've been chasing around getting nowhere, and you've set it up while my back was turned, haven't you?"

"Strictly in beta." It's hard to talk around a grin this broad. "But yeah, 2.0 is up and running. Sort of. Don't expect to see them waltzing in the ballrooms, but we might meet someone riding down the street. Someone who wasn't there last time we saw that view."

I suppose I could have cheated it, set up a script to walk you through, knowing where to look and who to show you. I haven't done that, and as it turns out I didn't need to. They line up to show themselves to us, as it seems, like pent-up visions released at last.

It's not even that odd these days, to walk down the street looking at your phone all the way. Or your friend's phone, as you do this night, hanging over my shoulder, holding on to my arm that way you never do when we're merely out together like a regular couple, doing our thing.

This must be our new thing. We don't make it to the end of the block before there's Mr Renton who kept the post office for twenty years, still in the apron he always wore on duty, beaming at us from the corner as he had beamed from the steps of his empire with all his clerks and telegram boys lined up in their uniforms beside.

It's impossible not to give him a cheery salute as we pass. Watching neighbours may think us crazed, perhaps. Perhaps not for the first time.

Around the corner, and where the new church stands, what we see on my phone is the old church, gone fifty years now but rendered more credibly, more solidly than anything around, we've had so many views to work with. No speculative reconstruction here, we know it from all four sides.

Today there's the back view of a farmer on a mule, apparently trying to ride it through the main doors of the church.

"Engine may need a few tweaks," I mutter. You just laugh.

We walk on across the flyover that bridges the expressway, seeing nothing of that because the expressway in its cutting hadn't even been imagined back then. Our view shows us only a country road, with wagons coming in from the west. Same wagons as yesterday, as ever. Not everything is scheduled to change, or subject to it.

Maybe I'm lulled by that particular, familiar view. Maybe we both are. Certainly we're distracted, suddenly all business, arguing as so often about whether there's any real point in releasing version 1.0; won't people get bored with seeing the same static views as they step out of their doors, the same static horses at the end of the street? Won't they just use the app a few times for novelty's sake, mostly to show their friends, and then abandon it when it isn't novel any more? Maybe we should hold back till 2.0 was ready, so at least we can promise change, if not—yet—animation...

And by the time we remember to look back at the screen, there she is. Right in front of us, staring directly at us, in her usual dreadful impractical whites. With her usual dreadful expression, horror constrained by inevitability, weary acceptance of the unbearable, as though she lives it every moment.

As ever, I want to comfort her with apples, or at least with platitudes: *you are stronger than you know, no one is given more than they can bear, you are still and always a survivor.*

What you want, even now, I have no idea. What you say is something else. Of course you're talking to her, not to me; my instinct was the same, it's just that you're the one with follow-through.

"We'll find you," you say. "We will." That's commitment, not desire. I can read your passions as readily as your code, and it's really not what you want. It's a desperate act, almost. No one could want to bring her anywhere closer than this, where she stares from the phone screen as though she were right there in front of us, as though we stood in her street or else she in ours.

The phone's power switch is right here under my thumb, but I can't turn her off, any more than I can turn away. Any more than I can dream of turning you.

One of us does have to move, though, and it certainly won't be her. Nor you, not without help. So I take your arm and nudge you, tug you, haul you into motion. Keeping the phone on her, keeping her in clear sight for you as we walk carefully around her. Somewhere servers are burning hot, running the numbers they're picking up from my phone, position and orientation, everything to hold her pinned in place, in view.

Smarter than I knew, those servers. They extrapolate a back view for her as we step weirdly around an apparently empty spot on the sidewalk: that fine white gown all laced and trimmed, with the long fall of her hair held in a bow we've never seen before and neither have the servers, neither apparently the cameras that caught her all over town a century ago. Even her profile is an extrapolation; we've never seen her anything but full-face, flying her distress like a flag.

Without the distraction of that terrible sorrowful stare, she seems—well, odder than ever, from the back. More out of place, though we see her standing in her own street, in what ought to be her own time. There are cars and trucks in the roadway, while she's dressed for a world of horse and carriage. Of course there must have been an overlap, in technology as much as fashion; it must have been commonplace to see horses and motor vehicles side by side, at least for a few years. Odd to our eyes, perhaps, but not to theirs. And country styles are always lag of cities, and some families must surely have clung to earlier ways of dress—and even so. Even calling her Edwardian is a stretch. My eye still wants to say that she's dressed purely Victorian. It's only my mind that revolts, that pleads an essential compromise. Here she is, photographed over and over, in pictures unequivocally dated to the 1920s. She can't be a Victorian, in anything but outlook.

"I will find you." You say it one more time, and this time it's personal, it's exclusive. It's not a common enterprise any more, you're not including me.

That's—well. Significant, of course. Hurtful, of course. Worrying.

WE see less and less of you in the office, I see less and less of you at home. You're spending all your days out in the field, tracking down archives that haven't been digitised. Wielding your charm on hapless archivists, scanning and uploading as soon as they succumb. Nights you're in the office alone, coding and debugging, refining search parameters, pounding keyboards as if brute force will hammer the data in hard enough to shatter walls of ignorance and obscurity, to break you through to where she lies concealed.

Not much can stand against you, when your blood is up. I know it; I never could. One night you come home late, and you come straight to me, which has become almost unusual; and there's a look in your face that is almost defeat, a tone in your voice that could foretell catastrophe as you say, "I found her."

Of course you did. She never stood a chance. I kick a chair in your approximate direction and say, "Sit. Speak. Show me."

You're holding a print in both hands, and all I can see is the back of it, with an ink stamp and those hand-written notations so familiar by now. Source and classification: which archive and where stored, whose work, who the subject (if known). A few strings of numbers and a few scribbled words, and that's almost more data than the picture itself can offer. Almost. We think we're visually driven, but appearances are deceptive and the camera always lies. There's a reason why prisoners of war have to hand over name and rank and serial number, rather than a photo ID. Faces are changeable, but words will pin you down. Words and numbers will always find you out.

You don't want to show me her face suddenly, seemingly, although it's so familiar by now. You're holding that print close to your chest, and not even reaching for the drink I pour for you.

"Her name's Amanda," you say, "Amanda Scarett. She was born here in the valley. Her parents were farmers—well, of course they were; that's what respectable people did, they wouldn't be in trade—and she was their only child. Their only surviving child."

"So?" And then, "Let's see," when you still don't move to show me.

And you sigh, and bite your lip, and lay the photo face-up on the tabletop between us.

And yes, that is certainly her face, that same face that we have seen and seen again, wracked and mute and frantic; and she's eighteen or twenty perhaps, and she's sitting in a stiff high-backed chair holding a stiff little boy in her lap while a man and a woman stand behind her, each with a hand on her shoulder.

I'm sure they're not actually holding her down, but it could look that way.

"So—those are her parents, yes?"

"Eveline and Harold," you confirm.

"So who's the boy? You said she was an only child."

"Only surviving child, I said. The only one to survive her childhood. I think this one's her youngest brother. Their last attempt. I looked up the records, and they pretty much went for a baby a year. If you read between the lines, Eveline clearly had a string of miscarriages and stillbirths, and the few she carried to term died in infancy. Like this one."

There's something about the way you say that, that has me looking again and a lot more closely. Seeing less clearly, the harder I try: as though focus were somehow shifty, or the recorded world lossy. A boy, a doll, a puppet…

"Wait," I say. "Wait. No… He's *dead* here?"

"Yes. Yes, he is. It was a thing some Victorian families did, to memorialise their dead children with a last family photograph. In the cities, child mortality was common enough that photographers could specialise. Not so out here, but even so, they found someone to oblige."

"And they made his poor sister hold the corpse? No wonder she looks so…"

"Yeah." And you reach to touch her face, just for a moment; and then you say, "It's worse than that, though. I said, her mother had a string of dead babies, boy after boy after boy, and their big sister was the only one that lived. I think they did this to her again and again and again. Maybe they meant to punish her for living, when all their glorious sons were dying one by one. I don't know, they might just have wanted something to remember every lost soul by, a sort of rolling successive family portrait—but I think it did something dreadful to her, deep inside."

"Yes." I believe you, absolutely. Well, of course I do; I'm programmed to. "Maybe you were right before and they were cult-religious, some weird isolationist sect like the Mennonites or the Amish. Dressing their virgin girls in white and idolising dead boys, they might have been."

"I suppose. Why?"

"Because else—oh, hell. Do you have a date on this photograph?"

"Yes," you say, with infinite reluctance. "That's the other thing," the thing you didn't want to talk about. Now, neither do I. I'm really sorry I brought it up. "It is dated, reliably. To 1872."

"Yes." Or rather, *no*. "We really didn't import any photos that early, did we?"

"Absolutely not. Nothing earlier than the turn of the century." We've been scrupulous about that, not to sour the timeline. This photo's not in our database—but you know that, you had to find it offline. The same must be true for any other, every other picture of her. That's why she always looks so out of place, wherever we find her; she's a generation too early to be there.

Which is a rock to run aground on, which is why we steer clear.

"We can filter her out. Can't we?"

"I don't want to do that," you say.

"Why not?"

"Because…because this may be all she's got. And it's got to be better than this." You reach to touch that photograph again—no, to turn it over. To deny it the light it feeds on. "Would this be how you want to go into eternity, exhibited with a body? Less important than the family corpse?" Because that was inherent, that the photo was all about the dead boy. "Well, now she doesn't have to. Now she gets to, I dunno, occupy the Bay. Here, there and everywhere. Like a game of Find the Lady, she's never where you expect to see her, because the software will always shuffle her off somewhere else. Maybe she'd enjoy that, after the life she had."

And I don't say a word about reification, I don't remind you that she's not any kind of conscious, she's barely even code, she's just data. If it's in my mind—well, it can stay there. She's in our system, after all, and apparently you want to leave her there.

I don't. I really, really don't.

"Maybe not," I say slowly. "Maybe it's worse, did you think of that? She surely doesn't look any happier now." Now I'm doing the same thing, reifying her: offering pseudo-life to a data packet, making a software object into a lost girl. A lost and sorrowing girl, a girl whose distress defines her. It's impossible to imagine her smiling, or at peace, or at rest. It was hard enough when we only ever saw her in other people's photographs, on the fringes of other people's parties. Now we've freed her up, we see her everywhere, and she's more alone than ever. It's as if the software itself has recognised her state of mind and reacted to it, giving her space. Or giving space to everyone else, perhaps, relief from her.

I'd console myself with the thought that I'm doing it for you, for the sake of argument, for us, for survival; only there's nothing in the least consoling about your face either, as I blunder on.

"Listen," I say. "It's a story, yes?" *It's a ghost story* is on the tip of my tongue, *she's a Trojan ghost,* but that's something else I'm going to leave unsaid. "There she was, this girl who couldn't ever be enough. Her parents kept trying to improve on her, child after child; and the newlings kept dying, and they made her pose with the bodies time after time, like a living example of her failure to satisfy. Potential energy outclasses any other form, right? Conservative principles apply; what you have, you want to hold. Dead sons outrank a living daughter.

"I don't know what happened to her in life, whether she went on surviving—"

"Oh, she did that," you murmur, amplifying rather than interrupting. "Hell, yeah. Amanda Scarett, died at eighty-six. Still a spinster, still on the family land. I looked her up."

"—but that doesn't matter," I go on, thinking *of course you did,* "because this was her perfect moment, the instant that defined her life. We all have them, and they don't have to be good. This is what she always goes back to, what she can never escape. That moment the photographer captured, with her dead brother and her own untouchable body and her parents' utter rejection, you can see that in their faces, how one more time they'd be willing to trade the living girl for the dead boy.

"And when I say that's what the photographer captured, it's not a figure of speech. No, bear with me: I told you, this is a story. It's science fiction, I guess, because there he is with this new machine that snares the light that reflects from her, through his unthinkable lenses onto his alchemical paper that'll hold it through the ages—and are you truly willing to tell me that there's nothing of her that goes with that, no vestige of self?

"I think something did. Maybe it wasn't captured by the camera, so much as driven by her own torment—but some essence, some hint of her soul at that perfect moment of her despair, passed out of her and into—well, into technology, photography, this new mechanical art. Which is why we see her passed from picture to picture, from one studio to the next: never part of a party, never dressed right because she was never actually there in the flesh, only in the image. She's all about the image.

"And I think she knew. What was left of her, that tiny memory of self, I think it remembered what it was, what she was, and what was done to her; but more than that, I think it knew where it was now. Where she was. Trapped in silver chloride, frozen motion, her suffering forever laid out for others to gaze at.

"That's what appalled her, see? Not her normal human unhappy life, she's stronger than that. She *survived* that. Intact, and for a long lifetime after. What broke her was this other thing, this half-life. No life at all, just time: like an insect trapped in amber, only still aware. A consciousness in amber. Silver chloride.

"And nowhere to go, no possibility of change, that's the killer. That should have been the killer, except that she survived that too. And then along we come with our clever scanners and our greedy servers, sucking up whatever we can find, changing its nature, taking this analogue of self and turning it digital, giving it a folly of motion, a scripted independence, a false equivalence of life.

"And she's still trapped, only now she's not a frozen portrait any more, stealing into the corners of other people's pictures. Now she's a puppet, and we have her fucking dancing in the street. And that's worse, don't you see? That's *worse.*"

You don't say anything, but that's all right. I'm not done yet.

"That's why you can't find her in the database. She isn't there. She's like a leaf in a stream, the system keeps her moving. Always skipping ahead. There is no rescue. No one can go back; history is full, it has no room for visitors. It's a book without margins, a tale told. History is complete, and we were never a part of it.

"Only the future has space for us. We can only ever go forward. And we've doomed her to hurry on ahead, in her old-fashioned clothes and her old-fashioned scenery, tossed on from one technology to the next, never human and never free, just an ever-closer simulacrum, until in the end we will be able to dance with her down the fucking street and believe it, feel it, taste and smell and all. And we'll use her and use her, and never feel what she feels, and never quite see her as she is, across that dreadful, terrible gulf. Always falling short."

Like a prisoner of war, it's the words that I surrender. You can have them all, I could always talk up a storm—but I need you to stop, think, step back. And I've already said you can't do that, I could never make you do that. History is full, and there is no rescue.

"We can give her something to skip for," you say. "Somewhere to skip to. To skip in, because she's there already. She only needs to look around and realise. Horror's just a habit, she sees what she expects; she's trapped because she thinks she is, no more. Hell is just a state of mind. This used to be called the Valley of Heart's Delight, remember, before the tech companies came. When she lived here, it was beautiful; she should have loved it. She still can. We can help, we can teach her how. We can rescue her."

WHAT hope do I have, to resist this? I gave you the keys to myself, and you are everywhere. Working from within. For myself, my only fear is that one day I will find you gone. For you, my greater fear is that one day somehow you will go.

Meantime, here we are. Here I am, facilitating what I fear most.

You do dressing-up, so I don't need to.

Later, you say, we'll call in all my friends to make a party that she's actually invited to, where she'll be guest of honour. You say that, but I'm not sure I believe it. All my friends have Victorian garb and they'd be glad to play, but nevertheless. I don't believe it'll happen, because you don't want it. I think you want her to yourself. You want to be the one she looks for, her focal point, the bridge-builder. The one who crossed the gulf.

I think you'd tear the bridge down behind you, if you could.

Looking at you through the viewfinder, in your finery and your new-grown whiskers, posed beside our cherry tree, for a moment you seem almost unreal, almost. One step across the gulf already, for all that I could step into view myself and touch you, hold you, fuck you right there under the camera's eye.

What you see when you look in my direction, I have no idea. I can no longer imagine what I am to you, more than a placeholder. I suppose you're in character already, and looking for her. Or looking to the future, version $x.1$, where you and she will waltz down the street together and I'll be the one watching from somewhere else, some technological absence. And you and I might live a lifetime yet—as she did, ever forward, ever further from her perfect moment—and talk and touch and fuck and never quite inhabit the same space. And how will I ever know what's gone of you, what more you might have been for me, what you've given to her instead? Love is lossy, by its nature; it makes strangers of us all, strange to each other and strange to ourselves. Will there be two of you, each growing apart from what you are?

Every touch of my finger on the shutter peels away another shaving of you in time, twice realised. And I can't stop doing this, though it leaves me with less and less for every frame I take. Is it you I'm unmaking here, or is it simply us? God alone knows what she will make of you, but nothing that I can reach or touch or recognise. My true love hath my heart, and she has yours; all that's left me is the fact of you, none of the art. Which will be a hard thing to look back on, when we must.

IN SKANDER, FOR A BOY

SKANDER: CITY OF EXILES, ASSASSINS, PLOTTERS and panders and whores. City of poets, of lovers, of embassies, liars of every hue.

Skander sits on every man's horizon. I gazed at it in contempt, where it lay like a smear of lit charcoal spilled at the sea's edge; I called for greater effort on the oars. These tideless waters had nothing to offer. Our own work would bring us in, see our task complete and take us home again. Untainted, if we were hard and fast.

RULF had sent us, raucous above a coffin in his high rede-hall. That was a memory to cling to, appalling and wonderful: torchlight on silver, shadow on bone. Rulf—Lord of the Seamarch, Kingslayer, the Iron Hand—weeping into his beard, roaring for mead, rejoicing and cursing and lamenting this death above any, that left him with no enemies worth the name.

The coffin had come by way of many hands and many holds, fetched in at last with a shipload of Rothland horses, breeding mares that had waited out the winter storms in Landrëas. Rulf had a fancy to be Lord of Horses too, to ride and rule inland as he did the coastal waters. It was madness, and so I told him—which might perhaps be a reason why he screamed my name above the coffin.

"Croft is dead," he said, thrusting a torch into the dark casket to make it evident. "Take ship to Skander, and bring me back the boy."

This was almost more stupid than his notion of turning sea-harriers into horsemen. I said, "How can you know this is Croft? All I see is bones." Bones with the meat boiled off them, ingeniously wired together in the figure of a man.

"Bones and hair," he said, showing me the long plait he had snatched up. That was coarse, blond gone to white: it might have been Croft's. Or mine, or his own. Any northman's.

"His name is on the lid," he said. It was: in silver inlay in a strange corrupt southern reading of our own strong runes, as though it spelled the name out with a lisp.

"Anyone can write on a box and put bones in it."

"And then ship it two thousand miles? Why would they?"

"To make you believe, of course, that Croft was dead."

"But he is," Rulf said simply, wafting his torch again. "He is here."

"You cannot know that."

"And yet I do. See his legs?"

I saw what he showed me, as he lowered the torch: how twisted the leg-bones were, how they had been shattered and brutally mis-healed.

"I did that," he said, as if I hadn't known it, hadn't been there. "These are the ways, the places where I had the bones broken and then tied up so they would set so bent he could never stand or walk again. Three months he screamed in the cesspit, before I was sure they were beyond any man's doctoring."

I remembered. All summer Croft lay in shit, and made sure that we all lay in the sounds of his pain and loss. I had thought that almost Croft's victory, rather than Rulf's.

And then he had been washed and dressed—in a woman's skirt, because those dreadful legs would never wear trousers again—and set in a skiff with the boy for deckhand and servant, and he had sailed into the sun's setting on his way to exile and death.

Eventual death. It was twenty years before his twisted bones came back to us.

I said, "Why do you want the boy back now?"

"Harlan, I have no heir. They tell me it is the gods' curse on my blood, for what I did to the old king his father. What I took from him. Some of that, at least, I can restore."

"He will claim the kingship."

"He is welcome to it, when I'm gone. I can adopt him, train him, make him a better man than Barent ever was."

"Rulf, you gave him to Croft. He will have been trained already, to despise you and all of yours. Will you make a gift of yourself, to a young man who is right to hate you?"

He shrugged ruefully, confused perhaps by his own sudden penitence. "Harlan. Fetch him back."

AT least the voyage home would let me see what kind of man Croft had made of the boy. If I judged it needful, I would keep him in chains and be sure at least that Rulf had to make his own mistakes.

We were two months abroad before we sighted Skander, a smudge of smoke in the east as we lost the sun, a sullen glow in the dark to guide us. Any other port on any other water, we would have held off for a daylight tide. Skander has no tides to wait for; and besides, I ached to be swift, in and out.

In, then, slow and steady on the oars, all sail furled. I was a windmaster and we had barely rowed all journey, but these were strange waters and this my own ship beneath me, manned on Rulf's gold and charged with his mission. I would be twice a fool to take a risk with her.

In fact we could have sailed right to the lamplit wharf and never scraped a rock nor jarred a timber; Skander's harbour is as deep and clean as legend paints it. We'd know, when it came time to be leaving. A man old enough to have grown wise always keeps it in his head, that he may be leaving swiftly.

That same old wise man knows it's good to come in slow and quiet. To seem tamer than you are.

I was old enough, even in my own eyes. I dragged my own long reputation like a twilight shadow at my back, but still: it had been a dreary voyage and the crew had seen every year of my age tell on me as we came. I was tired already, hungry only to go home. They were a pack of wolves at my oars, and I feared loosing them on the city. Any city, but Skander more than any: its reputation was longer, louder, lewder than my own.

I said, "The streets are full of lights. That's not a welcome, it's a warning. Stay close to each other, if you won't stay close to me. Keep away from shadows, keep watch on your bench-mates; keep out of trouble, because there will be no rescue here."

They had never looked for rescue in their lives. There was pity in their eyes, pity and contempt. Had I really fallen so far from my strength that I saw danger in an effete entrepôt where men and women alike dealt in silks and whispers, in smokes and perfumes and each other?

Even as we sidled up to moor, I thought I would be leaving half those men behind. Dead or enslaved, drunk or bewitched or carried off.

Well, they were free men—for now—and few of them truly my own. So long as I had hands enough, I would be leaving as soon as I had the boy. If necessary I could buy oarsmen at market, although I'd hate to do it. Slaves taint a ship's heart, and make a mock-man of her captain. I stared down the *Skopje*'s length and prayed to see enough of those faces back here in a day, two days.

And then my good ship bumped against the wharf, and there were small slim figures waiting for ropes and high shrill voices crying welcome, asking how they could serve us, what we might require. Whatever we might desire. Information, temptation: before one of us so much as set boot ashore, the bargaining had begun.

MY own boots were first, as was my right and duty. I leaped over the rail and landed two-footed and emphatic on the wharf.

I don't rightly know what I was stamping against: a snake's welcome, a hissing from the shadows? That was surely how I saw the city: as a nest of serpents all knotted together, spies and assassins and traitors in exile from a dozen different lands, poison and sorcery no doubt their weapons of first resort. Cowards and schemers all.

My head is a slow, dull thing. In my own country they call me Harlan the Wily, expressly because I am not. Rulf should never have sent me to Skander. He should have known, not to do that.

A voice hailed me; a woman stepped forward.

Smaller than me, but if she was smaller than the normal run of men, it was not by much. She carried herself with straightforward authority, and I liked that even as I was surprised by it, where I was looking for insinuation and duplicity.

"Are you the master of this vessel?"

"I am."

"Your name and origin?"

"Harlan, of Sawartsland; emissary of Rulf my king." I should perhaps not have said that, but I didn't even carry trade goods to disguise my mission. I have said it: I was not the man for this.

"I am Dzuria, harbourmaster here. My people will see to yours, and to your ship's comfort. You come with me, and tell me of your embassy."

"I will tell that to the prince of the city. There is a prince, I think?"

Her mouth quirked. "There are many princes in Iskandria, none interested in any tale but their own. Of course you must take your tale to the palace, but the chancellor's is the ear you want."

I sighed. "At home, if a man wants the ear of Rulf King, he walks into the rede-hall and bellows for him. I do understand that matters are arranged differently elsewhere."

She said, "In this city, truly, your best first step towards the chancellor's ear is through mine."

It was elegantly done. She cut me out from my crew and penned me alone, as she had intended from the first. My own intent, to use my king's name here the way I had used my axe and shield elsewhere, a brute swift way to the top—that was neglected early, abandoned swiftly, forgotten soon.

How much help I could truly expect from a harbourmaster, I had no way to measure. In my world, harbourmasters berthed ships and tallied cargoes, charged for wharfage and warehousing, their heads full of cables and weights and manifests.

They might have comfort in their offices, but not like this. She brought me to a chamber swathed in damask and lamplight, soft cushions and soft-voiced children who fetched sweet juice and fiery spirit, nutmeats and pastries, offers of anything more.

I batted them away with thanks and refusals. They smiled and shrugged, settled in the perfumed shadows in the corners of the room, watched me and their mistress both with a scrupulous, indefatigable care.

"Shouldn't they be in bed?" I grunted.

"Undoubtedly. Would you care to send them? I wish you joy of the attempt."

At least she didn't say *take them*. Even so, I was not inclined to be generous. I said, "You call yourself the harbourmaster; these speak to me more of a slavemaster."

"Indeed. Do you not take and keep and trade slaves, in Sawartsland?"

"We do, yes; but—"

"Not children, would you say?"

"Oh, children too, but not like this," scented and silk-clad and complaisant. The youngsters I bought or bred in my own house worked their share, just as my own children had, as my grandchildren did now. And fed from the same plates, ripped the same clothes ragged, rioted as much and were beaten for it side by side; and slept safe in a puppy tumble, free and slave together.

"I am sure not. There are none like these. Don't let their seductive ways deceive you. Some of our princes-in-exile, yes, they keep children for their bodies, for their beds; but these?" She stretched out a long arm to tug at the artfully tangled hair of one ingratiating imp that I took—not quite certainly—for a girl. "If you took one of these to bed, you would wake up sorry. If you woke at all. They are heartless, entirely without compunction, because that is how I raise them. Their perfumes and fancies are stolen, from any ship careless enough to let them aboard. Once goods are landed they are safe, because then they fall under my regard, but anything on shipboard is fair game. So is the crew."

"Do I need to warn my men?"

"If a man needs warning against such as these, he should perhaps have stayed at home."

Indeed; but we had Rulf's order at our backs, heavy as a blade and just as imperative. Staying home had never been an option.

I said, "Where do you find these dangerous children?"

"In the alleys, on the wharfs, some of them. Most I buy. And sell again, when I can find them places. It's the only way to keep them from the thief-masters and the beggar kings. And the palace. Besides," reaching out again, touching the smooth cheek of an adolescent boy as he refilled her goblet, "how else would I manage my harbour? I can hire men to do the heavy work, but these are my rat-catchers and bead-counters, my watchers and messengers. As you have observed, they never go to bed when they're supposed to. If you are my friend, you need not worry for your purse or your safety or your ship, while you are here."

"I hope I am your friend," I said, with enough urgency to raise smiles in the shadows.

"Good. I hope it too; it means I can be a friend to you. Tell me of your embassy."

I said, "When my king took the throne twenty years ago, the man he took it from had a son, a boy of fifteen. Rulf sent the boy into exile, sooner than see him as dead as his father."

"He sent him here, you mean, to Iskandria."

"Of course. Where else? In company with his father's warhammer, Croft, the finest fighter and the worst picker of us all, who chose to support the old king when all his friends had turned the other way. Rulf…punished him, but would not kill him. Which was perhaps a mistake. Rulf has spent twenty years being wary of the world and never quite comfortable in his chair. But Croft is dead, and Rulf hopes the boy will come back now to make a son for his side and an heir for his back."

"Not so much a boy now, if he was fifteen then."

"They are all boys, when they stay so much younger than we are. You know." There was grey and white in the dark woven pattern of her hair; she was younger than me, but not so much as it would matter. "If you were here then, you would remember: a boy, tall and slim and flaxen-haired, not yet come into his strength. And a cripple, a big man who would not be walking, who could not leave the boat without help. A small boat, and just the two of them to crew it."

She said, "Oh, I was here. I have always been here. But a cripple and a boy, in a small boat, this far? That sounds…ambitious."

"We are good sailors." Even crippled, even ungrown.

"Even so. There are storms, there are pirates. There is simple bad fortune, and they would seem not to be rich in anything else."

"Indeed—but we know they did come. At least, we know that Croft did. His bones came back to us." And someone had to send them, with knowledge and purpose both.

"Yes. If it was the cripple you were seeking, it should be Fenner that you spoke to. A boy, though, a prince in exile—well, we have a city full of those. You will have to go to the palace."

"Fenner? Who is that?"

"He is—no, he *was* one of those I saved my children from. A beggar king, for a while. He matters more these days, but he is still cripple-king in this city. He knows all the lame and all the lacking."

"It's good, no doubt, that they have a friend with influence," but Croft was dead, and it was the boy I sought.

"I didn't say he was their friend. He buys and sells, he deals in flesh as much as he ever did, only from a more exalted position now. We used to call him Fenner the Helpless, because he never needed any help. He would have known your Croft, and where to find him. If you want your boy, though, ask at the palace."

I grunted, nodded, sighed. Not the man for this.

"Meantime," she said, "rest while you can. Palace days start early, and run long."

ONE of her watchful children—this one a girl, close enough to a young woman that I'd have been watchful myself if she were mine—took a lamp and led me to another room of cushioned comfort. I ought to have asked where my crew had gone, where I might hope to find them. But I was tired, and ashore, and frankly weary of them; and interested in bed, a lot, and in the girl a little, because her mistress interested me greatly.

"Will Dzuria really sell you to another house?"

The girl gave me a quick smile. "Of course. Soon now, I think. How else would she afford new little children? Being harbourmaster does not make her wealthy."

Which was as good as to say that she was an honest harbourmaster, but I had gathered that already. She was probably an honest slavetrader too. I said, "Don't you mind?"—but the true question was *why don't you mind?*

If anything, she seemed amused by my naivety. "This is Xandrian. Here, everyone belongs to someone else. And Dzuria will sell me somewhere I can be happy, to someone who will be happy to have me. Why should I mind?"

I shrugged, and sat on the bed. My boots looked a terrible long way away. I thrust my legs out hopefully, and said, "You mean you trust her."

"Of course. She has fed me and dressed me, washed me and doctored me, taught me to run with others and to run alone—how could I not trust her?"

She hauled with a will at one boot and then the other. I thanked her heartily, and reached for my purse.

"Not in this house," she said, frowning mightily. "We don't take money from our friends."

Then she scudded swiftly out of the room, and it took me a moment too long to realise she had taken my boots with her.

WAKING slowly, stiffly in an unaccustomed bed after a long sea-voyage: there was nothing unusual in that.

What was unusual was to find myself alone, and depressingly glad of it. It gave me the chance to move slowly, to groan aloud as I stretched, as every joint ached, as vicious age stabbed me mockingly in one hip and numbed a foot entirely.

I cursed, and stamped until some hint of feeling came back. The stamping only hurt me more, which only made me curse more, which left me all the more embarrassed when I looked around for clothes and found a boy, a small boy squatting in the corner.

I stood quiet, breathing hard, under the grave weight of his stare. I knew what he was seeing—a particoloured giant, wind-burned at face and arms and throat, pale elsewhere and seamed with scars—and I understood the fascination.

He said, "My name is Salumehramahin, and I am yours until you no longer need me." Then he looked me deliberately up and down one more time and added, "You will need me for a long time, I think."

"Dzuria sent you, I take it?"

"Of course."

His dress was shabby and painfully white; I liked that better than the slippery silks of last night. At least he looked like a servant, not a whore.

"Say your name again?"

"Salumehramahin," he said, flashing a smile as white as his cottons.

"What do your friends call you?"

"Ramin."

"Where do I find breakfast, Ramin?"

"I could bring it to you."

"No, bring me to it: somewhere between this room and the palace, which is where I have to go now."

He shook his head ruefully. "You should have been there earlier than this."

Then he dressed me like himself, in a long loose shirt and baggy trousers, and offered me sandals that he said were the largest he could find in all the warehouses of Skander wharf. He said they would be too small. Which, yes, they were.

I have worn less, in my time. And been led by the hand in stranger, darker places, to worse meals and worse days too, though rarely so frustrating.

I broke my fast—and the boy's, at my expense, naturally—on flatbreads filled with a hot spice paste, standing on a street corner. Afterwards I washed grease from my face and fingers at the public fountain, thought briefly and enchantingly of the notorious baths of Skander—and set my jaw resolutely against asking the way. I was for the palace, sea-scoured as I was. In and out, as swift as might be.

RAMIN led me through winding alleys and shadowed arcades, with never a glimpse of our purpose until suddenly we came out into the light and there it was, four-square in front of us.

They call it a palace—*the* palace, as though this were the principality of the world—but in truth it is nothing so singular. There isn't even a wall, to mark it off from the common city. The first building of authority is set openly on a public square; everything else has been added where it might be, behind and to the sides and running away out of sight.

That gateway building stands high and square, cut of local stone, as stern in its age as it must have been when it was new. Beyond lay a hundred unlikely structures, each one vying with its neighbours to be taller or broader or deeper, brighter or more imposing or more absurd. Some weary exiles built their pavilions to look like home, to teach their children where they came from; others seized the chance to shrug away tradition and build jubilant fantasies, faerie-castles that resembled nothing real in any city anywhere.

Some had built true castles, sullen fortresses that spoke of their fears: assassination, instability, uprising. I thought they should look around and find other things to fear. With five ships and a case of gold, I thought I could take this city entire. Except that I did not want it, and neither would my king. It's always useful to have somewhere else in the world, a place that sits apart. Somewhere to send those enemies you'd sooner not quite kill.

And the children you dare not live with, those too.

I looked down at the child who hung so persistently on my arm, and tried to shake him off. And failed, of course; he was most earnest, tugging at me, "Come. There is a back way to the kitchens, I know a man there…"

I was sure he did. That was his Skander, and his experience: covert, insinuating, conditional. Not mine. "This is my way, my king's way," in through the front door to ask straightforwardly for what I wanted. Looking at me, they would see Rulf at my back, and all his ships behind him; they would not refuse me. *In and out.*

Little Ramin let go of me then, and put his hands firmly behind his back. "I cannot go in there."

"Nor should you."

"Nor should *you*," emphatically. "Dzuria said—"

"Dzuria is your mistress, not mine."

I straightened my shoulders and walked alone, under his diminutive sceptical gaze: up dry and gritty steps, between stout pillars, through an open door.

I was met with obsequious manners, with drinks and courteous conduct into one antechamber after another. Courteous to me, at least: they almost fought each other for the privilege of serving me, those big smooth rounded men. I was surprised that Skanderenes ran so large, until I remembered the native habit of the high-born in the matter of their officials. Cut young, a eunuch boy might grow and grow. This must be the consequence: this heavy, huge unmanning, this fatuous squabbling over the right to be subservient to strangers.

I sat and sweated in close confines, ate and drank what they brought me, demanded attention that did not come. I asked for the prince of the city, and was politely abandoned; I asked for the chancellor and was moved to another room and abandoned again. I wielded Dzuria's name, and they might never have heard of her.

There were always other supplicants coming and going, seeking an audience, being disappointed. If all day I saw one person being led into the presence, I was not aware of it.

I did wait all day, in ever-fading hopes. And talked to my fellow-hopefuls, though none of them could offer hope. Some had waited weeks, one months. *In and out* looked like a fool's dream suddenly. Tomorrow perhaps I'd come back with my blade and whoever I could find among my men, cause a rumpus, see what ruder manners might achieve.

Tonight, there was nothing to do but yield at last to brute implacability: court was closed, audiences were over, neither the prince nor the chancellor would see us now, we should all come back tomorrow.

I headed down towards the harbour, and was unsurprised to find Ramin dancing attendance on me before I was halfway there, smugly certain. "You should have come with me, not wasted your time with silly pompous eunuchs."

I wondered briefly how wise he was, to make such mock. For sure some of those same eunuchs had come to the palace by way of the slave markets; for a boy in need of a future, his mistress might deem that a reasonable road.

Over supper she said, "I'm sorry, I thought you understood. You should have gone with Ramin. The front door is hopeless. Even with the right bribe in the right hands, none of them will be seen to hurry. That might imply that money holds the power, not themselves."

I growled, and wished again to show them other ways to hold power. A fist gripping a broadsword, a booted foot kicking in a door.

She said, "The palace is divided, half and half. The prince has time and no authority, while the chancellor has authority and no time. Both men train their staff to keep petitioners away, for entirely opposite reasons."

I grunted. "How is anything brought to happen? Ever?"

"Oh, the city finds its way. All our business passes through the chancellor's hands; just, not through the front door. Ramin will take you back tomorrow. Be warned, he will probably scold."

"I don't doubt it." If he were mine—but nothing here was mine, except the *Skopje*. I wanted to step outside, simply to look at her. Wood and tar and canvas, pegs and ropes: I knew her absolutely and trusted her the same, and I could say that about nothing else in Skander. Not my crew, nor my new friends. Nor myself, even, or what I would do tomorrow.

Tonight—what would I do tonight? Drink, and listen to this woman.

Watch her, too. She had wit both ways, wisdom and humour; I would be happy just to listen. My eyes were still full of palace smoke, which made them sore and restless both at once, and I would be happy to close them and just listen. But then I would doze, I knew. The smoke had gone into my head and was numbing yet. So I kept my eyes open and my mind alert by dint of watching her. Her skin in the lamplight, how the lines were dressed in shadow like a web of softness laid over strength; her hair, that had been tempered and pinned close to her skull, was another heavy fall of shadow now. Her mouth was mobile, lightly mocking. Her eyes were steady, scrutinising, always honest and so not always kind.

If I'd been younger, I might have made a grand gesture of a grand offer, the courtesy of my body for her night's delight. She would have laughed me out of the door, I think, even if she had been a younger woman.

But then, if I had been a younger man, I would not have seen the value in her. There are advantages to the slow creep of age; there is recompense. Not everything rots at once.

When there was space, when there was a quiet fallen between us, I said that, or something like it.

Even older men can make fools of themselves. She smiled and told me to go to bed, and did I want a child to light me the way?

COME morning, true to her word, Ramin took me up through the city again. On our way I saw a sprawled heap in a gutter, a groaning sorry mess of a man I thought might have been one of my crew. Another day, I might have stopped—but he was Rulf's man, not my own. One of the young bloods; let him bleed. If he was bleeding. The dark wet stain he lay in might be wine, or vomit. It might be piss. Truth? I didn't care.

On another narrow street I saw a shaggy blond head lean out of an upper window. Again, I thought that was one of mine; and wished him well, as a man's dark arm reached to draw him back inside. I liked the lad. Indeed, I'd seduced him myself from his father's farm, before bad land and bad luck had the chance to sour him. Left to make my own choices, I chose well, on the whole. Rulf? Not so. He had been a lucky king, but he'd needed that, to offset his disasters.

Sometimes I was astonished that he'd ever won the throne at all, let alone held it for so long. That none of his wars had killed him, and none of his mistakes, and—particularly!—none of his friends.

That Croft apparently never even tried to kill him, even from exile. Where were the Skanderene assassins? The city is famous for its dealings with death.

Perhaps he'd had his bones poisoned, his hair soaked with bane. Perhaps Rulf was dying even now as he gloated and lamented over his fallen foe, as I chased about on his stupid, deadly errand here in Skander, here at Ramin's heel. Here in the chancellor's back yard, in his house, in his kitchens, where there was heat and sweat and hurry, loud voices, no time.

Ramin snared a servant, greeted him by name, said, "Where is the steward Cephos?"

And would have been answered with a backhand blow, except that I was there. I caught that blow before it landed, a hand's span from his head; held it the way a cliff might hold a hurled stone, unmoving, undisturbed.

I said, "The steward Cephos?"

"Please, you will, you will find him in the storeroom, down that corridor," a frantic flicker of his eyes to show me where.

I nodded graciously, and released his wrist. Ramin ducked ahead, to where indeed a man was checking sacks.

"Cephos! I have been looking for you!"

That earned him a slap too swift for me to intercept, even if I'd been inclined to.

"Master Cephos to you, little brat. And I have been waiting for you; I had word from your mistress. Yesterday, I think."

The blow was taken for granted; the unfairness of the rest reduced Ramin to spluttering incoherence. With a shrug, the steward turned to me. "You would be Harlan the Sawartsman?"

"I would. I need to speak to your chancellor."

"Yes. Come with me."

He took us through a side-door, and into another world: a half-world rather, between the domestic quarters and the public rooms. Rulf's rede-hall was a single vast and open space, where you had to work out for yourself who was king and who was carl, who lord, who stable-lad. Here the very shape and structure of the house separated servants from their masters. It was like walking within the skeleton of a great beast; internal walls were hollow, and within them ran a network of stairs and passages, narrow and awkward and secret as spies. Secret for the light-footed, at least, for the slender and flexible. Ramin was cat-quiet and cat-swift, the steward much the same. I knocked my head on low beams, stumbled over sudden steps, rubbed my shoulders against both walls at once.

We passed a dozen doors before at last the steward unlatched one and beckoned us through. I straightened my poor cramped spine with a grunt of relief—and struck my head one more time, on something that swung away from the contact and then back to hit me again.

This time I didn't even try to hold the oath back to a mutter. At my side, the steward flinched; behind me, Ramin giggled; ahead, someone laughed aloud.

I reached up to snare the rope-hung obstacle, a bar of polished wood like a ladder's rung or a child's swing. Just one of many; for a moment I thought we'd been brought into a spider's lair, the room was festooned with so many ropes and bars. A spider with a sailor's ken, knowing knots and bindings and how to rig a space so that no two ropes should tangle.

Beneath that web, two men: one standing, one lying on a couch under a coverlet of cloth-of-gold. Both pale, shaven-headed. I took them for eunuchs, one more layer of officialdom to be circumvented.

It was the older of the two, the man lying down who had laughed. He was grinning still. Glowering at him, wondering if he was sick or indisposed, I saw how the coverlet lay flat where his legs ought to have been; his body ended abruptly, just a little below the hips.

Now I understood the ropes and rungs. He was broad-chested, vigorous despite his age, despite his pallor; no doubt he could pull himself around this webwork as handily as any sailor aloft. Handier, without his legs' weight or the need for footing.

And he was grinning at me yet, waiting for something; and—

"*Croft!*"

I was the king's windmaster; the breeze comes at my calling. A gale, when I shout. I had learned long since not to shout withindoors, even in a hall. Even in Rulf's great rede-hall. In that close space, that day—well, I shouted.

I broke the room.

Those hollow walls splintered like bird-bones, shattered like window-glass. Ropes snapped and tangled, spars flew like straws. Ramin was blown clear across the room; I never saw what happened to Cephos.

Croft lay in the ruin of his couch, clinging to his companion, laughing and laughing.

LATER, in another room, first passion spent:

"They call me Fenner nowadays," he said, "hereabouts. Or simply Chancellor."

We used to call him Fenner the Helpless, because he never needed any help. I had never been the right man for this mission. Rulf had subtler thinkers he might have sent, souls as suspicious as his own. Blunt and trusting are poor qualifications for an ambassador, especially to a city as insidious as Skander.

"You seem...shorter than you were," I breathed, still barely trusting my own voice. Rulf and I were friends as two cats are friends, always sidelong in the corner of each other's eye; Croft and I had been friends as two bulls are friends, always head to head. I couldn't measure my danger here, or his own.

"Come, sit," he wheezed, hoarse from laughing, hauling himself upright on this other couch. "Drink with me. The people here make little stronger than bread beer—but I have all the palace as my plaything, which means half the world, and the better half. Our guests learn to be open-handed. I've a honey brandy from the Brach that would be worth the journey to Brachia on its own account, rowing against tide and current all the way."

Unexpected, abbreviated, very far from safe, he was still Croft. Of course I would drink with him. He wanted to talk, to tell me how clever he'd been, and how sly. We'd had the same conversation over and over, since we were boys together.

I sat the other end of the couch, where there would have been room even if he hadn't shifted, that space where his legs were missing.

"We thought you were dead."

"You were meant to."

The second man had carried Croft in here, as casually as one carries a child. Now he fetched us bowls of glass filled with a clear dense liquor, fire on the tongue and fire to the heart. And took none for himself, but settled wordlessly on the floor against the couch's arm, where Croft could reach out and stroke his smooth oiled scalp, tug lightly at his ear. Servant and lover, then—or I was meant to think so.

Croft had shaved his own head, and his beard too. That was my excuse for taking so long to know him. We look for what we expect to see, and make easy judgements: clothes, hair. Legs.

I said, "How does a crippled beggar, even a beggar king, rise to be chancellor in Skander?"

He snorted. That was not the question I wanted to ask. Even so, he graced it with an answer. "Painstakingly. A doctor fled here because his lord had died under his knife. I took the same chance, and lived. A man may shrug a burden off, and get by the better after. You might learn that, if you chose. I traded legs for influence; the city's prince was curious to watch the cutting and the healing after, and so I reached the palace. That prince is dead now, but I am here yet."

"Your bones are in Sawartsland, in Rulf's lap. Named and known." Unmistakable, or so Rulf thought. "Did you have your doctor keep your legs in pickle, till you needed them?"

"And then attach them to some other body, and hope they looked to fit? I might have done." He sounded pleased with me for suggesting anything so wily, so unlike myself. "But no: I bought a man at market and had my doctor break and bind his legs, just as Rulf had done with me. Then I kept him alive until I needed him."

For years, that meant: years and years, in pain he knew too well. And then killed him, boiled his bones, wired them neatly together and sent them to us. I might have said anything, nothing; it would make no difference now. I said, "What for, old friend? Is there some way of vengeance here, that I can't see?"

He laughed. "Oh, I have had my revenge on Rulf, although he doesn't know it. He has no child, does he?"

"None—though not for want of trying."

"Of course. He'd want a dynasty. He'll never have one. I sent him a woman long ago, a hedge-witch to poison his seed. No sons for Rulf King, however hard he tries."

It would never have been hard to put a woman in Rulf's bed, even from this distance. I wondered which woman and whether he had kept her, whether she worked her spells yet or one time had served for all time, a curse-bane lurking at the root. He had tried witches of his own, I knew, but Croft's must have been the stronger. No surprise, if he found her here in Skander.

He went on, "In the end, I knew he'd want Toland back. Adopted by the new king, sired by the old: that speaks of dynasty, what better? And what better way to push him into it than sending him my bones, letting him think me dead and the boy adrift? I knew you'd be the one to come, the king's windmaster. Perhaps you're right, perhaps this is still vengeance after all. I have stolen his posterity, and now I steal his friend."

Croft seemed content to smile and wait—not for the first time—for me to catch up with his meaning. I looked at the younger man, and back through time to when he had been younger yet; and spoke to him for the first time, said, "Well, then. If Croft has gone from crippled exile to beggar king to chancellor, what are you now?"

He echoed his master's smile, and said, "I am the chancellor's legs. As you have seen."

Which was to say that he was more than that, much more; but he would never be Rulf's son and never king in Sawartsland. I wondered if Croft had taken other measures to be sure of it, besides stealing the boy's heart and keeping him close all these years. I had taken him for a eunuch at first sight; I might not have been wrong.

It didn't matter, and I wouldn't ask. Not here, not now. I said to Croft, "I have the *Skopje* here, and I can find a crew, buy a crew if need be. I can go home, with this news or any. I don't see how you have stolen me from Rulf."

"A man can shrug a burden off," he said again. "And should do, where it has no value. My legs, your loyalty. The ship's your own; so should your life be. What do you have to go back for? Grown children and a bitter king, neither in need of you. A draughty longhouse cold all winter long, an ice-needle in your bones, and too many people always at your ear. They've had the best of you already; enough, now. More than enough. Stay here, and keep what's left."

"You're saying this was a trap for me? Not for Rulf at all?"

"Rulf would never come, you know that. A king without an heir, without children to marry off to build alliances? He hardly dare leave his hall. You, though: of course he would send you, and of course you would come. And once you were here—well. Harlan, stay. Find a new crew, sail new waters. Learn a city, the way you learned the sea. Woo the harbourmaster."

I startled. Perhaps I glowered.

He laughed. "What, did you think that she imagines all those children to be her own?"

Ramin crouched once more in his corner of choice, quiet and still, shrugging off his bruises. Who owns whom is always a question; in his mind, I thought, perhaps he owned me. Or perhaps he had traded me, or given me away.

In my own mind—well, I could see a small house, a quiet house, a great and welcome change from what I'd left, all that bustle and labour and noise. A boy to run errands and make a nuisance of himself, a girl who would know where my boots were; I shouldn't need more of a household. A house not too far from the harbour, certainly. Convenient for the *Skopje,* for a new life on and off the water; convenient for friends to visit, back and forth. Or to stay, either way. The harbourmaster if she eventually would, my blond farm lad in the meantime...

I said, "Why, whyever would you want that?" Apart from causing Rulf a deal of worry and frustration, which was no more than bread beer against the fiery spirit of what Croft had done already to trouble Rulf.

Sometimes, theft is an act of simple honesty. Everyone belongs to someone else, elsewhere as in Skander; but he said, "I miss more than the sea, and my legs. I have my legs," tweaking Toland's ear, simply to see him smile. He said, "I miss my friends. One friend," and so he stole me from my king.

THE BURIAL OF
SIR JOHN MAWE AT CASSINI

NEVER DID A MAN HANGED SEE such a funeral. Old Cobb leaned on his spade to watch the barges come down the canal in caravan, in smoky procession, each decked out with black solemnity. Crowds lined the bank, quality and commoners all intermingled, while open carriages and charabancs blocked the roadways behind. Gentlemen and coolies removed their hats as the cortège steamed slowly by; ladies bowed their heads, while their maids dropped a dutiful curtsey. Soldiers saluted, officers and troops together. They were not—quite—a formal muster, but a great many had chosen to turn out in full parade dress today, a scarlet glory against the green.

Flags were everywhere, at half-mast every one. Poles had gone up overnight at every measured furlong to ensure it. That had been a job of work. Cobb knew; he'd had the navvies in his bothy before dawn, drinking tea, smoking, grumbling. Now they too were beside the water, clean shirts and

a shave, grouped around the last pole they raised, just opposite the cemetery's watergate. Proud of their achievement, showing their respect. Mute
before their betters, awkward in any society other than their own, standing
their ground today. Cobb knew them intimately, them and their kind.
Perhaps he admired them, though he would scorn to admit it. Admiration
was for the idle classes who had time to compare this to that, others to
themselves. He was a navvy himself, in all but name. But for an accident of
birth, unless it was the grace of God. His mother had said the one thing,
parson the other. He needn't believe either. He was just glad of the red
stripe on his blue passport—*red, red, white and blue*—that said he was a
subject of Her Britannic Majesty, and Mars-born. This and that together:
the best of both worlds, as they liked to say. And give Venus never a mention,
they liked that too. Venus was in Russian hands, and the Tsar no friend to
the Queen Empress.

Cobb's birth was a privilege, maybe, but he worked as hard as any navvy
fetched up from Earth on a judge's warrant. Graves don't dig themselves.
Nor do cemeteries beautify themselves, even on a day with no digging.
Paths must be weeded, hedges trimmed. Old dried wreaths taken away,
fresh flowers laid. The route from gate to burial had been marked down on
a scribbled map and sent urgently to the city, to be sure that no one put a
foot wrong—and even so Cobb had taken time to string black ribbons from
tree to tree and in judicious places, swagged along the back of a bench and
garlanded around a sleeping cherub's neck, to stand as mute guide wherever the path divided. Nothing about today was spontaneous, though it was
meant to look that way. *Not our work,* Authority meant to say to any eyes
that watched, *we had nothing to do with this. The man died in his shame, at
our hand; all else is the will of the people.* That and, *See how the people feel,*
Authority meant to say that too. *They choose to honour him this way. That
should surely tell you something.*

Someone, from somewhere, must be watching. There was not a nymph
to be seen in the water, though, not an imago in the sky. That seemed appropriate. On such a day, they ought to keep their distance.

People said, *They're shunning us, they think all this disgusting.* Old Cobb didn't know about that. He didn't have the finger-talk, no one he knew had the bubble-talk. If there was an air-talk, no one knew it at all; who could talk to an imago? They wouldn't hold still long enough. Flibbertigibbets. The creatures lived their lives half backwards, as it seemed: growing old and wise and ever deeper, from vicious reckless nymph to naiad in the slow dark waters, and then abruptly young and foolish once again. Briefly, in mid-air.

Merlins, he liked to call them. People did, all up and down the classes. He'd heard the word from a widowed duchess and a weaver's boy. You had to call them something, after all; and *Martians* didn't apply. He was a Martian himself, born and bred. Red-blooded. They said that too, all up and down. Even the lordlings who might have boasted otherwise, bluebloods they'd be called on Earth. Not here. Red dust under their fingernails, despite a lifetime's scrubbing.

DIGGING graves is a profession and a privilege, not a punishment detail. To a man with the right mind, it's almost a sacrament. Cobb knew his work and he knew its value. In a smaller town, given a simpler church with a lesser congregation, he'd be sexton and respected. But Cobb was Cassini-born, raised within the sound of Thunder Fall, in the shadow of the cathedral rising on the flooded crater's rim. He had never thought of leaving. The sexton here was a most superior man, far above Cobb's touch, with airs and responsibilities both. Cobb was content to be gravedigger, and do the work that mattered.

No digging today. The spade was a prop to his comfort, not a tool to his hand. The cathedral might be unfinished; the cemetery had seen a century's use already. Of course the great families had their private vaults and mausoleums, stone-built, adorned with weeping angels and Latin mottoes, the reverence of ornament. Sir John's great-grandfather had been on the first Settlement ship. His grandfather was signatory to the Charter. From the day he was born, it had been known where he would lie in death: beside them in the family crypt, on the shelf that already bore his name. Only the date, this day was a surprise.

The date, and the manner of his coming. He might have expected pomp, but not disgrace. Disgrace *and* pomp. The unseemly rush to judgement, arrest and trial and execution should have been startlement enough, so hurried they were. That and this funeral too, this frantic elaborate fair, the very opposite of discretion or diplomacy or tact: startling. *We bend the knee to the merlins,* people said—the navvies had said it, around Cobb's hearth this morning—*when we stretch his neck so fast, because they ask it; we slap them in the face—for his sake, aye—when we bury him with honour, as we do.*

Just who had ordered the flags, the barges, the sense of great occasion would likely come clear only in time, in the account-books. Someone must be paying for all this. The crowds had not been ordered, quite—except the schoolchildren, perhaps, in their scrubbed and serried ranks, boys in Eton collars and girls in white pinafores, with flowers in their hands—but they had surely been expected. The schools must have been told, *you are expected.* The common people could simply be relied on. A public hanging at first light, a gentleman, a man of reputation, the whole city would turn out for that; and even before the body was cut down, the rumours must have started.

No one quite knew anyway, whether he was condemned for murder or for treason or for breaking the Charter, or all three. His trial had been held *in camera*, and the proclaimed verdict was conspicuously unforthcoming in its detail. Easy then to understand how quickly people accepted that his crime had been noble and terrible and strange, that he had died in the service of Queen and Empire, although the Queen would necessarily say nothing and the Empire was obliged to disavow it. The Viceroy was subtle or else craven, depending on your point of view, but could be disregarded either way. The city of Cassini meant in any case to say a solemn farewell to its fallen son. The funeral cortège was steam-up before dawn in the basin below the Fall; the poles stood waiting for their flags; authorised or not, informed or not, the city took a half-holiday to see him silent home.

GIVEN his choice, Cobb might have stood with the navvies by their flagpole. He valued their salty, uncouth respect more highly than the prescribed and public sorrow of the cathedral's clergy as they stepped from the leading barge onto the heavy timbers of the landing-stage. From archbishop to thurifer, their words and roles were written down; it all came easy to the likes of them. They could speak of honour and sacrifice and debt, exhibit all that was proper and not necessarily mean a word or a moment of it. Cobb trusted the navvies more.

He had his place too, though: just within the locked gates, ready to open them at need. There was no need—the archbishop himself did the honours with his plated key, and the lock turned sweet as any, because Cobb had bathed it in rock-oil overnight and only fitted it back an hour ago—but this was not a day to be taking chances. You could feel it. This was a day for history to remember, in books and in the home, in family legend. *You listen to your grandad, he was there.*

Here he was, and glad of a sort, however much he wished himself marginally elsewhere, just a little transported. Over there. The clergy stood for ritual, tradition, what was careful and proper and ordained from far away; the navvies for a sullen passion that rips the heart, the urgency of presence, the true spirit of the Empire.

The sexton drew the gates wide, with barely a glance at Cobb. He was in his whites, as was the dean and all the chapter too, with just a band of red at the hem of every alb as though the linen dragged inch-deep in Martian dust. Wherever it flew, from Westminster to New Shoreditch to the canalside today, the Union Flag wore that same red border now. In happier times, on church parade, the children sang their way around it:

Red, red, white and blue
These are my colours and my fealty too.

It was simple, stirring, cheerful, an unofficial anthem. Some days half the crowd would join in. That might be another way to spot the Mars-born: which songs they stood up for.

Cobb had a red handkerchief at his throat today. It jarred perhaps with his dusty dutiful blacks, but he was hardly alone. He'd have been hard pressed, indeed, to find man or woman or child who wasn't showing a flash of patriotic primary somewhere, along with their mourning bands: a ribbon in the hair, a buttonhole thread, the cuff of a glove turned back to show its lining. The schoolgirls' flowers were every shade of crimson, scarlet, cardinal, maroon.

It was like seeing all rumours confirmed, to see the hierarchy of the Church of Mars line either side of the landing-stage like an honour guard. The merlins would hate that, surely, if they ever understood it. What they demanded had been granted them, and this was the response: the letter of the law, and the spirit of the Empire. He was not a sentimental man, but even old Cobb felt a twist in his throat, a prickle behind his eyes. They did this well, he thought, his people. Each of them individually stood high today, and raised their neighbours higher. The Viceroy couldn't be here, of course, to see a man buried who had been hanged at his command—but the Widow at Windsor would hear of this through the aether, and nod, and recognise its worth.

The second barge carried the coffin beneath its pall of red, and the six men who would bear it home. Six troopers, drawn by lot—Cobb had heard—when every man in barracks stepped up to volunteer.

By the look of the fortunate six, every man in barracks had lent a hand to be sure they would not disgrace the regiment. From the plumes on their shakos to the pipeclay on their belts to the blacking on their boots, they gleamed and dazzled.

Before them, a single cherubic boy stepped ashore in a plain white surplice belted with scarlet. As the men shouldered their burden he stood quite still, gazing ahead through the double line of clergy and the open gates to the green of the cemetery, beyond the cemetery to the butterscotch sky, beyond the sky itself perhaps to very heaven: he seemed that innocent, that pure.

He might perhaps have had a signal, the twitch of a finger from the canon who was his music-master in the cathedral choir school. Perhaps it was the preternatural hearing of the very young, to catch exactly when the

pallbearers were ready at his back: the last deep breath, the rustle of immac-
ulately pressed serge and the creak of polished leather, the sudden silence
following. Or else there was simply a moment, when waiting was done and
the next thing had to begin. When the silence couldn't last a moment longer.

At all events, he sang. His lone treble rose like larksong, so high and true
it could carry perhaps all through the aether and back to the Widow herself,
to sing to her directly.

Red, red, white and blue...

Not a hymn, not a psalm. Not perhaps what the boy had been instructed
or expected to sing. The troopers—forewarned, perhaps?—didn't miss a beat
as they slow-marched behind him, their faces carved to solemnity, but Cobb
felt a stir along the lines of white. No one would say anything, here and now.
If Cobb was right, the boy was safe to be thrashed later; he might even lose
his place at school. He might think even that worthwhile in payment for this
moment, when the province's senior clergy closed ranks and marched behind
the coffin, lending their imprimatur to the simple schoolboy tune that lay
buried in every Martian's marrow.

Red blows the wind and free
From Mars to the Empress in the old country.

THIS is the order for funerals, wherever subjects of Her Majesty have land
and leisure wherewith to mark their loss. First comes the innocent, the cherub,
a herald of sorrow; and then the dead. Then the religious. The military, the
secular, the family follow on together, all one in the eyes of the Church.

Here came the mourners, then. The Mawes and their immediate rela-
tions, stiff with grief and shock: clad from eldest to youngest in severest black
except for those who had served the Queen Empress in her wars, whose uniforms blazed somehow brighter red than any. Officials and dignitaries from
the city, the men who had drawn up the warrant that hanged Sir John, determinedly not crept into hiding. The Viceroy couldn't lend his countenance to

the occasion, but they felt obliged or entitled or at least able, in formal civilian dress with not a mark of rank between them, not a mayoral chain or a hint of precedence to suggest that they came *ex officio*. Senior officers, by contrast, had all their medals defiantly on display. The man belonged to the regiment, and the regiment was here to acknowledge that. The *Arean-Messenger* was here in the august person of its editor, taking notes like any cub reporter, listing all the society ladies and the men of business who had begged or bought or commanded a seat in a barge, a place at the heart of this ceremony.

Anyone and everyone, and Cobb. He might not have seen the choirmaster's signal to prompt the boy; he did see the sexton's, aimed at him as the clergy shuffled by. A swift beckoning finger, *follow on*. Cobb might have ignored it, he had his place and it was not in that procession; but he had his curiosity too. Deep and dark and slow as a merlin naiad just before the change, unconfessed as his patriotism, rooted and grown in the same red earth. It stirred within him now, and of course he followed on. Spade in hand.

THE Sabaean Plain is broad and flat between its high-walled craters, broad and flat and fertile wherever it can be irrigated. The first settlers landed half a world away, but they were frontier folk by nature. Every canal was an invitation and an opportunity. They scattered, they spread, they settled. Inevitably they had contact with nymphs along the way, with naiads when they disturbed the crater lakes. That was before anyone had guessed the merlin lifecycle, before anyone had named the merlins anything. Of course there had been deaths, deaths and deaths. Settlers and soldiers died in droves, before the Charter.

Their first graveyard here overflowed, before ever there was a city on the crater wall to feed it further. Authority was wise, ambitious, confident; the Viceroy bespoke a stretch of land between three canals. As if to remind himself that he had been from home before, if never quite this far, he called it San Michele and gave it to the new Church for her people. Forbade bridges, so that the city ever after should call it the Isle of the Dead and see it as separate, contained, particular. See it from the crater's height, indeed, vivid green all year amid the cornfields, set like a jewel in its narrow bands of water. San Michele was a promise to the future: *here we lie and shall lie, white bones in red soil under a canopy as green as England's own. In perpetuity, in Mars. This world is ours.*

Along broad paths that were deliberately neither straight nor level, through groves of maturing trees, between tombs and monuments and stones already weathered as though a country churchyard had been laid out on the scale of a city park, they followed the coffin and the boy's sweet call to the final resting-place of all the Mawes of Mars. That name was cut above the low vault's entranceway; the iron grille stood open because Cobb had left it so this morning. The coffin was set down before it, on trestles he had laid out in the half-dark; the scarlet pall hung to the ground like a veil of discretion. Mourners gathered in a respectful half-circle on the grass, while the archbishop read the words of interment from a book held open for him by the choirboy. Earth to earth, ashes to ashes: a solemn symbolic handful lifted from a silver chalice and cast across the pall. They had come to Cobb for that too, as though soil dug by a real worker were more pure or more true. The archbishop wiped his hands after on a linen napkin. Even he must have red dust beneath his nails, unless he bleached it out.

Now the family stepped forward, to scatter their own thin handfuls and lay flowers on the cloth. Sir John's mother, his sisters, his young son. At least he had a son. The boy would likely have a time of it at school, but he'd carry the name forward another generation, and perhaps have the chance to redeem it. Find the chance, or make it. Here was a world of empire, barely scratched; a young man might do anything, if his family stood behind him. Or the regiment would take him, surely. Blood wipes away dishonour, and the Queen Empress always needed men.

Or young Mawe could lose the family name and disappear, he wouldn't be the first. Turn his back on all his people, in rage or disappointment or relief; take a mule and a dust-mask and a waterskin, strike out for the high country, *terra incognita.* Lord knew, there was enough of it. Away from the main canals, vast ranges still stood open to be farmed or mined or simply wandered through. If a man learned finger-talk, he could learn to survive. Or not. He could lose himself, lose his life, never come home to occupy his own shelf in the vault. It happened; Cobb knew. Traders and trappers fetched in bones sometimes, the shoddy remnants of a life abandoned. They'd bring them to him, rather than to the clergy. He'd bring them to God himself, in a private corner of San Michele in the quiet of dawn, untroubled by questions of identity or baptism or state of grace. There was no such thing as an unmarked grave; God marked the fall of every sparrow. So, Cobb thought, did the Widow. Even this far away, where sparrows were imported, rare and costly.

No call for Cobb's intervention today. Sir John had been given communion in his cell, before the hangman came; he was blessed on the gallows, before the drop. Now the troopers lifted up his earthly remains one more time, and bore him down into the crypt.

Not the archbishop, but the dean followed, and some few men in suits whom Cobb could not have named or rated—and the sexton, who looked back and again beckoned, *follow on.*

Cobb picked his way through the mill of mourners, following.

EVERY crypt and every vault is different. Cobb knew all of his, inside and out. This one, he had its every corner fresh in mind, he had swept and mopped them all in readiness—but he had never seen it quite like this. It was not at all how he had left it. The coffin was set down again on trestles, not his own; storm-lanterns glowed in niches all around. The troopers were dismissed. The strangers discarded their tailcoats and addressed the pall in waistcoats and shirtsleeves, scattering dust and flowers in casual profusion as they stripped the cloth away.

The dean's face twisted: anger or distaste or something stronger, contempt perhaps, unless it was disgust.

"Well, don't just stand there. Open it!"

Cobb looked at the sexton, the expectant circle, the unexpectedly cheap wood of the revealed casket.

He said, "I don't have a screwdriver, sir. With me, I mean. I didn't..."

"Your spade, man. Use your spade. Good Lord, don't tell me you have scruples? Does that look to you like anything deserving of respect?"

Actually, it looked to Cobb more like a crate than a coffin. And yes, he did apparently have scruples, shaped by the silent company around the walls, the long dead in their bones and boxes. He might have said something eventually, something of that, but he was always slow to speak; one of the men he didn't know was quicker to speak for him.

"Hardy, go easy on the man. He has no idea. God willing." And then to Cobb, gently, as he might speak to a child or perhaps a horse, "Set your mind at rest. This is...not as it seems."

"Indeed." The dean, speaking effortfully in his outrage. "A pantomime, no sacrament at all. You may use your spade freely, sirrah. You desecrate nothing that is not already defiled beyond recourse."

"Gently, though," the stranger urged. "The spade, by all means, if you have no crow to hand—but gently. Not to harm what lies within."

Was Sir John not dead, then? *A pantomime,* the dean called it. Had the execution been only show? That would be a bold move, under the public eye. Crowds could be fooled, though; Cobb knew. The people delighted in a grand illusion. They wanted, almost, to be fooled. And he had seen *Romeo and Juliet,* enacted by the gentry for the people's education. He knew about heroes playing dead for posterity, for the law, for love.

He lifted his spade with some energy, then, a sudden eager vigour. A *gentle* vigour, yes. The crate was rudely made and rudely lidded, nailed shut, not even screwed. He could slide the blade's edge quite easily between lid and case, and simply lean on it.

The creaking squeak of steel forced from wood; the lid rose up an inch. He moved to another corner.

Methodically, far from mechanically, Cobb raised the lid on all sides, then loosed it completely with one last heave and lifted it away.

Beneath was the Union Flag in all its red-rimmed glory, the flag that should have been Sir John's pall, except it was impossible. No man hanged could be seen swathed in imperial colours, whatever his rank, whatever his service. That was the edict, and it might have been written exactly for this occasion, so that he who shrouded the body—Cobb wasn't thinking *corpse*, not now—could deal justly by the Viceroy and Sir John both. Wrap him in the Widow's flag and nail down the lid, cover that over with a simple red. The letter of the law, the spirit of the Empire.

The flags that lined the canal path could be shrugged away—a random act, mute insubordination, the work of a few malcontents who would be dealt with later—so long as no flag draped the coffin or was seen to drape the corpse.

The corpse-presumptive.

The dean was here to witness for the Church. The men in their shirt-sleeves must be doctors, standing by to revive the body from its seeming death, its trance-state. No conscious man could lie so still for so long, in a box. Under a cloth.

Not Cobb's place, to peel back that cloth. He wished they would hurry; how could Sir John breathe, beneath its folds? If he were breathing. There was no shift in the fabric, not a hint of stir. The friar's potion had left Juliet seemingly beyond the gates of death. cold and still and breathless. The shirt-sleeved gentlemen had a leather bag which Cobb hadn't noticed till now, much like a doctor's. No one had carried that through all the obsequies, from barge to tomb; it must have been brought in before, like the trestles, and set down on an empty shelf. One man opened it, and yes: scalpels and lancets and scissors and saws, all the gleaming steel of the surgeon's art.

In a disregarded corner—but Cobb was looking everywhere now, disregarding nothing—stood a pile of wooden boxes strapped with leather. It was the furthest corner from the entranceway, deeply shadowed; no one standing outside would see. Cobb had never imagined that he held the only key; of course the family could come and go at any time. Even so: he thought all of this had been hurried in this morning, after he unlocked the crypt. He thought the family didn't know.

He wondered if they would be told, and when, and by whom. And how. Not, surely, by Sir John himself. That would be appalling, to meet him as an unexpected revenant, the rope's mark still about his neck. Perhaps they were never to learn. Sir John could rise again and vanish, take ship to another city or another world, take a new name and never be himself again. These few who stood here might be the only men who ever knew the truth, and Cobb was one. For what, the virtue of his spade? They could have thought to bring a crowbar and do the work themselves. To bear witness, then, to represent the people as the dean did the Church? Perhaps, but...

The boxes held coils and wires, valves and clamps, electrical machinery. The largest were batteries, into which one of the doctors decanted acid as he watched. Restoring a man to life, that might well call for some extremity of science, tamed lightning.

At last, another doctor stepped up to the crate and threw back the shrouding flag to reveal—no. Not a man's body. Not yet. A case of spun and burnished copper, rather, a coffin within a coffin. No doubt some complex instrument, a pressure-chamber of some kind that might hold a man preserved, until such time as his resurrectionists—

NO. Cobb might be old but his eyes were sharp, and his mind had not dulled yet. That...was not copper, no. And not the work of any man. It was shaped near enough like a highpine cone cut from its stem—round like a spindle, broad at the shoulder and tapering to a narrow foot, near enough like a man's shape if he were wrapped and wrapped until he lost all form else, near enough a man's height that a coffin-box might hold it—and the shape was intimately familiar. Not that colour, nor the way it gleamed in the lamplight, but Cobb knew it for what it was when he looked in honesty rather than hope.

There would be no Sir John rising from this tomb, today or any day. Sir John was not here.

On Mars as on Earth, trees grew by canalsides and overhung the water. As on Earth, they might have been planted there for shade or fruit or shelter, for beauty perhaps—if the merlins could see beauty, if they cared—or for other reasons more mysterious; but chiefly, it was believed, trees and canals went natively together in the merlin mind because they echoed the deep waters and the highpines, those massive trees that grew beside the crater lakes.

It was no coincidence, that a merlin chrysalis looked like a highpine cone. Boughs hung heavy-laden with those for half the Martian year. The first settlers had harvested them for foodstuff and for fuel, and felled the trees for timber. And died for it, many and many, before the Charter brought peace. Nymphs were quick and savage, but naiads, oh: if a naiad rose from the deeps, whole settlements were wise to run.

Survivors learned to be more circumspect, to keep their distance from the highpines. They watched—from distance, yes—and learned the merlin cycle: from nymph to naiad, unhurriedly, uncounted years coming to maturity in the deep waters, in the dark; and then the climb into air, the stiffening skin, the months of hanging sessile and dry among the cones, indistinguishable. They must have faced predators at one time, people said, to need such a disguise. It was impossible to imagine now. The Church had another argument, that God made the merlins this way to show that they were an element of nature and no different, no better than any other animal, only larger and more dangerous than most. They could point for proof to the airhead imago which tore itself free of the chrysalis and lived a short, gay, heedless life in flight. They could and did do that until the first bold settler—a woman, as it happened—learned finger-talk and spoke with the first wary nymph.

Then no one could deny their intelligence, although their origins were mysterious and their motives obscure. Even more obscure, once it was understood that the great ships that shuttled swiftly and silently between Mars and Earth were merlin-piloted. No one knew how or why, but sometimes a chrysalis would not hatch, its imago not emerge. Instead another choice was made, internally or otherwise. The skin would harden to this burnished shell, and the pupa would be cut away whole from its tree, borne off by imagines to become the living brain in a ship that spanned the aether.

"This," Cobb murmured. "This is what he died for."

"Indeed. And what a sacrifice that was." One of the shirtsleeved men— not doctors, no; scientists, anatomists, not here to heal after all—ran his hands over the textured surface of the stolen chrysalis. Awed and covetous and possessive all three, those hands, his face. "His life for us, for our future, for our race. He took this and had to row it across the lake, where the racket of a steam-yacht would have brought the naiads up. Even so, they knew; he was barely ahead of the imagines when he reached the safety of the city. No safety for him, he knew his life must be forfeit under the Charter. He thought it worthwhile. He told me so himself. I think it was the Viceroy's sense of humour, or else his sense of honour, that had us smuggle it here in the guise of Sir John's coffin. We've told the merlins that he destroyed it trying to open the thing, that he was mad, quite mad. They don't believe us, of course. They're hanging over Cassini now and watching everything—but they won't look here, they think it's revolting how we treat our dead.

"We'll be here some time, I expect," he said, "trying to understand the thing, and how to make it fly. You need to know that. If we can learn how the merlin ships are worked, if we can train it to fly for us, we won't be dependent any more. We can build our own ships, harvest as many of these as we need, and sail the aether as we ought, under the Pax Britannica. We could take our empire to the stars, and wouldn't the Widow love that?"

"But the Charter..." They couldn't think to hang a man for every chrysalis they took. There weren't that many heroes.

"Once we know," the man said, "once we have the wherewithal to fly ships of our own, we can write a new Charter. Or tear it up. We only negoti-ated because we need them to ferry us back and forth. When that's no longer true—well. We needn't live in fear any longer. The Army can subdue the creatures, sure. Exterminate them if need be. It may be their time. No one here believes that they built the canals, or the aether-ships either; they don't have the physical make-up for engineering on that scale, whether or not they have the intelligence. They inherited this world from some other race, or else they took it by force. The same must be true of the ships. Now it's our turn, perhaps, to take it all from them. This could be the first step on that journey, what we do here, what we learn."

Perhaps all men of science were so ruthless. Cobb looked again at the scalpels and the little saws, the drills, the electrical wires; and felt glad that the creature in its shell had no mouth to scream with, to eat like acid at Cobb's day. His days.

And turned to go, because surely this was why he was here, to understand this, that secret men would be inhabiting this vault a while with their experiments. Well, he knew it now; and the air would be cleaner outside.

And he had barely gone two paces before he checked, and turned, and said, "Sir John—where is he now? And when will he be brought here?" *And how?* would have been another question. Not in pomp, clearly, not as he deserved. Many a hero had seen a hurried grave, though, and…

"Oh, he shan't come here." That was the dean, interrupting coldly. "The archbishop has declared it. This far from home we must be stricter, more adherent to the rule of God's law and the Established Church. By any measure, Sir John's death was a suicide. He did what he did, he chose to do it, knowing what must follow. A sacrifice, yes—but he put his own head in the noose, and did it willingly. He cannot be buried in consecrated ground. You must do with him as you do for other executed felons, back at the prison, where his body lies."

Had Cobb thought that scientists were ruthless?

The hanged in this city were supposed to lack even an unmarked grave. Tradition would have buried them beneath the prison yard, but the merlins would not bear that. It was Cobb's task then to immerse them in a solution of lye for a few hours, until their flesh was gone. Then he was meant to crush the fragile surviving bone—with the flat of his eternal spade, yes—and scatter the powder to the winds.

"As I do for the others, sir, yes."

First the barrel of lye, yes, to eat off the corruptible flesh; but then—well, old Cobb knew the value of his work. It was a sacrament, almost. And he came and went between the city and the island, and no one ever wondered what he ferried back and forth, what he might be bearing in his sack. And he had his own private graveyard in a distant corner, where he brought lost men unsupervised to God, felons no less than wanderers.

There would be digging after all, this day.

THE KEYS TO D'ESPÉRANCE

ACTUALLY, BY THE TIME THE KEYS came, he no longer believed in the house.

It was like God, he thought; they oversold it. Say too often that a thing is so, and how can people help but doubt? Most facts prove not to be the case after all, under any serious examination. Even the Earth isn't round.

One day, they said, *D'Espérance will be yours. You will receive it in sorrow,* they said, *and pass it on in joy. That is as it is,* they said, *as it always is, as it should be.*

But they said it when he was five and he thought they meant for Christmas, they'd never make him wait till he was six.

When he was six they said it, and when he was seven and eight and nine. At ten, he asked if he could visit.

Visit D'Espérance? they said, laughing at him. *Of course you can't, you haven't been invited. You can't just visit. You can't call at D'Espérance. In passing,* looking at each other, laughing. *You can't pass D'Espérance.*

But if it was going to be his, he said at twelve, wasn't he entitled? Didn't he have a right to know? He'd never seen a painting, even, never seen a photograph…

There are none, they said, and, *Be patient.* And, *No, don't be foolish, of course you're not entitled. Title to D'Espérance does not vest in you,* they said. *Yet,* they said.

And somewhere round about fifteen he stopped believing. The guns still thundered across the Channel, and he believed in those; he believed in his own death to come, glorious and dreadful; he believed in Rupert Brooke and Euclidean geometry and the sweet breath of a girl, her name whispered into his bolster but never to be uttered aloud, never in hearing; and no, he did not believe in D'Espérance.

TWO years later the girl was dead and his parents also, and none of them in glory. His school would have no more of him, and the war was over; and that last was the cruellest touch in a long and savage peal, because it took from him the chance of an unremarked death, a way to follow quietly.

Now it must needs be the river, rocks in his pockets and thank God he had never learnt to swim. There would be notice taken, that was inevitable; but this would be the last of it. No more family, no one more to accuse or cut or scorn. The name quite gone, it would simply cease to matter. He hoped that he might never be recovered, that he might lie on the bottom till his bones rotted, being washed and washed by fast unheeding waters.

Quite coldly determined, he refused to lurk withindoors on his last long day. At sunset he would go to the bridge, *rocks in my pockets, yes, and no matter who sees, they shan't stop me*; but first he would let himself be seen and hissed at and whispered about, today as every day, no craven he. It was honour and honour only that would take him to the river; he wanted that clearly understood.

So he walked abroad, returning some books to the public library and settling his accounts with the last few merchants to allow him credit. He took coffee in town and almost smiled as the room emptied around him, did permit himself the indulgence of a murmured word with the cashier on his way out, "Please don't be troubled, I shan't come again."

And so he went home, and met the postman at the door; and was handed a package, and stood on his doorstep watching as the postman walked away, wiping his hand on his trousers.

THE package was well wrapped in brown paper, tied with string and the knots sealed. It was unexpectedly heavy for its size, and made softly metallic noises as he felt its hard angles shift between his fingers.

Preferring the kitchen in his solitude to the oppressions of velvet and oak, of photographs and memories and names, he went straight through and opened the package on the long deal table under the window.

Keys, three separate rings of keys: brass keys and bronze and steel, keys shorter than his thumb and longer than his hand, keys still glittering new and keys older than he had ever seen, older than he could believe, almost.

For long minutes he only held them, played with them, laid them out and looked at them; finally he turned away, to read the letter that had accompanied them.

An envelope addressed to him in neat copperplate, nothing extravagant; heavy laid paper of good quality, little creased or marked despite its journeying in with the keys. A long journey, he noted, unfolding the single sheet and reading the address at the top. His correspondent, this remitter of keys was apparently a country solicitor; but the town and the company's name were entirely unfamiliar to him, although he had spent two months now immersed in his parents' affairs, reading everything.

My dear lad, the letter said—and this from a stranger, strange in itself—*I believe that this will reach you at the proper time; I hope you may learn to view it as good news.*

In plain, you are now the master of D'Espérance, at least in so far as such a house may ever be mastered by one man. The deeds, I regret, you may not view; they are kept otherwhere, and I have never had sight of them. The keys, however, are enclosed. You may be sure that none will challenge your title, for so long as you choose to exercise it.

I look forward to making your acquaintance, as and when you see fit to call upon me.

Yours, etc.

HIS first impulse was to laugh, to toss the letter down, his resolution quite unchallenged, quite unchanged. Just another house, and what did he want with it? He had one already, and meant to leave it tonight and forever.

But he was a boy, he was curious; and while he would welcome death, while he meant to welcome it, *come, sweet Death, embrace me,* he was very afraid of water.

His hands came back to the keys and played upon them, a silent music, a song of summoning. Death could surely wait a day, two days. So could the river. It was going nowhere; he'd be back.

AND so the train, trains, taking him slow and dirty into the north country. Soon he could be anonymous, no name to him, just a lad too young to have been in the war, though he was old enough now. That was odd, to have people look at him and not know him. To have them sit just across the compartment and not shift their feet away from his, not lour or sniff or turn a cold, contemptuous, ostentatious shoulder.

One woman even tried to mother him, poor fool: not knowing what a mother meant to him, bare feet knocking at his eyeballs, knocking and knocking, *knock knock.* He was cold himself then, he was savage, gave her more reason than most had to disdain him, though still she wouldn't do it.

And at last there were sullen moors turned purple with the season, there was a quiet station with a single taxi waiting and the locals hanging back, *no, lad, you take it, it's only a ten-minute walk into the town for us and we know it well, it's no hardship.*

He wouldn't do that, though. Their kindness was inappropriate, born of ignorance that he refused to exploit; and he had no need of it in any case. It was after six o'clock, too late to call on the solicitor, and he didn't plan to seek lodgings in town. His name was uncommon, and might be recognised. Too proud to hide behind a false one, he preferred to sleep in his blanket roll under whatever shelter he could find and so preserve this unaccustomed anonymity at least for the short time he was here.

LEAVING the station and turning away from the town, he walked past a farm where vociferous dogs discouraged him from stopping; and was passed in his turn by a motor car, the driver pausing briefly to call down to him, to offer him a ride to the next village. He refused as courteously as he knew how, and left the road at the next stile.

Rising, the path degenerated quickly into a sheep-track between boulders, and seemed to be taking him further and further from any hope of shelter. He persevered, however, content to sleep with the stars if it meant he could avoid company and questions. Whenever the path disappeared into bog, he forced his way through heather or bracken until he found another; and at last he came over the top of that valley's wall, and looked down into an unexpected wood.

He'd not seen a tree since the train, and here were spruce and larch below him, oak and ash and others, secret and undisturbed. And a path too, a clear and unequivocal path, discovered just in time as the light faded.

He followed the path into the wood, but not to its heart. He was tired and thirsty, and he came soon to a brook where he could lie on his stomach and draw water with his hands, fearing nothing and wanting nothing but to stay, to move no more tonight.

He unrolled his blankets and made his simple bed there, heaping needles and old leaves into a mattress between path and brook; and only at the last, only a little before he slept did he think he saw the girl flit between trees, there on the very edge of vision, pale and nameless as the light slipped.

Pale and nameless and never to be named; nor seen again except like this, a flicker of memory and a wicked trick of the light. He closed his eyes, not to allow it passage. And breathed deeply, smelling sharp resins and the mustiness of rot, and so cleared his mind, and so slept.

SLEPT well and woke well, sunlight through trees and a clean cool breeze and no fear, no anger, nothing but hunger in him. With the river's resolution to come, all else was resolved; there was, there could be nothing to be afraid of except that last great terror. And why be angry against a town he'd left already, a world he would so shortly be leaving?

Breakfast was an apple from his backpack, eaten on the march: not enough for his belly, but that too was no longer the driving force it had been. He had higher considerations now; with time so short, a grumbling gut seemed less than urgent.

Oddly, with time so short, he felt himself totally unhurried. He would walk back the way he had come, he would find his way into the town and so to the solicitor—but not yet. Just now he would walk here, solitary among trees and seeking nothing, driven by nothing…

WHICH is how he came to D'Espérance, called perhaps but quite undriven: strolling where others before him had run, finding by chance what was his already, though he meant to take only the briefest possession.

The path he took grew wider, though no better cared for. Tree roots had broken it, in places the fall of leaves on leaves had buried it; but logic and light discovered its route to him, not possible to lose it now. It turned down the slope of the valley and found the brook again, and soon the brook met something broader, too shallow for a river, too wide for a stream. The path tracked the water until the water was suddenly gone, plunging through an iron grid into a culvert, an arch of brick mounded by earth. Steps climbed the mound, and so did he; and standing there above the sound of water, he was granted his first sight of D'Espérance.

NEVER any doubt of what he saw. He knew it in that instant, and his soul sang.

The house was dark in its valley, built of stone washed dark by rains and rains. Even where the sun touched, it kept its shadow.

A long front, with the implication of wings turned back behind, though he couldn't see for certain even from this elevation, with the house full-face and staring him down. A long front and small windows, three storeys and then a mansard roof with dormers; in the centre a small portico sheltering a high door, and he wasn't sure even the largest of his keys would open such a door. Wasn't sure that it deserved to.

No lights, no movement: only dark windows in a dark wall, and the sun striking brightly around it.

Between himself and the house there were formal gardens wrecked by growth, rampant hedges and choked beds; but the hedges and beds stood only as a frame to water. Long stone-lined pools were cut strict and square at the corners, though they were green and stagnant now and the jutting foun-tainheads were still; and below the gardens, lapping almost at his feet now lay the deeper, darker waters of a lake. No need for the return journey after all. No need for anything more, perhaps, now that he'd seen the house. He could run down the slope before him, twenty yards at a good flying sprint and he'd be too fast to stop. And so the plunge into cold cold water and the weight of his pack, the saturated blankets, even the keys helping to drag him down...

But this side of all that water, on the verge of unkept grass between trees and lake stood a building, a small lodge perhaps, though its weight of stone and its leaded dome spoke of higher ambition. Ivy-clad and strange, seemingly unwindowed and halfway at least to a folly, it must look splendid from the house, one last positive touch of man against the dark rise of the wood. And it would be a shame not to have set foot in any part of D'Espérance, all this way for no more than a glimpse; shame too to go on an impulse, on a sudden whim, seizing an unexpected opportunity. No, let it at least be a decision well thought through, weighed carefully and found correct. Nothing hasty, no abrupt leap into glory or oblivion. He needed to be sure of his own motives, to feel the balance of his mind undisturbed; there must be no question but that it was a rational deed, in response to an untenable situation.

So no, he didn't take the chance to run. He walked carefully down the steep slope and turned to parallel the lake's edge as soon as the ground was level, skirting the last of the trees, keeping as far from the water as he could. Looking across to the further shore, where the gardens' gravel walks ended in a stone balustrade and a set of steps leading down into the lake, he saw a man he thought might have been his father. Blindfold and blundering in the bright dry light, the man teetered on the steps' edge, on the rim of falling; and then there was dazzle burning on the water as a soft breeze rippled the sun, and when his eyes had cleared he could no longer see the man.

IT is a truism that anything seems larger as you get closer, that you lose perspective; but here he thought it was the other way, that his eyes had made him think the lodge small because they couldn't credit the house with being so very large. It must be so, although he wasn't looking at the house now to make comparisons. This near, the lodge took everything. Squat and massive it sat below its dome and drew him, dragged him forward; he thought that it was so dense it made its own gravity, and that he was trapped now, no way out.

The lodge had double doors that faced the water, too close for his liking, only three low steps and half a dozen flagstones between them. In echo of the house, there was a small pediment above the high doors, with columns to support it in a classic portico. Still no proper windows. He could see a thin run of glass at the cupola's foot, at the wall's height, held between lead and stone; but even with that, even at this season with the sun low enough to strike through the doorway at the height of the day, it was going to be dark in there.

No lock on the doors, though, no need to struggle with the keys. He climbed the steps, laid his backpack down, set his shoulder to one of the doors and pushed.

THERE was rust in the hinges, and it spoke to him: its voice was cold and harsh, it said "Guilty," and then it squealed with laughter.

He jumped back, sweating, clutched at a column for support and looked out across the lake again. Saw nothing, no movement, no man.

Stood still, listened; heard the blood hiss and suck in his ears, heard his heart labour behind his ribs, eventually heard birdsong and the soft lapping of the lakewater, a more distant rushing which must be the underground flow to feed and freshen it.

The door stood ajar, silent now. He stepped forward and pushed again, and it swung wide with no sound beyond the grating of rust in its hinges.

NOT a lodge, then. Surely a folly after all.

He stood in the doorway, and the sun threw his long and slender shadow across an enamelled iron bath. One of eight, all set in a circle, radiating; and at the centre a square tiled pit, a plunge-bath large enough for a dozen men to share.

There was nothing else in the great circular chamber except for wooden slat benches around the sides, dark with mould and damp. The walls were adorned with intricate murals, figures from history painted in the Pre-Raphaelite style, though the light was too dim for him to identify the scenes portrayed.

A bath-house, he thought, *a bathing-house.* This vast construction, and it was only a place to bathe, *ensemble* or *en famille;* and that with the lake outside, just there, wide and deep and surely more attractive.

Perhaps there'd been a club, a bathing-club, the local gentlemen anxious to preserve their modesty or their ladies' blushes. That or something like it: nothing else could explain so much labour, so much expense to such frivolous effect.

But frivolous or not it was here, and so was he. If D'Espérance could spawn a structure so large and strange at such a distance, then he thought his keys could stay where they were, safely in his pack. Something he lacked, to take him up to the house. He'd settle for this, at least for today. The child is father to the man; there were lessons here to be learned, aspects of the parent surely reflected in its idiot son.

He thrust the door as wide as it would go and then opened the other also, to let in as much light as he could, and allow the breeze to freshen the musty air. Some few cracks in the domed roof added a little further light to what the door gave, and that high circle of glass below the dome, but this must be the most it ever saw by nature. He thought they would have needed lamps, those who used it. Whatever they used it for.

Still, there was enough to see by. Stepping inside, he could see a gallery, circling just at the top of the wall, below that ring of glass—he wanted to call it a clerestory now—and the dome's curve: all wrought iron, the gallery, and likewise the spiral stair that led up to it from behind the door. *That must have been for strangers,* he thought, *for observers, non-participants.*

Now he was concerned about the murals, he thought at the very least they must be lewd. Some provincial Medmenham set he imagined building this bath-house, ambitious to reproduce the Hell-Fire Club in their own gardens. But lowering his eyes tentatively to look, expecting grave disappointment, expecting a grand fancy rendered simply sordid, he found nothing like it.

King Arthur and Excalibur he found, Oberon and Puck he found, Wayland in his smithy and other men or fairies that he couldn't identify, but all surely harmless even to his nervous sensibilities.

And all flaking, too, some cracking as the plaster bulged behind them or else staining darkly from beneath. Seeing one crack too long, too straight for nature, he went closer and found the outline of a door within the picture, found a painted leather strap to tug it open.

And tugged, and first saw the mirror that backed the door, that showed him his own shape marvellously moving in this still place. Then saw the closet behind the door, with its hooks and bars for hanging clothes, its slatted shelves for towels and other necessaries.

Closed that door and looked for others, found them regularly spaced around the chamber; and none hid anything more than an empty closet, until the last.

On the other side of the double doors was the iron spiral leading up; here, as though in secret reflection behind its concealing door, was a stone spiral leading down, leading into darkness.

Bold he could be, curious he certainly was; but he needed a light in his hand before he ventured those narrow steps. And hot food in his belly, that too.

ONE thing at least he'd learned in his time at school, though not from his teachers. Like many a boy before him, he'd befriended the local poachers for the sake of an occasional salmon or grouse to scorch over his study fire and eat with his fingers, with his friends. At the start of term he'd brought them bottles of brandy filched from his father's cabinet; in return they'd taken him out more than once, shown him how to make a snare and where to set a night-line.

Those skills would feed him now. There must be fish in the lake; there were certainly rabbits in the wood's fringe, he'd seen signs of them already. He hadn't thought to bring fishing-line or wire, why should he? He wasn't here for sport. But he could improvise. He had bootlaces, there were springy willow-shoots growing by the water. No need to visit the town, even to shop for what would ensure he need not visit again.

Sitting on the steps in the sunshine while water rippled before him, that water reflecting clouds and light and nothing of the great dark house, he reflected on the house; and almost felt he had a duty there at least, if none to family and reputation gone or a name that was meaningless now, himself the last shamed bearer of it. He should go to the solicitor, and ask how arrangements might be made. If he had to be honest, *I shall be dead soon and the house needs an heir,* then so be it. He could do that, once. More than once, he thought not; but once would be sufficient.

Something screamed in the wood behind him, with the voice of a young girl. He started, shifted on the warming stone, and went to check his snares.

Already there was a rabbit kicking, held tight around the neck and its feet barely in contact with earth. He gathered wood for a fire, laid it in the portico and lit it with flint and tinder from his pack; then he fetched the rabbit. Carried it still living to his fire, though it lay still as a dead thing in his hands, only its eyes alive. Those he killed first, with a pencil. Contrary to all his tutors' lessons he let it die slow and suffering, tutor himself now and pain all his lesson, the real world his theme.

"See it?" he whispered, poking with his pencil, digging gently. "See the light, little brother, see the *light?*"

What the rabbit saw, of course, was darkness: which was what he saw also, whichever way he looked, into the bath-house or out across the lake. Shapes woven from shadow moved in the shadows inside, avoiding the last of the sun's fall across the floor; or they moved darkly in the water, under the glitter of light.

Ragged gunfire sounded through the wood and birds rose like smoke, screaming on the wind. *A posse shooting crows,* he thought; but he still thought himself alone in this valley, and he didn't believe that anyone would shoot at crows with a .303.

Later, as his fire hissed under the rabbit's dripping quarters, he heard sounds of soft knocking, dull and rhythmic.

Sat and listened; and no, not knocking after all. Sounds of kicking. Slow, steady, unremitting, a foot thudding into flesh and breaking bone.

He tended his fire, but his hands were trembling now.

SITTING in the twilight, licking greasy fingers—not wanting to go to the lake to wash, not while it was light enough to see what moved within the waters—he thought he saw words scratched black across the red disc of the sun.

Guilty he thought was said again, and other words he couldn't read for the fire in his eyes, but they might have been names. His father's or his mother's, the girl's, his own. It didn't matter which. Any name was a betrayal.

He thought he should leave this valley before the games turned worse than cruel, before they remembered the real world and turned to blood. Not at night, though, he wouldn't leave at night. The wood had been friendly to him once; but there was coming in and there was going out, and they were different. He felt a little like an eel in a basket, trapped without trying. Come the morning, he'd test that. Not now.

SO he made his bed in the portico, on hard stone because there were too many shadows in the long grass moving, too many murmurs coming up. Between the wood and the water, even the bath-house seemed to offer something of protection.

Something, perhaps; but not enough. Waking in the cold night, he felt a moist warmth on his face and smelt sour breath, smelt blood.

Heard his own breathing change, heard his blood rush. Stiffened every muscle not to move, not to roll away; and thought there was no greater give-away, no louder announcement, *I'm awake!*

An unshaven cheek brushed his, dry lips kissed him, and he held himself rock-still. A voice moaned in whispers, and he wouldn't moan back. Then touch again and harder this time, hard to hold against such pressure as the man's face stropped itself against his. Skin and stubble and the bone beneath: and something else he felt, wouldn't open his eyes to see it but he felt coarse cloth, a blindfold.

And then there was nothing but the hard sounds of breathing, and the sounds of footsteps gone too quickly. He couldn't hear water, but he thought the man had walked straight into the lake.

In the morning he found a thread of linen caught in his own soft stubble. He tied it in a coil and put it in his wallet for safe keeping, where he might have put a lock of someone's hair; and no, he couldn't think of leaving now. Too much of betrayal already, too much of guilt.

Besides, the wood would never pass him through. He tested that. He went back to the culvert, and tried to walk the path upstream; and tree-roots tripped him, leaves hid hollows underfoot where he fell and hurt his ankle, might have broken it. Where the path slid beneath his feet and he could barely scramble back to solid ground, watching earth crumble into water, there he gave it up, there he turned and came back; but it had been nothing more than a token in any case, he'd only meant to scout.

NO escape from the valley, then. Not by the wood, at least. There must be a road, however ill-kept; but between himself and any road the house lay, massive and dissuasive. *My house,* he thought: a legal fiction, more of a brutal joke. Even at this distance, he was learning a little. The lesson was that

D'Espérance didn't belong, it wasn't owned. It might, on sufferance, permit; but he was not yet ready to confront what that would mean, being accepted by D'Espérance.

So no, not that way. He wouldn't even skirt the borders of the house; this was closer than he liked already, in its ambit even this further side of the lake.

Locked out of the wood, not ready for the house and no water-baby, never that, there was only the bath-house left him. This much he could encompass, heavy as it was, as it might prove to be. This much he could carry, for a while. *For a brief while,* his thoughts reminded him, and were still.

IN the best of the light, with the doors wide, he went in with a pale torch burning and opened the door to the spiral stair.

Walking down in sinking circles, he smelled must and mould and dead air. The flame flickered, making shadows dance around him; but that was only mechanical, the action of light unfiltered by strangeness, he could understand that and not fear it.

Distant sounds of rushing, like a hard wind contained: he thought of the culvert, and the hurry of hidden water.

The stair turned one final time, and brought him into a high cold chamber lined with brick, dark with moisture. This too was dedicated to the mechanical, though, and nothing to fear. His weak torch showed him pumps and boilers, copper pipes and iron, gauges and valves. His eye traced the run of pipes, what would be the flow of the water; he followed it, he learned it, he loved it. This was how he wanted the world to be, all in order and all explaining itself.

Until his torch went out; and this was not how he wanted the world to be, utterly dark and cold and empty, nothing in reach of his groping hands.

Groping, his hands found nothing but his eyes did. *Knock knock,* cool and stiff like fingers but not that, not fingers: lightly knocking against his eyes and knocking again like crooked fingers while he only stood there, too much knocked upon.

Moaning, he heard his voice say "Mama"; but all moans sound more or less like mama, and he hadn't called her that since he was a child, not since he was very small indeed.

He stepped backwards, away from the knocking; and kept his hands rigidly at his sides not to grope again, not to feel.

Not to find.

His feet found a wall for him, and he kept his shoulder against it until they came to the rise of the stairs. And so up, still in darkness and that rushing sound in his ears changing now, turning rhythmic, turning to kicks; and the door closed at the top but his barging shoulder crashing it open and his stumbling feet carrying him out into the cool and shadowed bath-house which was so much warmer, so very much brighter than what lay below.

AND still he couldn't leave, and wouldn't. Not if she were here too, and the girl somewhere in the wood, perhaps: that early glimpse no trick of light or memory, those sounds of kicking no folly of his mind.

He saw his father again across the lake, bound and blindfold, a khaki figure in an early light although the sun was setting.

Beset by his own senses, he struggled for that numb normality he'd worn like a cloak before. Horror was unexceptional, pockets were a proper place for rocks, one deep plunge and never rising after was a fit deed in a nothing, nothing world.

But poking at a rabbit's eyes wouldn't do it now, wouldn't keep him. Not where his father's eyes were too much on his mind, where his mother dangled always in his thoughts, where the girl might be watching from the wood.

What could keep him, the only thing that might keep him from the slip, from sliding through terror and into its undermath, would be to walk that slip's edge, to hang on terror's lips against its speaking. To go back into the bath-house and take possession of the dark below, where his mother currently possessed it.

GATHERING cobnuts and filberts at the wood's edge, his back turned to whatever threatened in the water, he heard a snuffling that might have been tears and saliva backed up in a sobbing girl's throat. He heard a scratching that might have been a girl's desperate nails digging furrows in the path, and then a steady heavy thud-and-scrape that sounded like nothing so much as a boot falling and falling, and its metal studs scraping on the path between falls as the foot drew back and lifted to fall again. He could hear breathing too, hard grunts tied to the same rhythm.

He lifted his head expecting to see her, expecting to see her kicked; and saw instead a bloated pink-brown rump swing and rub against a tree, hard enough to shake the trunk. And it swung away and swung back, thud and scrape, and it was only a pig after all: a great sow twice or thrice his weight, let forage in the wood or else—more likely, he thought, out here where no one was—escaped her sty and living feral. Unless D'Espérance did this too, throwing up animals unexpectedly and when they were most desired.

He needed this sow badly, and lacked the means to take her.

MEANS could be made, though. Made or found.

He slipped away quietly, not to disturb her at her scratching, not to startle her off into the depths of the wood where he might not be allowed to follow. If this was her current rooting-ground, then above all he wanted her to keep to it.

He blunted his knife cutting at ash-saplings, hacking them away from their roots. With the blade given an edge again on the granite steps of the portico, he spent the evening trimming and whittling until he had an armoury of sorts, three straight poles each sharpened at one end. He hardened the points in his fire, remembering an engraving in a book that showed cavemen doing the same; and the work absorbed him so that he forgot to look over the water before the light failed, to see if his father were there.

He still listened for the creak of rope in the bath-house or sounds of kicking in the wood, as he turned his spears in the glowing ashes; but he heard neither tonight, only the sow's noise among the trees. He might have chased her then, but that he was learning to fear the dark, or those things that were couched within it. Instead he trusted her still to be there in the morning, and lay all night fretting in his blankets, doubting her.

UP at first light, he found the sow moved on; but didn't need his acquired skills to track her. A blindfold man could have followed this trail, the broken undergrowth and the furrowed earth.

He caught up with her quickly, and with no hindrance from the wood: no tripping roots, no hanging branches tangling in his hair. There was hunting, apparently, and there was trying to leave, and they too were different.

Slowing as soon as he heard the sow's heedless progress, he crept close enough to sight her rump again; and ah, he wanted to do this hero-style, one mighty cast to fell her swift and sure.

But this wasn't sport, there was no one to applaud, and his spears weren't made for throwing. Silent as he knew how, as he had been taught, he slid forward into the wind and the sow never heard him, her great flap ears trailing on the ground as she snouted under leaves and bushes, eating nuts and acorns, eating insects, eating frogs.

At three yards' distance he set two spears to stand against a tree, and hefted the other in both hands above his head. The sow moved one, two casual paces forward, blithe in her size and strength, and oh she was big, she was just what he needed; and he took a breath and ran and thrust, all his strength in his arms as he stabbed down, driving the spear's haft deep as he could into the sow's flank.

She screamed, as he was screaming as he stabbed: high and shrill both of them, vicious and unrestrained. But he thought she'd run, or try to; and she didn't run. She turned, although her hind leg failed her where the spear jutted from it, and her eyes were red in the shadowed wood, and her festering yellow teeth were snapping at him; and he tried to jump backwards, and he fell.

Sprawled on his back, he looked up into a canopy of branches baring themselves for winter, and he saw his mother twist above his head, lolling at the rope's end. Her bare feet swayed and turned, one way and the other, feeling in the absence for his eyes.

He screamed again, and rolled; and though he only sought to roll away from his mother, he was sprayed with slaver from the sow's jaws as her bite just barely missed him. Gasping and shaken he scrambled away, and the sow strained to follow, hauling her weight unsteadily on three legs, slipping and rising again, squealing in pain and fury.

Up at last, he wanted only to run; but his eyes snagged on his two spare spears, and this was what they were for, after all. He'd never expected to finish her with one. So he snatched up a second, holding it two-handed again against her sheer mass; and as she came at him open-mouthed, he rammed its dark point into what was soft at the back of her throat.

And barely released his grip in time as her jaws threshed about its haft, jutting out between them; but she was a spent force now, crippled and gagged, blood colouring her leg and frothing out between her teeth. He could take time to recover his last spear, time to consider his aim before thrusting.

Trying for her heart, he didn't find it. She fell away, though, all her efforts on breathing now, no fight left in her; and he could work the spear deeper, turning and thrusting and leaning on it like pushing a stick into the earth. At last something vital gave, be it her heart or her spirit. One last shudder, and then the slow moan of leaking air with no breath behind it, and she was dead.

And he lifted his head, ready to howl if he needed to; and his mother was gone, there was no body dangling, wanting to knock, *knock knock* against his eyes in this dappled daylight.

HE butchered the sow where she lay, bleeding on a bed of dead leaves. There was no other choice; he couldn't possibly have dragged her back to the portico for a cleaner dismemberment.

He hewed at her with his short-bladed knife, and this was butchery indeed, up to the elbows in blood and ankle-deep in the run of her spilt guts with the stink of her rising all about him. The knife slipped often in his slimy hands, so that he added his own blood to hers; but he worked all day, and at last had all the pieces of her laid out on cool clean stone under the shelter of the pediment. Then he could wash, he could strip his fouled clothes off and wash those also, naked under the cold sun; and briefly he had no fear of the lake, he watched only with exhaustion and no hint of terror as dark shapes rose to question his shadow only a little further out, where the lake-bed suddenly fell steep away.

BECAUSE he had no other way to do it, he built a slow fire beneath one of the iron tubs in the bath-house, and laid pieces of pork inside it on a bed of well-scrubbed stones. As the bath and the stones heated, so fat melted and ran down to spit and hiss on hot enamel; and this was what he needed, not the meat.

While the lard rendered, he made crude pots from clay he'd dug with his fingers from the lake's edge. Baking in the fire's ashes, several of them cracked or flindered; but some survived well enough to use, he thought.

Pork for dinner, roasted dry but he wouldn't heed that. The skin had gone to crackling; as he crunched it something roiled and stirred the water, far out in the centre of the lake. He heard his father cry out in the darkness, and he heard a staccato rattle of gunfire; and he heard his mother's slow choking; and louder than any, louder than all of those he heard the sounds of kicking.

HIS father came to him again when he should have been sleeping. Wet serge warned him, smelling strongly in the damp air; cracking his eyelids barely open showed him an outline against the sky, the glint of moonlight on buckles.

He heard boots shift on stone, he heard each separate breath like a groan. But no kiss this time, no touch at all; and after his father was gone, what he heard until he slept was his mother's rope creaking in the wind, as she dangled somewhere close at hand. He wouldn't open his eyes again to look, but he thought perhaps she was up between the pillars of the portico, that close.

IN the morning, he scooped a potful of lard from the bath and set it to melt by his cooking-fire outside. Threads drawn from his blanket and plaited together made a wick; he laid that across the pot and let it sink, with ends trailing out on either side.

When he lit them in the shadows behind the bath-house door, they made more soot and smell than light; but they made light enough to work by. Light enough to reclaim the cellars from his mother, perhaps, though she could dangle as well in light as darkness.

She couldn't knock, *knock knock* at his eyes in the light, and that was what counted.

HE made as much light as he could, three lamps each with two wicks burning at both ends, twelve guttering flames to save him. He carried them down one at a time, and even the first time there was no body swinging at the head of the stairs, nor any at the foot, nor in the chamber below: only the boilers and the pumps and the constant rushing sound of water.

By his third trip down, coming from light into light with light right there in his hands, he felt secure until he looked more closely at the machinery. All the surfaces were coated in a sticky black mixture of dust and grease, generations old; but two words gleamed out at him in the light he'd brought, shining where someone had written them with a finger in that clagging muck. One of course was *Guilty,* and *Coward* was the other.

One quick sobbing breath, staring, seeing the finger in his mind—fine and delicate for sure, trembling a little perhaps under the enormity of it all—and then he turned abruptly, and saw the box of tools in the corner, half-hidden under dark and heavy piping.

A galvanised iron bucket, and a wooden box of tools: hammers and screwdrivers and wrenches, everything he could possibly need. No can of grease, but he didn't need grease now, he had his bathful of rendered fat. He could sieve that through his shirt to get the grit out. Not first, though. Cleaning came first; and first for cleaning were the boilers that bore those two accusations, those truths.

DAYS he worked down there, days and into the nights sometimes, cleaning and greasing and taking apart, sketching plans and patterns of flow with charred sticks on the tiled floor. His parents left him largely undisturbed, his father no longer crossing the lake, his mother only distantly dangling. If they were making room for the girl, if it was her turn now, she was being slow to show; and he wasn't waiting.

Not consciously, at least. Consciously, he was learning how to plumb.

AT last, the turn of a great brass stopcock brought water gushing through the pipes. The furnace burned hot and fast on gathered wood; and as soon as pressure started to build, the first leaks showed where rubber had perished and his rabbitskin-and-porkfat improvisations wouldn't hold. He patched as best he could, and set the bucket to catch the worst of the drips. It didn't matter, he was only testing the system, and there was a drain in the floor in any case. If it wasn't blocked.

Sweating, he refilled the furnace and threw a lever, and the pump started to knock, *knock knock*. Knocked and failed, and knocked again. More leaks, jets of steam now, clouding out the light; briefly he thought the show was over for the day, *knock knock* and nothing more.

But again a knock, and a faster knocking; the rhythm changed abruptly, hard and steady and unfaltering now, and he thought of course of kicking; and the girl came walking to him out of the steam and oh, she was so afraid.

She wore white, as she had when last he saw her. Her fingers plucked at the fabric of her dress, her eyes were wide and panic-lost and all her body was trembling. Her mouth shook so much, at first she could say nothing.

There was nothing he could say, and nothing he wanted said between them; but she tried, and tried again, and at last,

"They shot your father," she said. "They took him out and shot him. For cowardice," she said; and she had said all this before though not like this, not so dreadfully afraid. "There was a court martial and they found him guilty, and they shot him."

Her voice had been hard before, hard and accusatory. *You lied to me,* it had been saying, *you're a coward too.* There had been no tears then, and none of the pleading, none of the terror he saw now in her pallid face.

Then as now, he had said nothing at all; then as now, she had gone driving heedlessly on, far past what was honourable or decent. And yes, he was an expert on honour by then, he'd seen it from both sides and knew it better than any.

"Your mother," she said, though she clearly, she so much didn't want to. "That's why she, why she hanged herself," she said. "For shame," she said, "she hanged herself for shame."

Let herself dangle in the dark for him to find when he walked clean into her, her bare toes *knock knock* against his blinded, desperate eyes.

"You should do that too," she said, "why not? Why don't you? A coward and the son of a coward, and your mother the only honourable one among you all, why don't you just jump in the river? Too scared, I suppose," she said, answering herself. "I should have known then, when I realised you were a water-funk. Once a coward, always a coward. Like father, like son…"

And that was all she said, because it was all she had said the first time. After that it was only crying out, and grunting.

And now as then, and this was what she'd been so afraid of: that it would happen again as it had, that it would have to.

And of course it did. He swung wildly, and felt the solidity of her against the back of his hand as she sprawled at his feet; and *feet, yes,* already he was kicking.

Kicking and kicking, but not to silence her this time, not for shame. Only because she was there, as his parents were intermittently there, in their intermittent deaths; and the thing was there to be done, and so he did it.

Felt better, second time. Not good, never that; but better. She cried, but not he cried. No choking, no fire in his throat or eyes, neither anger nor grief could find him. Fear might have found him, perhaps, but he wasn't afraid of this.

Neutral at last, he kicked until his feet lost her in the steam, until she was entirely gone from there.

And then he felt his way up the stairs and out into the bath-house where a couple of taps were hissing and spitting, scalding to his hand as he turned them on.

He scrubbed one of the baths as best he could, and washed every piece of clothing that he'd brought. He laid them out on the portico steps, and came back naked to fill the bath again.

Lying back with his eyes closed, with burning water lapping at his ears and the corners of his mouth, he thought that nothing was finished, even now; but it didn't seem to matter. Let his father stumble blindfold against death, let his mother dangle, let the girl come for kicking when she chose. Or when he called her. The world was wider, much wider than this; and here he was only on the fringes of it yet, he hadn't even been up to the house.

LATER, in the darkness, when his clothes were dry, he thought he might walk down to the lake and into the water. He would be borne up, he thought, and carried over, because in his pockets he carried the keys to D'Espérance.

BUT actually, he slept; and in the morning he walked the other way, he walked into town looking for the solicitor.

WHITE TEA FOR THE TILLERMAN

TERRIBLE AS AN ARMY WITH BANNERS undoubtedly is, a single man can be worse. A quiet man, a sober man, a man with drab clothes and delicate manners. He has passed the gates; he is within the walls; he is within the palace, at the throne's foot, where she must serve him tea and listen to his embassy.

The army is at his back, at his beck if he should call for it. Its banners are in his eyes. He is the blade at her throat, unless he is in her heart.

The tea is served in simple celadon. She hopes he will despise it, but his tastes are as fine as his comportment. He praises its lines, its colour, its age and fragility; all his words are honed, double-edged, speaking to her land as much as her porcelain. She wonders if he will crush the cup between his fingers, to show her its beauty broken.

Instead he sips, and the sophisticate in him overrules the diplomat for a startled moment.

"Exquisite!" he declares. "May I ask...?"

"It is white tea," she says, thinking *the tea was a mistake; he wants us now, where before he was only obedient to orders.* "My people harvest the leaves too soon, still in the bud, and dry them hastily. The result is delicious, but that is happy accident, no more. It is hard to be patient, to cultivate the plants to a proper age, when there is a dragon on the mountain."

"A dragon?" He does not—quite—splutter in his tea. "My lady, that is ridiculous."

"Of course. We know, you and I, that dragons only fly at night; but it is the peasants who must do the work, and they are a timid and credulous people."

Briefly, she thinks he is uncertain, whether to challenge her own credulity. Instead he says, "I cannot direct my lord's decisions," which is a blatant lie, for he is most clearly the tillerman for that ship of state, "but his soldiers could certainly stand between you and any dragon, if you only accept his protection."

He means his army and its banners over her lands, her heart in his possession. She says, "Do you think so?" and sends for the dragon's tooth.

"Like a baby," she says, "it is shedding teeth as it grows," as she shows him the great curve of the tusk, half the height that he is, more. There is blood on the root of it, still sticky.

He says, "My lady, I have seen an elephant's tusk before."

She says, "Ah, I have not been so lucky. I have never left these lands; and how would we keep an elephant here, on these slopes, where there is no forage? We cannot keep a cow."

He bows to her, disbelieving; but she knows that he has seen no cattle on his journey, for there are none.

IN the night, the palace resounds to the beat of slow leathern wings. Perhaps he is suspicious, perhaps he thinks that servants are flapping hides in the darkness; but later there are screams from distance, and great swathes of fire score the mountain like tracks of lava.

In the morning, the air is full of smoke and he can see black devastation where there were tea-bushes in ordered ranks before. This is not the time to ask how many harvests will be lost; she is busy in the courtyard, where they have brought the night's survivors, a dozen peasants dreadfully burned.

He finds her kneeling by a boy whose face is molten, who cannot catch the breath to scream his pain. At her nod, a knife makes wet work of his ending. Her face is bleak, her voice savage; she says, "I cannot use a dragon, as I do these my people; but when it has destroyed us utterly, do you not think it will turn its gaze downriver, to where it might find many men marching with bright banners…?"

TERRIBLE as an army with banners undoubtedly is, a dragon is most definitely worse. He makes a swift way homeward, to forestall his lord's advance. The swiftest way down is the river; the only boat to hand is an old rough sampan, with an oar for a tiller and a hard, withered scowl for a tillerman.

Great men must sometimes stoop to humble commons; they share a bowl of tea. "White tea," the tillerman says, sneering at his startlement. The man was bitter, but his brew was not. It was hot but nothing more, insipid, without savour. "Leaves cost coin; what man of us has that to spare, for tea? White tea, we drink." And then, to make it clear, "We boil water, that's all. There's nothing in it."

ASHES TO ASHES

because it is bitter,
and because it is my heart

SOONER OR LATER OR TOO LATE, every pilot touching in at Dock finds their way to Parry's on the Margin.

There's a sign out over the sheetwalk, but that's not designed to be helpful. It doesn't offer guidance, far less an invitation. It doesn't even say as much as *Parry's*: just an elegant sweeping *P*, grey on grey. You need to know where you're going, essentially. Or have someone take you in.

It's not a bar, although you can certainly get a drink. And pay for it. Parry likes to call it the rest between bars. It's certainly not a club, it's not private in that peculiarly public sense, there isn't a membership list that excludes you. Find yourself on that problematic doorstep, you're welcome to come in. Just be aware. There's a whole lot happening in Parry's that is really very private indeed. Most of it is not your business, and it would be a mistake to make it so.

MERCY Mercy walks in like a blow to the heart, like a benediction.

Spacers run tall, but Mercy's taller. And nothing in the Margin is ever quite clean, but she's clean all through; and sharp as a chef's knife, with that inward curve that talks of too much sharpening, of steel worn dangerously thin at the core.

She's picked someone up out there on the walk. Young and male and vividly lovely, exactly the type to be sucked up and drawn after as she passes. Not a pilot.

He steps into Parry's in her wake, and for a moment he only stands there, occupying the doorway, stunned by the calm.

Out there, that side of the door, the station gropes into nothingness like a half-curled spider. The head, the part that occupies the least space—where this boy has strayed from tonight, where he truly belongs, whatever he wants to think—is called Base. The rest, the most expansive part, the embrace of it is called Dock.

Dock encompasses those stretching legs where the great ships pause, and everything that serves them in their hesitation: storage and supply, loading and unloading, repair and re-engineering, customs and record-keeping, contact and communication. And local traffic, of course, to and from every planet and moon in this system; and recreation, yes, that too. Hence the Margin, out on the sheetwalk here: where everybody comes when they have an hour or a day or a long dreary month to kill before they can ship out. That transient population numbers sometimes in the thousands and never stops talking, moving, drinking, dancing, fighting, fucking. Never.

And then there's Parry's. In the Margin but not quite of the Margin, unless it's the very heart of the thing: a haven for anyone who needs to catch their breath, have a conversation, look someone in the face. Share a meal, take a shower, start again.

Anyone's welcome, any time. Parry never sleeps, and never turns anyone away.

You just have to put up with the pilots, and remember that it's all about them.

MERCY Mercy is the least of them, the best of them: the least work, the best company. She walks in and everyone smiles. Her boy catches the backwash of that warmth and smiles himself, a little uncertainly, a little buoyed: willing to coast in on her welcome, aware that he's taking a liberty. It's a nice display, unexpectedly bashful. Anywhere else, it might have won him acceptance in his own right. Not here. He's not a pilot.

Mercy cosies up to the counter, where Parry's already pouring.

Her long fingers engulf the glass, lift it in a toast to him, to the room, to the company. A dozen glasses are lifted in response, from colleagues. Peers. In anyone else it would be an impertinence, and everyone else knows it.

Her boy, of course, knows nothing. He reaches past her to proffer his ID, to pay before she can. Parry shakes his head. Perhaps he rolls his eyes a little. He says, "It's on the house."

"Oh. Excellent. What is it?"

"Coryatric lemon," as though that means anything, as though it has ever meant anything other than *expensive*. As though anything else could matter.

"Oh!" He knows nothing of anything, except the price; he says, "Make that two, will you?"

Parry says, *"Hers* is on the house."

"Oh." He knows nothing of anything, and all he knows about price is that he can afford it. "Well, I'll have one too, in any case."

This time Parry charges his ID, and the kid conspicuously doesn't look to see how much that cost. Now everyone else knows what he knows, for all the good that'll do him.

Still: here he is, with the best imaginable companion. Mercy Mercy is a passport into better and brighter and darker conversations than ever he could have broached alone, for all his money and all his youthful beauty and all his practised educated charm. And he has the grace to know that, and to acknowledge it. He sips his drink and slides into her shadow, follows in her wake, not quite erased but self-effaced. And that's charming too, and beautifully done, as though he were after all wiser than his years. Perhaps he is. Everything's ambiguous out here on the Limb; what isn't liminal is problematic.

Mercy Mercy leads him to a table where four or five are sat together (it depends how you want to count: is that devolved clone one entity in two bodies, or two minds with but a single thought?) and hooks herself a chair by means of one long, long leg. She sprawls at her ease, and looks up at him with a smile that's open and easy: not an invitation—it's not her table, after all—but certainly suggestive. So he fetches a chair for himself and perches modestly on the edge of the circle, still somewhat in her eclipse. Really, he's managing this unexpectedly well.

"So," says Mercy, "who's new?"

Her boy, of course, is newer than new, but that's not what she means at all.

Around the table there is—or are—Ten Barry the clone(s), who will cheerfully answer to either name or both together (and always want to be asked about the other eight, in order to be mysteriously evasive in reply). That's not new, of course. That's repertoire.

So is Brone, the hulking Shutterself entity: the pilot without a ship, the lone traveller who never leaves the station, who has barely ever even been seen to leave Parry's. It has a room in the back and a seat in here; that seems to be enough, by and large. If this is anyone's table, it must be Brone's. No one would thinkingly choose Brone for a host—that vast and disturbing figure, swathed in blankets, sipping an unidentified liquid seemingly through a translucent hollow finger—and yet people do choose to sit here when they can, when there's a chair and space to squeeze it in. Brone speaks about as often as it steps outside, but it exudes some sense of calm or comfort, of homeliness. People feel better, sitting close.

Brone's other side, there's Quest. Yes, of course that's his real name. It's the one he answers to, the one that everybody uses. What's more real than that? If anyone out here is still using their milk-name or the name on their paperwork, it's more than they'd admit to. The only history that matters, the only records that anyone would look at are a pilot's logs. You are where you've been, and how swiftly and safely you arrived there, and what you delivered along the way.

Quest is like a distillation of every downsider's fancy, what a pilot is and ought to be. Lean and ageless and experienced, he's a cynic and a mystic, both at once. He wears his journeys the way downsiders wear their years, on the skin and in the eyes: he's a faraway look that doubles with an intensity of focus. Asked if he has another name, he'll say Vision. He can't compete either with Brone's depth of silence nor with Mercy's bright engagement, but he doesn't need to. There's nobody here to compare with Quest.

Last at the table there's Maellelin, who might as well be a deliberate exercise in contrast. She's small enough to look ridiculous in this company, needing a booster seat to reach the table; and she can only ever fly her own ship, because she depends on its adaptations. In downsider terms, she's too short to reach the pedals.

But Maellelin has adaptations of her own, that make her a phenomenal pilot. Her eyes are five times human-standard size, and they don't only see wavelengths unreachable by default. Whether it's the eyes alone, or the eyes in combination with her other alterations—she is said to have enhancements on the molecular level, in her brain and throughout her nervous system—Maellelin is one of the few who can look directly into the chaos of n-space and see actual structure there. She can find her way without benefit of software or luck or strategy, intuition or long experience; hell, she can find her way without drugs, and that's priceless. Even passengers feel safe, with Maellelin.

Besides which, she comes with her own ship. Which is the opposite of priceless, because everyone knows what a ship is worth, which is more than anything else that anyone has ever tried to pay for.

MATHEMATICALLY, human space itself is vanishingly small. They call it the Limb because it is long, attenuated, stretchy; and because limbs are coherent, reliable, solid. Reassuring. Apply the actual maths and it's more like a whisper in the wind. Nobody does that kind of maths, it's too dispiriting. The other kind says that we have occupied and colonised dozens of systems, in a long throw from home base out into the dark. It's a pathway, progress from point to point, with settlements at every stopping-place; and pilots are the invaluable linkage, the golden threads that stitch it all together. Where would we be, without our few—our vanishingly few—pilots? Alone in the dark, that's where. Seriously alone, because we've never met any other rational creature. It's Fermi made physical, a philosophical question answered in the actual: we really are apparently on our own.

When it's asked in Parry's, *Who's new?* actually means the opposite, *Who's still alive?* Because there's only one way to know for sure, and that's to find them here. Veterans accumulate, they localise, they seek each other's spaces. Parry's is a node, when everywhere else is just a destination.

Maellelin lifts her sharp little chin, and uses it to point into a shadowed corner. "Ferrel is," she says. Meaning not *Ferrel's new*, because they all know him intimately; but *Ferrel's back*, now that is new. That is news.

That is a call to duty, or else a call to arms. Mercy Mercy looks, and sighs; and turns to her pretty boy and says, "Enjoy your drink, sweetie," and walks away without a backward glance.

FERREL wears his shadows like a cloak, like Brone its blankets, a wraparound mood that no one is invited to peer beneath. No one, ever. Which does—bizarrely, almost unthinkably—include Mercy.

Which does not—of course!—keep her from trying. She thinks it important to try. Perhaps it's only important to her, but that's enough, surely.

Besides, he's a pilot. Pilots are rare and precious, and tend to come broken, one way or another. Survival is a damaging business.

It's Ferrel's table, and he's alone as ever. Mercy Mercy touches the back of an empty chair, raises a questioning eyebrow. He shrugs. He truly doesn't care; he can be just as much alone in company. Or just as little. This could be his great failure, his entire incapacity to leave humanity behind. However hard he tries, however far he goes, he's always got himself for company, and they don't come more human than that.

She sits, and just for a moment, her fingers shift to touch his glass. Like the eyebrow and the shrug, there's a whole unspoken conversation going on here, except that this one's more of a monologue. He doesn't trouble to shrug this time. They've unsaid it all before.

Pilots don't drink while they're in port, off duty, away from their ship. Nor do they smoke, nor drug: no intoxicants. Downtime is about reacquainting themselves with their bodies, living inside their skins. They seek out strong flavours and vivid experiences, and all of them in real time, unmitigated, undisguised. Sex is popular, commitment is not; hence Mercy's boy, casually acquired and just as casually abandoned. If he's still around later, she'll pick him up again, maybe. If he's lucky, if she's back in the mood. If Ferrel doesn't turn even that sour and unrewarding.

Pilots don't drink, but Ferrel does. And worse than that, he blinks up at her and she can see that he's still taking hexumeth. That's the pilots' survival tactic out in n-space, the only edge they've got. It slows things down around them, buys them time; and it stretches them out, it gives them room and reach. They love hexumeth. Out there.

In here, that's something else. Nobody likes to see a pilot using in normal space. It isn't safe for them, or for anyone. What they can see, what they can tell, what they can touch: there's nothing neutral here, nothing harmless. Nothing clean.

Nothing except Mercy, who is clean all through. What gift she has, that sees her go into n-space and return in safety, time after time—well, that's been hotly debated, but there's an emerging school of thought, a drift towards consensus.

She feels it, is what they say in every port and station. *She finds her way by feel. She's another skincrawler, except for her it goes deeper. Call her a bonecrawler, the first of her kind.*

In the universities, they say, *She has empathy, a layer of empathic response that underlies all her sensorium. She doesn't question n-space, she listens to it reflexively.*

A man who was neither dock worker nor neuropsychologist said once, "She's a one-way mirror who dreams of broken glass."

Be that as it may, she sits with Ferrel and observes the niceties. You never ask a pilot where they've been; what does the destination matter, when it's all about the journey? You buy them a drink, except that he has one already; and then you say, *"What's new?"* It's meant to draw out the true story of their trip, whatever they can bring themselves to share. Awful warnings, generally: snares and pitfalls, rockfalls, deluges and plagues. Everything's a metaphor. N-space is a mesh of possibilities, mischances, ways to go awry. And that's a metaphor too, it's really not a mesh at all, nothing so organised. Some say it's a mess, hopelessly unstructured, "we could have ordered things better"; only then you're into the whole metaphysics of travel and existence and who ordered what, who had the power and who the authority, and you really wouldn't want to go there.

It's hard to go where you do want when there are no maps and no routes, no trails to follow and no practical directions. When those who've survived the journey can only talk about it in images and references that are not your own, a whole system of semiotics that you don't and cannot share.

Nevertheless: pilots still do this. Neurotically, relentlessly, they seek each other out, pin each other down and ask for stories. Sometimes all they can do is wonder at how strange the other has become, and nevertheless.

Ferrel says, "I saw something. Way down deep, where no one goes but me."

Everyone always thinks that they have it hardest, that they're boldest, that their risks are the great risks and their journeys the great journeys.

Mercy says, "Honey, everybody goes deep. One way or another."

"Not like me," Ferrel says. "I could show you, if—"

His gesture speaks to the alcohol, but that isn't what he means. It's only that the drink is in a glass, it's contained, it's something he can point to. What he means is the hexumeth, which is in his bloodstream and his tissues, nothing to show except the distance, him to her.

"Ferrel, you know you shouldn't do that. Not here. You have to come back to ground, or we'll lose you altogether. None of us wants that. We've all seen too many drifters out there."

That's what they say, but the truth is almost opposite. The drifters are the ones they never see, out there or anywhere: they're the ones who don't come back. The missing faces, the undelivered cargoes, the ships gone and long gone from the roster. People assume they just got lost in n-space, but no one really knows. Occasionally a pilot reports a sighting, another ship out there in the fog and the confusion; but people see so many strange things, and no two pilots ever see the same. Those reports are not considered reliable.

What is reliable, what is certain: no pilot reported lost has ever turned up later or elsewhere, and no ship has ever been recovered. They walk a borderline, who choose to go for pilots. One step over is all-time gone.

"Not out there," Ferrel says. "In here," meaning *all through the human polity, throughout our reach and culture*, meaning *in ourselves, in our being, in our deeds*.

She hears him, down deep. And almost reaches for his drink, although she never does that.

"Tell me," she says. He's drunk, he's high, he's on hexumeth; but if he's drunk and high and on hexumeth—he of all people, a pilot; and in here of all places, in Parry's—perhaps there's a reason.

"It's what we do," he says, "what we've always done, although we didn't know it. What we bring with us, out of the Blue."

To scientists, and so all through the polity, it's n-space: another dimension or a distortion or a practical dreamscape, n for nightmare. But no pilot can be a scientist, or not for long. It's easier to be a believer, even in a faith of one.

Perhaps it's some hangover from faiths long superseded, that pilots call it the Blue, that place they go where no one else can follow. Perhaps they're only hankering after ancient history or a sense of continuity. Something to hold on to.

"What's that, then, Ferrel?" The terrifying thing is that she believes him, before she even knows. He's a pilot; he brought his ship safe to Dock, and then he came here. If his mind has broken, it's since he berthed. It's because of this, of what he's found in here. Not n-space has done this to him, not the Blue. That only made it possible, perhaps.

"Ignorance," he says. "Misinformation, lies: that's what we ship, one system to the next. One year to the next, one generation, all down the line. We tell them we're so special," he says, "we're so important, their indispensable lifeline. How would they ever hold the polity together, without us? We few, we sacred few, all that stand between them and isolation, every system on its own again and humankind alone again, in the dark…"

"Well, we are. Alone, I mean."

"No," he says. "No, we're not."

"Wherever we've been," she says, "it's just us. We've never found other intelligent life." Even Brone the Shutterself entity, even that is human, of a sort. Far and far from baseline, but human yet, human after all.

Ferrel says, *"We've* never found intelligent life, no"—and there's such despair in his voice, he's so irretrievably broken, she reaches over the table to grip his hand. She never does that. Pilots get willingly, wilfully physical with the world, with passing strangers, with any body they can—but not with each other as a rule, as a fixed rule. That's not a place they care to go.

After a moment, he says what he's been building up to all this time, what he's been dodging around.

"I was out there," he says, "down deep," he says, "and I saw, I saw a ship."

"Ferrel, we all see things we think are real."

"Yes," he says, "yes, we do—and you know what? We're right. Just that once, that little way, we're right. It's all we've got. Then we come back in here and tell each other we were wrong, just that once, that little way…

"I saw a ship," he says again. "Not like the stories, the incredible designs, the great living ships or the webs of coherent light. I'm sure those are all true too, I'm sure there are aliens all through the Blue, but I saw one of ours. Not recent, not current. Not one of us. It must have been centuries old, but still. Human-built, for sure. It used to have a number on the side. Mostly gone now, space-dust and time, I couldn't read it. I can't tell you who flies that ship. Who flew it.

"But that's the point," he says, "it wasn't adrift. It was...purposeful. Travelling. Going somewhere. The way we do.

"I could feel her," he says, "the pilot, working her way through the Blue. I guess, if two ships come that close, it's going to be because their pilots work the same way, more or less. Think the same way, feel the same, something. We could've connected.

"If I'd been sharper," he says, "we could've talked. I could almost hear her; I could almost follow her. I did try. But she slipped away from me, going somewhere I couldn't quite reach.

"And that's when I saw it all, so clear. That's when I understood, just when I lost her.

"They're not lost," he says, "the ones who don't come back. Not the pilots, not the ships. Not drifting, no. Going somewhere we can't get to, because we're not good enough.

"We thought they were the failures," he says, "but it's not them, it's us. They're better than us. They don't just hobble from one system to the next, the way we do, bound to human space and human reach. We fall short and turn back, where they go all the way.

"And not alone," he says, "they only have to go alone the first time, from us to them. To break through. That's where all the other races are, Mercy: on the other side of the Blue, where you and I can't go. Not good enough.

"We thought we were the stars," he says, "and they were the fallen, but it was the other way around. We fell back, where they went on ahead.

"I thought," he says, "I thought if I kept on taking the hexumeth, if I tried to find another way of seeing us, in here, I could maybe see a way to bring us all through together.

"Of course I was wrong," he says. "Why would I ever think otherwise? I've always been wrong, that's the point. Like all of us," he says, with a perilous sweep of his arm. Mercy barely snatches his glass away in time to save it. "We're the rejects," he says, louder now, snatching it back again. "What's the point of keeping clean? Going out, we're never going to get there; coming back, we're always going to know."

Now, they are. She is.

Mercy Mercy looks around, at all those pilots looking back at her; and she can't think of anything except how she's going to tell them. What she's going to say.

Maybe she should start with drinks all round. Not coryatric lemon.

I AM DEATH'S BROTHER

I am Death's brother, his shape and shadow. I am his bonds-man, his major-domo and his messenger. Where I open the door, Death enters. Where I touch his mouth, he speaks.

E WAS MY BROTHER, AND HE was late. I sat by the open window, waiting; and at last he came, with a flurry and a snap of short wings, falcon shape, my brother David.

He stood on the sill, edged in moonlight: a small bird, sharp, eyes like razors. Then he changed. Shifted. Dressed himself in his proper body.

And was a boy, my brother, naked and shivering against the stars. I closed the window and pulled a dressing-gown over his lean shoulders. He put his arms around me, hugging me close.

"Kit." His voice was breathy, tight with exhaustion and magic remembered. "Oh, God." He felt feather-light in my arms, as though his bones were hollow like a bird's. Even through the thick wool of the dressing-gown, my fingers could count his ribs.

"Come on, David. Move." I hauled him across the room to the fire, and let him drop. "You get warm. I'll make some coffee."

LATER, we sat on the floor with our hands wrapped round heavy pottery mugs, watching the flames like feathers sliding over cherry logs while he tried to tell me how it felt.

"Flying, it's… I don't know how to say it, but it's like there's nothing left, nothing of you. You're all wind and fire, with no limits and no laws. It's not like simply putting your own mind into a bird's body. I leave David behind, down here with you. Out there I'm just flying. Or running, or whatever, it doesn't have to be a bird. Or not moving at all. Morton taught me trees."

He rubbed at last summer's scar, high on his forearm, and I knew what he was going to say.

"It's no good trying to tell you. There aren't any words for it. Morton could show you, though—or I could, now. It only needs one quick cut. My blood and yours. Then you'd have it too, and I could show you, we could be together…"

I shook my head, hard against the pleading in his eyes. "No, David. Still no. I *can't*. And it's not the cutting, you know that. The whole thing scares me. It's like you're not real any more, when you can be something different every time you blink. I need to know what I am. You could lose hold, so easily…"

He grinned then, and punched me. "Who says I'm not real, little brother?"

That stung, as it was meant to; I was taller than David, and half a stone heavier. So I hurled myself at him, and we wrestled across the polished floor until I had him pinned in a corner with his arms down at his sides and my knee in his ribs. He blinked up at me, and smiled.

For a moment my hands went numb, and my leg where it was touching him. I dropped a foot, falling through him—or where he had been—onto my hands and knees. And found myself eye to eye with a coiled, swaying cobra.

I jerked back with a yell, cuffing at it frantically. The snake trapped my wrist in a loop of its own body, then spiralled up to curl around my throat. It butted my cheek affectionately, like a kiss; then I was numb all across my neck and shoulders, and I could feel David's weight pressing into my back as he held me in a vicious armlock.

"Give up, little brother?" he asked tauntingly; but before I could speak or move he let me go, running his fingers through my hair, almost an apology.

"I wish you wouldn't do that," I muttered, tossing another log onto the fire.

"I know. But you always win if I don't." He yawned suddenly, and we went to bed with hardly another word passing between us. I dreamed of black wings, beating hard enough to blow the stars away and let the true night in.

WHEN I woke up next morning David was gone again, leaving the window open and a single brown feather in a corner of the sill, trapped in a cobweb, shifting in the breeze. I lied for him as so often before, saying he'd gone off early to do some fishing with Morton; then I kicked my way down the path to the river, feeling that something precious was being stolen away from me. It wasn't jealousy. I was jealous, sure, but it wasn't that.

My brother's keeper—I'd been David's keeper for years now. I'd looked after him, fought his battles for him, held his freedom in my hands; and now he wanted to wrest it away, and give it to an old man with unquiet eyes.

When I reached the river, I dropped onto my back in the grass and watched the birds. Starlings, finches, a single rook—and suddenly two falcons, coming out of the sun to hover directly above me. That was my brother, with Morton. You wouldn't get two together naturally, not hunting.

We watched each other for a long time. They moved hardly more than I did, just turning a feather or a wing-tip to hold themselves still above the meadow. Then one flicked away across the water and the other followed, after a second's hesitation.

"David…" I scrambled to my feet to watch them, two specks keeping low, quickly lost against the brown fells. "Be careful…"

I went back to the same spot in the afternoon, taking some of David's clothes with me in an old rucksack. Just before sunset he came to me, a solitary magpie. *One for sorrow.* The old rhyme was nonsense, of course—but I would have been happier if Morton had been with him.

David dressed slowly, shivering, tired as ever, but with a strained look that was new about his eyes. There was none of the exultant weariness I was used to; the set of his mouth was angry, or tearful.

We walked back towards the cottage in silence; but as we passed through the neglected orchard, I reached out a hand to stop him.

"David, what is it?"

He picked an apple off the ground, worm-eaten and rotten.

"Nothing."

"Come on. This is me, remember? Kit. Your brother."

Looking at me, his lips twitched into a half-smile. "All right. But it's still nothing. Only that Morton…asked me to do something, and wasn't happy when I said no."

That worried me. I didn't trust Morton, even when he was being friendly; he had too much power to be safe. If ever he found cause to use that power against us, there might be changes which even David couldn't find his way back from.

"What was it?" I asked. "What he wanted?"

"It doesn't matter." David's face shuttered, and I knew he'd never tell me. "Just something I don't want to do."

He tossed the apple in his hand, then hurled it suddenly, far between the trees, to splatter against a wooden pig-trough by the gate.

"Come on, little brother," he said, slapping the back of my neck. "I'll race you home. The long way, through the wood."

So we ran; and as there was no one to see, I raced a fox, and a deer, and a white horse that for one fleeting, laughing moment was a unicorn.

Over the final hundred yards David twisted from shape to shape like a mad boy, badger to hare to snake to beaver; so at the last I just managed to catch up and get to the door before him.

I subsided panting onto the stone step, and watched until he twisted eventually into himself, naked of course, his clothes lying forgotten on a path in the wood.

He glanced down, and laughed. "Well, at least I'm still human."

And as he went past me into the cottage, I heard him repeat it under his breath. "Human. At least I've still got that. And I won't give it up; not for anything."

I wondered just what it was that Morton had offered, and what he had asked for in return.

DAVID spent the next three nights in his bed and the days with me, in his own shape, fighting and fooling the way we used to. I was glad, but I didn't trust his mood; he was wound-up and edgy, always glancing at the sky, watching the flight of hawks and ravens.

"He'll come, sooner or later," he told me one night in our bedroom. "I'm not hiding from him; he was angry, but that will have passed by now. I just don't want to see him, that's all. He'll only try to persuade me again. There's nothing more I want from him, I told him that. But he'll come."

And he did come; but when he did, he came to me.

IT was early one bright, windless morning. I left David asleep and went walking, up through the woods to the hilltop behind. When I reached the summit, I sat on a moss-stained boulder and stared out across the barren moors, feeling the strength of this old country, and the unconcern.

I sat without moving until a shadow caught my eye, flickering over grass and stones, speeding towards me. Glancing up, I saw a buzzard coming down fast, wings folded and talons thrusting forward. I flinched back, throwing one arm across my eyes as the sun glinted off steel-grey claws.

Somehow the bird checked itself in mid-air, a yard from my face. Its head lifted in a mocking, triumphant screech; then it dropped to the ground beside me, and I knew it was Morton.

He was an old man who sat at my feet now, blinking up at me against the sun: old and slightly foolish-looking, his skin pale and pimpled like a fresh-plucked goose. But there was nothing foolish about his eyes, stagnant pools of murky green breeding who knew what beneath the surface; and he spoke in a bubbling, scalding voice, a voice like boiling water.

"Well. It's the other one. Not the one I want; not yet. You're the one who won't, is that right?"

"I don't know what you mean," I said sullenly, trying not to let him see how scared I was. "I'm not interested in changing shape, if that's what you're getting at."

"Boy into hawk won't go, eh?" He chuckled to himself, a soft sound, dangerous as falling snow. "Well. Tell your brother…" His voice was suddenly angry and his body blurred at the edges, losing distinction as a thousand shapes threatened behind his opaque eyes. He paused, then went on more calmly. "Tell your brother this. All things have a price; and I have given him all things, so he must pay all prices. I mixed my blood with his, to give him wings when he asked; now he must mix his life with mine, because I ask. Tell him this." Morton stood up, and shadows wove and rippled around him, so that I could no longer see that he was naked. "And tell him also this: that I will not ask again. Next time, I compel."

With that he was a bird again, a maddened eagle, wings beating about my head and razor talons tearing at my clothes and skin. I turned to run; he clung to my shoulder long enough to rip my cheek open with one stab of his beak, then he spread his wings and let the sky lift him to itself.

I found David down by the river, lying on his stomach, one hand in the water. He jumped up when he saw the state of me, my shirt in rags and blood all over.

"Kit, what...?"

The question died somewhere between throat and lips. He stood rigid, turning ash-white behind the fire of his anger. "Morton. Wasn't it? It was Morton!"

I nodded, and dropped down to splash water onto my torn cheek. I could feel it now, burning like a brand across my face, and I knew that Morton had marked me for life.

I told David what Morton had said, and what he had done. I was sitting half-turned away from my brother, watching the river; but behind me I could sense him shifting crazily, one shape to another, as though in his fury it was too much of an effort to hold even his natural form for longer than a moment or two.

When I had finished I heard a coughing growl and screaming, the rage of fur and feather; but when finally I turned to face him he was a boy again, flint-eyed and spitting.

"He has no right! Curse him, he has no *right...*"

"Don't be a fool, David," I said, alarmed. "He's stronger than either of us, there's nothing we can do."

He shook his head, reaching out to brush a gentle hand across my cheek. Even that light touch snagged a gasp from me, and David showed me red on his fingers.

"Blood and blood, Kit. First my blood, and now yours. It's enough. I won't be blackmailed into anything; and I won't let you be hurt."

"David, he's stronger than you are! You can't touch him..."

He smiled, as a cat smiles in the night. "Yes, I can. Anything he can shape, I can shape; and I'm younger and faster than he is. Don't worry, I'll catch him."

He didn't say what he would do when he did catch Morton; but just before he took the falcon's shape and left me, he touched my cheek again, and his face told me everything.

He was my brother, and there was death in his smile.

I waited for him all day, down there in the water-meadows, watching the sky and calling uselessly into the wind. No one answered me; but at last a shadow came out of the red sun, a great buzzard hurtling across the grass.

It came to ground and shaped itself into Morton, damp and sweating, streaked with something dark.

He laughed at me and said, "I left your brother in the orchard. He's waiting for you. And so am I, boy. Blood calls to blood. Boy into hawk goes twice, with nothing over."

Then he was gone, I don't know in what shape. It might have been a beetle or a spider, or any crawling, vicious thing. As far as I was concerned, he simply vanished.

I stood for a while, staring at the space where he had been; then I turned to trudge slowly up the hill towards the orchard, knowing already what I would find there. Those wet streaks across Morton's chest and arms, showing almost black in the dim, heavy light of sunset—they couldn't have been anything but blood.

I found him lying in the open near the old pig-trough, where Morton must have dropped him; but it wasn't David, not any more. Dead, he was just a bird, a falcon with its heart ripped out, blood on its feathers.

Not crying yet, I cradled the tiny body against my ruined shirt, cursing mindlessly under my breath. It was so pointless; Morton hadn't needed to kill him, I was sure of that.

And he'd been spiteful, too. He hadn't even given David back his own body to die in.

Holding the warm, sticky raggedness that was all he'd left me of my brother, a blind anger seized me, shaking me out of my fear and even out of my grief. What was it Morton had said—that he was waiting for me? That blood calls to blood?

"Then let it," I muttered. David had told me where it lay, the power to change shape; you could inherit it, or you could take it from anyone who had it, simply by mixing a little of their blood into yours. And heaven knew, I had enough of David's here.

The gash on my cheek had clotted and dried long since, during my vigil by the river; but there was a sheath-knife on my belt. I drew it out, catching a silver gleam of fish-scales on the moulded handle. The last time I'd used it was to gut fish that David caught for supper one evening, shifting from otter to heron and back while I watched and felt jealous and just a little afraid.

There was far more of David in the memory than there was in the dead falcon in the grass. That was where the loss and the heartache lay, in the past, and the future; the present was only anger, and action.

But even so I was crying now, at last; watching through tear-blurred eyes as my hand laid the knife-blade against my forearm and jerked savagely down and across. Watching as the fresh blood oozed out and began to trickle over my skin. Watching as I smeared blood from the bird's corpse, dead David's blood into the cut, blood meeting blood, shape meeting shape...

I watched as I cried, cried as I waited for the hand of change to touch me.

I didn't know what I was doing. Living blood gives power; but David was dead, and Death has no shapes in his gift. He had no body, until I gave him mine.

So it was as a boy that I went to Morton. Not the boy he knew, not Kit; Death had taken me half into his own country, and it showed. I was a quicksilver, slipshadow figure, the colour of moonlight on deep water, eyes of dust.

Morton gaped at me, and I could smell his terror.

"What...what do you want?"

"Blood," I said. "You promised. Blood to shape me. You said you would be waiting."

My voice might even have scared me, if I could have remembered how fear felt. Spiders, perhaps, should have such voices, grey and powder-dry.

"Yes—yes, of course. Anything..."

My arm was bleeding still, from the cut I had made. Morton opened his palm with a razor, along the line of an old scar; and I caught the blood on my finger as it dripped. He flinched away although I hadn't touched him, and waited silent in a corner as I mixed his blood into mine.

It hurt, this time. Where David's death-touch had been a gentle, kissing change, Morton's was the shock of fire meeting ice, the threat of destruction.

I dropped to my knees, fighting the pain, burning as I began to lose the limits of my shape. There had to be room for both life and death; I had to find room, or I would be nothing as David was nothing, and Morton would have won after all.

At last I found that room, or made it. Each absorbed the other, and I both. I was a changer now; while Morton watched from his corner, boy went into hawk, or the echo of a hawk—still dust-grey, death-grey, with nothing of life about me but bright drops of blood falling from one wing.

I flew to a tree outside the hut, and waited. When Morton came I challenged him, a hawk's scream shivering the air. He owed me more blood than I'd been given; he owed me for David, and I wanted it all.

He fled, and all that day I hunted him from one shape to another, silent and close as his shadow. A thousand times I could have caught and killed him; but I hung back until at last, cornered against rocks, he turned wearily to fight. I shifted to falcon shape, for David, and struck.

I didn't really kill him. Rather, death passed into him, through me. There was no struggle, simply a rushing as I touched him, a liquid sound, and he was dead.

MORTON was the first, and the only one I wanted. There have been others since, there are others every day; but I take them at random. I am not God.

Like Lazarus, I live in exile from my life, always moving. Usually a bird or a cat, shadows of love; a fish when I meet water. Rarely now a boy.

And where I go Death follows, taking people and animals as lightly as the wind takes a feather, all the life that I choose and touch.

I bring death, as surely as a storm brings rain; but I am not Death.

I am Death's brother, his shape and shadow.

LUKE, HOMEWARD ANGEL

KEEP YOUR PERSONAL SPACE IN A public place, other people will always muscle in. If you don't like that, if you're not up for it, don't lay yourself open. Stay home and hide your secrets, store your secret treasures where they're safe.

Me, I moved everything that I value to the Bodega long ago. My being there, it's like an invitation: *here's my life, come look, come share...*

Which they do, and sometimes I regret it. That's the point.

THE Bodega is a pub, of course, in the traditional English manner: so much so that they had to remake it a dozen years ago, do it out in Olde Traditional style, wood and leatherette and framed prints on the walls to be sure you got the point. That's when it got the name. Before then it was the Black Bull and genuinely traditional, small dark rooms full of dogs and back-street betting, tiled walls yellow and greasy with nicotine, the high cupola in the lounge bar so layered with grime inside and out that you couldn't even tell its glass was stained by intent, bright colours clouded into grey.

Now all the internal walls have gone, the dirt has gone, so have the dogs and the old clientèle. At night it's a student pub and a theatre pub, loud and busy, good for music and bad for conversation. By day, though, it's pretty much ours and we keep it to ourselves.

To me, the Bodega is an office and a playroom and a place for lunch, for drinks before dinner and a brandy on the way home after. I have business meetings there, I have dates there; I have been known to sleep there, but that's largely accidental and they generally wake me up for last orders.

The regulars there, either side of the bar: they're familiar in the good sense, we're easy with each other. They're friendly without being intrusive, they put up with my odd habits and my odder friends, they know not to trouble me much. If you wanted to say they were my second family, to go in my second home—well, the Bodega is a free house. Say what you like.

THERE are half a dozen booths in line abreast, opposite the bar. Not traditional English pub style at all, but very Olde Traditional; it looks like it ought always to have been like that, like family pews in a country church. The last of the six is mine, by custom and habit. I walk in and I walk directly to it, I toss my bag and jacket in and turn towards the bar. Ordinarily, by this point Jim will be pulling my first pint for me.

This particular day, this far from ordinary day, I couldn't see whether he was or not.

The Bodega is three rooms knocked into one, so the shape of it is irregular. My booth is the last in line because that's where the space suddenly narrows, three or four yards of blank wall butting in. Obviously, if you give a pub some blank wall, they will fill it with a games machine. As a general rule I can see past the machine, but not when someone's playing it.

As a general rule, no one is. We've learned better, and we teach the students as they come, if they're too slow to work it out for themselves. All games will beat you in the end, that's inherent, it's the house percentage and it's written in; but this machine is special. I should know, it's pretty much my fault.

There's been a rash in recent years, of quiz machines in pubs. Pub quizzes, TV quizzes, the quiz as board game, art form, joke: as a nation we're obsessed with trivia and our own absorption of it. Of course there are machines. They swallow pounds and offer questions, offer cash in bucketloads and pay it out in cupfuls. Young men argue over multiple choices; the loudest are not always the most accurate, which is how the manufacturers reckon their profit.

Initially, they forgot to reckon with us. Me, and people like me: those who are good at this, who frequent pubs and have drunk trivia since boyhood. If you knew the length of an ell without thinking, the name of the last man to walk on the moon, who scored in Southampton's FA Cup triumph and who wrote Naomi Campbell's novel 'Swan' (which is not Naomi Campbell), then there was money to be made. In bucketloads. For a while there, a good part of my living came from my playing these machines in every city I could reasonably reach.

When they got wise, they rewrote the algorithm, such that the game was no longer worth the candle. They gave the machines a psychological edge, a hypnotic quality, to lead you down your own particular primrose path to a place you couldn't go. How they did that, I do not know and never will. But I stopped winning enough to pay the train fare, and so I stopped travelling; and soon I was fighting just to hold my own against the machine in my own pub, so I stopped playing altogether. If we were still engaged in any kind of duel, that machine and I, it was my goal to get it out of there, to make it so unprofitable that the owners would take it away.

The young man playing it this day was no one I'd seen before. I would have remembered. Believe me, I would. He looked about nineteen, old enough to be legal but a long way short of being sussed. About anything, really. It was December, there was a wicked easterly coming in from Siberia, and he was wearing a loose and ragged jumper with nothing underneath, bare skin showing through all the holes. His jeans were ancient, ripped and rotting, none too clean; he had a pair of worn and battered deckshoes on his feet. No socks, no laces. He might as well carry a banner, or a brand: *no compromise, no limits.*

His hair was dirty-blond, by nature and by practice; it looked as though he cut it himself, or chopped at it rather whenever it grew to annoy him. He probably did think that, that it grew only to annoy him. I thought perhaps that many things annoyed him.

Including this game he was playing, that kept feeding him questions. He gave it answers and it responded only with another question, or sometimes with a triumph of trumpets and another gush of coins.

He was winning. He was winning and winning, as I used to do, and it wasn't meant to be that way. I couldn't do it; I couldn't believe it of him. Even of him. There was something about him, beyond the clothes and the stance and the concentration; even beyond the striking, astonishing beauty of him, and that distillation of carelessness and charisma he seemed to splash around in lieu of soap and water. His face was perfect in profile, and under the dirt his skin was honey-gold over a lean body caught in that exact moment of achievement, where you know it's never going to be this good again. And I still thought there was something more, some extra shine he had to hook the eye and hold it, as though he was himself the focus of God's burning-glass: the core of him too hot to touch, too bright to look upon.

Whatever. The body of him was too solid to look through, so I walked around him to the bar. And picked up the smell of him as I passed, wood-smoke and spices; and saw a curious puckering of the skin at the back of his neck and running down under his jumper, first hint of a flaw and I thought it might be massive, catastrophic, just the fringe of some great scarring event that had left his spine and shoulders marked for life. Something about the way he stood with his back exposed to the room, hiding nothing: it was almost a declaration, *look at me, see my damage, how I suffer here…*

Or perhaps I was just reaching, overreaching, stumbling badly. He was playing the game, watching the screen, of course he had his head down and his shoulders hunched against us; and I could displace it as I liked, disbelieve it if I wanted but the fact remained, he was playing the game and winning.

I collected a pint with less grace than I usually manage, and then went back to stand behind the boy, unashamedly watching. From here I didn't have to deduce it, I could see the dreadful molten scarring on his shoulder-blades, showing clear through the holes in his jumper. I could also see how inept he was with the machine, the clumsy jab of his finger at the buttons. Again and again, his black and bitten fingernail stabbed down; again and again the screen would flare, his points total would flicker upward, another question would be offered. I thought these machines were psychic, but this one was getting nowhere near him.

I watched for a while, for a long time, for however long it takes to drink a pint when you're fascinated, when you're numb, when you're ignored. Then—well, I shouldn't have done it, but I did.

"You haven't got a drink," I said.

He looked round for the first time. Not startled, not distracted, not irritated except in so far as the world irritated him altogether. His eyes were a cold, cold green, and his voice was husky with youth or disuse, perhaps both.

"No," he said. "I don't like to ask for things."

"That's all right, I'll do the asking. What can I get you?"

"Hot water. From the tap."

"Hot water. Right. Pint?"

"Yes."

I was being facetious, but he seemed to mean it. Okay, fine. I went to the bar and asked nicely. Jim's face twitched, but he's had stranger requests; he ran the tap without comment till the whole sink area was billowing with steam, then he filled a pint glass and passed it over. No charge.

Thin glass, no insulation: I walked hurriedly over to the boy, "Here you go, then," *and take it swiftly, please, before my fingers blister...*

He did that, reaching out a hand without looking, gripping the glass precisely, neither his fingers nor his face showing any reaction to the heat of it. He kept his eyes on the screen and punched buttons with his left hand, no less awkward than his right had been, no less accurate. I wanted to say "I don't know how you do that," but it would have sounded fatuous.

Then he lifted that scalding glass to his mouth and drained it in one long, oblivious swallow, and I really didn't know how he did that. It was like a conjuror's trick, a fakir's fire-eating to impress the credulous, except that I was all the audience he had and he gave a convincing impression of not giving a toss whether I was impressed or not.

Perhaps that was part of the performance. If so, I suppose that it was working. I said, "When you're finished with that game, come and talk to me if you'd like to. I'm just over here."

"I know where you are," he said. And he said something else too, he gave me two different responses with no link between them. "How could I ever be finished with the magnitude of God's creation?"

That took me a while, as I sat in my booth and watched him, sipped my beer and waited to see what he would do. At last, I thought I had it figured. The machine asked him questions about the world, about facts in history and geography and science and the arts. By definition—or by his definition, at any rate—God had created the world, so all these facts could be seen as a chart of God's work, a map in many disciplines. And he was, what, reporting it? Reviewing it? Recording it? I wasn't sure, but there was a relationship, clearly, so long as he was working the machine.

It never occurred to me that he might have meant to be ironic. Looking like that, dressing like that, having that kind of intensity—of course he was a believer. The only question was what exactly he believed, and what he did about it. What he'd be prepared to do.

I don't generally encourage strangers, and certainly not missionaries. I was intrigued, though; perhaps I was enchanted.

And perhaps he would play that machine until the pub closed or the fuses blew. At last, though, it tried to make a pay-out and made a harsh ratchety noise instead, one that I knew of old.

"No more money in it," I called, across the short distance that separated us.

"Do you suppose that I use it for money?" The words might have sounded angry, but he didn't. From his mouth it wasn't a rhetorical question at all.

"Whatever. It uses you for money, and it can't play without a stake. No more questions. Come and sit down."

He pressed a few buttons in ignorance, at random. And elicited no response and so did come over, and did sit down.

"Do you want another drink?" I asked.

"No."

I did; but I also wanted an excuse to stand up, to walk past the machine, to look down into its hopper and say, "Hey, you haven't taken your winnings."

He only shrugged. I scooped them all up, several double handfuls, and deposited them on the table in the booth. In front of him, but they'd be in front of me too. A religious fanatic and his money should probably be parted, and I was just the man to do it.

To prove which, I held back a couple of quid under my thumb, and took them to the bar to buy my beer. Jim had seen the boy's winnings, he'd heard the machine's emptiness, he knew its history and mine; he said, "What's the story, then, is it faulty or what?"

"I don't think so. I think he's just better than me." Better than anyone, I thought he was, impossibly good—which was, more or less, what I'd said.

Jim snorted and said, "I'll get someone to check it over in the morning." We'd been fighting for a long time, he and I, over that machine. Time was on my side, it would have to go when the next new thing came along; in the meantime, we locked horns regularly over its continued tenancy.

I paid for the pint, pocketed the change and went back to my booth. The boy had scrunched himself sideways into the near corner, back to the wall and shoulder hard against the partition, legs almost up on the seat. I sat down opposite and asked, "What's your name?"

"Luke."

I waited for the reciprocal question, *What's yours?*, but it didn't come, so I tried another tack. "What are you, a student?"

"No."

"What do you do, then? When you're not winning a game that can't be won?"

"I lose, of course. There's nothing that can't be lost."

Except a sense of humour, I wanted to suggest; nineteen-year-old gloom is inherent, it's in the job description, but it doesn't have to be unrelieved. Perhaps he wanted me to pursue it, but deliberate obliquity is tedious, and question-and-answer is a brutal form of conversation anyway. Instead I started to talk about the game, about how it had been rewritten—genetically modified, I may have said—specifically to work against me and people like me, and how impressed I was that he could circumvent that programming and beat it anyway.

He listened, he said nothing except "I'm not like you," which was manifestly true. He could embody grace even in awkwardness, but the converse was also true, that he could seem to shrug even in stillness, he could listen and still be heedless. I didn't think he was bored, exactly, so much as entirely unconcerned; I've never felt myself so unnecessary.

And then the door opened and a man came in.

HE was a stranger, another stranger, almost a surprise in itself in the Bodega in mid-afternoon; and he stood in the doorway and looked around, and he said, "God bless all here."

And Luke, unseen in his corner and not looking round the partition, not curious, Luke spoke softly in response, where only I could hear him, and he said, "He will not do that."

By the law of averages, I was sure that he was right; only that I was also sure he didn't mean it statistically, I thought he meant it specifically and imminently. I only didn't know whether he was making predictions for the man, for himself, for me or for whomever else.

And of course whether he had any talent for prophecy, I didn't know that either.

WHEN the man reached the bar, he spoke again to us all, through my silence and Luke's, through other people's conversations, through the music on the juke and the rival jingles from the slot machines. This time he said, "A round of drinks on me, for anyone who comes up and says what they would like."

You couldn't call it the world's most generous gesture, there weren't a dozen of us in the house; and you couldn't say that we stampeded to take advantage. We're not a trustful group. There was a deal of looking around, of watching to see what others did. Still, he started laying money on the bar and Jim seemed happy with it, so one by one we drifted over. Each of us was greeted with a handshake; to me he said, "I'm Jon, Jonathan Pitt, and you are…?" When I told him, he said, "David, excellent, good to meet you. Ask at the bar for whatever you want. And do take something back for your friend, if he's shy. What does he like?"

"Luke? Hot water. If he'll take it. I'm sorry, I hadn't realised he was still…"

He was, he was very still, curled in his inner corner; Jon must have had sharp eyes to spot him there.

"It doesn't matter, not in the least. It's an easier way to meet everyone if they come to me, but if they won't, I'm not too proud to go to them. Hot water, is it? I'll help you carry."

I didn't exactly need help with two glasses, but I was glad to let him take Luke's. On the way I said, "What's this in aid of, the buying drinks all round?" You see it in saloons, in Western movies; I'd never seen it in real life, in England.

"No better way to meet people," he said, "and I dislike being solitary. Luke, hullo. My name's Jon."

"I don't think so," Luke said, not moving else, not reaching to shake hands and not sliding up to make room on the seat.

Jon laughed. "No? Well, perhaps it's not the name that I was born to. It is what people call me, though, and that's more useful. I'll sit with you, David, if I may. If you don't mind being at the centre of things."

"I usually prefer the margins," I said. "But, what things? And what centre, come to that? Just the three of us, we hardly..."

"Not for long, the three of us," he interrupted. "You'll see. People aren't good at taking something for nothing."

He was right, of course. Buy someone a drink, there's a sense of obligation; in a near-empty pub, it's awkward and embarrassing to ignore the benefactor. One by one my fellow drinkers came over, glass in hand, to say thanks and introduce themselves again, to linger and listen, to try to understand who he was and where he was coming from.

It wasn't easy. People gathered round, drew up chairs or dragged stools over from the bar, and I felt more and more hemmed in, trapped even; Jon talked and the same thing happened, I felt his words building up like walls around me, or like sliding partitions in a maze, fluid and shifty. Meanings were motile, stability was a dream.

Strange that I'd been anxious about laying myself open to a religious diatribe. Luke mentioned God in casual contexts, as though they were on familiar terms, and yet he'd shown small interest even in conversation, let alone conversion. Jon mentioned God not at all, his talk was all of the human spirit and human achievement, and yet he was an evangelist to the bone.

And I'd got myself pinned like a pawn, like an amateur. Getting to the toilet would be hard, getting away would be harder by a distance. I was bored, annoyed, regretful—one free drink was not worth this much aggravation, it simply wasn't—and there was nothing I could do but listen, keep my counsel, not get involved.

Jon was involving his audience, of course he was, good evangelists always do. "What do you think, Michael, am I right? Is it too much to ask, that the government take a step back, that they allow us our traditional freedoms? I don't even think that 'allow' is the right word there, is it, Steve? Our freedoms are our own, and government has no voice to speak against them. The tradition here is that everything is permitted, except where it's specifically forbidden; they assume too much, if they think we'll let them make our liberty conditional on their approval. Government is and must be by consent.

It is we who allow them to govern, not they who allow us to live within their narrow notions. Jim," who'd come across ostensibly to collect empties, but let himself be caught listening in, "we need more drinks, the same again for everyone, but we need your opinion too, you have a stake in this. What kind of culture is it, that makes laws about when and where a man can have a drink…?"

If all this sounds like a political rant, it wasn't. His subject might have been politics, but his purpose was religious. He didn't want debate, or even agreement; he wanted converts, believers, I thought he wanted to lead a long march and call down plagues on Westminster until his people were let go. What he would do with them then, I couldn't imagine. If it was hard to work out where he was coming from, it was harder still to see where he was going, where was his Promised Land. *Trust me, I'm a visionary* seemed to be the gist of what he said. I suppose visionaries have always led people by the nose, and blindly. Me, I wanted to know a lot more about his particular vision before I would offer him anything remotely approaching trust.

Still, he had something, a charisma that reached far further than free drinks. I stayed, I listened because I had to, I was wedged in by his own body and the others packed around; the others, though, they stayed and listened because his voice had a spell in it. He was touching more than a nerve here, he was touching their hearts, and it had been a while maybe, for some it had been a long while. The Bodega of a weekday afternoon is no place for the heart-whole or the contented soul.

I thought I was untouched, immune; even I startled like a dozing fawn when the outer door banged, and then the inner opened. A group of office girls, out early: they moved towards the bar then hesitated, seeing the single group of us so intent and the pub so empty else.

Jon said, "I don't think we need any more now, Jim, I think we'll be enough."

"Yes. Yes, of course…" And Jim was up and moving towards the girls with his arms spread wide like a man herding idiot sheep, and his voice was saying, "Sorry, ladies, we're closed today, this is a private party."

Once he'd chased them out, I heard the bolts slam, up and down. I'd heard that sound before, often and often, but never from the inside. Then Jim came back to his seat, to the tight little group of us waiting; and Jon went back to talking, while I went back to wondering what he wanted. No one else seemed to care, they were content just to listen, to be enchanted. All except Luke, who I thought really truly didn't care.

Jon had seen that too, or something like it. He said, "What about you, then, Luke, what are you thinking? Do you have any questions for me?"

And Luke said, "I have a question. Why do you talk about government and these little matters, when all the time what you mean to talk about is God?"

"Why do you think of God," Jon countered, "when I talk of government?"

"Because you do too."

"Well," he conceded, "perhaps. But that is the real world, and human kind cannot bear very much reality. You have to make allowances for our poor mortal flesh."

"Is your flesh mortal?"

"Oh, yes. Yes, of course. We may all be made of stardust, but everything's recyclable. What goes around, comes around. Even experience is recycled into dreaming. What do you dream of, Luke?"

"I never dream."

"Perhaps you should try sleeping, once in a while. But what do you aspire to, what's your greatest desire?"

"Restitution." And he shifted his shoulders against an absence of weight, a responsibility ripped away.

"Ambition is always to be admired. Even that, though—it is achievable. In time."

"I have lived in time for too long."

"Or for long enough, perhaps. That is not yours to judge, neither mine. But we mustn't ignore these others and their needs. I think perhaps we all seek restitution, one way or another. Anthony, what's your greatest loss, what would you most want restored to you?"

We knew his answer before he spoke. I thought perhaps Jon did too; I thought this was unkind, and still somehow aimed at Luke, spelling out a little loss only to remind him of a greater.

Anthony's awkward, wrinkled fingers played with the wedding band he still wore, that he would still have worn even if his knuckles weren't too swollen to release it, and he said, "I want my wife back. Nothing else in the world. Sad, isn't it? When the only thing you want is impossible..."

"Nothing is impossible, Anthony."

He laughed, like a cough of pain. "She's dead. And she lived just long enough to divorce me first, so it was twice I lost her. You want to tell me you can bring her back from that?"

"I don't want to tell you anything. I want you to tell me, how to make you happy. That's all it takes."

Light falls in colours onto the floor of the Bodega, where sunlight strikes through the great stained glass dome in the roof. Sometimes you can even see the colours in the sunbeams, where the dust dances; sometimes it can look like shadows etched from light.

I was gazing out across the room, across the heads of all my gathered friends, only because I couldn't bear to be looking at Anthony. I found myself looking at patterns of colour and light, like angled columns hanging in the air; they were darker than I'd seen them before, darker than seemed reasonable, and I thought they were shifting, shaping themselves in a slow weave into something more solid than dust.

I thought that Anthony might stand up and push his way out through the crowd at any moment, and I really didn't want him to do that. I was suddenly afraid of what he might find lurking at the back there, where the light fell. *We may all be made of stardust, but everything's recyclable.* Dust and starlight might be recycling themselves into some brutal simulacrum that would lisp and shuffle in mockery of Anthony's twice-lost love. Or worse, into the thing itself, actually her, dragged out from where she lay rotting and forced back to the man she'd fled; or worse yet, her as she had been, young and happy and still in love. Jon had done nothing yet, nothing but talk, and yet already I thought he could do anything; I believed in miracles, I suddenly had faith and dreaded to see it justified. No man should have that power, to press the dead back into the hands of the living.

Anthony didn't move, though, except to huddle closer in upon himself. Dolly laid a sympathetic hand on his arm, which only drew Jon's attention to her.

"And you, Dolly? What's the dream of your heart?"

She blinked, hesitated, told him. Told us all.

"I want a child."

She was what, mid-fifties? That at least. And she wanted a child, and I thought Jon could give her what she wanted. I thought he could make one whole and bespoke, or else just reach inside her and wake an egg, make an egg if necessary, break down a few cells and put them back together another way. That couldn't be hard. Not against what I thought he was doing already, back there where colours stained the air where it ran thick with dust. I was glad suddenly to be penned in my corner, furthest from whatever was forming behind the crowd, all those bodies between it and me.

Furthest from the back, of course, meant closest to the front, next to Jon. No point holding my breath, or trying to move as little as he did: he was intimately aware of me, and ready to make that known.

"Wait," he said to Dolly, "wait and hope. To let go of hope is the only sin that cannot be forgiven, the only act of folly that cannot be redeemed. David, now. What of you, what are you yearning for?"

I could have lied, and said I lacked for nothing; I could have lied, and said I'd lost too much. But he would know, and all these people too. They'd seen Anthony and Dolly strip themselves bare; I couldn't cheapen that. But I didn't dare feed what was happening here. It was too cruel already, too monstrous. I could see the faces of those people standing with their backs to the light, and they knew. They had none of them turned round to see—scared or snared, was there a difference?—but they knew something was building there, and nothing kind or welcome.

Besides, I didn't have that kind of all-consuming hunger. All my losses were small in comparison, all my failures were mean affairs. Which surely gave me the right to choose, so long as it was an honest choice, something I did most seriously want. And something he couldn't or wouldn't give me, something unanswerable...

Like the game, the quiz-game that couldn't be beaten, except by...

"Luke," I said, "I want to be like Luke," and not to beat the machine, or not only that. "I'm not like you," he'd said, and I wanted that not to be true. I wanted to be eternally nineteen again and beautiful and damaged and in need of restitution, in search of it, in hopes of it. In the moment that I thought of it, I said it; and almost in that same moment I was sure how the exchange would go, how Jon's eyes would widen and then contract, how he would say "That's impossible" and I would say "I thought nothing was impossible" and he would say "Not to God, but what I mean is that I can't do it." And that would break the spell of him or I hoped it would, cut us free of his charm and interrupt his creature still a-borning, make a stillborn thing of it, spare Dolly the brutal reality of her baby, let us all avoid our desperate, dreadful wishes.

But Luke forestalled it all, that story as it played out in my head. He screamed, and though there was a long trailing "Noooo!" at the heart of it, the body of that scream was all revulsion. And he reached across the table in the booth, and if he'd been a fraction slower I'd have had just time enough to be afraid. But he outreached my fear, he outreached me and seized hold of Jon and pulled him up and up. The two of them rose high above the rest of us, and nobody was saying any of those things you say when a fight breaks out in your local, "Stop it, Luke, leave it, it's not worth it, calm down or take it outside," still less trying to get between them. This mattered, this was a battle for our souls or our sanity, something on that order. I could hear soft cries from the back, the sound of someone spewing; I couldn't see through the bodies, what lay behind them in the pools of sunlit colour on the floor. I didn't try, more than one swift glance. I didn't want to look away from Luke.

I was wrong, though, we were all wrong, and we saw that soon enough. This was not a battle, nothing so even-handed. It was an execution. Jon had said his flesh was mortal; Luke proved it, to us and to himself. His own flesh must be something other, unless it was simply pure and original and unadulterated, not after all recycled; no human hands should or could be so strong. Like a leopard he dragged his prey up high, out of all reaching, atop the partitions that divided one booth from the next. Jon's struggles seemed weak, a gesture, nothing more; I think they were not, only that they were immaterial to Luke.

"I know who sent you," he hissed, "and why you came. Not for them, not for any of them. It was all for me. I was going home, and you were sent to test me. Or to trip me."

"And will you see that and choose to stumble anyway," Jon gasped against the grip around his throat, "will you come so close and turn back now? Don't you want to be free?"

"My freedoms are my own, and God has no voice to speak against them."

Neither did Jon, any longer. Luke's grip tightened, and that one-handed strangle must have been enough, was probably enough to break Jon's neck as well as choke him. Not enough for Luke, though.

Gas fittings are a feature of the walls in Olde Traditional pubs. Sometimes they're even original, there really are pipes in the walls and genuine lamp-holders surviving. In the Bodega, there's just one ironwork arm jutting out of the plasterwork a couple of feet below the ceiling. Jim hangs a paper skeleton from it, every Hallowe'en.

Luke held Jon at arms' stretch above his head, slammed him against the wall and released him. He hung there, grotesquely broken, suspended in air; we all took a while, too long to realise that his skull had been pierced by that iron spike.

People were leaving already, walking backwards, groping blindly behind them to find their way while their eyes stayed fixed on the dark and dangling body, beside it the bright vision that was Luke. I heard the bolts on the door drawn back; I heard footsteps, faster footsteps, almost a stampede; I didn't hear a word, not a single word from anyone.

Jim retreated behind the bar. I saw his hand move towards the phone, pick it up and then just hold it, dialling no one.

By the time Luke jumped lightly down, there was no one left in the bar, bar the three of us. The three of us and Jon, perhaps. I was the only one who hadn't moved at all. From where I sat, I could see the body weirdly foreshortened above my head, all feet and tapering; I could see the spatter of blood on the dado rail, where it was dripping down.

Luke scooped up handfuls of his scattered winnings, and fed them back into the machine. Storing up credit in heaven, I thought, great credit.

Then he began to play, and he lost and lost and lost again. He couldn't remember who founded Rome, or who wrote *The Rights of Man;* he didn't know where the Okavango lay, or what was the capital of Belize. He seemed bewildered, bereft, entirely disconnected. Once he glanced over in my direction as if for help; I offered him a shrug, no more, and he turned his head back towards his losses.

After a while, after a slow and breathless while, he straightened his back, although it seemed to hurt him. As he walked out, his foot slipped in something slimy on the floor. He didn't look down to see; no more did I. Perhaps it was only vomit.

EVERY DAY A LITTLE DEATH

or

THE CLOCKMAKER'S APPRENTICE

WHEN WE COUNT THE CLOCKS THAT tell the time, there are always more than we think. We find them everywhere we can; we watch the sun, we watch a shadow lengthen on the ground to say how late it is. We keep calendars to say how many days there are to come, and journals to say how we have used what days we've had. We calculate moveable feasts, and give names to the days when the seasons turn. We're more nervous than we know. We try to pin time down with numbers, with measurements, with standing stones and mechanical devices, candle-clocks and water-clocks and pendulums and bells.

There is a reason for it, for this obsession, and it makes good sense if you happen to be human. Monkey see, monkey do; we learn by imitation, we've always been best at mimicry, and we look for comfort in homoeopathic doses, hollow copies of the real thing. We bottle history in plays and songs, we tell each other stories that make-believe the world—and we surround ourselves with toys that cut time into smaller and smaller slices, separate and survivable moments that are short enough to do no harm, only to help ourselves forget that in the end there is just the one clock for each of us, one clock that counts.

ABU bin Hassid was a clockmaker in Baghdad. Did I say a clockmaker? No, I malign him. He was *the* clockmaker, the fat one, the king of his craft. He had served kings; he could have lived in the palace and served the Sultan himself and drunk pearls in vinegar all his days, as the saying is. But he was a proud one, the fat one, and he preferred to have the Sultan to come to him. He had started his life in the souk, he said, and he would end it there. He did, he said that, often. Of course he had started as a thief before the old clockmaker caught him and kept him, beat the worst out of him and beat his own trade in. Abu didn't often tell that part of the story. And of course in the end he was hardly in the souk at all, building his own little palace of a craft-house within sight of the Sultan's, with high walls and barred windows and great mutes for guards at the gate and no one knew what secrets kept within, along with the gold and the jewels and the precious tools of his work. He might speak expansively of his people—"the poor are my tribe," he liked to say, especially when he was speaking to the rich—but he took care to keep them outside his house. His was a private showroom, and the less money you had the more private it became.

HIS guards were carefully trained to keep it so. They might have no voices to plot against him, but it was remarkable how expressive a silent giant with a massive scimitar could be, when he was seeking to suggest that your purse was too light to work the latch on the gate.

Accordingly, our Abu felt a twinge of annoyance one hot afternoon, when he came in from the courtyard to find a man looking around in the workshop. It was a tall man, a stranger, dressed in a dusty and unpromising robe. At first sight, he should never have talked his way past the guards. If second sight had shown him to be wealthier than he appeared—a traveller, perhaps, who carried his money in diamonds and preferred not to show it in his clothes, no foolish precaution in these troubled times—then Abu should have been summoned immediately. In any event, the man should never have been allowed to wander freely this way, into the workshop or the warerooms or who know where. Abu was at a loss to understand how that had happened, when he himself had been in the courtyard and had seen not a shadow move; his men would be at pains, indeed at extreme pains to explain it to him later, with whistles and gestures in lieu of words, grunts and shapeless cries in lieu of—well, in lieu of nothing, really. Grunts and cries could be whipped up from anyone, whether or not they had the gift of tongues.

Still, the man was here, whether or not he ought to be; and he had a precious thing in his hands, a confection of frothy gold and diamond.

"Sir, sir, please, put that down…"

The man showed no signs of doing so, but turned it over in his fingers as though he had never seen such a thing before. Well, and so he had not; it was unique.

"What is it?"

The voice must of course have come from below the hood, where his face was hidden in shadow. It didn't feel that way. It felt as though it spoke from everywhere at once, as though the world itself had spoken very, very softly, and the echo of it resounded in Abu's bones.

"It's a clock, sir, a very special clock…"

"It looks like a castle. A castle made of sand."

"Yes, sir, yes, a clock in the shape of a sandcastle. See, the turrets turn to show how the minutes pass, flags rise to show the hours; and all the case is gold with diamond slices for the windows, and please, sir, it is very precious and fragile," by which Abu meant 'valuable', "so if you wouldn't mind just setting it down quite carefully on the workbench there…"

"I am accustomed to handling fragile things," the man said mildly, "and someone always thinks them precious."

"Even so, sir. It is not for sale. It is a gift for His Magnificence the Sultan," by which Abu meant that his own skin depended on its safe delivery, and that therefore it was very precious indeed.

"I do not want it. It pretends to be one thing pretending to be another, sand shaped into a castle, when it is neither; and it pretends to do something more, which is to count the passage of time, which it cannot."

"Pretends? Sir, I make the finest timepieces in all Baghdad! And this one is a true clock, it strikes the hours as the flags rise…"

Indeed it did so now, ticking and whirring and chiming suddenly in the man's hands, raising its little flags of jewel-chippings on a gold ground in designs that flattered the Sultan and God in equal measure, because Abu was a careful man. The man's sleeves fell back as he held the clock up into a fall of sunlight; Abu blinked, and tried to tell himself that it was just the dazzle deceiving him. The man was gaunt, no more than that, no doubt a desert traveller; if he seemed bone-bare, well, that was just a metaphor. Wasn't it…?

Abu had been a thief and a liar all his life, but he still found it hard to deceive himself, and in honesty the sunlight wouldn't do it for him. If beauty was only skin deep, this man should perhaps not keep a mirror in his house.

"Remarkable," the man said gravely. "Such noise, such fuss—and all such nonsense, to pretend that time can run mechanically, always the same distance between one sunset and the next, to be counted off by cogs and spindles. I prefer sand, myself." There was sand in his voice, like the tides of ages, dry and merciless.

"Sir, if you have no interest in my work…" He meant to sound angry and dismissive; he was afraid that the words came out more pleadingly

"That was what I came to discover. I have heard speak of Abu bin Hassid, and I came to see what it was that you did. Well, now I have seen, and it is not worth the doing. No matter. I do not judge. The world may miss your clocks, but no doubt there will be others."

"Sir, who are you, to come into my house and speak so?" Like any dishonest man, Abu liked to be sure of his ground. He had a fear in him now, and he needed to be certain that he should.

"I have been called the clockmaker's apprentice," the man said, as though he had puzzled over the title himself, "because I sweep up what God discards. You may play at being God, with your machines that hammer time into a chain of links; but time moves on unregulated, sand slides through glass and I do my work as I must. Abu bin Hassid, we shall meet again."

"How, how soon...?"

"What, can your clocks not tell you? At the time appointed, then. It will not be long delayed."

Then the man turned and was gone, and it was hard to say whether he had walked away or not, whether he had passed through the door into the court or gone some other way not open to Abu. This much was certain, that there would be no point in challenging the guards. If they had seen the stranger coming, they could not have stopped him; Abu thought that they would not have seen him leave. He knew many stories of those who tried to keep a watch on Death, to bar him from their houses, from their lives. They never could.

No, Death must come. The trick was not to be there, when he did...

ABU sat for hours while his clocks chimed all through the house, while the sky grew as dark and secret as his thoughts, while the moon rose like the lamp that his servant brought to lighten the little space around him, though that only served to make the great house darker yet to his eyes. He had always seen the span of a man's life like a thread, wound around a spool by the steady ticking of a clock. Now he could see his own life like a thread cut free, and the loose end winding closer. It was hard to think, against that brutal ticking. But still, he was a clockmaker, and so was God; had Death not said so? He understood the workings of the world, none better. And there was no one better able to adjust them, given the proper tools...

SO he sat all night and drew intricacies in his head, because a clockmaker is a man of hidden ways and subtle understanding. And in the morning, he washed his head and hands and went out into the city without his breakfast. He really didn't think that he would need to eat.

First he went down to the river quarter, where the real poor could be found, and the powers that live among the poor if you know where to find them. Abu had a mind like one of his own clocks, it ticked over and over and never allowed that a moment passed was a moment lost; he remembered everything.

He remembered to leave his bodyguards behind him, which was good for a man who did not wish to die. He remembered to turn left here and right here, and not to look behind him as he went. He remembered the smells of these alleys, all the separate smells, the damp and the food and the dirt and the fear. He remembered his own fear, those times he had ventured further than he had excuse or courage for.

Above all he remembered this particular door, and who waited behind it. Old witch, old crone, old meddler: she had always been old, he thought. She was old when he was young, she would be old now but still perhaps no older, he thought she had reached a perfectibility of age and had no need to add to it in this world. For sure, he thought, she would never trouble herself with dying.

He hoped that she might help him now, though not with her own solution. He had no interest in growing witheringly old. He thought that he would rather do the other thing, and step away from Death by stepping back.

Abu bin Hassid, clockmaker to the court, to His Magnificence himself and emperors of other lands: his steady, ticking mind was curious to see how scared he was, as he passed through that door.

AN hour later he came out again, unchanged, unless perhaps she had given him something more to be frightened of, after Death and her. Something at least she had given him; he carried it in a pouch inside his robe. What he had given her, we need not enquire. Some things never were meant to be told in stories.

He went from there to the cattle market, outside the city walls. He bought a fine she-camel, he who was too fat and satisfied to travel, and ordered her sent to his house with saddle and reins and riding-stick, all that might be needful and all of the best quality. The dealer was doubtful, managing to imply without ever quite saying that she would never stand beneath his weight. Abu was a hard man to deny, though, and his gold was a soft persuader.

Then he walked on, he who never walked anywhere, past the horse-lines and the ox-pens to the slavers' compound, where he visited his old adversary Muazzar bin Muazzar in his tent. Muazzar was a lean man, a quiet man, and if he had vices they were not of the flesh. He and Abu despised each other, but each was preeminent in his trade, and each liked to buy the best. When Muazzar had need of a clock—usually for a gift, to flatter a reliable client; he was not a man for trinkets—he would come to Abu; when Abu needed more guards or other servants for his house, he brought his trade to Muazzar and no one else.

On this day they drank coffee together, ate sweetmeats, exchanged news and pretty compliments; and when time came for business, Abu said, "Muazzar, I want a boy today."

"Do you, indeed? To what end?"

Abu chuckled. "I shall make an apprentice of him, and pass on all my skills. It is time I made provision for my age."

"That may be true, but as I remember, the last boy I sold you for that purpose, you strangled him."

"He was stealing from me."

"The sweepings from your floor, I believe, Abu."

"Even so." Abu's face clouded; the phrase had an uncomfortable echo. "The sweepings from my workshop floor are dusted with gold and precious things. I sweep my own shop now. This boy shall not touch a broom, I promise you; nor shall I harm him. I will be as careful of his health as I am of my own."

"Well, I do have a boy that might suit, a bright lad, well set up, only unfortunate in his choice of father. The man is a drinker of arak; it is a sin expensive of health, of position and of money, and he is made bankrupt by it. His creditors have seized his goods, his house and household by way of restitution. I had the boy cheap, and I will not sting you for him."

"None the less, you must be recompensed for time and trouble. You know that I am generous with my purse, Muazzar." This was how the two men expressed their contempt for each other, in a duel of underpricing and overpaying. To come off worst in a deal was a victory; their struggles tended to counteract each other, so that victories were few and far between and most of their exchanges were grudgingly allowed to be fair.

"Well. Let us see the boy."

A clap of the hands, a word to the servitor, and the boy was fetched. Abu was pleased with him, on the whole. He had perhaps been too hungry for too long and he had some growing still to do, but his body was straight and his eye was sharp. He was a little sullen and a little scared, but that mattered nothing. Abu offered a price in gold; Muazzar was appalled, outraged that an old and favoured client should so cheat himself. He refused to take anything more than the same number of coins in silver, and that was too high…

And so they bargained, and came at last to a figure that satisfied neither of them, by virtue of its being more or less the market price for a boy not trained to any work.

THE boy was called Hussein. Abu took him first to the offices of the city scribes, to adopt him legally into his household and name him heir to all that he possessed. While Hussein was still gaping, they went on to Abu's tailor, where new clothes were ordered to replace the shabby rags that he was wearing; everything from riding boots to a traditional clockmaker's welchet, and all to be delivered that same day.

And so home, where Abu introduced Hussein to all his staff with the strict injunction that they were to obey the boy in all things, as scrupulously as they did himself. Then, just the two of them, they went to the strongest of his storerooms, where there were no windows and the door was iron-barred. "I will show you my treasures, lad," he said; but first he locked the door behind them, and then he opened the pouch that he had bought that morning, at what cost we do not know.

STORYTELLERS need not be spies, under an obligation to report all that they have seen. No matter what Abu did in that dark room, or with what craft he did it. For us it is enough to say that the door opened again in the twilight of the day, and it was the boy Hussein who came out smiling. He locked the door behind him with great care, and summoned all the household.

"A dreadful thing has happened to our master," he announced. "An 'ifrit came and took possession of him, and he raves. He is sleeping now, but mark me, when he wakes you must not listen to his madness. Nor should you fetch him imams or a doctor or a lawyer, whatever he may demand. Only feed him through the bars here and see to his comforts as best you can; I will keep the keys, for fear that his blandishments should move you to a dangerous kindness. Do not under any circumstances seek to force the door, or the 'ifrit will destroy you all. I ride to find a magician who can drive the creature out. In my absence, be watchful, beware! Let no one in to see him, and above all, do not let him out!"

And then he dressed himself in his fine new clothes and saddled the camel in the yard and rode away, and all the house stared after him in mute astonishment.

FOR days he rode and nights he slept in caravanserai, buying his food and entertainment with Abu's coin. When he came to Samara, he felt it seemed that this was far enough. He sought out the finest clockmaker in the town and showed him a paper written in Abu's hand, commending his son Hussein as a skilled apprentice, highly trained, needing only experience in another man's workshop now.

The clockmaker—a good man, you will be pleased to hear, whose name was Sharif al Tarkas—grunted, and said, "Abu bin Hassid's name is known throughout the sultanate. I have seen his clocks. But I had not heard that he ever had a son."

"I am adopted, sir. The city scribes will confirm it, if you ask."

"What, shall I send all the way to Baghdad to have some pox-scarred clerk's warranty? Those are easier forged than this," and he waved Abu's paper dismissively. "I will believe it when I have seen you at work. Come, here is an old clock, foul with dust and sand; let me watch you clean it."

That done, there was a bezel to cut, an ornate clockwork to be assembled, all the testing tasks that Sharif could conceive. By the day's end he was exhausted, but the boy was still smiling. Sharif did not quite like that smile, but he was an honest man, as well as a good one; he said, "Well, lad, I have tested what I can, and I would keep you without the name you bring, without the testimonial. You have the eye, the gift, the skill; your father must have trained you all your life, to bring you on so far so young. I suppose you must go back to him one day, but till then, your home is with me. Come back now, and my wife will find us food and a place in my house for you to spread your blanket."

A few days later, the boy was watching his new master's stall in the general market, where they sold mostly simple timepieces to simple people. He was pining a little, perhaps, because Samara is not Baghdad. Then he saw a familiar hand trail among the clocks on the stall, touching, assessing, dismissing: a hand that might never have known any sins of the flesh, or the fleshy.

He was nervous, but he had always been bold; he lifted his head and met the stranger, eye to eye.

For a moment too short to measure, he thought perhaps that he had startled Death.

Then, "You have changed your face, Abu bin Hassid."

"I have, and my body too. I left the old one for you in Baghdad."

"Did you so? I have not been to see; our appointment was here in Samara. And I have found you here. You are still yourself, Abu bin Hassid. You cannot hide from me."

"I don't need to hide," our Abu said, with a kind of anxious smugness. "You have found me, of course—but you cannot take me now, out of this borrowed body. I am not Abu bin Hassid, I am the boy Hussein, his adopted son. Hussein is not fated to die today; God himself would not allow it. You need old Abu's body, the fat one. Go back to Baghdad, you will find it there, penned up and waiting for you."

"With the boy's spirit trapped inside it—and as you said, he is not meant for me today."

"It is a puzzle for you," Abu said, smiling and satisfied. "But you cannot save him, I have come too far; take my spirit and this body dies, before you can fetch him to it. You need one body between the two of us today. Take his, take Abu's. It is written so, and men at least will understand it. Otherwise he is a madman, an old man pleading to be a boy; and the boy might live another sixty years in that body, which would make him the oldest man in the world before you would let him die. It is a wicked trick of mine, I am sure, and God will punish me; I will face that when my time comes."

"Your time has come."

"But not yet gone," said Abu, picking up one of his master's clocks from the stall and turning the hands backwards, to show Death where they stood. The clock was more intricate than any other here, and was surmounted by a clockwork figure that struck a bell to mark the hours; and yet the whole device was only pocket-sized, if you had deep pockets. Your pockets would need to be deep, to pay its price. It was a showpiece, not really meant for sale, only to catch the eye; but Death said,

"What cost would that command?"

"Oh, I thought you were not interested in our work?"

"Suddenly," Death said, "I find it very interesting indeed." And he drew, from what must have been a very deep pocket indeed, a purse holding nothing but pennies. "How many of these do you want?"

IN Baghdad, in the strongest storeroom in the city, a fat old man sat huddled in a corner, surrounded by the most precious wreckage imaginable. He had begged and wept, he had raged and cursed, he had broken open boxes and poured jewels out through the bars on the door, but he could not buy his freedom. The more he raved, the more the guards backed away from him. Of course they could not speak, to urge him to be patient, to be at peace, to pray and trust in God and the boy Hussein, who had gone to seek help for his affliction. Before long their silence had driven him to smash boxes for the simple sake of smashing, for the chance to break anything that was Abu's.

His great body was too heavy to bear such passion for so long. His hands trembled now, his heart laboured in his chest, and his spirit was almost broken. The tears had dried in his unaccustomed beard, and he had no more weeping in him; bewildered and exhausted and afraid, he barely raised his head when he realised that he was suddenly no longer alone in the storeroom, although the door most certainly had not been opened.

He had no light in there, beyond what was grudgingly let in through the door's bars, but the figure before him seemed to blaze in the shadows, as though it stood in another kind of darkness altogether.

"I know who you are," he said, shying almost at the sound of the voice that said it, Hussein's words from Abu's mouth. "But I am not, I am not the man you want, the monster Abu…"

"This I know," Death said. "And yet, that body has to die today, it cannot live; and your own is far from here, where you could never reach it."

A lost spirit is a desperate thing, restless beyond recovery, fading and howling in the desert. The thin boy choked in the fat man's body, but he made no further protest. Let it be as it was written; his was a cursed life, and he could not change it now.

Death reached into his pocket, and drew out a clock that gleamed darkly golden in the eerie light. Hussein would rather have expected an egg-timer, glass and sand, his life equally frail and equally short.

While his eyes were still on the clock, he was aware of Death's other hand in motion suddenly. So swift the movement was, he couldn't say whether there had been an implement used, something long and bright that existed only at that margin where speed was a measurement of sharpness, or whether it was the hand itself that he saw, blurring as it stretched towards him. Nor could he say quite what was done, what was cut or pinched off or plucked out. But it seemed to him that the hand, unless it was a tool, had slipped somehow inside this vast body that he inhabited now, and yet he had not felt it; and while in there, in here, that tool—unless it was a hand—had done something drastic and irrecoverable. He felt like a ship cut loose, adrift; there was abruptly nothing solid under his hands, no certainty in him anywhere. He was detached even from his misery, from his despair.

He stood up, if you could call it standing; he looked down, and saw Abu's body slumped on the floor at his feet, and thought lightly that this would probably be a powerful moment in a man's life, if that were his own body that he looked down on. And then he saw that he had no feet, no body at all that he could register, and suddenly it was a powerful moment in his own life, except that he thought that he couldn't really call it life. More like the other thing, though he didn't want to use the word, with Death standing right beside him. It would have seemed like lèse majestée, and possibly led to confusion.

Instead, gazing at the figure of Death which was somehow brighter now, or else the world was more shadowy, he said, "Isn't the clock supposed to chime or something, to show that my time is up?"

"That might have been a good idea," Death said, "if it were true. But I have stopped the clock. You would need to chime it yourself."

And Death's hand moved again, and this time it was clearly empty. Hussein felt it close around him like a cage, like bitter iron, constricting, squeezing; and then it was gone but the grip was not, he was held and confined in a cold world, a world of wheels and teeth. For a timeless moment, nothing moved. Then, one by one, those terrible wheels began to turn...

THE day was not over, though the sun was very low. Abu in his stolen body had packed up his timepieces and carried them back to his master's house, with a small sack full of pennies. Now he was cutting cogs in the last of the light, smelling what vagrant aromas slipped into the yard from the kitchen to promise good eating to come, wondering how vagrant his master's younger daughter might prove to be if he could slip her from the kitchen and out into the dark. He was hardly at all thinking of Death and his great defeat, the long-awaited triumph of man over the oldest enemy. Or the triumph of one man, rather. He didn't intend to share it.

Nor did he at all expect a cold shadow to fall across his work, especially as the sun was behind his shoulder. He glanced up and felt his young heart race for a moment, before he could control it.

"I have said, you cannot have me today."

"And yet I will. Your body I have already, back in Baghdad; now I want your spirit."

"If you slay this body, you slay the boy; and that you cannot do. Have you forgotten?"

"I forget nothing. And I did not speak of slaying. You left your proper body, to borrow his; I have brought him with me, to reclaim it."

A silence, brief and wary; then, "I have not finished with it yet."

"Neither have I finished with you."

Death took the clock from his pocket, and Abu almost, almost understood. "In there? But how...? It is a mechanical contrivance, a toy..."

"And what more is your body, or the boy's? God is called the great clockmaker, remember, and I am his apprentice." The little bell struck, light and silvery: once and again and then again, erratically, although it had been better made than that and the hands of the clock were moving not at all and stood nowhere near the hour.

And it seemed Death was tired of talking then, or else he was irritated by the chimes. His other hand reached out and might perhaps have seemed to slide within the body of the boy, unless it passed behind, if it could be behind from every imaginable perspective. It came out clenched around something that could not be seen, although it was transparently there; and it passed into the clock and came out empty. And then it reached for the clockwork figure that struck the bell, that was striking and striking. It drew something forth from there, and slipped it back into the boy's body.

The boy caught himself suddenly, on the very edge of falling, like a man who is dozing and startles awake. He shuddered, and rubbed his hands across his face, and then drew back and looked at the hands minutely. Then, because he had nice manners and was perhaps still a little bewildered, he lifted his head and said, "Thank you, sir. But, please—what am I to do now?"

"I think you are to be a clockmaker's apprentice," Death said.

"But, but I do not, I have not the skill..."

"You will find that the hands remember, they have had a master craftsman guide them; and the head can learn. It is probably a better life than a slave's. There is property that belongs to you in Baghdad, but you should not claim it yet. You might prefer not to claim it at all, as there will be some uncomfortable questions that come with it. If you stay to make your life here, your new master is called Sharif al Tarkas, and I understand that he has a daughter. The rest you must discover for yourself."

And then he turned and was gone, as though he had stepped from sunlight into shadow, but all the shadow had been his own. Hussein blinked, and gazed down at his hands for a while. Then he picked up a small brass cog and a delicate tool, and sat cutting teeth until a dark girl with teasing eyes came to call him in to supper.

IF Death had a house, there would be a room in that house where he would keep a table, which would be Death's table, and he would sit at it; and at his back there might be the ever-swelling hiss of sands, innumerable sands, but on his table there would be a clock. Just the one, and with a muffled bell. And Death would be aware, he would count its every tick, as he is aware, he counts every grain of sand that slips by for each of us; and Death's clock would never need winding, and every tick would be a little, just a little as though the pendulum were a razor, and with every swing it scythed the finest imaginable shaving from an endless, breathless, unstoppable scream.

ANOTHER CHART OF THE SILENCES

SOME PEOPLE THINK THAT A BREATHLESS hush is the natural state of the universe, as darkness is: that sound is like light, a rebellion of angels, a thin and fierce and ultimately doomed attempt to hold back the crushing weight of utter stillness.

THEY'RE mistaken. White noise is universal, it's woven into the fabric: the sound of the Big Bang infinitely elastic, infinitely stretched. In the beginning was the Word, and what we hear is still the scratch of God's pen on the paper as he made it, as he spoke it, as he wrote it.

I hear it, almost, on a daily basis. I sit in the Silence Room in the Lit & Phil, the quietest place I know, where even the books are bound and gagged, tied shut with strong white ribbon; and when I'm alone, when I'm not turning pages, when I listen past my lungs' breath and my heart's beat and my belly's churn, I think I can hear the faintest possible scritching sound, inherent in the air. White noise: but actually this isn't that everlasting, ever-fading echo of the slam of all existence. This is something entirely other, contained within walls, within covers. Books telling their own damn stories. I swear to you, it's true. Go in, sit down, sit quiet, you can hear it for yourselves. It's there, it's always there; it's the sound of all those books. Rewriting.

DEATH is a deception, it's a trick. It's a game that books play. What do they know? They want to keep everything, unchanging and for ever. They take what is liquid, mutable, permeable, life; and then they fix it like a dye, set solid. Historically, what are the three most scary words in the language? *It is written.* You can't argue with that.

BUT the rules change, surely, when the books rewrite themselves. Somewhere—downstairs, probably, on a shelf in the Silence Room—there's a book that's rewritten the border between life and death, unless it just scribbled something illegible in the margin. Like this:

IT was a Saturday morning, and I was alone, content, down there at the large table with my back turned to the room. I had charts spread out before me, and an ocean in my head. That afternoon I'd have the real thing beneath my keel, and I ached for it already; but out there, quite often I would ache for this. When a man can measure his happiness coming and going, he should probably be grateful.

What's good can always be lost, or broken, or taken away: by our own carelessness, by other people's clumsiness, by envy or greed or disregard.

The door opened, at my back.

There were two of them, I could hear that in their footsteps. Both male, I thought: the length of their strides or the sounds of their shoes, perhaps the timbre of their breathing. One was older than the other. By a distance, by a generation.

I heard the squeak of chairs at one of the little alcove-tables, and turned back to my papers.

Then I heard another kind of noise: not incidental, not the haphazard sounds of bodies in motion. Steady, irregular, deliberate.

And familiar, and I didn't believe it. I still didn't turn to look, but I listened, and was sure. Those were the sounds of chessmen being set out on a board. And this was the Silence Room, it says so on the door, they must have seen; and it is impossible, *impossible* to play chess silently.

I didn't turn, but my back was stiff with outrage. They paid no heed. They played, and every move was an offence; and soon—of course!—they started talking.

It's not conversation, exactly, but talking always counterpoints the play. Some moves have to be discussed, some lingered over like a line of beauty. And this was an older man and a boy, a youth, so the game was a lesson also. The boy had that abrupt, husky teenage way of talking, stumbling over his words; it jarred me every time he spoke.

I could have swept up my papers and stalked out. Perhaps I should have done; hindsight aches for me to do it, for another me to have another chance. *Matthew, I'm sorry. Look, I'll go, and all things will be different for all of us, amen…*

I didn't move, though. Even that would have been a statement, an accusation, awkward for everybody. I stayed, they played, I seethed and nothing further happened until the older man left the room in the middle of their game. He might have been fetching coffee, he might have been visiting the toilet. It didn't matter. He was gone; and some imp of the perverse felt it right that, just as the door swung closed at his back, the boy's mobile phone should ring.

Then I did swivel round in my chair, I was too blindly angry to keep still. The boy knew; he was already looking in my direction, even as his hands fumbled for the phone.

"Sorry…"

"If you were sorry," I said, "you wouldn't answer it."

He flushed, suddenly and thoroughly; and glanced down at the phone, stabbed it with a finger, lifted it to his ear. Hunched over it as though that would help, and muttered "I'm in the library."

Something in that, the flush or the defiance melted my anger in a moment. All the pent-up rage flooded out of me, leaving me hollow and brittle and defenceless. Then I did have to move; I slipped out and went walking through the library. I went to old friends, old books, sailors and travellers: Hakluyt's *Voyages,* Ibn Battutah.

When I went back down, when I could face it, the older man was packing chess-pieces into their box. The boy was standing by my table, looking at the charts and my own notes where I had left them.

He saw me and flushed again. "What are these?"

Earlier today, any other day, I might have been angry. Now I was past that, in unknown territory. "Nautical charts," I said. "Soundings, landmarks, everything a sailor needs to know. These are contemporary; that one's three hundred years old. Well, you can see," the paper crumbling at its edges.

"Are you a sailor, then?"

"Yes, I am. Don't touch that."

It came out perhaps sharper than I meant. He snatched his hand back as though I'd burned his fingers. So then I had to give him balm, a little. "No harm, only that it's fragile." It's odd how possessive you can be, towards what is not your own. Tom Turner's chart was mine by rights of intimacy; I knew it better than any man alive, I knew it the way you know your lover's skin, their every expression, the rhythms of their voice overheard on someone else's phone. Soon I hoped to know the chart better yet, from the inside.

"So why do you bother with it? The new ones are better, yeah?"

I confronted the intricacies of explaining that marriage of art and craft and science to a teenager, and sighed. "The new ones are more accurate, of course. GPS, satellite imaging, they're exact. But this is beautiful, and it's the work of a sailor, not a machine. This is real mapping, drawn to a human scale, one man's expression of his world and its dangers. It's the original, not an engraving; look, you can see the pen-strokes, sometimes you can see the pencil-lines beneath."

He wasn't interested in pencil-lines. "What dangers?"

Did he really know so little? I took a breath to tell him, but the older man interrupted.

"Leave it, Matthew. You're not meant to talk in here." And then he nodded at me, and walked out. The boy blushed one more time, mumbled something incoherent and was gone.

THE next week, they were back. This time, the boy Matthew came straight over to my table. I had to glance up then; he smiled, put a finger to his lips, set something down by my elbow.

It was his mobile phone. He left it there like a promise, *look, no calls today.* Or it could have been a more aggressive message, *look, it's in your hands now, up to you not to answer if it rings.*

I fairly swiftly gave up any hope of working, and went to watch the chess.

The old man frowned up at me once. Matthew didn't lift his head. His determination not to was so obvious, he reminded me of me.

Halfway through the second game, the old man left us abruptly, without explanation, as was his apparent habit. As the door closed behind him, I said, "I haven't the faintest idea what to do if it rings, you know. Except throw it at your head, obviously."

"No worries. I switched it off."

"Thank you, then. Though you're not supposed to be playing chess in here either."

"I know, but he won't be told. Thing is, he hates it when people come up and comment, criticise, make suggestions—"

"Uh-huh. While he's gone, then—pawn to king's bishop five."

"Eh?"

"Here." I showed him, on the board. "Just a suggestion."

"Yeah, but—he'll take it, won't he?"

"Yes, of course."

"So what am I supposed to do next?"

"You're supposed to work that out for yourself." I gave him back his own smile from earlier and left him to it.

I sat with a book in my hand and listened to the gameplay. I heard him make that sacrifice, and how he used it to queen another unregarded pawn, and how he won the game thereafter at a merciless canter. I heard the triumph in him; I heard the moment when he remembered I was listening, when he wondered suddenly if I'd give us both away.

Not I. I sat quiet, and he came across to scoop his phone up as they left, and neither one of us said a word.

THE third time, he came in alone. He laid his phone down at my side, and then he said, "Grandad can't come today, he's sick."

"I'm sorry to hear that."

"Would you, would you like a game?"

I could have said my work was too important. But that would have been to say that he wasn't important enough: true, perhaps, but cuttingly unkind. Besides, it was working on me again, that gawky charm of the adolescent, the way he laid himself open for the rebuff.

So I said yes when I shouldn't have, I broke a silence where it mattered most, and of us all, I've paid the least price for it. Betrayal can be like that.

CHESS is a bridge between strangers, between generations. Get them talking, and everything's fair game.

Sometimes the less people say, the more they tell you. Matthew went to school, he went home. He spent time with his grandfather. He didn't want to talk about his parents, nor much about his life. He didn't really want to talk at all. Rather, he wanted to listen. He wanted to hear about my boat; he wanted to know why I spent my Saturday mornings in here with dusty old charts and books, when I might have been out on the water.

"Look," I said, setting the chessboard aside and reaching for that despised paperwork, "here's *Great Britain's Coasting Pilot,* published in 1693. A naval captain called Greenville Collins spent seven years charting the entire coastline. It's our first detailed, practical survey; it changed inshore navigation for everyone. But look, look here…"

I showed him the chart of our own waters, and let him find the problem for himself.

"There's a bit missing," he said. "What happens here?"

There is, indeed, a bit missing. A neat blank square a mile offshore and two miles on a side, where even the rhumb-lines and the bearings break off, where Collins has delineated emptiness. It's unique, throughout the forty-seven charts of the survey.

"The most dangerous rocks on this coast," I told Matthew, "that's what happens there. They've been wrecking ships since Roman times. People around here call them the Silences."

"So why didn't he, you know…?"

"Chart them? Because sailors are superstitious folk, and those rocks have an evil reputation. It's a known hazard, and every captain tries to steer clear; but they say it's like the Sirens, something lures them in regardless. You know about the Sirens?"

He nodded. "We did Odysseus in school. The sailors stuck wax in their ears."

"They wouldn't do it here. Collins' crew simply refused to go near the Silences, they came close to mutiny. Hence this absence. A local fisherman,

Tom Turner, made and printed his own chart, here, but that's drawn from observation more than measurement. Tom was a sailor, not a surveyor. If you compare his plan to this, from the Admiralty, which is put together from satellite photos, you can see how inaccurate he was."

Matthew nodded uncertainly.

"I want to make my own chart of the Silences," I said. "I want to do it Collins' way, using his instruments."

"Aren't you scared?"

"Rocks are only dangerous if you're careless. The Admiralty charts are quite clear about depths, currents, the shoals that are hidden at high tide. Though I'll tell you what's interesting, they had to rely on satellite imaging because GPS doesn't work around the Silences. There's some magnetic anomaly that interferes."

"No," he said, "I meant, aren't you scared of the Sirens?"

"Would you be?"

He shook his head, grinning, suddenly all cocksure boy. And then someone else came into the room, and we had to move or else stop talking. He helped me carry all those papers across the corridor to where there was a larger table and permission to speak, and somewhere in the shift and flurry of it all either he begged or I offered, I truly can't remember which. Either way, a day's sailing was the prize.

"Not without your parents' permission, mind."

"They won't care."

"Even so, I'd better come and meet them."

Another shake of the head, this one quite urgent. "Talk to Grandad. Next week, if he's better. He'll be in."

HE was better, he was in; we did speak. In the Silence Room, naturally. When sin slides into habit, that's when you'd best beware. Careless talk costs lives.

I said, "I'll just give him a day's run, see if he likes it. I'll undertake to bring him back wet, cold, filthy, smelly, starving, exhausted and intact."

That was good enough. The following Saturday I found Matthew waiting by the kerb outside his house, chewing his nails with doubt of me. He brightened in a moment, jumped into the car and said, "Did you bring any wax?"

"Wax?"

"For the Sirens."

"Oh. No, not today. We're not going near the Silences."

"Aren't we? I thought…"

He'd thought we were heading for adventure, danger, high risk on the high seas. I disabused him.

"Today, we sail in circles. Well, triangles, largely. Way out, where we can't hit anything. You'll learn the ropes, you'll learn to say 'aye aye, skipper,' you'll make mistakes by the yard, and by the time I bring you back, you'll have learned how to sail. Next time we go out, you'll still make mistakes, but at least you'll know what they are."

I was deliberately making it sound like school. He sulked, a little, but that blew away as we came down into the marina.

"Which one's yours?"

"There." I pointed along the floating jetty. *"Sophonisba."*

"She's enormous," he said, in the tones of someone who'd been looking for disappointment and hadn't found it.

I hid a smile and said, "Big for one, certainly."

"I really will be a help, then?"

"Oh, yes. You really will. Not today, though. Today you'll just be a nuisance."

He grinned contentedly and followed me as I opened her up and showed him over, stem to stern. Then I tossed him my spare waterproofs and said, "Turn off your mobile, before you zip them up. Sailing's about getting away from all of that, being out of touch."

"You mean it's about the silences," he said.

If he thought that, he'd never been to sea without an engine, but I knew that already. He had a whole new world of sounds to learn, from the creaking song of rigging under strain to the slap and hiss of waves against the hull to the half-human cry of a gull over deep water.

Me too, though, I had my own learning to do that day, my introduction to the teenage wall of sound. The groans and curses I'd expected, but not the sudden yelps and whoops, nor the singing in a breathy monotone, nor the jokes, the jabber, the utter inability to keep quiet.

We tacked back and forth until he was comfortable with the sheets and stays and winches. Then I let him take the tiller, while we went around again. He didn't raise a protest when I decided that was enough, and turned for home; he saved that for later, once we'd moored, when I introduced him to the mop and bucket.

I took him home in the state that I'd promised, drained and overloaded both at once. As he stepped out of the car I said, "Next weekend, then? Up for it?"

"You bet," he said, with as much relief as anticipation. "Thanks, skipper."

SATURDAYS, we played chess and sailed; Sundays we sailed and played chess. After a month I decided he was ready, we were ready, captain and crew. Next week, the Silences.

We started early, in perfect weather, a steady offshore wind and a smooth, swift sea. I offered Matthew the tiller; as he came to take it I saw wires dangling from his ears, disappearing into a pocket.

"What are you listening to?"

"Oh—my new phone. Birthday present. Doubles up as an MP3, it's brilliant."

"Not on my boat, if you don't mind."

"Well, but it's too early to talk. And I can still hear you…"

"Even so. Turn it off, please."

His face was foul, but he did as I asked. And took the tiller, checked the course, did everything he ought to. Best leave him to it, I thought, show some confidence and let the wind blow the temper out of him. I made my way forward, settling into the bows where I could watch for trouble and eventually for the Silences.

At last there were nubs on the horizon that were not other yachts' sails. I called out and pointed.

"Where?" he asked, trying to peer past the mainsail.

"Fine off the starboard bow. Come see; I'll take the helm."

"Aye aye, captain."

I watched him scurry forward, then came about onto the other tack. We'd sail by on the seaward side, to give us both a good look, before we came back inward.

As always, the breakers were easier to spot than the rocks themselves, a sudden stitching of white water in a grey swell. The Silences lay low in the water, but there were no savage currents to beware of, no tidal suck; it was hard to understand their reputation. I took plenty of sea-room none the less, running no risks with my beloved *Sophonisba*. We'd need to be closer on the return leg; at this distance I could barely distinguish rock from spray.

I murmured as much to Matthew at my side. And turned my head for his reaction, and of course he wasn't there, he was all the way forward. I felt as though I had fallen through an unseen door. There was no one in the cockpit with me—and yet for a moment there had been no question about it, an absolute presence.

I couldn't recapture that brief certainty, any more than I could understand it. Let it go, then; stranger things happen at sea. I glanced forward, and saw Matthew coming.

Matthew frowning, puzzled, a little upset. As he jumped down beside me, I saw those earphone cables again.

"Yeah, yeah, I know. Sorry. But I was on my own up there, just looking, and—well, I thought it needed a soundtrack, that's all. It's no good without music. Listen, though, just listen…"

I thought the world made its own soundtrack, but I wasn't sixteen. He held out one of those earphones, gesturing, impatient for me to share. Reluctantly, I listened.

Nothing.

Or no, not nothing: white noise. A steady swish and slurr of interference, the echo of God's heartbeat.

"I think your gadget's broken."

"Only it's new, and it was working fine, and then it just went..."

New toys do just go, sometimes; but I looked at him and remembered what he was clearly remembering, something I'd said before.

"Take the tiller, I'll go and see what's what."

Down in the cabin, no little lights glowed on any of my expensive equipment. No GPS, no radio, no radar.

No warnings, and no way to cry for help. We were on our own.

On our own in clear weather, open water, not a worry in the world. I glanced back out at Matthew and saw him startle as he looked aside, as though he was looking for someone he knew was there and then not finding them.

I did that, I thought.

"Not your phone," I told him. "It's all out, all the electronics."

"You said, that's what GPS does around here."

"I know I said it. That doesn't mean I believed it. Are you happy to go on?"

He shrugged. "You're the skipper."

That meant *yes, for God's sake, why not?* with a subtext of *I don't suppose you will*. I surprised him, then; I didn't let him down. I just nodded, and took the tiller.

Sophonisba was still sailing sweetly, over a sea like glass in motion. The Silences were a presence, but no threat; I wanted to be closer, to see them better, to sketch their profiles from the seaward side. Half a dozen times I caught myself letting her drift in towards the rocks, half a dozen times I nearly sent the boy for a pad and pencils. Each time I checked the motion, checked the words before I was committed to them. In honesty, I didn't want to speak. There was a hush to the air, to the moment, that words would only spoil.

A moment stretched, not ended, becomes momentum. A word not spoken gives us impetus. We ran by the rocks, and it was the easiest thing in the world to throw the tiller over, to gybe, to let her headway bring her around and all the way around, until the sail could catch the wind again and take us back down inside that line of rocks. Sailing can be like that sometimes, where wind and water seem to be unusually willing. Here there might have been currents after all in air and sea together, circling the Silences as a storm circles its dead centre, drawing a path that we could follow.

Between rocks and coast there was room to tack and turn, there was water enough beneath the keel, but a good sandy bottom within the anchor's reach. Now we weren't sailing, we were surveying. We dropped anchor half a mile off the northernmost rock, and established our position as best we could by landmarks and estimate, by telescope and eye. Then we turned towards that chain of rocks and I took bearings on each of them with an authentic period compass, calling the numbers for Matthew to write down.

Surveying by running traverse is a technique as old as the compass rose, and we had practised it up and down the coast till we could do it without thinking. Suddenly, though, it was hard to keep focus. Water sang past the hull, urging us to movement; wind whispered in the shrouds like a summoning, like a question, *why the delay?*

Only the rocks were patient, and they needed to be. Perhaps they could afford to be. My eye kept shifting, caught by a spume of water flinging high or the eerie stillness in the lee of a rock. My mind drifted another way, into fancies. I thought I heard footsteps aboard *Sophonisba*, out of my sight. I thought I heard cries on the wind, greetings and questions, as one sailor might call to another across a gulf of sea. There were other boats in the corners of my vision, that were only gulls or clouds or nothing when I looked. I could see the same effect in Matthew, the way he shied suddenly and stared around and couldn't concentrate.

I didn't talk to him about it. I didn't want to talk at all. My own voice sounded harsh and alien here, calling numbers; his was an untuned string, a dull vibration, flat and grating.

At last we were done here. We could weigh and set sail, reckoning speed against the clock to know how far we went before we let the anchor go again at the southernmost point of the Silences. That was hard; there was such a temptation to let her run, to come about on that helpful wind and work up the seaward side again, closer in this time…

But I turned her head into the wind, all the air spilled from her sails, Matthew dropped the hook and we were there, with all the work to do again, bearings to be taken on the same rocks from this new position. Later I could mark those two positions on a chart, draw in all the bearings, and where each pair crossed should be definitive, *this rock stands here.*

Find the rocks, take the reading, cry it out. Listen for the boy to call it back—but how much more you hear in the emptiness behind his voice, how hard it is to care for what you tell him, or for what he says…

Was it him who moved to draw the anchor up, or did I send him to it? Were we finished, had I checked my figures, or did I skimp the work?

Did we have an argument, or did I dream it later, whether we should sail round those rugged rocks again? She was my boat and I was captain, but did he win against the odds, to take us southerly, homeward, away?

I don't know, I can't remember. I know that the sun was setting and I was on the tiller, I could see the city's lights tainting the sky ahead which meant that it was later than I liked, later than I could understand. He was trimming the sails, quiet and confident; on that thought he glanced back at me in the cockpit and said, "So when do I get to go solo, skipper?"

"You don't."

"Oh, why not? She's built for one to handle, and I can do it, you know I can…"

"The insurance is in my name. She can't go to sea without me. Sorry."

He groaned and sighed and made faces, as he ought; and then he said, "So how's about that night sail you promised?"

He was right, I had promised him stars and moonlight and the extraordinary potency of the sea at night. We settled on the following weekend; then he dropped onto the bench beside me. "What happened back there, that was really weird, wasn't it? Or was it just me…?"

"Not you," I assured him. "I think you coped better than I did."

He shrugged. "They are haunted, those rocks. The old sailors knew. We should've listened."

"We did listen. Once we got there. But I think the Silences listened back."

That was how it felt, at least to me: that they were attentive, interested, listening. I thought he was wrong, though, it wasn't the rocks that were haunted. The rocks just were. It was the water, the wind, the liminal world about them that held more than it ought to. If there are ghosts, that's where they abide, in the shift between state and state, that blur where you can't say *this is water and this is air* or *this is life and this is death, that was then and this is now...*

I didn't say any of that to Matthew. We were better being quiet, I thought, each of us finding our own place to stow what had happened for mulling over later. Or for rejecting later as a fancy of the day, the rocks' reputation, a desire to be impressed. Strange things happen at sea, but they happen inside our heads as much as they do on the water.

It was full dark before we berthed in the marina. When we were done cleaning up, Matthew reached into his pocket with a half-smile that might have been wider if the day hadn't been so pressing. Still, he was a boy, he'd prepared this, he loved it; he said, "I've got a present for you," and handed me his old mobile phone.

I gazed at it blankly. "I don't use these things."

"I know, but you should. I want you to. Look, we can play chess," and he touched a key and the panel lit up, already primed, *P—KB3*. "We can text moves to each other, see? I'll show you how. And if you never tell anyone the number, then you'll know it's me, every time it rings."

And clearly he wanted me to think this was a good thing. I thought his loneliness was showing, brighter than I'd seen it before; so I let him teach me how to text, and how to make a call and answer one. Then he gave me the charger, jumped on his bike and was gone. I sent a message after him—*P— QB3*—to await arrival, and locked the boat up. Checked the spare key was still hanging on its line below the water—and no, I didn't really think the ghosts had taken it; I always check, it's a neurosis—and then I headed home. Thinking about ghosts, already finding ways to rationalise.

Halfway back, the phone beeped. In Morse, *SMS*, twice. I ignored it. Five minutes later it rang properly. I sighed, pulled over, picked it up.

"Hullo, Matthew."

"Did you get my text?"

"Yes."

"Only you haven't sent your next move. Aren't you going to bring the queen out? You always bring the queen out."

"One of these days I'll surprise you. But right now, I'm driving."

"Oh. Right. Sorry..."

It wasn't just a lesson in his loneliness, it was a lesson in his youth; at a guess, no one else he might call would have a licence, let alone a car.

When I got home, I sent him the move he expected. And spent the rest of the evening answering his texts, his moves, at five minute intervals. When I wanted to go to bed, I realised that he hadn't told me how to turn the damn thing off. I phoned him to ask; he just giggled, and said goodnight.

A couple of nights later, I did have a good night, I had a really good night. Until that damn phone started up. I apologised, didn't answer it, promised to leave it at home in future. Presumptuous of me, she hadn't promised me a future; but she only quirked an eyebrow, and asked if I couldn't turn it off.

"I don't know how," I confessed. "He won't tell me."

So then of course I had to explain, and she pealed with laughter and took it from me and nor would she tell me how to turn it off, but she did switch it onto silent running.

"Vibrator effect," she said. "So you'll know, but it won't bother me."

AND a couple of nights after that, I had to phone Matthew and cancel our night sail on Saturday.

"But you promised…!"

"I know I did, and I'm sorry, but something's come up."

"Well, get out of it."

"I don't want to." I might have lied, of course, but it was just too much trouble. "This is too good to get out of."

"Oh, what is it, then, a woman?"

"Yes."

That silenced him, but only momentarily. He was passionate, he was furious, he was almost tearful and pleading; mostly, I thought, he was jealous. Deep-down, fiercely jealous. He would not be placated, I would not be moved; we both said some harsh things before I hung up on him.

I regretted that, of course, the way you do. Not enough to call him over the next few days, but enough to keep the phone charged up and close at hand. It was still and silent all week, until the Saturday. Saturday evening, when for him we should have been out at sea already, watching the stars appear and hoping for the Northern Lights; when in fact I was in my bedroom, trying to decide what to wear.

I was running late already, I didn't want another confrontation; it was my turn to be resentful, that he should try to elbow his way into my evening. I threw the phone onto the bed, and ignored it.

It rang three or four times, in the half-hour that I took to get ready. That felt deliberately intrusive. When I went out, I deliberately left the phone behind.

And had a good, a very good time, and so I guess did she. At all events, she came back home with me. I left her in the living-room with Miles Davis and the Macallan, while I made that traditional hasty scour of the bedroom, changing the sheets and hiding what else must be hidden.

And there was the phone, and the screen showed half a dozen calls from Matthew; and I suppose this was part of the scouring, to sit on the bed and listen, not to leave unfinished business hanging over what lay between here and morning.

Half a dozen calls, but only one message on the voicemail. He sounded faint and frightened, far away. He said, "I'm sorry, skipper. Really, I am. I was, I was angry with you, and I thought I could manage her on my own. I didn't mean to come this far. I don't know what happened, I got too close and I couldn't see the rocks but I don't think she hit anything, she just turned over. I'm, I'm up under the hull and I can't get out. I called for help, I tried to call you and then I called my grandad, and he told the coastguard. I think I heard a helicopter one time, but I guess it didn't see us. It's gone now. And my battery's going, and then it's going to be all dark in here, and I'm so cold already, I can't keep my legs out of the water and I don't, I don't think anyone's going to come…"

THEY didn't find *Sophonisba* till the morning, drifting keel-up off the Silences. They never found Matthew at all. His body should have been there, trapped inside the yacht's hull, but it wasn't. Perhaps he tried to swim out, in the end. They say that bodies are seldom recovered from the rocks there, something in the current holds them under.

It doesn't matter much to me, where his body is. He won't need that again.

Nor do I think the rocks have him, in any sense that matters. Rocks have no reach, no stretch beyond themselves. All their strength looks inward.

I looked for Matthew on my boat, when they gave her back to me. That they couldn't find him, didn't mean he wasn't there. I even sailed her, when she was fit for it, back up to the Silences. I called his name into the wind, but he didn't show. Why would he?

I sold the boat, in the end. She had nowhere left to take me; and I didn't lose Matthew, in losing her. I take him with me, everywhere I go.

I still keep the phone charged up, as he told me to. I keep it in my pocket, mostly. Always set to vibrate, to silent mode. That way it needn't disturb anyone but me, in the Silence Room or elsewhere, anywhere.

Mostly, it keeps silent on its own account. Sometimes, though, quite often, it does shiver into life; and I do answer it, every time. At night, I keep it beneath my pillow and I sleep alone, so that if it wakes me, I can pick it up.

I'm too much of a coward to ignore it. I'm afraid that if I do, I'll find another message on the voicemail. I don't want that. I'd rather be here for him, every time he calls. I'd rather listen to his silence, to his listening: white noise, the hissing attention of the universe, that slow dragging pulse of nothing that—when you listen, when you wait, when you give it long enough, as I have—pounds in your head like surf over shingle, like breakers on a rock, all the surge and suck of the sea.

TERMINAL

unspeakable journeys
into and out of the light

E STOOD ON THE TOWER OF Souls, and watched her fly.

SAY it another way, he stood on the high-stacked bodies of his Upshot kind,
but that was nothing: filing. Bureaucracy. Paranoia.

It was the locals, the natives, the dirigibles—she called them *dirigistes*,
but that was ironic—who had built and named this height, who gave a value
to these discards. Black discs, each one identical, each one uniquely coded:
each one the residue of a human passing through. A carbon footprint, she
liked to say.

At other terminals, other Upchutes, the discards were racked in vaults, in
coded order, physical back-ups of what the record said: never needed, simply

because they were there and known to be there. What greater security could anyone ask for? Here, they stood in another kind of order. As soon as the dirigibles understood what the discards were, what they meant—in so far as they did understand, in so far as free-floating bags of gas could understand the motives and intentions, the physics and biology of meat and bone, of mammals—they had taken possession, demanded it. They saw humans walk into the 'Chute, they saw them gone, and only these discs remaining; they claimed the discs, and built—well, this. A tower. A Tower of Souls, just as they built for themselves, their own waymarkers, their almost-holy statements, *we were here*.

It made sense, he supposed. It was the same message, even. And there was no risk, however much the bureaucracy disliked it. Dirigibles were as careful of every discard as the most paranoid could wish. Just, they layered them into a tower, high and broad and solid, mute testament to how much traffic this terminal had seen in its century of standing. The Upshot might not be many, reckoned against downside populations, but they did like to keep moving; every stopover, every staging-post meant another discard, another disc.

This tower was tall enough by now to be a feature of the landscape, standing higher than the terminal roof, though the spire of the 'Chute still dwarfed it. The landscape could use a few features, he thought, weary of endless wind-blown plains; which was surely why the dirigibles built their towers, and just as surely why she flew from here, and why he clambered up behind to watch her.

It was only by grace that the dirigibles allowed it. *Hard-earned grace* he liked to say, but she wouldn't have it so. She said that grace could never be deserved; it came as a gift, the soul of generosity. Like flight, she said, to earthbound creatures; like transit to the Upshot, immeasurable grace.

Even on a low-grav world, flying was still a matter of faith as well as engineering. He always said he himself had faith too much; he believed very firmly in the solidity of things, and the susceptibility of air. She seemed to believe what people told her, and the evidence of her eyes. Therefore she flew, while he kept himself grounded. He watched her soar, and checked her equipment scrupulously, before and after. And talked to her, mid-flight—

"How's the wind?"

"Easy; always easy, this late. Fresh at dawn, but that's fun too. You should try it."

"What can you see? Tell me what you see."

"Nothing new. The sun's so low, the spire's shadow goes all the way to the horizon like a road, so straight—but you know that, you can see it from down there..."

"Not so far. My horizon's a lot closer. And for me it is a road, I could walk it if the sun stayed still."

"You do that, then. I'll hold the sun steady, I can almost reach her from here..."

"Not so high! Don't fly so high. I told you before, keep the tip of the spire in your eyeline and stay below it. That suit's not rated for heights above a thousand metres."

"Well, it should be. I'm fine. Anyway, I can too see the spire..."

"Only by looking down. Don't lie to me, I need magnification just to find you. Come back."

"Coming! Whee—!"

"—Not like that, not all at once! Woman, do you want to see me die here?"

"Sole purpose of dive. Ready to catch you when you fall. I thought it would be ironic."

—because he thought he was her anchor, her tether to the fixities of life. He really thought she needed one.

HE thought they all did. So too did the downsiders, legislating for the Upshot community. Set free to roam as far as any 'Chute could fling, essentially rendered into information, they must necessarily be tethered by that same information: a backstory that led all the way, traceable through every separate body, every discard, to the one that they were born with, however long ago. Identity was absolute, and paranoia was the key. If one mind, one personality could migrate from one body to another—and have that body grown specifically for them, to a DNA-weave of their devising—then how could anyone be sure that the person they spoke to today was the same person they were speaking to yesterday? The body might match entirely, but that meant nothing any more. Questions of identity had to be cut entirely away from the physical; which meant by definition that no Upshot could be allowed two matching discards. They called them discards, even while the bodies were still growing in the vats, to emphasise the temporary; and every DNA profile was one-use-only, and whenever someone went through a 'Chute they were fitted into a discard not quite entirely at random. They might emerge as any racial mix and any gender, any body type; the only certainty they had, they would not be the person that they had been going in. If no one looked to recognise an Upshot from one trip to the next, if identity was carried in the mind and not the body, then no one stood in danger of deception. Paranoia was a virtue; people's private codes and passwords were intimate, intense, not to be stolen or given away.

Like all the Upshot, his life was an open book, a matter of public record: how he had been flung out of school, out of the army, out of any discipline he'd tried; how in the end, almost in desperation, he had been flung into orbit to work on terminal construction. His home world wouldn't tolerate a 'Chute downside, but they had the schematics and the skills for an orbital platform, and chemical rockets to get there, and the benefits were too great to ignore. So it was built, and in the building of it he found a life he could cherish. The intimate spaceside disciplines that his and his co-workers' lives depended on; the extraordinary physicality of working roustabout in a suit, in vacuum, in nul-g; the extraordinary physicality of his co-workers in the dorm-ships, inter-shift, where rules and limits seemed all to have been left behind, downside; the constant call, no, suck of the stars, which were not a background to his new life so much as the vessel that contained it.

And then at last the 'Chute was finished, and he was eager in the queue to be away. His original body was abandoned, crushed and dried, compacted and coded by the process that his people had signed up to, compulsory para-noia. He'd been flung far and far, to another planet and another job, building mineworks for a new colony. He might have stayed, he might have found himself a family and another life again. In fact, though, he had been she in that new incarnation. After so long as a male, the shock of change was enough to be dealing with; pregnancy was something else again, and not to be considered. Besides, it was a wild ride, this being flung from one body to another. Why, whyever would he only taste it once...?

So he'd gone on, from that world to another, and another; and like most of the Upshot, he'd acquired the taste first and then the habit of it. And after a while, of course, he began to understand its deeper meanings—functional immortality, to be brief, in a life constantly refreshed by new horizons, new opportunities, new flesh—and he had yet to meet anyone with a good reason to offer, why he should turn away from that.

Here, now, he'd met her, who offered him the opposite.

THE suit she flew in stretched into webbing between arms and legs when she spread-eagled, which gave her not quite enough lift to glide in this thin air; even the teasing tug of gravity here would be enough to haul her down to ruin from a height. Extra lift came from the impellers at wrist and ankle. Eventually, with practice, she'd get fine control the same way.

Eventually; not yet. That day she came down fast and awkward, even when she wasn't trying to scare him into a cardiac arrest. Diving she was good at, that sudden plummet where her body was cooperative with all the other forces acting upon it; she was made to fall, as they all were. A steady descent was something else, unfamiliar, unnatural. Unappealing, perhaps.

He watched her come down, said,

"I don't suppose even you can miss the planet, but you're sure as hell going to miss me. You'll miss the whole tower, if I don't jump to catch you."

"So jump," she said. *"Take a chance."*

She swooped in, tumbling as she tried to brake and stall and so drop neatly to his side, to prove him wrong. Tried and failed, tumbled catastrophically and would have overshot and fallen thirty metres to the ground, out of any hope of control or recovery. It wouldn't have killed her—probably—and the Upshot always have the option to move on from a broken body *in extremis,* though the move might be unwelcome at the time. Still, he leapt—too high for his own comfort—to catch her ankle, and his weight was enough to pull her down, while her momentum rolled them over and over on that broad platform and they had cause again to be grateful how many of their kind had been this way before them.

When they stopped, where they stopped, she pulled her helmet off and shook her hair loose and grinned at him, sweating and exhilarated. He could only hold to the lean solidity of her and marvel at his privilege, at her trust, at how close they were to the edge.

"You see?" she said. "My chevalier. Always ready to catch me, should I fall."

"Always bruised," he said, "from needing to."

"Yes. Ouchie. Worth it, though. Worth every bruise and every bleeding scrape."

And she was, of course, worth all of that and more. Much more. The Upshot could be as heedless with their hearts as with their bones and bodies, in a life where staying put was stagnation, another life entirely; where moving on—even if they moved together—still meant other bodies on other worlds. It was hard to commit to someone who might be another gender next time round, was sure to be another type, as would you be too. Physical attraction faltered in those shifts, and they were too abrupt to mend in other ways.

He'd never learned to be so casual in possession, of himself or of his lovers. They had been few, then, necessarily; there had been more pain than plenty. Upshot or downside, people mishandled his heart as they did him, mistaking his intensity for passion, his failures for greed. He hurt, and moved on, and took his hurting with him.

It had been a burden, but she freed him. Not of his nature, none the less she delighted in it; and yes, she would come on with him, the two of them together and let the 'Chute fling them where it would, into anything, they could survive it. If she fell, he would be there to catch her; when she flew, he would be there to watch her. One day, perhaps, he could learn to fly himself...

THEY lay sprawled and sore together on the Tower of Souls, and here came a dirigible, flying above them. Or floating, perhaps, if one could float with purpose. At least some of the time they did that, they had purpose. They couldn't have built this tower otherwise, nor their own.

They built nothing else, that he knew about. Until the first tower was discovered, people thought they only drifted on the wind. Some refused to call them sentient, arguing that they had no more need of intelligence than they did of buildings, engines, any product of mind and work together. Great bags of gas, feeding from the medium they floated in: why would evolution burden them with brains or self-awareness?

Then someone spotted the first of the towers—its shadow, rather, seen from orbit like a needle laid dark and unnatural across the land—and that wasn't a question any longer.

That they had language took longer to discover, and still needed machinery to decode it. They spoke metabolically, drifts of shadow and substance beneath a semi-translucent skin; they needed a day to share a greeting, a month to have a proper conversation. They'd intertwine dangling filaments to stay together, to keep a stray gust from interrupting. Not often, though. He supposed, if you had to reorder your digestion—the closest way he could imagine it—to communicate by gastric rumbles, nothing so simple and convenient as farting, you'd be frugal. You'd save it up. And want to be damn sure the other party was paying attention; repeating yourself would mean going back to the beginning, filling your stomach, starting the whole process again.

So no, this dirigible wasn't going to talk to them, nor them to it. By chance or by intent—he couldn't guess which—it was going to pass directly overhead, and all he could do was watch. Observation of course was inter-action, but it did feel a little one-sided. He had no idea whether the dirigible reciprocated, whether it saw him too or how else it might be sensing where he was, what he was, what he did. Somehow, surely; but it had no discoverable eyes, nor any other organ that the xenobiologists could identify as sensory. Precious few organs of any kind, the way he'd heard it. Dirigibles were seem-ingly careless of the bodies of their dead; after the first few curious post mortems, so were the scientists who studied them. Inside the collapse of the ripped glassine tegument they could trace a few membranes and a primitive digestion, some hint of a nervous system trailing through the fronds, ten-drils, call them what you would that hung below. That was all. What fluids, what gases, what more solid masses might hold the mind of a dirigible could still be only guessed at.

A century of study? What was that? It had taken long enough to under-stand how much the piercing mattered, that they never found a body not torn open.

THIS one—and if he'd seen it before, he couldn't tell; they really did look all the same to him—seemed to hover a while above them where they lay, though the things moved so damn slowly it was hard to be sure. Maybe it was only caught in an eddy of air, some freak of turbulence caused by the tower or the great spike of the 'Chute behind it. At any rate, he had plenty of time to gaze up at it. The sun on its flank drove light and colour through its skin and deep into the gaseous swirls within, he'd seldom seen so much of mystery; and there was the great dark shadow of a soulstone in its belly, unmissable, enough to make anyone wonder how for so long they had not been missed from the corpses.

On Earth, some birds swallowed gravel and stored it in their gizzards to substitute for teeth. On this world, a mature dirigible untethered from its parent needed some substitute for absent mass, something to keep it upright and manoeuvrable against the wind; and so it would ingest what the first people here had termed keelstones, or simply ballast.

It had needed time, linguists, computers to come close to understanding what the dirigibles called them, which was—or might be—soulstones.

SHE was quicker to recover from her plummet, his grab, their mutual tumble. Also, she was possibly—no, certainly—less curious about the alien that hung over them, its wafting filaments not so far at all above his face. He had jumped for her; he could jump for this too. He wasn't going to say so, for fear she might try it. She wouldn't think of it on her own account; her attention was otherwise, on him. Her hand was on his clothes, in his clothes, unzipping as it went.

He said, "Don't, not here...!"

"Exactly here," she giggled, "and—oh, here, too. Why not here?"

"Look up."

"I've seen. So what? If it's watching, who cares? Who *knows?* It can't tell anyone; what would it say? Take half a year, just to misunderstand us..."

That might be true. Perhaps thought was as slow as conversation, where it depended on the leak of gases through semi-permeable membranes. Or whatever they did, however they did it. It didn't matter. He felt observed, considered, weighed in judgement; never mind that he couldn't understand the judgement, there were other things he equally couldn't do under others' eyes. Tendrils. Scrutiny.

He pulled away from her questing fingers, hasty to fasten his clothes again. She pulled faces at his back; he knew it, he could feel them. Sometimes he couldn't believe how young she acted. She might still have been in her earliest sequence of discards, barely left home, despite what the record said. It was rare to have come so far and give no signs of being older than your body, not to have picked up even a cynical veneer; he joyed in her enthusiasm, and mocked it, and felt as baffled by her as a dirigible must be.

THE way down the tower was a perfect spiral ramp, built into the solid structure as soon as the dirigibles understood that if they raised this thing, people would insist on climbing it. It had taken them a while, three metres or so of accumulated height, to come to that understanding, so the ramp only started that distance above the ground; below was smooth solid wall of stacked discards. In this gravity, three metres could be jumped either way, up or down, but the need to do it amused him every time.

Just as well, when little else in the climb or at the top amused him. She delighted him constantly and disturbed him constantly, kept him on the razor edge of anxiety; sometimes he felt like a parent, having to watch his child fly. Which was absurd, she was older than he was, with a trail of discards twice the length. She didn't like to talk about the past, though, so he never pressed her to it; which made it hard to remember that distance travelled, when all he saw was the bright youth of her body and all he heard was the dizzy enchantment of her voice.

Today he heard that voice laughing back at him, he saw that body a turn below, disappearing a turn and a half ahead; she took the steep smooth ramp at a bounding run, while he walked it like a model of good sense and cursed her in a steady monotone. Even now she couldn't let him be easy, no, never that.

At the foot of the ramp, the flat platform; the jump. And her waiting below, making as though to catch him; and tangling her arms around him, stretching for a kiss and getting it here in the tower's shadow, regardless of whether the dirigible still hung overhead; and walking that long shadow as though it really were a road, for that way lay home, more or less; and walking it hand in hand then arm in arm then closer yet, her arm around his waist and his slung over her shoulders as she tucked herself beneath it: she as shifting, as restless, as physically demanding as he was patient and willing to take whatever came. Willing and wondering and never demanding anything, for fear of losing whatever it was that he had already, her whimsical devotion or her trust.

Home for now, for here was a canister habitat, dropped in from orbit to accommodate the first arrivals, those who built the terminal long ago. It had been his, till she arrived; now they shared it. There was more comfort in the newer dormitories, but he'd preferred the option of sleeping single, a cabin to himself and nearest neighbours a walk away. Now he had her, constantly in his sight, and isolation was another kind of blessing. The Upshot were not body-shy, they couldn't be; when every relocation meant another body and the old one left empty for disposal, shed like a dead skin, what was there to protect? And yet, he wanted privacy from his own kind as much as he did from alien observers. He could never be comfortable sharing a bed in a shared room, in earshot of others.

It was also true that he could never be comfortable with her, in company or alone, but that was another matter. Nothing that she said or did worked to his comfort or content. She kept him nervous, alert, constantly watchful; other people had to tell him he was happy.

She said, "How will we choose where to go next? When we move on?"

He never had chosen, not like that. He stayed where he was until the work was done that he'd signed up for, or until he'd done something so stupid or so graceless that staying no longer seemed to be an option. Repercussions made an effective motive force. Then he'd contact the Bureau and ask about jobs elsewhere, take the first that came available, take the fling.

Now, with two of them, he supposed it would be different. He couldn't even imagine now, what it would be that would make them move. Both at once and both together—how could that work?

He said, "You choose. I'll follow you." There was always work for a roustabout, out on the edge; empires overreach themselves, always, and their peoples scrabble to keep up. But—it struck him, suddenly—what if she chose to go inwards, towards the centre of things, the ancient settled heart-worlds?

She was here, though, now, not doing that; her record showed a face turned always to the ever-expanding frontier, as his own did.

She smiled, and said, "Yes. I'll do that. You tell me when."

Which should have answered his own unspoken question, but this was what she did, she taught him anxiety: it might be his to say, but he wanted to please her, he wanted to pick just the right time. How would he know, how could he tell when she was ready...?

He guessed she'd make it clear, when the time came. She seldom did ask a question without having the answer right there in her grasp, held up for him to see it.

THE dirigible shadowed them, all the way back. Actually, with the sun so low, its shadow never touched ground where he could see it, but it lingered in the air above and behind them as they walked, in the corner of his sight if he only turned his head a fraction. He wondered if they had curiosity, these creatures: for sure they had some sense of life beyond themselves, that first gift of sentience, or else they would never rip open each other's corpses and salvage the soulstones, to build towers like fingers breaking up out of the soil.

That was all they did build, all the mark they made on their world; grazers and drifters, they needed nothing more. Sometimes he thought he was much the same: he grazed on a world's interest, and then moved on. He left more solid monuments behind him, but that was camouflage, meaningless, the excuse and not the purpose. They intrigued him, with their towers of the dead. Something they memorialised, though whether it was the dead or the death or the survivability of stone, he couldn't tell. 'Soulstone' was the best label anyone could offer, it was hard to call it a translation and even that hint of religious significance made him suspicious, but the facts were undeniable. They did salvage the keelstones of their dead, and build them into towers, and revere those towers; they did do the same with the Upshot's discards, to the point where it had needed slow discussion and eventual consent—grace, she called it—to allow people the climb up their own Tower of Souls, to give them a vantage-point and a view across this dreary landscape.

To give her a launching-point to fly from.

ALONE for sure, canister'd, contained, with the door dogged shut behind them: here he could shuck his clothes off, peel hers away from sticky skin and make her sweat again before they washed, before they sprawled again in the ruin of their bed and she said, "Low-g, I do love it. When we fuck, we fly. It's so new—"

And then she was abruptly silent, until she said, "New to this body, I mean—"

Which was just as stupid, because they'd been doing it for months now, since she'd first occupied that body.

He said nothing, and she heard that; and turned her back, drew her legs up, huddled herself against him and shivered in their shared heat.

"Who was she?" he asked—which was stupid in itself, because if there was one question he knew the answer to, it was that one. The record said exactly who she was and who she had been.

"You mean, who am I?"

"Yes."

Her voice had shrunk within her, as she was trying to shrink within herself, to be unnoticeable. His arms were around her, but that was a helpless gesture, a mockery of protection. She said, "I was downside, of course, just a girl, but I ran errands to the terminal. For my father, or for anyone who'd send me. I loved it there. I met her, and we were friends. My first adult friend, my first alien friend. She'd been so far, seen so much; I couldn't get enough of her.

"And she stayed, longer than…longer than most of you do. Long enough for me to grow to adulthood, way longer than anyone stayed there, on my homeworld. It wasn't a welcome place to be. They allowed the terminal, they used it for trade, but the Upshot were confined to the compound and none of us were let leave. They said it was our religious duty, to keep within the bounds our god had set us; I think it was political, they thought too many of us would leave if any went. But I wanted, I wanted to go. So much, I wanted it…

"And then she said she wanted to stay. She was tired, she said, and she wanted to grow old in a body she was comfortable with; and she'd met a man she'd like to make a family with. It was illegal, of course, but she worked in records and her friend drove trucks in and out of the compound all day long. Between them, they could make it work. Except that the Upshot keep such careful track of their people, not like mine; she needed someone willing to be sent on in her name...

"She said she'd change the record, so the machines couldn't see I wasn't her. And of course, once I was here, whole new body, *official* body, then no one need ever know. She gave me all her codes, her passwords, everything. I only had to be careful not to talk too much, about that life I haven't had.

"And I've messed it up already, first world I came to. You won't, you won't *tell* them, will you? You won't tell *anyone...?*"

He wouldn't need to. The woman had lied to her. A terminal's local records could be overwritten, perhaps, by a skilled hand, to fool the 'Chute's internal logs into believing that this body being presented for discard was the one supplied however many years ago to such-and-such an Upshot personality. Internal logs and local records were audited, though. Necessarily, of course they were; and no hand was skilled enough to hide the marks of its meddling from audit. Besides, there was the physical record, tissues taken from the body at time of discard to be matched against those taken at time of issue. Those matches were always made.

She had, how long, a few months more at most? He wasn't in records, he didn't know the frequency of audit. Only the certainty. All the Upshot knew. And that woman had sent a downside innocent into this all unaware, purely for camouflage, a placeholder to distract attention for a while, until authority caught up. She would have known when the next audit was due; likely she timed all this to happen immediately after the last, to buy her the maximum time to slip away with her lover. Planets are large; even a cooperative government might struggle to locate two people who've had time and motivation to bury themselves in new identities far from the Upshot compound.

Meanwhile, this girl, authority would know exactly where to find her. And would come, detain and question. She would confess; she could do nothing else, and it didn't matter anyway. Her body would speak against her.

And then—after how long, how many days of terror and despair?—they would put her in the 'Chute, and send her nowhere. The body would be a discard, recorded, preserved, as they all are; her self would be lost information, deleted, irrecoverable. She'd be dead.

People called them immortal, the downsiders did, but they were very wrong. Everyone dies, in the end. Accident, negligence, deliberate choice: their own, or someone else's.

Everyone dies; everyone lies. He said, "Don't worry, nothing terrible will happen. Just be careful, and don't let it slip to anyone else. You're with me now, I'll look after you." Ready to catch her, should she fall. "We'll move on soon; if we just keep moving for a while, we can leave trouble behind, and give you enough real planets to talk about, you won't even have to remember you've got anything to hide. I promise. We'll ask about work tomorrow, register as willing to transit. Meantime—well, this is meant to be a rest day. Let's do something wildly unrestful…"

So they did that, though she was tearful and needy, so little like the woman that he'd known these last months; and then he teased her, tempted her into showering and eating before he took her quietly back to bed and held her till she slept.

And lay awake all night, deliberately, keeping vigil over his beloved; and in the morning, early, when she roused, he brought her coffee and bakies in bed.

When she rose, he had her flying-suit laid out and ready:

"Sun's just coming up," he said. "You could have an hour in that dawn wind you love so much, before we have to get serious. Could be your last chance. When a job comes up, they won't hold it open if we don't go stat."

"Come with me?"

"Of course. When did I ever not?"

She purred at him, and wriggled into the suit's cling. "Promise not to shout, if I go high?"

"Promise to be sensible, and I won't shout. Of course, if the wind should happen suddenly to lift you higher than you were ready for, I'd have nothing to shout about, would I...?"

"I might have to dive quite suddenly too, to correct for that."

"So you might."

SO they retraced their steps of last evening, through the clear shimmer of the dawn. When they reached the Tower of Souls he boosted her up to the ramp-platform, though she really didn't need the help, and followed with a barely-graceless scramble.

They climbed the truncated spiral to the broad top, and he wondered aloud what the dirigibles would do when the logic of that spiralling ramp had brought the whole edifice to a point, to match the 'Chute it shadowed.

"Start another tower, of course," she said. "Why not? They've made plenty for themselves."

Which was true, of course, they had; dirigibles had few offspring and long lives, and there were nevertheless many towers. But none of those seemed to be finished, they were all works in progress, waiting on another death. This that they built for human discards had a necessary terminus, and he wasn't sure how they would deal with that.

Still, at least he wouldn't be here to learn.

He checked her impellers and webbing one last time, and kissed her, and let her go.

She leapt from the tower, arms and legs astretch and impellers hissing. She caught the air, or her suit did; seized it, climbed it, conquered it.

Went high and higher, and he said not a word.

Surmounted the spire tip of the 'Chute, and higher yet.

Was a glory, a shimmering speck in sunlight, a mote of something lovely.

Until the impellers failed, all four of them at once, all at the utmost of her flying height.

He had no magnification, but he knew. Her voice would have been in his ears, screaming the news of it, but he'd killed the sound long since.

He knew the moment when it happened, and he knew what she did to save herself; how she spread her arms and legs to use the webbing as much as she could, to drag what little speed she could from her disaster. How she tried to spiral down towards the tower, where he waited, ready to catch her if she fell. He was her solution; surely he would save her now.

How the webbing ripped loose in a second and final calamity, and then she had nothing that mattered: no hope, no steerage, nowhere to turn.

HE stood on the Tower of Souls, and watched her fall.

KEEP THE ASPIDOCHELONE FLOATING

"**W**ELL, THEN," SHE SAID SOFTLY, MENACINGLY. "Give me one good reason—*one*—not to kill you. Here and now."

I don't take prisoners, she was saying, *I don't collect ransoms. The living are too much trouble.*

There were heavy splashes from astern, as the captain—the *former* captain—and his officers went overboard. No trouble at all.

I said, "There's only one ocean. One. All the waters of the world, all intermingled, all *talking* to each other, and they're under us right here, right now. Listening to you. Weighing you, weighing me. Is that good enough? Big enough?"

"It should be," she said. High sun glinted off the pocked blade of her cutlass. Another splash came from aft; I didn't look around. Down below, someone screamed: thin and hoarse, I thought it was a man. Or had been.

Her eyes didn't flicker, her blade didn't twitch. I was counting on that. She was solid: sure of herself, sure of her crew. Nothing to prove.

"It really should be," she said again. "Enough. But—you don't buccaneer. No one ever called you Pirate Martin. Did they?"

"No," I said. "No, they never did."

"No. And I don't carry passengers. So…"

The blade was like liquid sunshine in her hand, hot and ready. She'd do this herself if she had to; God knew, she must have had practice enough. She really didn't want to, but she thought she'd do it anyway. She'd be famous, maybe: the one who put Sailor Martin down, the one who sent him to the bottom at last.

That's why she didn't want to. It's not the kind of fame a person looks to carry, even on land. Out here, on the attentive waters—well. If she was hesitating, that was why.

Unhurriedly, I said, "I can cook, though."

Now I'd surprised her. She blinked, took her time, said, "You can?"

"Yes, actually. I can cook for you." Not buccaneer, but feed her and her crew: that, yes. Nothing in that to sear my conscience or darken my long story more than it was dark already. I wouldn't be feeding prisoners, conniving at their capture. What my new shipmates did to those they took—a swift blade and a splash astern—would be on their souls, not mine. I was comfortable with that.

I'd be hanged regardless, if we were taken.

I was tolerably comfortable with that, too.

"Good, then." Her cutlass slammed back into its sheath, and she turned towards the poop. "Help my people get this mess cleared away, I want to round Dog Point before sunset. You're ship's cook, but I carry no idlers; you're starboard watch, and you'll scrub and stow and haul like any of them."

"Aye aye," I said, "cap'n."

FOR once in my life I was aboard a naval frigate, rather than a merchantman; for once in my life, I was on the passengers' manifest, rather than the crew's roster. I'd come aboard at Port Herivel, seabag on my shoulder and my name like a whisper rolling up the gangplank and across the deck before me: *Sailor Martin, that's Sailor Martin; he'll be luck for us, good luck in tricky waters...*

The captain welcomed me to his poop deck and his table, would perhaps have given me his cabin too if I hadn't insisted on bunking in the gunroom with his junior officers.

"Those pipsqueaks? Unbreeched boys, I warn you, they'll keep you up half the night demanding stories."

"That's my intention," I said cheerfully. "Perhaps I can teach them something. Youngsters listen to me."

He grunted and didn't argue, for whatever brief good that did him. Not half an hour later, I was followed up the gangplank by a woman in black veils and her two servants, one a dusky matron and the other a boy.

I stood by the taffrail and watched while the captain and his first lieutenant went to greet her. After a minute, the captain called for his steward and there went his cabin after all, gifted necessarily to the lady. He took her through to view her accommodations; her servants followed with the baggage; the first lieutenant came thoughtfully up from the afterdeck to join me.

"Who is she, Number One?"

"Florence, Lady Hope. Says she's sister-in-law to Sir Terence Digby, king's man at Port St Meriot. That's barely out of our way, and we're only running cargo anyway; the old man said we'd take her. Between you and me, I don't believe he likes the idea, but..." A shrug said the rest of it: that even the navy bowed to politics, and a wise captain did nothing to aggravate the civilian power.

For a little time, I thought of reclaiming my seabag and treading spry down to the quay again, seeking another ship. I knew Sir Terence, by more than reputation; I knew why the king had sent him to Port St Meriot, and why he'd gone. I knew he had no family, in or out of law.

But I was ever curious, it's my besetting sin and why I can never quit the sea. I held my tongue and settled into the gunroom, amused the lads and tried not to interfere too badly with ship's discipline while I kept a weather-eye on the lady and her people.

She herself kept her cabin, didn't join us for dinner, rarely showed above-decks and never without her veil. She was in strict mourning, seemingly. Gunroom gossip said it was for her husband, or else her lover: either way, the man who had brought her from England and then had the discourtesy to die of yellow fever, leaving her with no alternative but to fling herself on the charity of an unfortunate but obliging relative.

Her boy had little enough to do, and was apparently glad—at first—to have the freedom of the ship. I found him everywhere, from the lower hold to the higher rigging, gambling with the idlers or racing the midshipmen from deck to masthead and down the shrouds again.

After our second day at sea, though, I saw him mostly in the company of the boatswain. Who was a bully, as are so many of his calling; and the boy looked less than happy now, red of eye and bruised of spirit, bruised of body I suspected as he slunk about, obedient at the big man's heels.

Well. No doubt that would be a lesson learned. No doubt he'd find it useful. Myself, I spent my time in pursuit of the abigail as she laundered smallclothes in a barrel of fresh water, stood over the cook in his galley, sat to her needlework high on the foredeck in the late of the day.

Her name, she said, was Delia. Tall and broad-shouldered as her mistress was—convenient, she said, for fitting dresses—she was good-natured and open with it. Firm of purpose, knowing her own mind, finding her own course in life and cleaving to it. Free to do that, serving her mistress because she chose to: "I was never slave. I wouldn't have stood that. A person should be free. If she ain't born to it, she should take it."

As she spoke, her eyes roved the ship, the crew, the set of the sails, the horizon. I didn't need to keep watch myself; I could depend on her to do it for me.

NO surprise, then, when the look-out hailed the deck: "A ship! Hull-up, two points off the starboard bow!"

Really he should have seen her sooner. I rather thought Delia had, though from the foredeck we could make out only the scratch of her masts on the skyline. She was adrift under bare poles, so the man had some excuse, but even so I thought he'd probably face a whipping come Sunday, when his officers would have time to attend to it. A warship with a skeleton crew such as ours, reduced by disease and desertion, too few to work the ship and man the guns at once: she needed fair warning above all, to close with friends and keep her distance from any threat.

I should probably have said something to the captain, that first day. Too late now. Captain and first lieutenant both were halfway up the shrouds, telescopes in hand, to see for themselves.

Before their polished boots hit the deck again, I could see the first smoke rising from the other ship, a greasy smudge against the sky.

"She looks to be a whaler," the first lieutenant confided, while his captain paced the windward side of the poop alone, considering. "A derelict, in trouble. We'll go to help. It's our duty."

Duty could bring a rich reward, salvage-fees on a vessel full of sperm-oil and ambergris. I held my tongue. Nothing about this captain impressed me, from his own indecision to the quality of his officers to the manners of his crew. I wouldn't interfere now. I distrusted even his ability to run away.

Even the wind was a conspirator, lying handsome off our aft quarter; in less than an hour we were drawing alongside. Even in his cupidity, the captain wasn't entirely stupid. He'd had the guns loaded and run out, so that we had at least the appearance of a wary warlike vessel in His Majesty's vigilant navy. Every officer bore a loaded pistol, every man went armed.

Even so, that was just routine. The ship was really not expecting trouble.

Even so, I was still exploiting my privilege, lingering on the poop with the officers of the watch, just to see what happened.

What happened first was that Delia swung up the companionway to join us. There was no sign of her mistress, nor their boy.

Delia might be free but she was a woman, a passenger, a servant. The captain merely stared; the first lieutenant moved to evict her as swiftly as he might, as rudely as need be.

"Madam, by all that's holy, you may not—!"

She forestalled him, with a swift nod of her turban'd head towards the other ship. Where a plain red flag had broken out astern, and a boil of men erupted from below.

"My God, sir, they're pirates! Hard aport! All hands, bring us about!"

Delia said, "I'm afraid you'll find that my man has cut your steering chains." Her man, she said, not her boy. I pictured her supposed mistress, as tall and broad of shoulder as she was herself, veiled in solitude. And wondered, a little, what the boy was up to.

The man at the wheel cursed, as it spun freely in his hands.

"Belay that order! All hands to the guns! Fire as they bear!"

"Unfortunately," Delia said, "I don't believe your guns will fire. I'm afraid my boy has been fooling about in your magazine since we boarded, mixing powdered glass into all your gunpowder. He's a skittish lad, so you may be lucky; but if he's done his work properly…"

The first lieutenant tested that, jerking the pistol from his belt and levelling it straight at her face at no more than two yards' distance. She simply stood there, waiting.

He pulled the trigger. There was a flash in the pan, a sullen smoke, no more.

He flung the pistol furiously at her head. She ducked, and when she straightened she had a cutlass in her hand, drawn through some cunning slit in her skirts.

She was just in time to meet his blade with her own. She was a big woman, but even so: a hanger with a man's weight behind it should have been enough to finish her quickly. Somehow, it was not. They fought from leeward to windward, and when they came bloodily apart at last it was she who stepped back and he who slumped boneless to the deck.

That the captain and his other officers had only stood and watched, transfixed—that said all that was necessary about the ship's command. By the time they saw their brother officer fall dead, it was too late to recover. A man in skirts came bulling up from the afterdeck, with his veils thrown back and pistols in each hand; grapnels were already flying across the rail to drag the doomed frigate closer, while the pirate crew came swinging aboard on ropes.

There was fighting down on the quarterdeck, but none up here now. Everyone waited for the captain; what they saw at last was his sword-belt hitting the deck as he let all slip.

AND that was the battle, more or less: how His Majesty's frigate *Milford* fell to a pirate queen, with never a shot fired in anger.

And how I found myself eye to eye with her, shortly afterwards; and,

"Will you spare the boys?" I asked.

"Perhaps. If they swear to follow me, and if I believe them. Boys can be taught. Don't waste your time pleading for the men. You might be better served by pleading for yourself."

"Perhaps, but I don't plead. Ever. You know my value, you know what I am. You choose to keep me, or you don't."

"Well, then…"

AND so I found myself ship's cook and standing a watch, everything next worst to a pirate true. I saw the boys I'd slept with herded over onto the bait-ship, where no doubt they'd be tested and tested. I watched, and wished them luck, and hoped that some at least might survive, for a while at least.

One boy remained, as Delia took possession of her new flagship: the lad she'd brought aboard. I saw him come up from below, scrupulously cleaning his knife. A little later, I saw men carry up the bloodied ruin of what had been the boatswain.

Well, small blame to the boy for that. I remembered the screaming, and still blamed him not at all; I had a fair view of what he'd done, as the men swung the body overboard, and still not. I never did like bullies.

The boy came up and glanced at me, and seemed surprised; turned to his captain with a questioning glance, "Why's he—?" and won the only proper response, a quick cuff to the ear.

"He's our new cook. And you're his galley slave, till I say otherwise. Get below, the pair of you, and see to the crew's dinner."

HIS name was Sebastian, he said. That was the most of what he said for a while, caught in a fit of the sullens as we scrubbed and chopped. He held our captain too much in awe to disobey even my commands let alone hers, but he was bitterly resentful. He really didn't understand why I was still alive, let alone why he should be set under me.

Matters eased between us when I contrived to let him think that he was really there to watch me, to stand by with that good knife of his in case I tried to poison his captain or set the whole cursed ship aflame.

After that, it was easy enough to get him talking. He was barely twenty yet and mightily pleased with himself and the wild tangle of his life, bubbling over with it, spilling stories. He'd been a stable boy in Jamaica and then tiger on his lady's curricle, until he was snatched in a tavern and pressed into service on a buccaneer. Twelve years old, stolen for his pretty face and given the same choice that faced those boys on the bait-ship today: swear fealty to a pirate and knuckle under, or die.

Sebastian had sworn, smart boy, and survived. Longer already than most pirates did; and somewhere in that lucky life, he'd fallen in love with it. Like any boy he could be vicious and fearful, passionate and sentimental by turns, hungry for adventure and hungry to sleep in the sun. Playing cabin boy to a pirate crew had fed each of those urges and more; serving Delia had brought him to the point of worship, her total devotee. I could have found no simpler way to win his heart myself, than to let him talk about her.

I hadn't planned to win his heart at all, I hadn't planned to stay—one cruise, one port, I'd be away—but even after so long at sea, the sea can still surprise me.

So can a boy. Even after so long, so many boys.

I had him stir the porridge for loblolly, not to let him ruin his precious knife hacking at the navy's salt beef, harder than the barrels it was kept in. In the end I fetched a mallet and a sharpened caulking-iron. Between my pounding and his giggling, we agreed that it was wondrous condescension on her part, that she would eat this with her men; and that let me ask, "How does she come to lead a crew of men, white men, in any case?" There had been women freebooters, there had been black freebooters; probably there had been black women; but not as captain. I was sure of that.

"We elected her, of course. It's the tradition." Then he pulled a rueful face and went on, "I think it was a joke. Our last captain was no use, he lost us too many prizes and sailed us into trouble, time and again. We were hiding out, hungry and afraid with the navy at our heels and hunting. Delia had been the captain's doxy, that's why she was aboard. She was sensible, someone to listen to. Even so, it was a joke. We wanted rid of the captain before he got us all hanged, but you never call for a vote unless you know who's going to win it, and there were too many men who wanted to. That's dangerous. Nobody dared stick his neck out until Double Johnny got drunk enough. He called the vote, the captain asked who stood against him—and Johnny named Delia. Because he thought it was funny, or because it was a measure of how much we despised the captain, or because he was so drunk and the rum so bad hers was the only name he could remember, hers the only face he could make out. I don't know. I think it was a joke.

"But he named her, and when the captain had quit laughing, he asked if she would stand. And she said she would. He already had his hand on his cutlass, he knew just how this would go: of course he'd win the vote, and then he'd kill her, and then Johnny, and that would be that.

"Only he lost the vote. We all hated him that much, and we all loved Delia. So we voted her in. And then he tried to kill her anyway, but she was ready for him. She had a loaded pistol in her skirts, and she blew his head away.

"I think we thought she'd stand down after, and let us have a proper election for a real captain. Only she didn't do that. She took it on herself to be a real captain. She found us safe harbour and led us to a prize; and then we wouldn't have let her stand down if she'd wanted to. She's hard on us, but she's kept us alive all this time; and now we have a warship," unthinkable bounty. And he might want to give all credit to his captain, but he still did keep a little for himself, how clever he'd been, playing servant all those days while he quietly sabotaged the gunpowder and never gave himself or his companions away.

He wanted my applause, so I gave it him; then I traded stories with him. Soon enough his eyes were bugging out, as he finally understood just who I was. Or thought he did. He'd have known it sooner if he'd listened to the crew of the *Milford*, but he was a boy: full of himself and his own daring, listening at first to nothing and nobody but his captain. And then to nothing and nobody but his own sorrows, once the boatswain had him. I had apparently entirely passed him by. I might have been wounded, if I didn't understand him all too well.

Still, he made up now for that neglect. I was famous, all around his limited little ocean. He'd heard the common stories about Sailor Martin and wanted to test them, to hear them again from the source. *Did you really...? Is it true that...?*

He was a boy, he could readily be squashed at need. For now I talked more than I ordinarily do, I told him more than I was entirely comfortable with. I wanted an ally, perhaps a spy, certainly a bunkmate. He was still pretty; he'd do.

PRETTY and willing and trained, as it turned out. Better than willing, awed and grateful. I had worried that the boatswain might have killed his pleasure in the act, but one night's careful negotiation took us past that. Gentleness was a revelation to him; so was anything that didn't directly marry my cock with his arse. Soon enough he was melting-hot under my hand, far past caring how roughly I handled him. He was rough himself, with the unexplored strength of the young; making me grunt was a triumph, apparently. Even if it cost him extra chores in the morning.

I took cheerful advantage of his body, day and night, this way and that: any excuse to fuck him at any opportunity, any excuse to heap work onto his wiry shoulders. The more I left to Sebastian, the more I could sprawl at my ease on the foc'sle on a bed of coiled rope in the sun. The captain didn't mind, so long as she and the crew ate three times a day; and she'd been light on crew even before she had to divide it between two ships. Really, feeding those she'd kept on the *Milford* was no burden. Not to me, at least. Sebastian grumbled, but even he didn't seem too outraged.

Our consort, the *Nymph Ann*, showed herself to be a true old whaler by her lines, when she wasn't pretending. She'd probably never been much of a pirate, but she'd made a good bait-ship. Now she offered a good shake-down to new crew, those navy boys. From my rope throne I could watch them being put through their paces, up in the rigging and around the deck, swabbing and holystoning and hauling sail. I saw one of them flogged on a grating, two dozen strokes of the cat; next day I saw a rope slung from the yard-arm and thought I was about to see one hanged.

And so I did, nearly—except that they hung the boy up by his heels and just let him dangle, for punishment or amusement or I know not what. For a while he writhed and begged shrilly, loud enough to carry across the water, while the old hands laughed at him. Soon enough he fell quiet and only hung there, and they grew bored and left him.

They might have left him too long, he might have died, if a boy can die of a blood-flood to his brain; but he saved himself at last, pointing and squealing, trying to cry out as a good boy should.

Someone looked, and called a proper warning to the ship's master at the wheel. He responded with a bellow that sent hands swarming up aloft; I suppose one of them must have taken the time to cut the boy down, if only because he was in the way of the fore course's falling.

The *Nymph Ann* veered close on our starboard, within hailing distance.

"Whale, cap'n! The boy saw her blow!"

"Where away?"

"North and two points east. If he could see her, the boats can reach her."

The captain hesitated, but only for a moment. Then she nodded, yelled her approval, started yelling orders to our own crew.

A simple cruise makes a decent shakedown—but hard sudden work, the chance of danger and the chance of profit makes a better. Pirates and whalers are close kin, half of them have been the other thing at some time; we had enough experience between the two vessels, maybe enough boats too.

What boats there were went overboard, and collected crews to row them. Harpoons came from the *Nymph Ann*, cables from our own locker, courtesy of His Majesty.

"Sailor Martin: do you whale, if you won't buccaneer?"

"I've served," I said, "on a whaler."

"Take a seat in the gig, then. Pull an oar, if you can't throw a harpoon."

I could, but not as well—I was sure—as the lean tattooed creature crouching in the bows of the gig as we pulled away. The whale must have shown again, because voices called down to us: directions, exhortations, blessings on the day. Nothing excites a crew like first sight of a blow.

Nothing is harder than to catch sight of your whale from a little boat on the swell. We rowed to where we thought she had been seen; our ships were no help, having to work up against the wind, soon left behind.

We rowed and craned our necks around, seeking and seeking. We were a fleet of three, the ocean is desert-vast, and whales can swim far and far underwater; I thought we were safe to lose her. I thought we had lost her already. It was almost a relief. Our crews were learning their work, whaling or pirating or both together; and Sebastian was in *Milford*'s other boat, and if we found no whale then he was at no risk. That sat more easily in my mind and on my stomach. I hadn't expected to worry for him, but—

"There! There she is! She's logging!"

She was; and she was a cruel unlucky fish, that we should find her adrift, asleep in the water, almost impossible to spot from a boat unless you came right on her, as we had.

Once spotted, a logging whale is easy to spear. We coordinated by voice and eye, gathered all three boats together, hit her with three harpoons at once.

She dived straight down, our cables whipping out hard and hot, fit to take a man's arm if he tried to grip one. But she couldn't stay down long, she couldn't go deep, she'd had no chance to breathe; soon enough the cables slacked as she rose and breached.

Rose and breached and dived again, and now she was dragging us, and what could three cockleshell boats, two dozen men do against such a monster? This was the perilous time, when a boat can swamp or turn turtle, when a whale can turn against a crew, a fluke can splinter planking, men can die.

We hauled on the oars, legs braced: backing water until the shafts bent and our shoulders popped, until we had to yield or something broke. Then we let her pull us, until we'd recovered enough to strain again.

We worked her and worked her, each boat in turn or all together; she hauled us hard, worse when she stopped diving and only swam because she needed the air. Our little boats sheared through the swell, flew off the peaks and slammed back into the troughs, again and again. I never thought they'd survive; I never thought we would. It's always a surprise after a Nantucket sleigh ride, to find yourself and your mates intact.

If you do.

I watched Sebastian's dory when I could, when spray wasn't cutting at my face like knives, when the gig wasn't flying or smashing down into the whale's wake or tossing so hard that we could do nothing but hold on. We lost oars, we lost sight of anything outside that eggshell, we lost hope; we never lost the whale though I thought we must at any moment, the rope would break or the boat would break or the harpoon's barbs would tear free of her blubber and strand us in mid-ocean.

None of that. She slowed, the world lost its madness, the sea settled back beneath us; we recovered what oars we could and backed water one more time.

You can brace and look about you, both at once. Heaving, I turned my head and looked and looked. There was a dory, there were men in it, braced as we were, bending their oars against the whale's pull. Salt spray blinded me and I had no hand free to wipe my eyes; sun was setting, and I had no good light; I had no breath to bellow his name. Nothing to do but haul and wait, haul and wait until that fish at last stopped fighting.

Then, when she lay floating, as still as we had found her, wheezing in great bubbling salt-stink gasps; then we could call from boat to boat. I held my tongue, having nothing useful to say, but youth is loud; I heard Sebastian exult at finding himself alive yet, nothing worse than wet and sore.

I heard him call my name across the water. I heard him hushed peremptorily, hoarsely: "Quiet, lad, no chatter now. You'll start her again. Who has a lance?"

From beyond the dory, no answer. I wasn't sure if there was still a boat.

Our own harpooner fumbled in the shadow of the bow, found a lanyard, pulled it in. Blessedly, it hadn't snapped in the fury of the whale's wake or any of the impacts of the boat on water. At the end of that rope rose a long iron shaft, cruelly bladed. Once that had been in the gig with us; I hadn't noticed it go, being too busy keeping myself aboard. Lucky it hadn't taken one of us with it, or at least an arm or so. A whaler's lance is wicked sharp; it needs to be.

The dory had apparently lost its own. Poor whale. The harpooner stood in the bows as we rowed slowly in beside the floating monster. She was aware, I think, that we were coming; her fins stirred, but feebly. No danger of Sebastian's voice starting her now. I thought she was utterly overdone, we'd exhausted her beyond recovery. Even so, she had sent one boat, eight or nine men to the bottom; and all whales are female, like ships, but this one truly was. A bull would have been half as long again, maybe twice the weight. More spermaceti in its head, more ambergris in its belly, more oil in its blubber—but twice the power too, many times the temper. Never mind boats, full-grown bulls had sunk ships in their time, in their fury. I doubt we would have survived a bull, any of us.

The dory pulled up beside us at the whale's flank. Sebastian didn't risk his voice again, so recently scolded, this close to the monster's shadow. He didn't risk standing, either, let alone the leap I was half dreading: from one boat to the other, his to mine. I saw an arm wave wildly, that was all, and knew him in the murk—and, God save me, I did wave back.

And then very suddenly needed both hands for holding on again, because the harpooner plunged that vicious lance in through the hide of the whale, deep in, probing for lungs or heart or anything that mattered. The great beast spasmed, though she lacked the strength to surge beneath the water. Perhaps she only shrugged in pain; perhaps she meant to swamp us. One small eye caught the last of the sun, gleaming in the vast dark bulk of her head, making her seem more intelligent than she was. Perhaps.

That little movement raised a wave that forced us from her side. Our harpooner left his lance jutting from her flank, preferring to let go than dangle, ridiculous and at risk. By the time we'd baled and caught the oars and pulled ourselves back in, the dory had our place and a man there had the lance.

A man? No—a boy. Sebastian, of course: on his feet and taking a man's task, wanting to impress me. Pulling the lance free of her flesh's suck with one swift draw, that sweet unsuspected strength resolved into grace in shadow; letting the dory's drift carry him a yard down her flank before he drove it in again, power and spring and determination, knowing himself under my eye, coiled at the heart of my anxiety.

Again she flung herself about in the water as that vicious needle struck deep into her innards. Again, her wash forced the boats away. Sebastian was too slow to let go, too young to understand the need or else too focused on twisting the blade, probing for her heart, wanting to be the one who slew her cleanly. He found his platform suddenly gone altogether from beneath him; I saw him hang by both arms from the dipping lance's shaft, and then I saw her roll him underwater.

And then me, me too, as though her one movement had carried us both down. I swear, I never chose to dive. There I was, though, swimming through the dark in quest of him. Something on her hide glowed phosphorescent, like moonlight trapped in water; weed or living creature, I couldn't tell, but by that faint illumination I found his shadow as he sank.

Of couse he couldn't swim, what sailor can? Apart from me, of course. Rumour says that I could log like a whale and drift like a derelict and never need to shift a finger in effort, that the sea would bear me up.

Rumour is an ass. In this and many things. I swim because I learned to swim, the way I learned to handle boats: with work and time and practice.

I swim for the same reason that I sail, because I love the sea, not it loves me. Because it is dark, because it is salt, because it is deadly. Because it is bitter, and because it is my heart.

Dark, but not obsidian; deadly, but not mortal. Not necessarily mortal.

Bitter, but not unbearable. I saw Sebastian, by the grace-light of the whale's hide. I struck down and reached him, found him still clinging to the shaft of the lance. Desperation or good sense, whichever, I had cause to bless it now. If he'd let go, he'd have sunk; if he'd sunk far from that gentle light, I never would have found him.

He wasn't about to let go now, even though I'd found him. I wasn't about to allow him. If he ceased to clutch at the lance, he would clutch at me instead; then we'd both sink. I have seen men drowned by their friends, and I didn't mean to join them.

The whale meant for both of us to join them, but I too can be dark and salt and deadly. The beast had rolled deliberately, I thought, to hold Sebastian under the water. His eyes were screwed tight shut, so he was no trouble to me, if no help. If he'd been looking, if he'd seen me, he'd have lunged, I think. I didn't even touch him. I only laid my own hands beside his, and twisted that lance as sharply as I might.

Poor thing, she'd been trying to shake the boy loose and shed the pain. Now here it was again, worse than before; what could she do but roll up to the air again, and breathe, and suffer?

Sebastian's death-grip was tight enough to fetch him out, no chance of shaking loose. I hung on by grim purpose, through the wrenching tug of that roll; and there we were, breaking back into the world, gasping and coughing and holding on, still holding on as we dangled and kicked above the surface of the ocean.

And there was the dory, seeing us, pulling back to the whale's side: giving us something to drop into, if Sebastian would only let go.

At least his eyes were open now. He stared at me, wild, frantic—and then twined his legs around my waist, a death-grip too late to do harm, and swung us both back and forth.

Working that lance-head in the whale's innards, back and forth...

Finding something, I know not what, but something that mattered. Slicing into it. Bringing one last brutal spasm from the beast, and then a groaning stillness.

The dory came back for us again, and this time I let go, this time it was my turn to practise my death-grip on the boy, wrapping my arms around his shoulders so that all my weight hung from his determined hands.

He laughed in my face, and held on that one last second, long enough to kiss me. Then he let go, and we fell.

Bruisingly, into the crowded boat: oar-handles and benches and other men contributed all their share of bruises, but mostly mine came from Sebastian. He seemed all elbows in my grip, and all deliberate, and all delight. Wet lithe muscled boy, once again exultant and alive; I had to cuff him hard to make him let go, and then again just to calm him. He spat blood and grinned dizzily up at me, settled between my legs there on the boat's boards in the awkward cramping space between the rowing benches and other men's feet, and said, "What now?"

Said it to me as though I were captain, as though the decisions were mine. It ought not to have been true—but the dory fell silent, as though all the men there were waiting on my answer. Across the water I could hear the silence in the gig too, matching.

Into that delicate moment, dying or dead, the whale let rip an abrupt and tremendous fart. Which shattered the tension nicely, throwing us all into gales of laughter; and in the subsiding cheerful chatter that followed, I took an easy charge.

Got a rope around the whale's tail, not to lose her in the encompassing night; joined both boats together with another, for the same reason; said, "We'll just sit out the darkness, lads, and wait for the captain to find us in the morning. She'll come. She'll have to: can't hardly handle one ship without us, let alone two."

"How's she going to come, then, if she can't—ow!"

I suppressed my boy handily, amid another ripple of laughter, and asked who had rum or hard tack in their pockets, tobacco still dry in a pouch, anything to share around to see us through the waiting.

LATER, we sang; later still, we slept, those who could, sparing only those on watch. Sebastian could most likely sleep through a hurricane; I hoped to have the chance to prove it, another day, another voyage. For now I cradled the slumped weight of him, felt the slow seize of stiffness in my joints, learned that it is possible for a man's parts to be both numb and excruciatingly painful, both at once.

WHEN he woke, he was youthfully, outrageously limber. Also he was youthfully and outrageously heedless, teasing me and disturbing everyone, knocking men out of their slumbers as he mocked and stretched, making the whole boat rock as he scrambled to his feet to peer into the dawnlight for his beloved captain.

In the end I pitched him overboard, left him to squawk and splash for a minute before I let a man thrust out an oar for him to snatch at.

As we hauled him in dripping over the gunwale, he was still squawking, but not in protest now. He'd swallowed too much water to be coherent, or else he was just too angry—but he was a good boy, he kept pointing and making noise until we turned, until we looked, until we understood.

The sky was pearling to the east, the other way, the way I'd pushed him. Westward was still dark, but it was too dark. Not sky-dark, not even storm-dark: a rising arc of shadow split the night, cut away the stars. Now, in the hush of experience, I could even hear the sounds of surf breaking against rock.

I had not thought we were that close to land, but the whale had hauled us far and far, out of all reckoning.

"Good, then," I cried, pounding Sebastian between the shoulder-blades as though it were his achievement, as though I didn't just enjoy pounding the lad. "Landfall will make our wait more comfortable; there'll be water, sure, and green timber to raise smoke, to tell the captain where we are. Out oars, lads, and haul away. We'll haul our catch to dry land, and be dry ourselves…"

SOMETIMES I am wrong and wrong. Even now, even still: wrong and wrong and wrong. We came ashore in the false dawn, with our false hopes high; and found ourselves cast on a hard rock, hard and bare and empty. No trees, no habitation and no water. One of the hands talked of an island he'd seen rise overnight, a seething volcano building itself in fury from below; but that had been far to the east, half a world away. There were no such stories here, save the ones he told. In the end I sent him to the high bleak peak of this rock, to keep watch for the captain. He'd have no way to signal her, but she should come in any case, as soon as she sighted land.

If she were anywhere on our trail, anywhere near, she'd come. Even if she knew what little comfort this place offered, she'd still come. Any sailor would. We love the sea, and turn to land like a needle to the north. She'd know to find us here, sure as storm.

Meantime—well. There was no fresh water, and no timber for a fire except what we'd brought with us; and no sailor would ever burn a boat.

Even so, more than one hand sat on the ridge-rock shore and dangled bare hook-and-line into the tugging sea. Hope springs eternal, and you can always eat fish raw; and it was always possible that the captain wouldn't come.

That was a possibility we didn't talk about. Every man held it private, in the back of his own skull, with all that that implied.

To one boy, it didn't occur at all. Sebastian was full of excitement, empty of doubts. As full as he needed of rum, perhaps, that too: I thought the men had been topping him up, for his reward for being first to cry land or just for their amusement.

He was a happy drunk, happy and confident and trusting, almost impossibly pleased with himself. He couldn't keep still, but he didn't want to walk. The rock felt rocky under sea-legs, and his triumph floated large and alluring just offshore; he wanted to row around the whale's corpse and relive the whole adventure, show me the jutting lance and tell me how clever he'd been, how kind I'd been to come after him, how wonderfully we'd worked together.

I didn't mind, so long as he did the rowing. One lean lad shifting a heavy gig: the work of it would burn the rum out of his bones and maybe even still his restless tongue. Also, we'd find a privacy on the water that I hoped to celebrate, in the whale's shadow and down between the benches, doubly out of sight from shore. The men would speculate wildly and mock cruelly when we came back to them, I hoped with every justification in the world…

Sitting in the stern, manning the tiller, I got to watch his face as he pulled: all strain and anxiety until he had her moving, until his confidence came back. Then concentration, the determination to do the thing well, not to catch a crab, above all not to splash me more than he could help; then awe at the simple size of the thing, his achievement, the tales he could tell as we came into the windshadow of the whale. A more simple smile, when he looked at me.

An unreadable expression, when he looked over my shoulder at the island at my back. He had no breath spare, but his eyes were speaking for him. I twisted around, and saw a sea-cave rising broad and high, just a little way along the coast from where we'd come to land.

"That," I said, turning back to the boy, "looks big enough to shelter the *Milford* and the *Nymph Ann* too. You may have found our new hideaway, lad."

"Oh, I didn't..."

The protest was breathless and instinctive and utterly meaningless; he thought he did, I could read that all through him. The mighty adventurer, slaying beasts and leading us to treasures. He was almost unutterably pleased with himself.

"You were the first to see it," I said, feeding his imagination happily. "We'll call it Sebastian's Cave—"

"—Sebby's Cave, they'll call it, only you call me Sebastian. You and the cap'n—"

"—All right, Sebby's Cave, but we still won't go in there till we have torches. It's dark, and anything could be hiding out already."

"I want to go now." A dead whale, a tale told had lost all its attraction suddenly, in the face of an adventure not yet lived. It would be the same with me, I thought: right now I was all the world he lived in, as the captain had been before me; sooner or later, I would be a tale told.

It was a boy's life, that was all. Sooner or later, perhaps he'd be a man.

I felt unutterably old, and played that hand as I had to: "I know you do, but we'll still wait. You don't want them calling it Seb's Folly, because it's where you went to die. It looks like a mouth, half-open, ready. Just pretend you can see teeth hanging down, and wait till we have lights. Now row me round to the other side of this fish."

He pulled a face, but then he pulled the oars. Still a good boy.

Still a boy: he sulked, and complained about the stench of it. I laughed, and said, "You should be used to that, sleeping down below. You should *get* used to it. Wait till we flense this fish, before you worry about smells." *Then wait till we fry it*, but I didn't say that. One step at a time. Little by little, let him learn. "Now ship those oars, and come here."

TIME and tide, the movement of small vessels on great waters. Sex in the scuppers. It's all one.

While I had his clothes off, I gave him his first swimming lesson. Unless the whale had done that, and all I had to do was reinforce it. All I wanted him to learn was not to panic—whch made it really a lesson in trust, which started as it had to, with trusting me. "Let go of the gunnel, Sebastian. Just let go. It's perfectly safe. I'm here, and I won't let you sink…"

Eventually I had him with his arms hooked over a floating oar, kicking furiously for shore. Soon enough, I thought he'd trust himself; sometime after that, he'd learn to trust the water. And probably start calling himself Sailor Sebastian, thinking himself immortal, *the sea will hold me up.*

At the moment he was all effort, more splash than surge, and that good oar was all that held him up. I paced him in the gig, one slow stroke and then another, easy work. I was ready to pluck him out if he exhausted himself entirely, but I thought the whole crew ought to thank me if I brought him back weary to the bone. He could sit in the sun with his good knife and make himself useful as well as decorative, pick limpets from the rocks, give us all something to chew on while we waited for the captain.

WE couldn't make smoke to guide her, but oh, she was good. Not four bells in the afternoon watch, and there was a bellow from the peak, a wildly waving figure, our watchman running and slipping and sliding down the long slope, risking bones and softer parts to bring us news.

"I'd have sent the boy up to you," I murmured, once we had him safely gathered in, "if you'd only waited."

Sebastian just looked at me, and went on sharpening his knife. I grinned. "Go on, then. What did you see?"

"She's coming, she's there, she'll be with us by sundown…"

"No. What did you *see?*" There were other ships in these waters, and few of them were friends to us.

He saw the point, nodded, stuck to his guns despite: "Two ships, mast-high. One warship and one whaler, I rate 'em—and don't tell me I don't know the *Nymph Ann*, for I do."

"She might have been gathered in by a king's ship. Which might have sunk the *Milford*, if the captain made a fight of it. If she could. Or the king's men might have taken both, hanged everyone, might be coming now to hang the rest of us."

If they were, there was little enough that we could do about it. Still, we all trooped to the peak to watch the ships' approach. Of course they were the *Milford* and the *Nymph Ann*, that was clear soon enough; we had to wait to see the scarlet shock of the captain's flag, to be as certain of her.

WE had her gig; we had to row out to fetch her. Sebastian insisted on pulling an oar, only so that he could lay claim both to the whale and his cave, before any other hand got the jump on him.

Cap'n Delia could manage him, better than any of us. Better than me. She gave him everything he deserved, in due order: praise and encouragement; mockery; a stinging slap to the head when he wouldn't subside.

Finally, after she'd seen all that we had to show her, after we'd brought her to land, she said, "Well, then. There's work to do. Food and grog for all you marooned lads and the lads who came to save you; Martin, see to that. Use the galley on the *Milford*; people will be busy on the *Nymph*. She still has all her try-works from her whaling days, but they're down in the ballast, largely. Someone wriggly needs to haul them out. Sebastian, that's you, and those boys we took from the navy. You'll be in charge down there, but that's not an excuse to slack. I want everything out and set up tonight; you don't get your grog until it is. Don't drink the bilge-water meantime. Sorry, Martin, but we need to boil down that fish before it starts going bad. You'll be on your own today."

THAT was nonsense, of course, and she knew it. You're never alone in a ship's galley. Even with half the crew on another ship and half the remainder ashore, with the watch reduced to a bare skeleton few, there's always someone with time on their hands and oil on their tongue, hoping to wheedle a jot of rum, or else a handful of soft tack and a dip of it in the slush.

I had company, then, and I could put them to work, but I did still miss my boy. Which was unexpected and curious, interesting to watch in myself, not easy to understand. Not easy to shrug off. Boys are like deep-ocean swell; they come, they go, there's always another on the way.

This one—well. Apparently I wanted to ride the wave awhile.

I could do that. I could afford the time. That's something I've never been short of.

A hasty dinner for all, then, as each mess of men was relieved in turn. No time for the salt meat to soften, so I gave them hasty pudding. When every mess had been fed, I watered rum for the grog and took that up on deck to serve it out. Last in line, as ordered, came the boys: sodden and stinking, exhausted, elated. Arms around one another's shoulders, leaning into each other even before the rum hit them.

Last of all was Sebastian, proud of his command and proud of their work, determined to show me. I'd seen it all before, but still: for his contentment, I let him row me ashore one more time, a lamp in the gig and fires on the shore to guide us. Not till after I'd dunked him in the sea one more time, though, in the tropical sunset glow. I called it a swimming lesson, and forbore to fetch the scrubbing-brushes.

The men had roamed all over this rock-bubble island while I was busy, and found no beach. Some way down the coast from Sebby's Cave, though, the rock shelved out almost level, like a lip. Here they'd hauled the whale ashore already, secured her carcase with rocks and ropes, drained the spermaceti out of her skull and begun to flense her carcase. Come morning, they'd open her belly for the ambergris; in the meantime, no reason not to start rendering the oil out of her blubber.

The *Nymph Ann* was too old to have try-works built into her deck, all bricked about for safety, as the modern whalers did; so the great iron pots had been set up ashore on tripods, with empty barrels stacked behind and slow fires already lit below them. Those would burn night and day now, until we ran out of either blubber or barrels, depending.

"See, these are the blanket pieces, these long strips we cut straight off the fish. I did one myself, this one I think," nice boy, honestly laying claim to the least of the stacked strips, the shortest and most ragged, "till Twice Tom took the flensing-knife off me. Then we cut 'em into blocks, the horse pieces, I don't know why they're called that; and then they're sliced down for the pot. Bible leaves, Tom says these sheets are called. He wouldn't let me cut those, he says I'll take my hand off..."

He was likely right. I was grateful to Twice Tom, and impatient to quiet my boy, to stop him bubbling over with what I already knew. I knew too well what the bubbling pots would smell like, all too soon; I'd sooner be back aboard before then, or at least on the other side of this island. Besides, the reek of rendered whale-oil clings to clothes and hair even worse than the smoke of a smudge-fire, and I'd only just washed him.

I kissed Sebastian, then, to silence him, and guided him away uphill. He was too tired for the long haul back to the ship, it'd only make him quarrelsome if I tried to take him far from his triumphs; too tired to sleep, he could yet be charming company if I only flattered him a little and taught him a little. The island offered no softness, but we'd contrive.

"Sailor Martin."

Hers was the one voice I couldn't ignore. She was sitting alone in a blaze of starlight, halfway up the slope; I swallowed my sigh, settled on a rock below—the perfect courtier, attentive and obedient and not threatening her status—and tugged Sebastian down at my feet, let him settle against my legs, played with the damp straggles of his hair while I waited to hear what was on her mind.

"I had a look inside that cave," she said, "after the men's dinner, before my own." I knew it; her lamps had been lit from my galley fire. "It's not as deep as I've seen them, but it's even higher inside than it is at the mouth. It'll take both ships with ease, even at the height of the tide, and not a sign to see outside. I wouldn't want to be caught in there in a storm, mind, but if we need to duck a king's ship, that's the place. Hell, I don't think this rock is even on their maps; it's not on mine." And hers, of course, had been the king's before. She'd have nothing more recent or more reliable than the *Milford*'s charts.

"That's good news," I said, which was true, but irrelevant: good news for her, of little interest to me, not what she meant to tell me.

"Yes. Somewhere to run to. All we need now is a reason to run." Here it came. "The *Nymph Ann* doubles very nicely as a whaler, and now we have an honest cargo to prove it. We don't need to take it to Port Royal and let those thieves bilk us for a tenth its value; we can head for Port St Meriot and deal openly for once. Only, not with me on the bridge."

Well, no. News of a black woman pirate captain might have spread through the islands already; even if it hadn't, news of a black woman whaler captain would still raise too many questions. It wouldn't be believed.

"The master can stand in for you," I said.

"He can—but so can you. Everybody knows you, everybody trusts you—and you know Sir Terence Digby. I thought we might pay a call. Word on the water is he's giving a ball."

Likely he was. Everything in its season, and this was dancing weather. Light muslins damped with sweat, candlelight on gold brocade, military boots and dainty slippers, scents of jacaranda and musk in the fevered air.

I understood her perfectly. I said, "I still don't buccaneer."

"You don't need to. You only need to be there, in port, visible. Master of a whaler with her holds full to bursting. Of course he'll invite you to his dance. Of course you'll ask to bring your chosen men: your mate and the surgeon, the specktioneer and the skeeman. A couple of likely boys you think the navy might like to look over. That's your part, all I'm asking. We'll do the rest."

I could imagine the rest. She'd be in the kitchens, with a few more men: fresh fish from the harbour, perhaps, or vegetables from market, rum and sugar syrup from the hills, something. And all Sir Terence's guests in all their glitter, the finest jewels for a thousand miles—and no prisoners, no hostages. She wouldn't change her customs on dry land. The cream of the navy would be at that ball, all the senior officers and most of the young hopefuls; why would she ever leave them living behind her, knowing her face now and hot for revenge? They'd scour the ocean till they ran her to ground. Better to hew a hundred heads at a stroke, leave the navy and its government rudderless and adrift, leave no one to come after her.

"That's not what I signed up for," I said mildly. "I'm the cook."

"You are. And, for the moment, a man of mine." If that was a warning, it was pleasingly oblique: no threat, simply an observation of what was owed and owing. "Think about it. We'll be days here, salting that fish down."

She rose and left. I'd have stood to see her off, but Sebastian had fallen asleep with his head in my lap. For a long time once she'd gone I only sat there thinking, watching the stars wheel slowly around the sky while the moon dallied with the horizon.

WHALEMEAT for breakfast—of course!—with biscuit-crumbs fried in the grease. The crew gorged, men and boys together; the only one not groaning as he rose was Sebastian, and only because I'd rationed him.

"Oh, why?"

"Swimming lesson later, and I don't want you seizing up with cramps. You've eaten enough. The cap'n wants to move the *Nymph Ann* into your sea-cave first, then the *Milford* after, see if they both fit. Go climb the mainmast, see if you can touch the roof as she ducks under."

He went off happily enough, knowing that if he went up aloft on either vessel he'd be raising sails rather than fooling with the cave roof. The master was a disciplinarian with a ready rod, and the captain was probably worse; and half the men were ashore wrestling with the whale, so it'd be a lean crew managing some tricky sailwork. In honesty I thought it'd be easier to put the men in boats and tow the ships in, but there was pride at stake all around.

Pride has never been my problem. I cleaned up in the galley and then went on deck to watch the *Nymph Ann* through the cavemouth. Looked for my boy but couldn't spot him: not high in the cross-trees, he was probably hauling ropes down below. No matter. Even a vigorous swell couldn't lift the whaler anywhere near the roof; the master kept her on a perfect line and she headed slowly into ship-swallowing darkness.

The *Milford* would be next, but not me. I've headed often enough into damp uncertain nights, I didn't need another. The little boats were all busy, ferrying the working crew from the *Nymph Ann* back to the *Milford*; I gave Sebastian—and everyone else, but I did hope that Sebastian at least was looking—an object lesson in the confident swimmer's entry to the water. One neat dive, down and down into the measureless ocean; I could almost see the island from its underside before the water threw me up again, up and out like a breasting dolphin, vigorous and free.

I swam ashore and dried off in the sun, walking over rocks: first to the try-works just to see how the men there were coming along: to stand upwind of the seething pots and counsel care with the ladle there, count the barrels filled and sealed, count the exposed ribs of the flatulent giant carcase.

And then away, up the rising curve of the hill that was the rock that was the island; and soon enough down again, to a high cliff-edge that I sat on with my feet hanging over. And leaned down to look and no, not a cliff after all, the mouth of another great sea-cave. And I thought about that, and the stars in their slow shift last night, and the way the moon had seemed to drift on the horizon; and I was almost expecting Sebastian's hail when it came, in that way that lovers do anticipate each other. I was almost commanding it, indeed, that way that lovers can reach out in extremis.

I said, "The captain let you go, then?"

He sat contentedly at my side, swinging his bare heels above nothing: utterly trusting, utterly vulnerable, soon to be utterly betrayed. "She said the men at the try-works don't want me and nor does she, and there's no point leaving more than a watchman on an empty ship, so she sent me to find you."

"Uh-huh." He was, I guessed, my bribe or my persuader, a little of both; she held him in her gift, and offered him to me. He was ignorant but willing, sweet and savage and desirable. I was something close to desperate, even this close to the sea. Normally, properly, that's all that matters; but nothing was quite normal now.

"Go back," I said, holding my voice steady with an effort that I could only hope he was too young to hear. "Go to the captain and say I sent you, tell her this: that Sailor Martin says there's a storm in the offing and a king's ship nearby. Tell her to bring back all the men she can, and stand by. She may need to move both our vessels out to open water, but she shouldn't do it yet. Just be ready. Tell her that. You take an oar and help to ferry, get everyone aboard if you can. Tell her that we'll watch the try-works, keep the fires going, feed the pots. Just the two of us, we can manage that between us. Leave the gig with the *Milford* once you've got them all aboard, and come back with the bumboat. Then we can get to the cave when we need to, to bring word of the storm or the king's men. Tell her that."

He stood, straight and slender at my side; he stared around the long horizon; he said, "I don't see a storm. Or a ship."

I said, "Sebastian. Which of us is a green brat, and which of us has been at sea for ever?"

He grinned. I waited, and soon enough I saw that smile slip as the weight of what I'd said, the reality of it sunk into his head.

I nodded. "Tell her nothing is immediate, but it'll blow up fast when it comes. She needs to be ready now. She should fetch the look-out down, if she doesn't want to maroon him. I'll keep watch. Go."

This time he went, urgent and easy, trusting me as he trusted the rock beneath his feet, as he trusted his captain too.

THERE was a look-out high on the mound of the hill, watching all the wide ocean. He too would have seen nothing, neither storm nor ship. That didn't worry me. He didn't have my name. The captain might flog him just on my word, that something was coming. It wouldn't be just, but no pirate looks for justice.

Besides, I didn't think he stood in too much danger of her whip.

I sat brooding on the brow above that sea-cave, waiting for something to show. Too long, I thought I'd waited, before at last the sea seethed and surged below me to speak her coming. She was late, she was slow on her own behalf. I guess it takes time, all night and half the day, for the heat of slow fires to scorch through a shell as thick as rock, as hard.

Her head was as massive as a ship itself, thrusting forward like the ram of some unimaginable galley before it rose clear of the water on a neck too long, too monstrous. Her eye might have stood for the rose window of a cathedral, if those were ever glassed in black, a single untraced lens.

She looked right at me; I could see myself reflected in that glossy horror, just as a diver sees his own self rising in the stillness of a pool before he breaks it.

I thought she didn't even need to eat me; her eye would swallow me down.

SHE'D need to be faster than this. I was already running, while she deliberated. Over the rise of her unthinkable shell and then down, down to where smoke smudged the air, where the bumboat rocked in the water, where nobody yet knew anything.

Where a figure stood waiting—and a second, rising to stand beside him. Two men, two: and neither one slim as a willow, neither one rushing to meet me…

I was coldly, painfully breathless; it took time even to gasp, "Where's Sebastian?"

"Cap'n took him. She said he's your boy, and you're cook; it's his duty to polish the ship's bell, she said, and he could do that while we all waited for you. Is it coming, then, that storm o' yourn?"

She knew, then. Not the facts or she'd have one ship out by now and be working for the other; but she knew something, not to trust me, something. She was changing her habits after all, using long-established custom to hold one boy hostage. For now, for this little time I had...

Not long enough to take the boat and row that little way, to find any useful truth to tell her. Not long enough to do anything but get there, whichever way I had.

I turned my back on the bewildered men, left them to their smoky fires and seething pots—not long!—and ran again.

Along that flange at the water's edge and up the shoulder of her shell, to the high edge above what we had taken for a sea-cave: where our two ships lay in companionable stillness, where their crews had gathered in secrecy and darkness. Where I had sent them, to a cold destruction. Where the captain held Sebastian, but would not hold him long. One way or the other.

STRAIGHT to that high edge, and straight over.

I have dived into water so still I could see myself come at me. I have dived into the steady swell of the deep ocean, where nothing but myself disturbed the water for a thousand miles all around.

This was...not like that. Even as I went, I could see how the sea's surface bent and stretched below me like a mill-race at a sluice, as great things shifted out of sight.

Down and down I went, purposeful as a hurled knife. As I plunged through the broken surface, I felt the water's familiar grip, tight as a sleeve closing about me; but I could feel the first slow tug of dreadful currents too.

Too fast to be seized, I went down and down, as far below as I had been above; and further yet, far enough that I really could see her underside this time, the plastron of her shell. Clad in barnacles and weed but unmistakably floating, more like a vessel herself than an island; and here came her flippers, ponderously unfolding to pull her down below the surface, to cool that fierce hot spot on her back.

Unfolding from behind those great arches we had taken for cave-mouths, that I'd only understood late and slow, and too late now. What must it be like within the shell there, on board ship and still not understanding, knowing only that the great cliff of the cave-wall was moving, lurching forward, crushing one ship against the other and both against the inside of her shell, heedless as a man crushing snail-shells underfoot?

What must it be like in the captain's head, thinking *he knew; Sailor Martin saw something, knew something, sent us all into the ships exactly for this, because he knew...?*

Never mind the captain; I was looking for my boy.

Either one of the ships might have been lucky, might have been popped out like a bottle from a cork—but I'd have seen the shadow of her overhead if she was, parting company from the vastness of the turtle, bobbing away. I did look, up into the brightness of the sea-sky.

No ships, no. The great broad blade of her flipper, undelayed by whatever ruin she had wreaked on its way—and here came the first fringes of that ruin, splintered timbers and twisted ironworks, heading for the bottom.

Timbers and ironwork and a boy, floundering, frantic. Sebastian, with the ship's bell on a rope around his neck, a terrible brass weight to drag him down, sounding his knell for him as he went.

She hadn't even bound his hands or feet: just belled him and thrown him overboard, as soon as she felt the trap close about her. Let him struggle as he would, the bell would bear him all the way, irresistible. That was a cruel touch, one last vengeful fling at me, though I ought never to have known it.

Except that I was here, and down he came towards me; and she had taken his good knife, of course, but I had mine. I caught the bell first, and severed that rope with a slashing cut; then I caught my boy.

And shook him hard, and held him until he remembered his lessons, not to panic, not to flail about; and then held him and kicked for us both, kicked for the surface.

We were too deep, too short of air. Even I don't have gills, to breathe salt water; and I couldn't breathe for him. His mouth was closed yet, but his eyes were bulging; he couldn't last. And there were men in the water all around us, not all of them broken or dying yet, dead yet; and those jagged plunging timbers, those were a danger too, though the men were worse; and—

Men in the water and a woman too. Of course she'd never learned to swim, the captain; of course she had weights of her own beneath her skirts, weaponry and harness and whatever else she chose to carry against ill-chance, gold and more. Here she came, easy to know in the chaotic waters with her skirts puffed out around her like a jellyfish, like a ship's bell…

Like a bell, yes. Yes.

EASY to know, easy to reach. Poor Sebastian was dragged by his neck again, though this time it was my arm curled about him; and I dragged him below the margin of his captain's skirts and thrust him upward, past her kicking legs to where the billowing fabric still trapped a bubble of air.

Just a bubble, but enough: enough for him, for now. I held him by the body, and felt it as he gasped, as he breathed and breathed.

Then pulled him free of those entangling skirts, and didn't let him see her as she fell below us: faster now, with that last buoyancy stolen from her, dwindling into the dark. He didn't need that face in his memory, those mute curses on his mind. He barely knew what I had done there, only that I'd found him air from somewhere.

Air for him. None for me, and I can't breathe water—but I can hold my breath longer than most, and think while I do it.

And look around, and see the vast bulk of the turtle sliding by, and act against all obvious good sense.

Tow my boy *towards* that surging shadow, not away.

Perhaps he thought that I was mad at last, mad for lack of air perhaps; he tried to kick against me, to pull me back.

He had no chance of that. I took a tougher grip and towed him on, into the currents of her passage.

Turtles use their front flippers to drive them forward. Their back feet do quieter work, acting as vanes against the water. I wouldn't have risked this if she was coming at us, but that lethal front flipper was past already.

Besides, we were committed now, caught in the turbulent suck of the water she threw back. Rolled over and tossed about, I clung and kicked and maybe prayed a little; and saw what I was looking for, a break in a mighty wall, a gateway not quite blocked by the massive limb protruding through it…

YOU can trap air in a skirt, until it leaks out in a thousand streams of bubbles. You can trap air in a bell, and it won't leak; make a bell big enough, you can lower a man to the sea-bed and have him breathing all the way.

How much air can you trap in a cave, if your island takes a dive?

ENOUGH, there'll be enough.

I hauled Sebastian in, and the water flung us up, and there was air; and even a hint of light, that same phosphorescence that had clung to the whale. Enough to show that we floated in a chamber where half the wall was rigid shell and half was shifting leather, the obscene leg of the thing. It looked like seamed rock, but no rock ever moved with such purpose, this way and that like the rudder of a ship under steerage-weigh.

Everything about her was slow and mighty; she had no reason to heed us little things. I helped Sebastian pull himself out of the water, up onto a ledge of her leg, and found just strength enough to follow.

Then we lay against each other and only breathed awhile, painfully, gratefully.

When he spoke at last, his voice sounded strange in that strange space, distant and muffled and hollow all three. He said, "We, we're inside it. Aren't we?"

"Her," I said. All ships, all whales. All giant turtles, seemingly. It felt right. "I suppose we are."

"Like Jonah."

"Something like Jonah. Not swallowed, though."

He thought about that, then said, "What happens now?"

I didn't know, but lying's easy in the dark. I said, "She won't stay down long. When she rises, we'll go out and see where we are, who's about. There'll be someone to signal, or land we can reach. We'll be famous, shipwrecked mariners who survived Leviathan, like St Brendan survived Jasconius."

His head was on my thigh, wet and warm and welcome. He sounded sleepy, like a child; he said, "You're famous already."

"I am, I suppose. Not for anything particularly praiseworthy. Just for surviving, mostly; and here I am again. Doing that. And here you are, doing it right alongside me."

"I'll be a part of your story." No self-deception there. The fact of it, the act of it, the being with me: that could only ever be temporary, in the nature of the thing. He knew. But the story of it, that goes on for ever.

"You will," I said, toying fondly with his ear. "And you'll tell it yourself, to Sir Terence Digby yet; he'll invite us to his ball, and we'll dress up fine and dance all night," and take no prisoners and do no harm and perhaps Sir Terence could find a berth for him, some other life that he could love, not buccaneering. And perhaps I'd be there with him for a while, be a part of his story, however briefly told. "It'll be a masked ball, naturally. You can go as a pirate boy, you'll like that. Yo ho," I said, "Sebastian."

FROM ALICE TO EVERYWHERE, WITH LOVE

T HE PROBLEM WAS THAT SOMEONE HAD to go. Slowly, irrevocably, actually go.

The aliens, when they came, were…properly exotic. Difficult to see, difficult to understand. Their ship pulsed to indetectable rhythms; chilly computers sweated to find a pattern they could analyse.

The aliens brought a machine, the great phase-transmitter that stands on Salisbury Plain. With painful caution, they explained its function. They demonstrated; one by one, they entered the machine and were gone. Transmitted, relocated, somewhere else. Other aliens would come by return; there would be two-way traffic. The speed of light is the speed of information and light is an idler, but they would come.

It would not work for humans, yet. The phase-transmitter needed a template to work from. Uncountable numbers of these machines were spread across the Galaxy, and each of them would have to examine a living human before it could accept one in transmission.

Before humankind could take even a single phase-jump to the nearest station, someone had to go the slow way, in the ship.

Alice Temple had spent her life immersed in the science of language: first as an academic, then—since the aliens came—as a practitioner. At the same time, she had raised a husband and two children from idiocy to independence. She had achieved respect within her profession, renown outside it: and still she was unsatisfied.

Not bitter, not malcontent: short-changed, rather. She had done the best and the most that was available, and it wasn't enough. It had been too easy. Success ought not to be this cheap.

It was she who found a way to communicate with the aliens; of course she was on the panel that decided who should leave with them. She sat through days of interviews with bright, healthy, noble young volunteers—and in the end, she said no.

"No," she said. "It has to be me."

It had needed her to make the aliens comprehensible here on Earth; it would need her again, to make humans comprehensible elsewhere.

When the others were done arguing the point, they argued outside it: her age, her responsibilities, her entitlements. She might make the journey in cold-sleep, but it would still be thirty years at sub-light speeds. She could come back through the machine, but even so: her parents would be dead, her unborn grandchildren would be having children of their own, she'd be out of her proper time, adrift. Better to dwell gracefully in her achievements, and leave adventure to the young…

It wasn't about grace, she said, nor yet adventure. It was necessary: to the project, to the planet and also to her. She needed to do this thing.

She was right, and finally they confessed it. When the alien ship left, she was the one in the cryotank.

She remembered being the one who went into the tank. Now she was the one coming out of it, with the deep knowledge in her bones of time and distance passed. She was still herself, this was still her body, but something had shifted between them.

This place, this time was not her own or anything like it. Just a terminal, a switching-place, a depot on a cold moon: there was a phase-transmitter constantly busy and a spaceport too, just as busy. Only living matter could go through the machine. Everything else must be carried, by old-school traders prepared to spend lifetimes in cold-sleep between brief spells ashore.

They took her to the machine, and it...engulfed her. She felt its slow and intimate examination like a reverse of the cryotank, endless awareness of going nowhere.

Once it had what it needed, it gave her back to herself; they said she could go home. Immediately, if she cared to: be the first human to pass this way, through the phase-transmitter to Earth.

"And then what?" she asked.

Why, then humans could transport here, at light-speed at last; and the young, the vigorous, the bold could go onward in ships to open up new routes to other planets, other vistas...

"What for me?" she said. "If I go home?"

They couldn't answer that, but she could. A little brief celebrity and a resumed lifetime of disappointment, of feeling that there should have been something more.

The alternative, of course, was to go on. Someone else could carry the message, that this portal was open to humans now. Before anyone arrived she could be well on her way to the next, beating a trail forwards.

But oh, this was an achingly slow way to the stars, eked out one body, one gateway at a time.

She mused, she argued with herself; at last, she asked more questions.

Yes, they said, the portal could be reconfigured, looped around to send its message to itself; but...

Yes, they said, the data stream could be divided, to make two copies of the same individual; but...

But, they said, catching on at last, the process would be lossy. Neither one of her would be what she was now. Not so sharp, not so vibrant. Less Alice.

Yes, they said, the iterations would still be perfectly good templates for the machines.

Yes, they said, if the beam could be split once, it could be split a dozen times. But...

The next dozen cargo-ships to leave each carried a passenger. Like a starburst, Alice sent herself to a dozen other portals; and then again, a dozen each from each of those. And so on and on, fading and multiplying, slicing herself thinner and thinner until there was not enough Alice left to sustain a living body. Five billion living bodies.

It wasn't really humankind that flung outward to the stars. It was Alice.

LIVE AT MALY'S

EVEN IN THE SILENCE—AND THERE must be silence, occasional, transgressive, or how could there be music, how else could music happen, how come?—but even in the silence, in the dark, in absence, music squats at the foot of Maly's stairs. Organic as compost, patient as yesterday's rain: soaked in, waiting. Here.

THE young leach light and beauty from the world around, as bread draws salt from a soup. You do it yourself, all unheeding. You do, though. You make me look old and drab, when I'll have you know that I am neither.

Yes, yes. I know all that. Be easy. What, did you think you were here by your choice, only yours? I stepped into this of my own volition; at least one of us had to know what we were doing. Pup.

No matter. If you shine, if you put me in the shade, it's not your fault. It's just your age. You'll get over that. Eventually. I'll wait.

IF music is a situation, Maly's is a state of mind. Here, now. This is where it is, this is what it is. This doorway, these stairs descending. Everything else is a story. Maybe it was on 42nd Street before; maybe it was Bleecker Street. Is that what you heard? Believe it. It might as well be true. The world reshapes itself; every life is its own arrangement.

You don't think you arranged me? Arrogant young…

Never mind. Come down.

DOWN the stairs, and there's Maly: where he always is, waiting at the bottom. Just this side of the music. Maybe there's a door, or a felted blanket hanging in the entry; things change, but not Maly. This is his process, that he sits in a cubby at the foot of his stairs and checks you over. If you're carrying an instrument you're in, free and clear. If not, well. Options are open. If he likes the look of you, if you look hungry or earnest or sincere, if he thinks you'll take away more than you're bringing in, then he'll charge you a dollar and you can stay all night, eat on the house, share whatever comes around. Someone puts a bottle in the pot or pot in the bottle, maybe you get lucky, maybe you get high for free. Don't count on it, but there's always water and there's always ice. You'll need that, it gets hot down here.

If you look like a rich kid slumming, if you look like you're in the wrong business—A&R or the media, say, anyone who sucks money out of music—or if you look corporate at all, Maly will sting you for everything he can, at the door and in the club. And he'll make sure you understand that, and if you choose not to pay, if you turn around and go back up the stairs, that's your loss and no skin off his nose. None at all. He never wanted you, though he can always use your money.

What's that? You, personally? Oh, he'd skin you, if you came here alone or with that gang of privileged buffoons you're pleased to call your friends.

Not tonight he won't, though. You're with me, and I get in on the nod. Old friends, Maly and me. His casa is my casa.

IF music is a motive, Maly's is the means and the opportunity. Carry an instrument, make yourself at home. So long as you're willing and able to play the thing, that is: people will notice, if you try to cheat. You don't want his finger tapping you on the shoulder, his thumb gesturing towards the exit. That's the walk of shame, and we will watch you all the way. And you'll never get back in, there is no forgiveness here. Maly doesn't forget a face, and not even beauty serves as an excuse. Not even youth.

When she came the first time—yes, her, the girl in the corner there, sitting alone, sucking all the light into herself—even Maly didn't know what to make of her. She wore those ragged clothes that might be slumming-chic or simple meanness or genuine poverty or an expression of art, and she came with a crowd who dressed nothing like her, who seemed barely to know her, who expected to pay through the nose for the privilege of coming in.

He always talks to them all, there are no group rates at Maly's. Come her turn, she said she was a musician, she said she sang. No instrument on show but her speaking-voice, and that was instrument enough; it got her through the door.

Except that then she sat—there, yes, in that corner: it's a club full of corners, deliberately so, and that one's hers—and didn't sing and didn't sing, and he lost patience in the end. Tapped her, sent her out the long way, under everybody's eyes.

Yes, he let her back. Yes, that's exceptional. She is. Hush. You'll see.

HERE, sit here. This is my corner. Discreetly central, as corners go. I don't want people staring, but I like to let them look.

At you tonight, they can look at you. Nobody's going to see me, except in your shadow, some wizened clutching greedy thing. It's all right, I don't mind. How could I? It's true enough. Close enough for jazz.

No, stop that. Even the young and beautiful only have a limited licence to misbehave, especially in here. Especially in here with me. I actually do have a reputation, and you actually could do it damage, so be good. If you can't be good, be kind. You can manage that.

Why didn't I bring you before? You weren't ready before. We weren't ready. You don't bring a date to Maly's. This place is about opening your eyes, not dazzling them or blowing smoke. Hush now. Watch the band; you know they're watching you.

HOW can we know the dancer from the dance? If music is a river, Maly doesn't only shape its banks. He finds the streams to feed it, diverts them when he must, raises groundwater, regulates the flow.

Too many poor images, weak metaphors? Never mind. Keep Yeats in mind, and watch the band. See how they shift places, instruments, personnel from one set to the next, even from one number to the next. "This is my grandfather's axe. Father changed the handle and I have changed the blade, but still. Grandfather's axe." This is Maly's house band: never the same line-up, never the same repertoire, and nevertheless. Something abides, some essence that they pass along like a baton, like an inheritance, like a gift. It's not in the phrasing, it's not in the tempo, nothing so simplistic; it's not a style or a genre or a mood. Nevertheless. The house band carries a house brand, as it ought.

IF she carries a brand, she wears it hidden. Something has marked her, for sure: but what she shows, what she wears out front is the pain of it and the uncertainty it's left her with, her tentative habitation of the world, that mermaid attribute of walking on knives and not wanting to sing for her supper.

What happened, the way I hear it, one of Maly's boys was out posting flyers for the club and he heard her busking. Just herself, her voice, for a theatre queue. He fetched her back, I'm told, and asked Maly to give her a hearing—but she wouldn't sing for him, or else he wouldn't ask her to. He doesn't do auditions, unless it's her who doesn't. I've heard it either way. No matter. She came, she didn't sing—again!—and this time he let her stay, he made her welcome. No pressure now, only the possibility. I don't really know what changed his mind: something in her, or something in him. Some confluence between the two of them, a meeting of hearts unless it was a dissonance they both could recognise and value, two blades laid edge to edge across and against each other. Something. You'd need to be there, perhaps you'd need to be them to understand it. I don't think you'd want to stand between them.

Anyway. She comes here, yes; and sometimes, yes, she sings. Not for her supper, that's abundantly clear. She eats anyway.

Yes, yes. We can eat. See that boy in the apron, picking his way between the tables? You could call him a waiter, if you wanted to. You could call him over, tell him we want Itza Chicken.

What is it? It's an opportunity for you to ask what it is, and for half the club to answer "It's a chicken!"

It's a pun, yes, but it's not a joke. It's a meal, and the best you'll get tonight. Roast chicken, salad, bread. Half shares, one bird between two; treat it as a picnic, eat with your fingers, and the parson's nose is mine.

IF music talked in metaphor, Maly's would give it a frame of reference, but it's not like that. Not here. Music *is* a metaphor, perhaps, but only in the sense that the map is not the territory. It can still show all the territory there is, it can map it one-to-one. Music contains the world, and Maly's contains the music, so where does that leave us?

Right here, yes. In the enfolding heart of paradox.

Sometimes I think that's what she doesn't understand, how there is nowhere else to be when the dark draws in, how nothing matters more than what happens here, how Maly's house band will save the world if we will only let them, if we will only *listen*—but what do I know? I'm a raddled old roué with a toyboy at his side, and—

Yes, yes. Don't interrupt, I'm on a roll here.

I don't know what she's thinking. I don't know how she's hurt, or what to do about it. We can save the world, we can remake the world with music, but we can't save her. That's all I know. There she sits in her poor determined beauty, and she wears her damage as blatantly as she wears those ragged sweaters, and we all know she's got nothing underneath, that's all there is. And Maly will feed her any time she comes in, and any of us would give her anything she asked for except that she'll never ask, and none of it matters a damn, it doesn't mean a thing. What she carries, whatever it is that she carries, it's not just worse than we imagine, it's worse than we can imagine.

We can't save her. All we can do is pay her the courtesy of knowing that, of leaving her be and letting her get on with it.

Maybe she's the necessary sacrifice, the year-king, the child under Omelas. That might almost make it easier to bear, if someone somewhere thought that all this mattered. Don't look at me, though; that's not my line. Not my line of work, faith and eschatology and such. You know me better than that. I live on the surface of the world. I only come down here to listen to the music.

The map is not the territory, but I like maps. I like artifice, description, flights of fancy. If I want to think there's something else occurring, that cartographers know more than I do, that they're laying down lines of power and beauty that carry meaning on beyond the margins of the chart—well, you can't blame me for choosing to believe in the significance of art.

You can't. You, of all people. You are a work of art, and I chose to believe in you. I choose to. You're here, after all, with me, and you say that you're staying. I either believe that, or I walk away. Do you see me walking?

No, we can't dance. Not here, not now. I'll take you dancing another night and somewhere else, if you're that determined to make a fool of me. Somewhere it won't matter. Be still now, drink your drink. Smoke that bong, that *bhang* if it comes this way, and listen to the music. Close your eyes if you need to, if it helps you hear better. This is important.

No need to keep an eye on her, she won't sing yet. Not for hours yet, perhaps. Or not at all. The trick is not to mind, or would be. I haven't mastered that myself—but then, I've heard her sing.

IF music is a measure, as light is, maybe Maly's is the unit that you count by; fixed and certain, unalloyed. What it is you're counting, that would be something fluid and determined. Determinable. Light counts distance, but music—

How long? How long has Maly—? Don't. Don't ask. That…isn't even a question, not down here. We don't count years. Or, no: better to say that years don't count. Age counts, perhaps; that's unvarying. We could stay for ever, we could go back up just in time to catch the heat death of the universe and it would make no difference, time couldn't touch us. I'll always be twice the boy you are tonight, the band will still be saving the world, and she—

Well. Maybe she'll still be in her corner. She can sing; that doesn't mean she will. That's what Maly had to learn, that performance is not an obligation. It isn't always going to happen. It's okay actually to sit mute, not to use what you've got, not to give a thing. It's not like we'll run out if everybody doesn't give their all. Music supersedes time; there's always more.

Maybe she's running out on herself, on her gift, but that's another issue. That's hers to address if she chooses to. Again, there's no obligation. She owes nothing to her art, and nothing of art to the world. She could keep her mouth closed all her life, and we wouldn't have a word to say against it.

What? No. Flatly, no. Oh, talk to her by all means, if you want to—you might learn more in an evening than I have in however long, she might just tell you flat-out what troubles her, she might tell everyone who asks: how would I know, when I've never asked?—but don't flatter yourself, it's not you she needs. Youth and beauty she has already, and that running talent like a tap she tries to choke off; she'll always be younger than you, it'll always be an advantage, and what else do you have to offer? A listening ear, I grant you, but she's a roomful of those already, and makes scant use of it. A hand to hold? I don't suppose she'd want it. That's not what ails her—or if it is, I've misunderstood her all this time, and so has everyone. If she wanted company, she'd have more than she wanted; they'd be circling her like wolves. There's something in her, though, she has the trick of it to keep them all at bay: a shark-repellent, a cold equation. You too, even you, it works on you. You say you might go over, but you don't. In all your heat and tenderness, you still hold your distance. Hold to me.

LOOK at her, just look; God knows, it's easy enough. The light all leans toward her like candle-flames in draught, it cradles her beauty like eggshell in the palm. It wants to measure nothing but the distance to her skin, and finds that little dash too far. Light doesn't see as we do, what's bitter or broken or gone bad.

No, I don't think she's bad. Nor mad, that either. She has that self-seeding sadness that only grows worse with the years, that'll tangle her entirely if she can't weed it out; but where it comes from, how to stop it, what to *do*…

Mostly, we leave her alone, in hopes that that's the right thing.

Sometimes, we hope that she'll sing.

HUSH now, and keep still. Breathless still, like the rest of us. See where she comes?

Out of her corner and up to the front, picking her way between tables: almost clumsy now within her grace, so eager she is, so urgent to step up, to sing out, to be free of what she carries.

Maybe it takes time to build, like a bath filling; maybe then she has to sing, like a bath overflowing. Maybe it hurts to swallow, maybe she can't keep it in.

This is how it ought to be for the old romantics, for me: young people with their talent ablaze, uncontrollable and vicious, running free.

Running to the stage now, running to the mike. Barely a glance at the band, a muttered string of chords perhaps to lead them out together and bring them home at last, a gesture with her hand to beat the time.

The drummer catches that, he's used to this; he leans into the rhythm of it, fetches the others along.

The girl on sax steps forward, blows a phrase. Checks our fretful singer with her eyes, wins a nod not as strong as approval, not applause, more like direction: *yes, go that way, that's the way.*

And so it is, and so she does, and so they do. The bass follows the drum, the piano skitters along behind the sax, runs ahead like an eager dog, waits for everyone to catch up; they all catch a breath, a moment, a hanging pause— and then she sings, and they trot on obedient at her heels.

IT'S a song without words, necessarily, inevitably; but you wouldn't call it scat. That has too many connotations, and they're all wrong. Wrong-headed. There's nothing comic here, and she's not riffing on anything you've ever heard, nor I either. She's laying down something fundamental, telling a truth deeper and newer than language, a fresh revelation.

IF music is a lever, strong enough and long enough, then Maly's is the place to stand, the place she's chosen.

She's the fulcrum.

They may say she carries the weight of the world on her shoulders, and of course she does—but not the way they mean it, not a helpless hopeless sorrow. Not like Atlas either, doing it as punishment or penance, holding up the sky. Keeping the status quo.

She heaves, she tilts. She moves the world.

She moves the *world*.

SHE sings, and something...happens. Or something doesn't happen: the same thing. That earthquake off the Philippines? Doesn't raise a wave. A drone that went astray comes back to base, its missiles undischarged. Guerrillas in Guatamala or Gabon don't raid a village in the early day, don't catch everybody sleeping, don't leave a strew of bloody corpses in their wake.

That's what she has, it's what she does. She sings a new world, a new way, a shift from one track to another. And yes, it costs her, in damage we can see and more for sure that we cannot; and, what, you want to *help?* You want to make her feel *better?* You want to stop this dead, this thing she does, this little faltering miracle she buys for us, this step back from grief unbearable?

No, what she has is bearable. You can see that. She bears it rather well.

IF music is an interrogation, Maly sets the questions. His house, his house band: it's almost clinical, almost cruel. Certainly it's ruthless. But so's she, in her way. Ruthless with herself, at least. She isn't keening here, she's not lamenting how she suffers.

She suffers, and she sings; they're separate. That matters.

So do you, yes. We all matter, so long as she's up there doing her thing. Her two things, the singing and the suffering. She needs witness, and we can bear it. We can bear that, at least. It's all she asks of us; it's all she offers. Nothing ever happens down here, or to us.

Nothing ever stops, no. Not for us. Push comes to shove, as it does, it's really not about us any more.

We can leave, yes, if you want to. When her set is over. Most people won't, not for a while yet. They'll have another drink, think it through, check their cells for coverage, for news. They'll see us if we go, they'll watch us all the way—but that's okay. We've done our bit, we've been here when it mattered, we've let her sing. That's what we do, it's implied consent. She's allowed to shift the world, if someone's listening.

She's allowed to suffer, sure. That too.

I'm sorry. You weren't ready for this, were you? You're so young. I forget sometimes how young you are. Once she sits down I'll take you home, if that's what you want. And I'll make a little prediction, just between us: when we head for the door, listen out. Just as we leave, as we go to climb those stairs? You'll hear the whole damn club give a little sigh, barely more than a breath, just enough to know that they've noticed. Don't be surprised if we get a quick tucker on the drums to see us out, or an air on a penny whistle. They're a romantic crew, and they'll be glad to see me happy; you don't know how good you are for me, or how long they've waited to see you come. But it's more than that, there'll be a relief in it too. They'd be glad of anything, almost, that isn't her. Something they can step back from, something they can smile at. Something they can applaud.

No one claps for her, no. She couldn't bear that, we wouldn't do it. She's like church; some things just aren't appropriate.

See, see now? See her go? See her step down and blunder back towards her corner, to her drink. There'll be drinks headed her way all night, as long as she stays. As long as she stays there. People will be praying that she won't sing again.

Come on, then, you. Let's hit the road. I want a drink myself. And silence, yes. Blind waiting animal silence, and a storm no longer pending: that sense of something cut away, something to be grateful for. And you.

GOING THE JERUSALEM MILE

TEN DAYS IN EVERY YEAR—EASTER week, the solstices, All Souls'—the canons of the cathedral have a great many chairs removed and a vast square of canvas taken up from beneath them, to reveal a labyrinth laid out in lines of bronze and time on the stone flags of the floor there, a channel worn by centuries of barefoot and chilly faith.

I think they're mad, entirely insane, and I have told them so. That cursed measure should be dug up and melted down, it should be ripped out and filled in, ploughed under and cemented over. That tainted bronze that marks the path should be cast into ingots and then into the sea, into the deepest trench of the deepest sea, where no man might ever see or touch it. Let it do harm to demon-fish in the darkness, I don't care. The labyrinth should be deleted, expunged, destroyed; beyond that, I dare not go.

No blame to the good canons, I guess, that it is not. Small lives are small concern to them, who overlook a thousand years of history in stone and height and symbol. Easter congregations flock to walk the labyrinth, jostling each other from its concentricity; its fame draws in tourists and townsfolk with forbidden cameras and outré shoes, both tolerated for that short season for the sake of money in the offertory boxes. In winter, pilgrims walk from the north, from distant Scottish churches, timing their long marches to reach us on the shortest day. Our labyrinth is the end, the point and purpose of all that walking; by candlelight and prayer they shuffle, round and round and back and forth like dancers to a spoken beat resounding down the generations. The summer solstice looks southerly, to churches from the chalky lands, the lands of flint and furrow. Their pilgrims burn candles too when they come to us, and carry crosses as a sign of fealty.

They hardly need to do that. It gives them pleasure, I suppose, to give themselves a little pain. Their coming is token enough that this is a crusade, Crusading-Lite, in search of a diet deliverance. They'll find no pain else, beyond what they bring on their own behalf.

It's called the Jerusalem Mile, our precious labyrinth, this way they walk, white-worn stone with brass edgings polished to a razor's edge. It's carried a special dispensation for the better part of a thousand years: the old or the infirm who walk this way are reckoned to have walked enough. No need to go further. They count equivalent to palmers, as though they too had been to the Holy Land and prayed in the holy places and scattered greenery in the dust and been forgiven for their pains. Form is function; the intent is taken for the deed and carries the same remittance. So a thirteenth-century Pope said, at least, declaring a local indulgence which the Church has maintained through the Dissolution and all points since. The current dispensation doesn't actually speak about indulgence, far less Purgatory, but they will still insist that a special blessing attaches, especially to the elderly and sick. How God might feel about it all is not recorded.

So they have their special pilgrimages at the turnings of the year, they have their mass migrations over Easter; all that gives them licence to have postcards by the font and local TV every now and then, mentions in dispatches and a presence on the Web.

What happens for All Souls' is very different, and they keep it quiet when they can.

On the second day in November—or the third, when the second is a Sunday; like Easter, All Souls' is a movable feast—the massive doors of the cathedral are locked against the world. Visitors and worshippers both are redirected to other churches in the diocese. Those who must be let in, those with authority or special dispensation find no service before the great altar nor any chairs in that greater space beneath the tower, where transept crosses nave. Only a wide circle of candles burning, and a patrol of sidesmen to lead the faithful to the Mary Chapel in the apse.

They preach a shortcut to heaven, a lesser gate to which they hold the key; and they do guard it, you see, on All Souls' Day when the desperate turn their avid eyes on any key that turns. They just don't guard it well, not well enough.

SHE was my wife, she was my love and she was stained with acid failure, the vitriol of lack. That was almost the first thing I loved about her, how she wore her defeats like tattoos on her skin and on her tongue. How she was as a child I can't say, we met first at university; but the way her family used to watch her, mongoose-wary before a cobra's spite, I think that says a lot. That a watchful, wary mongoose is always a good bet against a cobra, that possibly says more. Whatever she took on, always, she did expect to lose.

I overreached myself to win my place at Durham; she did the opposite, bidding for Oxbridge and failing, falling short. That was the inherent lesson of her life, that she could never learn her lesson. She must always aim high, and always be disappointed. She would have stayed to read for a master's and a doctorate, to have been a don, but that her academic ambitions couldn't survive her second-class degree. She would have been a management trainee and afterwards a manager, she could have been head-hunted around the world from corporation to multinational corporation, but that she never quite made it through the selection process. I guess the interview boards could read that hint of second-best in her CV, could measure how she burned passionately but somehow not quite bright enough.

I think she would have married another man than me, except that none of them would offer. I know she dated plenty. Even after I left Durham, even after she followed me down, still it took her a long time to settle for what she'd got. I don't know yet, will never know how far she felt she had to fall, before she could fall for me.

We did marry, though, and I at least was happy. I like a bitter marmalade, a green apple, a touch of sour to underlie the sweet. I liked it that her dreams outran her frantic grasp, whichever way she snatched; I liked it that she could not keep from snatching.

She was my wife; she wanted to be the perfect wife, homemaker and helpmeet. She learned to cook, grimly. She learned to sew, to keep house, to serve coffee and biscuits to my friends, to smile of a sort while she did it. She learned to knit, before ever she had anyone to knit for.

That was the next, near the last and near the most perfectly dreadful of her failures. Perfect wife must needs be perfect mother; and for the longest time, the worst time she could not quicken. That was the word she used herself, *quicken*, as though to underscore its opposite, herself. The opposite of quick is not slow, but dead. She began to speak of herself as shrivelled, barren, bereft. She never suggested that I should take a sperm-count. Like everything, this had to be her inadequacy. All her bitterness was turned against herself, like a scorpion that stings its own body in its frenzy.

Doctors tried to help her, but they could not; their failures were expensive. In the end, despairing, she fell back on childhood certainties and went to church.

Threw herself on the church, rather, on the fickle mercies of God. Even this she had to do in full measure, to perfection, to extremes: as though only monomania or fanatical devotion could store up enough treasure in Heaven to buy her the child she burned for. Sunday worship at our parish church would never do, it must needs be the cathedral and services daily, twice daily when she could. And flower-rosters, polishing the brass and speaking to the bishop, prayer-meetings and bible classes and retreats. The Dean was an old high Anglo, who seemed to hear the shiver of a bell when the Host was lifted;

she went to him for private confession, and learned to cross herself and bob towards the altar.

I'd go with her Sundays and holy days, no more. I had no greater trust in God than I did in doctors or thermometers or hope, blind hope. Some women are not made fertile; children are no more a right than life or liberty or luck. At last, I thought, she must accept that, and turn her fevered eyes elsewhere. Meanwhile, I loved her for her hunger, for this latest face of pain.

APRIL, come she will, and Easter with her. Of course my love, my wife, my dear despairing wanted to walk the Jerusalem Mile. Many a woman has made pilgrimage for the sake of a child, to confound an arid womb; some have come back pregnant. We could not afford the Holy Land, but this petty substitute was easy.

On Palm Sunday, all the congregation can be palmers. The chairs and canvas are all cleared away before the doors are flung open to let the people in for Matins; in lucky years the sun beats in through stained windows to throw the colours of the saints across the floor there, and those who sit behind can watch the quest of light across shimmering brass and stone. Then during the recessional the bishop leads his ministers, his choirs and his flock in that same quest, down the aisle and through the labyrinth in a long, long line all searching for their very own and golden city, all marching to Jerusalem. Some carry palms or other greenery in token.

It is not, of course, truly a labyrinth. It could not be; we're dealing in symbols here, and there are no false turnings, no dead ends for those who take the high and narrow way to God. No, the path defines the great circle quadrant by quadrant, as though it were a compass rose, not so much a spiral as a succession of switchbacks. The way into it comes from the north, from the cold, hard not to shiver at the thought of it, ice at your back; turn clockwise and follow the rim around until suddenly you're sent back, don't step over the line and you retrace your course just a short pace closer to the centre, bumping shoulders with those who come behind. And come back almost to where you started and so turn again, and again and yet again; each time a shorter walk and a more sudden turn, and you come at last to where a single step could have you standing on the central cross, X marks the spot, except that you may not cross that thin brass filament and so it leads you through to another quadrant and the start of a slow unwinding that takes you back towards the rim again.

Four quadrants, in and out and the same again, like the steps of a country dance; and indeed this is country religion, old-time religion and in the end there is a simple procession, for the path strikes clean and clear from the western edge to the heart of the circle and you can walk it with your eyes uplifted, fixed on the high altar and the rose window beyond, the east and the everlasting dawn beyond that, the rise of a hope imperishable.

My wife cherished a hope she could not believe in, but still she did hope, she needed to, she had to yearn and stretch. Faith does not accumulate, but blessings are heaped up upon the faithful. Persistence might pay off, she thought, she hoped. She never gave it credence.

I went with her, of course, to the cathedral. I was her witness, her counterpoint; I might not share her vision nor her need, but everything else I shared. We sat, we stood, we knelt in proper order, we sang hymns and heard the sermon and said Amen. She crossed herself and took communion, and so did I, though it was only she who shivered under the momentous weight of it all. It was her own dark stare that made me shiver, how her eyes followed every movement of the ministers while all the time I knew that her attention, all her focus lay on the great open space behind us, the revealed mystery on the ageworn flags of the floor.

After the final blessing, Bach rolled over us more sonorous than the bishop's voice, and more imperative. The organist was alone, left out, the only one who could not walk to mercy; perhaps he thought his fingers on the manuals, his feet on the pedals would be fit substitute if he only worked them hard, a double substitution, a pilgrim playing in lieu of a pilgrim labyrinth in lieu of a proper pilgrimage. I had heard him often, but I never heard him find such power. It set my skin to shiver again, just to listen to it.

My wife was shivering, fidgeting at my side for another reason altogether. She could always do patience until it came to the point, the purpose, the last sprint to the line. Then she would rush, and stumble, and so fall. She could blame exam nerves, poor interview technique, any number of superficial causes; the truth of it went deeper, to her soul. When she saw what she wanted, she must snatch, she must hurl herself at it; and what she wanted was always out of reach. Deliberately so, I thought sometimes. She set herself impossible targets in order to fail because that was what she did, that defined her. Or else she was simply afraid to succeed, afraid of what might follow. She was not desperate for children, I thought, until it was clear that they would not come easy to her; they were not crucial to her happiness until it was clear to her that they would not come at all.

I knew this, I think she knew it too. And yet she was desperate, and they were crucial. That was the heart of her unhappiness, that she truly did suffer, even where it was suffering of her own construction. And so she fidgeted and fretted at my side while the bishop paraded down the aisle in stately measure, and all his clergy and the robed choirs behind. Then came the sidesmen, slowly down the lines of pews and the massed ranks of chairs, gesturing out the faithful row by row.

Our turn and she was up and eager, into the shuffling single file, jostling the man ahead in her impatience. He was broad, impassive, ideal; unable to elbow him aside, she fell quickly into step, into that near-mindless state that the English call a queue.

More like a slow conga-line, perhaps, with no kicking. We did move in time with the music; like queuing, counterpoint is hypnotic, in a way that harmony can never be. And I did settle my hands on her hips, in a purely protective gesture, *don't jog the guy ahead, be steady, be calm*, though she shrugged me off, twitched away in short order. This was a holy place, not made for mauling. Besides, I'd never been given licence to offer that kind of protection. I could follow behind her if I chose, but she always went alone to face her demons, her failures, the precise measure of her falling short.

Shuffle-step weaving back and forth within the narrow brass lines that defined the maze, within the footworn channel, easy for the blind to find their way. So many of us that we might as well have been blind, we couldn't see our feet for the crush of others' bodies, just trust the one ahead and follow close as the turns got tighter, towards the centre of the circle.

Clergy and choir and congregation, filled out with the vapid and the curious: too many people already in that slow dance to the music of time. And then they let the children in, the Sunday-school children who usually picked up their parents after service; of course they could not be excluded, today of all days.

Most tagged on obediently at the rear, still some distance short of the Jerusalem Mile. Others did not. They spotted their parents somewhere in the slow-grinding mill of the labyrinth, or else they pretended to, for the simple fun of squirming through the crowds. We had been tight but organised, a steady state, slow water in the channel set; now suddenly we were buffeted unpredictably from any side, squeezed and shoved out of line and it was hard even to keep our feet, let alone be sure where they were treading.

Once warned already, I didn't reach out to wrap shielding arms around my wife. That was my failure, although later she would call it hers. So I was too slow to help, I was helpless when a boy cannoned heedlessly into her legs. She was knocked out of step, out of line, sent stumbling across the brass fillet that divided one quadrant from the next.

Kind hands caught her, gripped her, held her upright. I stepped across and put my arm around her, too late; looked back to the line that we had come from, but already our place was gone, the gap closed up and our neighbours moving on. Meanwhile these generous folk were making room for us in this new channel; I nudged my wife to take it. There was no going back.

She had lost the easy rhythm of the dance. All her movements were stiff and spasmodic now; her head kept twisting as she cast wild glances over her shoulder, trying to see where we should have been, how much we'd cut across.

"It won't matter," I whispered, a useless litany. "How can it matter? God will understand, God saw…"

She didn't, she couldn't believe me; but God perhaps was listening to my distraction, or else to her distress. We came eventually to the circle's centre and the cross set into the stonework there, where it points due east towards the altar. Those ahead of us moved on, following the straight path out of the labyrinth. We stepped forward, she set her foot deliberately at the focal point of the cross, the centre where the two arms meet—and she gasped, and clutched abruptly at her belly.

"What is it, what's wrong?"

"Nothing," she whispered, straightening slowly and feeling, probing with nervous fingers below her waistline. "Nothing's wrong, no..."

"But you were hurt, something hurt you."

"Not hurt. I felt, I don't know, a shifting? As though some little part of me had moved, fallen into place after a long time twisted..."

And she stared at me with a wild, frantic hope that seemed to plunder all the logic of the world and leave it, me, entirely bereft.

"Just wait," I said, all that I could say. "Wait and see, that's all. It might be nothing," a torn muscle from the shove, wishful thinking, constipation, anything. "Come on, I'll take you home."

"Not yet, not now." Her eyes moved towards the Mary Chapel in the apse. "I said a particular rogation to Our Lady, I need to go and thank her..."

"No. You need to lie down, you need to rest," *you look insane, and sound it,* although I would not tell her that, how could I? "We don't know yet if there's anything to thank her for. Even if there's been a miracle," she'd like the thought of that, I thought, "we still have work to do, you haven't quickened yet. Unless you're following Mary all the way, like a virgin?"

"Hush, not here, you can't talk like that here," but she was giggling breathily, like the girl she must once have been, digging her way out through accreted years of disappointments. That was miracle enough for me; I gazed on in wonder. It was like a transformation in reverse, the chrysalis tearing open to release someone much younger, much less formed...

And uncertain, and easy to direct. She came home with me, because I told her to; she went to bed in the middle of the day there, because I said that it was best. I let her doze behind the curtains for an hour or so, then took her a bowl of soup and a cup of Earl Grey with lemon, sharp and scented and suggestive. I sat on the bed and took my shoes off while she spooned the soup, my shirt and tie while she drank the tea. She looked at me doubtfully; I grinned at her.

"How are you feeling?"

"Fine. Rested. Thank you…"

"No pain, no discomfort?"

"No, nothing."

"Good, then. Only one way I can think of, to learn whether it really was that miracle you've been praying for. Yes?"

"Oh, yes. Please…"

SO we did, and it was, or it seemed so. For a while. Almost immediately, she announced that she was pregnant. Except that a month later, it seemed that she wasn't after all. She insisted that she'd lost a baby, and our doctor said that very possibly she had; many women lost their first, he said, especially where they'd had such trouble conceiving. Keep trying, he said, stay hopeful.

So we did that too, at my insistence against her revitalised depression, her overweening misery: "We don't know for sure that you did miscarry, but if you did, it's only proof that you can carry to begin with. You can quicken. And if you can carry, you can keep it. So we try again, and next time we'll be more careful…"

Months of that, and at last I proved a prophet, against my own expectation. She was pregnant, this time the home tests and the doctor's both confirmed it; and she was determined, this time there would be no more disasters.

A hard time she had of it none the less, though she stayed at home and often stayed in bed, like a woman of her grandmother's generation playing out the rules of a classic confinement. She was sick every morning and not well at any time, pale and anaemic and distressed. She ate despite her lack of appetite, she demanded special diets from midwives and nutritionists, any-thing that would benefit her baby regardless of what it did to her. She tried to drag herself and me to antenatal classes, but was too unwell too often; in the end they told her not to come again, and it had taken little persuasion from me to have them do it.

She sat out the last trimester of her pregnancy entirely at home. I only wished that she could have enjoyed it more, a rare treat, an indulgence. She was anxious, always, for the baby; otherwise she was simply sickly, enjoying nothing, only enduring, her gaze fixed ferociously on the closing goal, full term, the point and purpose of all this suffering.

It came as it must, with the rotation of the calendar. She was in no fit state to attempt a normal birth; I had booked her in for a caesarian months before, and she'd barely had the strength to argue. Her lips twitched, though, as she accepted it, and I knew she'd write it down as yet one more of her failures, that she couldn't bring a child into this world without medical intervention. Not a great failure, though, surely not significant against the achievement of the child itself, the grail discovered...

AND so the taxi-ride to hospital in the fortieth week, the overnight bag at last needed overnight, surgery in the morning. Scrubbed and gloved and gowned, I was there to watch; I saw her opened up and her baby, ours scooped out slimy, weakly kicking, wet and frog-like with a frog's thin croak of a voice to match.

It was a boy, hers, ours, our son; we delighted in him, of course, what could we else?

But he was not well, not vigorous, more grey than pink and undersized, ill-fed by her placenta. They kept him days apart from us, in an incubator, breathing bottled air and feeding from a tube. My wife had no milk to offer him, in any case. She needed special care as much as he did; when she saw him, it was from a chair where I was wheeling her.

She recovered slowly, and so did he; they both gained strength, and won an exeat at last. I brought them home together, he cradled in her arms, and then fed him from a bottle while she slept off the effort of the journey. He was thin and jaundiced still, his skin flaking and a disturbing dullness to his eyes, an air of being exhausted already by the world and finding no good in it.

WEEKS, months later he had not improved. He was still scrawny, yellow, uninvolved, showing little interest in food or the world or us, barely moving in his cradle, barely crying. He seemed to endure, and nothing more than that: as though there was no more than that, and nothing to be hoped for.

My wife grew stronger in her body, but that was little help. No strength could ever be enough to shoulder the weight she dragged behind her, the intolerable burden of her guilt.

She blamed herself, of course, she had to. One more failure, more terrible than any: our son's weakness must necessarily be his mother's fault. She might have blamed her diet, but did not. She might have blamed her exercise or lack of it, her lying in bed, her constant sickness; she did not. She blamed the Jerusalem Mile, where she'd met her blessing.

Her broken blessing, as she explained it now, because she had made a broken pilgrimage. "I should have gone back," and never mind the crush, the impossibility of it, "I should have walked the proper route, the full route. You can't cheat God and not be punished for it."

"You believe that God would punish our child," I said, "because you got jostled in a labyrinth?"

"Because I let myself be knocked from the proper path," she said, "oh, yes. Besides, it's not his punishment. Look at him; he doesn't suffer. It's we who pay the price, in watching him. That's how it is."

ALMOST, the doctors seemed to agree with her. They could find no other cause for his disconnection. He was in no pain, he carried no infections; I asked to see his notes, and what they said was *failure to thrive*. It sounded not too dreadful, until a specialist told me that a child could die from failure to thrive; it could be a cause of death on the certificate.

I did not tell that to my wife, but she knew it anyway. She didn't need the diagnosis. And if she knew what ailed him, she knew the cure too. She must walk the labyrinth again: no worse than that. With our child in her arms, and properly this time, prayerfully and undisturbed.

We were too late for Easter, even if she'd been prepared to risk the crowds again, which she was not. She petitioned the Dean and Chapter, that she might be allowed a private, solitary passage. They refused her. They turned down many such requests, they said, each year. Reluctantly, they had to. If they allowed one, they must allow them all; it was not their task to act as arbiters, to say who deserved the privilege and who did not. The work, they said, would be unfeasible, so much time and labour it took to clear the cathedral floor...

Privately, to me alone they said they thought we should look otherwise for causes and for cures. This was not Lourdes, they said, there were no miracles at the heart of the Jerusalem Mile. It was a gesture of faith, not a task undertaken for reward. If God chose to bless the pilgrims, that was his affair. There were no guarantees, from the cathedral or from heaven.

I knew all of that already, but my wife did not and would not learn it.

She asked to join the summer pilgrimage, when the southern churches sent their devotees to walk up for the solstice. Again, she was refused. She was not strong enough, they said, to join the march; or if she was, her baby most certainly was not. And this was an opportunity for others, not for local people. The bishop and congregation would pray for our baby, gladly, next Sunday and every Sunday; let her be content with that.

She was not, of course, though obedience demanded that she should be. She subsided, largely onto her knees; it was God and the Virgin she pleaded with now, not the unresponsive diocese. She threw herself ever more vigorously into cathedral life, as though she struggled to make herself indispensable. If she hoped that way to change their minds, I thought she was wasting her effort in a losing battle; but my judgement was based on those private conversations, which I could not admit to her. I stayed quiet, stayed at home, cared for the baby in so far as he needed or allowed it, which was not far at all. He remained unresponsive, uninvested in the world.

CAME the autumn, late autumn, first blast of winter weather; first touch of chill to my soul, as at last I understood my wife.

"You can't. You can't do that."

"I must."

Oh, we said more, we said it otherwise and often, but that was the gist, the thrust of everything we said. What I thought impossible, she thought imperative. I argued all the dangers, but in the end there was no argument. It takes two to argue, and she would not; she was simply resolute, determined, immovable.

Vulnerable too, open to betrayal. She understood that and expected it, I think. It would be another manifestation of failure, that she had hidden her purposes too scantily, betrayed herself to a man who must betray her.

So of course I did not, I kept quiet and only watched as she manipulated herself onto one more rota, the long night's vigil for All Souls'. Simple fire precautions demanded that a watch be kept on all those candles, but that was only common sense, not a religious obligation; it was the sidesmen who drew up the list of volunteers, and neither Dean nor Chapter thought to oversee it.

My wife put her name forward, and my own. They were so used to her volunteering, there was no question to it, no surprise. When she said we'd take the dog-watch, alas, she said it to a retired Navy man, who laughed at her. He knew what she meant, though, even before she stammeringly explained it, and he put us down quite happily for the graveyard shift.

I could not be happy, but only force could prevent her, force or treachery, and I was capable of neither.

SO I helped her wrap our sleeping son against the weather and myself carried him out to the car, as I had carried him in, his first day home. I settled him into her lap and saw them both securely belted before I drove the short distance to the high stark vision that was the cathedral, so lit against the darkness that there was no way to tell that simpler lights burned within.

It was a little before four in the morning. Only the wicket door was open, a private way into solemnity, *like a side door into heaven* I thought and did not say. This was not a night for symbols, not All Souls' in the cathedral with the candles aflame and my wife setting her feet, our child's welfare on a perilous path. I wanted nothing to mean anything beyond the thing that it was. *This is a door and nothing more, it leads into the cathedral, nowhere else; and there, that circle of little lights, those are candles and nothing more. They are not guards, nor wards. The shadows that surround them are not, are most certainly not moving except as the flames move, flickering in the draught of our arrival...*

They were altar candles, as fat around as the span of my two hands together, knee-high against me as they stood on the stones. The couple we were relieving, students from the theological college, said that none had needed attention during the four hours of their watch; they had prayed and read psalms to each other, kept a casual eye on the candles, felt themselves cheerfully redundant and wished us more of the same. Then they went away to their no doubt separate beds—all this great space to play in, and they read psalms to each other!—and left us to our own more dangerous occupations.

The wicket had barely slammed behind them before my wife was moving towards the candles, our son so muffled up in blankets against her chest, so habitually still and silent that the students hadn't even realised we had a baby with us.

"Wait," I said, and went to throw the bolts that fixed the little door within the greater, to keep us private and undisturbed. That done, I turned round to find that she had been overtaken again by that terrible hurry that would not brook any proper preparation, had not waited at all.

She had moved two candles, the two most crucial, those two that stood tall guard at the entrance to the labyrinth. She had set those two aside, set her feet between brass and brass, set off again to walk the Jerusalem Mile.

Set off alone, without me, unprotected: this night of all nights, this most deadly, with our child in her arms.

ALL Souls' is the day of prayer for those in Purgatory, those souls doomed but not damned for the sins of their lives. They must suffer a given time, perhaps a long time; but the prayers of the Church are effective, they can win remission for the faithful departed, and on this one day all the churches pray together. The priests wear black vestments, and say the office for the dead; in some places, monasteries, houses of the holy, they start at midnight and pray for twenty-four unbroken hours. Laying up treasure in heaven, perhaps, hoping to reduce their own future sentence by serving time for others now.

When it's four in the morning in England, it's midday or later in the far east, there are powerhouses of prayer out there that have been running a good twelve hours already. There are souls in Purgatory that have felt an easing, a lifting, a glimmer of hope unlooked-for; and now they look, now they're hungry for it, now they will swarm to any chink of light.

That's why the cathedral is closed, why the Jerusalem Mile is guarded by prayer and candle in this vulnerable time. There are uncountable souls in Purgatory, they are immeasurably suffering, we cannot know how many or how much; but this we do know, that they crave release as water craves to flow. Whoever can offer a shortcut to God's grace, whoever holds the key to a way out does well to guard it well, All Souls' Day when it comes.

IT had come, and my wife had opened the way in her own desperation. Against all policy and all advice, against my urgent pleading she had let loose a world of spirits for the sake of our sickly child; and she had done it without me, ahead of me, alone.

NOT let them loose on our world, she wouldn't and couldn't be that irresponsible. Set them free to run heavenward, rather, along the selfsame path as herself; she knew the risk to herself, and had discounted it.

The risk to the baby had to be discounted in its turn. Children die, from failure to thrive...

BY the time I reached the circle, she was advanced far into the first quadrant, but it was heavy going. She walked as though braced against a wind that blew on her back, as though she waded thigh-deep in a force of water. I have said, it was no good night for symbols; I mean this almost literally. Almost. Her long hair licked and whipped about her face; even as I approached the entrance to the labyrinth, I could feel the tug, the chilly flow around and past my legs as if all the cold thoughts in the world had massed together and plunged towards the warm.

How many sly souls could race that path to glean an undeserved forgiveness, seizing this rare chance before some wiser vigilant came to close the way against them? I cannot answer that. Uncountable numbers, at any rate. I felt them like wind and water, like the bite of a vicious storm; I could barely stand amidst their hurry.

I could watch my wife ahead of me, see the precious care she took to walk within the lines of brass, see how her loose clothes only emphasised her weakness as they were pressed against her skin, clinging to her body, showing her spare flesh and bone as if they were sodden wet. I could wonder how ever she managed to keep upright, where it was so hard for me who was so much stronger; I couldn't see the baby at all, but I could wonder also about him, how he would survive this. Whether he would survive it.

Before long I felt a button go, I heard my first seam rip. Before either one of us had reached the second quadrant, we walked in rags. My wife was hunched over what she carried, to offer to his blankets the poor shelter of her back, as though she had not given him enough, too much already.

Well, we could go naked and cold in a cathedral. There must have been holy fools run skyclad here before. Worse, far worse were the cramps that jerked and twisted my muscles with every step, the pains that danced electric along my nerves, that lashed me from toes to teeth. I know I sobbed, I may have screamed; I must have cursed God and the Devil and all souls trapped between. I felt like Caliban, tormented by cruel Prospero and his untame spirits: a creature of mud and mockery, whose suffering could count for nothing in this mad dash to redemption so why not make him suffer?

Or perhaps it was not so deliberate, perhaps it simply happened, perhaps a human body must bleed and break caught up in so much spirit, too solid to hold together. Perhaps our every cell yearns for disintegration. I cannot tell. I only know that I left bloody footprints smeared in the stone channel where I trod, smeared over gleaming brass where I stumbled. I know that I ached, I hurt, I suffered every step of the way, as though like Christ I shouldered all the sins of the world on my way to a sham Jerusalem, and paid the price of every one.

And my wife was ahead of me, who had suffered too much already; and she held my baby in her arms, whose life had seemed to be a dreary weight of suffering, and I did not think my wife's body was any protection to him. No more was I, I could not even reach them.

BACK and forth, up and down, the path contained within its wider circle: I trod on knives, there was broken glass in every joint and ground glass in every breath, I was buckled and bowed before ever I came to its end, almost crawling by the time I toppled at last into the centre.

Here was blessed stillness, the unblinking eye of the storm, relief from pain; here the spirits fled, were lifted up, were gone to their cheap-bought deliverance, forgiven us and all sins else.

Here I fell full length on ice-cold stone, and for a while only breathed, because I could.

Slowly, slowly I pushed myself up onto trembling hands and knees, crawling for real now; and crawled the little distance to where my wife lay crumpled, collapsed, ripped and raw like the rags still clutched about her, the bundle still held to her belly.

She was breathing too, but barely: the faintest flutter of air at her lips, weak as a dying wick's flicker before it drowns in wax.

Somehow she found enough air, just enough to shape a word, our child's name, no more.

I had to force her hands apart, where her clawed fingers had sunk deep into the tattered tangle of what had been good woollen blankets. *Rigor mortis conturbat me;* it seemed premature, if barely so.

I took the bundle, and unwrapped it.

Looked once, just the once, to see what my wife's desperate miracle had made of her child, ours; and heard the soft rattle of her dying beside me and was glad of it, rejoiced at it almost, that she might never have to face what she had done. A baby's bones are weak, are soft; they can be snapped like candles, or they can be shaped like warm wax, squeezed and moulded.

I cradled what remained, what had been boy as it snuffled at me, as it stirred; and I gazed down at where my wife was slumped and gone, and thought her greedy beyond redemption, though we lay at the heart of the Jerusalem Mile and fresh from a bitter pilgrimage. Some sins, I thought, can never be forgiven. I could hope only that God agreed with me.

DRAGON KINGS PLAY SONGS OF LOVE

R AIN IS THE PROVINCE OF THE dragon king. In days of mud and flood, in days of drought we make procession to his shrine and make offerings, make sacrifice, make ourselves heard if we can. If he does not listen, we take his image and put it out in the roadway, in the hard sun or under the thunder until he will intercede for us. When the rains stop at last or when at last they come, we deck him with flowers and carry him back below his roof, singing him all the way.

SOMETIMES, when the rains have come as they ought or when the summer's light is a kindly fierce shimmer on the waters in the paddy, when we are easy with the gods or they with us, a bonze will come walking over the hills, bareheaded and barefoot. He will squat below the tree at the heart of our village and look to us to feed him, as we do. He will not take shelter even under the headman's roof. Instead he will sit out in rain or sun and cry the praises of the dragon king, saying that we should do the same. We do not need him, we do not heed him, but he is a bonze; we give him rice and greens and palm-heart wine. We give him what time we can spare, a little in the evenings, for him to shout at us.

He is always wet or dirty, often both. While we are working and he is not, out of his hearing and after he is gone, we call him the mudman or the mockman, who does whatever is least wanted. He would fetch water to a river, we say, plant flowers in a meadow. We never see him when the rains are late, or when they last too long and we lose all our harvest. We have no village priest, and do not look for one; we can deal when we need to with the dragon king.

THAT year of change, the rains came on time and filled the lakes, filled the rivers. We planted rice and hoarded all the water that we could. Summer would come, bronze and baking; a long summer would dry the paddy and leave us desperate even before the tax-gatherers came for their share, who shared our crops but never shared our lives.

Long or short, summer would come, but was not here yet. Even the first rice was not cropping; there was precious little in the storage baskets, and we lived off forest gleanings. It was far too soon for gatherers. There had been no runners, no message-birds; no one was watching the road. It was a day like any other, one more day of our ordered lives, quiet under the eye of the August Jade. And then, quite suddenly, it was not.

THEY said I was too old for the forest. They said it respectfully, *you shall not go, not you, it is not fit*; they meant something entirely other, *the forest is for the fleet and fearless, it is for the strong and the sharp-sighted, and you are none of these.*

They said all of that, and it was true besides. So I was in the paddy with the other old women and the little girls, treading dung into mud between the green shoots of our hope and prosperity, and there was only us to see his coming when he came.

He was perhaps not looking for a welcome, looking deliberately to surprise. Unless I give him too much credit. There is the court, and the wiles of the court; and then there are the eunuchs, and the wiles of the eunuchs within the court, and these are boxes within boxes that I played with once, but that was long ago. I may have lost the way of it. At all events he came, the Emperor's eunuch, in all his pomp: not quite his master's pomp, but it might as well have been, played out for peasants.

Sound travels fitfully here in the hills. On the right day, on the right wind a cry will carry clear to the next village; on another day it will be flung back in our teeth, or else it will roll like thunder around our little valley and twist with its own echoes in a skein, turning and turning like fish in a basket. That day no noise would carry through the trees or between the rocks. It waited to run free, perhaps, across the paddy waters and the river pasture; and so we heard nothing until the men were there and filling our roadway, filling our heads with their drumming and their trumpets and their drumming feet.

Now we looked up, startled from our dark reflective waters. We saw the banners first, where they ripped the breeze like the finest and most delicate, most flexible of knives; and the bannermen below, where they ran six abreast with the banner-poles strapped to their backs and whipping to and fro, red and gilt.

Behind the bannermen came the musicians, and the sound of them like another banner, flying over all; then came the soldiers. Six ranks of six, swords at their sides and javelins crossed at their backs, and they ran with that loping trot that eats the miles, that could carry them all the day and half the night in chase of their master's whim. I knew these men, I had known them at the further end of my life, at the further end of the empire; I had never thought to see them here.

They were followed by canopied palanquins in line, curtains swaying against the dust of the road. The largest had eight burly men to bear it and trappings of Imperial yellow, the Emperor's dragon crest rising proud from its roof.

"Oh, is it him?" the little girls, the old women hissed as they gathered around me in the paddy. "Is it the Emperor?"

They moved to kowtow, to fling themselves face down in the muck and water, to drown themselves before their lord. One stupid girl, I had to seize the back of her neck to stop her.

"Himself? Of course not. Do you think he travels so far, and with so few?"

They gaped, that so very many men might be dismissed as so few. "He is in exile, the Emperor, here on Taishu…"

"I know what he is, and where." A boy, fled in fear with nowhere to hide.

"Well then, why not here in the hills? You think yourself too clever, Ma Yi. He could come here. Perhaps his doctors send him from the coast; perhaps his enemies drive him from the city."

"No," though I was less scornful with it. "The Emperor moves with his army; this is nothing. I have seen." I had also seen the line of men who came behind the palanquins. Young men not used to work, not dressed to run: their robes bore yellow ribbons to show who they belonged to, their shaven heads glistened with sweat, their long queues whisked like horses' tails as they struggled to keep pace.

"Run to the forests," I said to the fleetest and sharpest of the girls around me as porters followed, as more soldiers followed them, "run to find the men. Say that guests have come here, from the court."

"Who is it, what do they want, can we say, Ma Yi?"

"You can say the Emperor's chief eunuch is here, with an escort." Why he had come, whom to escort, I would not tell them yet. My message would bring the women too, wives and daughters; more news than this might have them hiding, and who knew, who could say what trouble that would bring? Twice six times six was a great many soldiers.

TWICE six times six and the bannermen, porters and musicians, eunuchs and mandarins too: that was a great many mouths to feed. The soldiers could eat rice, but would want all the rice we had and more besides. The mandarins would be courtly men, with courtly appetites; we scoured each other's memories even as we hurried home. Which of us had buried a pot of pickled cabbage and not yet dug it up, was there meat still smoking in anyone's chimney, whose were the ducks on the pond? Everyone hoarded, openly and in secret; everyone would give up what they had, to save the village. Hungry soldiers would loot our stores, but hungry mandarins might have their soldiers kill.

By the time we reached them, the mandarins had stepped out of their palanquins and were standing in a group below the village tree, where its blossoms gave them shade. The idiot Gao was staring, dribbling; I might have stared myself, we might have stood and stared all in a group at the sight of the Emperor's chief eunuch seated on the headman's stool, on the steps of the headman's hut, talking with Old Grandfather.

It could be one of the old man's better days. At least he had been headman once, before he lost his strength, his strength of mind. And at least he was kneeling in the dust at our visitor's feet, not being familiar. His beard was wagging, but not too much; he might even be listening more than he spoke.

"What should we do, Ma Yi?"

"What we have been speaking of: gather food, and cook. No use a gaggle of women kowtowing to hungry men. Bring towels and scented water to them, where they are. Where are the soldiers?"

"In the river meadow, don't you see, old woman?"

"Old enough that I have seen more than ever you will; small wonder if my eyes are tired now. Take cauldrons and charcoal to the meadow, take all the rice you can. If they see us try so hard, perhaps they will open the porters' sacks; we may end with more than we give up to them."

"Ma Yi!"

That was Old Grandfather's voice, and that was his arm, like a twig in leather, beckoning to me. So at least one woman did kowtow to one hungry, dusty man. I hid my face in the dirt while I listened to that whining, shrilling voice declare my life, like a hand in mah jong.

"Ma Yi is only a peasant, only a woman of this village, but she has been wife to an Emperor!"

"You should explain that, old man." His voice had the eunuch's softness, the unfettered power of the mandarin and the burr of the north, such as I had not heard together for thirty years.

"She was a flower when she was young, Excellence, a songbird, she could dance like a leaf on a breeze." His voice carried truth; he knew, he was old enough to remember. So was I. "Our lord in those days sent her as tribute to the Dragon Throne, where she was wed to the Great Emperor himself, to her eternal honour and our own."

"Indeed? I served as page in the court of the Great Emperor, and I know the list of the names of all his wives. I do not remember Ma Yi on that list."

I lifted my head an anxious hand's breadth from the dust and said, "Forgive him, Excellence. He is inclined to be boastful. I was never wife to the Emperor, but only *kuei jên.*"

"Ah. A concubine, quite so." And the lowest rank of concubine, never elevated, never giving a child to the Throne. I lowered my head, but, "I know the lists of the names of all the concubines, also. I still do not remember Ma Yi."

My head had to rise once more. "The Great Emperor was pleased to call me Xiang Yu, Excellence."

"The Great Emperor was pleased to call several of his girls Xiang Yu, in succession. Well. Perhaps I do remember, then. I never learned their faces." I thought perhaps that I remembered his, now that I could peep at it. Take fifty years away and the boy might still be seen, inquisitive, examining, learning. Remembering.

"When the Great Emperor died," Old Grandfather went wheezing on, learning nothing, "she was sent back to us, with gifts and treasures…"

"Was she so?" I could see him consulting lists in his head, details a long generation old, from the reign of the father of his young master's father. I hoped there were not too many details in his lists, what gifts might have been given to a *kuei jên* dismissed into the world. "One does not expect to find Imperial beauties in a peasant village. Neither Imperial gifts and treasures. I should like to see those, before I leave. Not now. Is that your headman coming?"

"Is it? I expect it is, Excellence, yes…" Old Grandfather would be peering; I could hear rushing feet and voices. I began to shuffle backwards, an old woman feeling very much exposed.

"And is this tea?"

"Yes, yes, Excellence, tea and rice cakes, look…"

"Well. No doubt I can drink it. Ma Yi, stay. You will know what I want, better than anyone here."

"Yes, Excellence." I was sure of what he wanted; I could say it for him, if he told me to. I was half afraid that he would.

WHEN enough stools had been fetched from other huts, the mandarins left the shade of our tree and came to sit in line along the step there, like a court in judgement. All the village had gathered; soldiers came up from the water meadow to keep a clear space before their masters, but they were hardly needed. None of ours was stupid enough to press too close. Some would be wishing they had stayed hidden in the forest. If some were not, I thought they should have been.

The chief eunuch lifted his hand. His voice had the lash of authority, no kindness to it.

"My name is Da Fo, and I speak for the Dragon Throne." He had no need to say it; his robe was a flame to the eye, as yellow as the law allowed. "You will know, your Emperor has come to make his home on this island," *in this benighted peasant country,* his face seemed to be saying, "until the rebels can be destroyed and the Dragon Throne return to the Forbidden City. On his journey here," *in his retreat,* "many of his treasures have been lost or left behind. To his great sorrow, that includes the flowers in his Garden of Felicity." Not his mother, not her attendants; but all his father's other wives and all the concubines, dead or abandoned in the rush and terror of the war or else sold en route, bartered for food or transport or gold to smooth his way. His mother would have arranged it, insisted on it, taken personal care to see that it was done.

"The Emperor is your guest, for this short time; you will see that it is your duty to restore his loss. I am sent to gather fresh blossoms to enchant his eye, to enliven his days and perfume his nights." The Emperor must have a harem, for his honour's sake; he must father sons, for the sake of his dynasty. He was still a boy, but old enough for that. There would be marriages, no doubt; his generals and lordly advisors would be eager to provide daughters. The Son of Heaven needed more, though, he must have women enough to people a city. Hence this travelling party, come to pick the young, the beautiful, the easily trained.

Ours was a small village, a poor village, and daughters came expensive. We had few girls to show him. Some of those were young and would be easily trained; only one was beautiful.

Her name was Mei Mei. Her hair was bright jet to the eye and silk to the fingers; her skin was like buffalo cream, thick and smooth and fragrant. She had grown in our valley like a jewel in the mud, utterly unexpected, an utter delight. All the men wanted her; she was not married yet because her father was a greedy and an indecisive man, who could not choose one offer above another in case a better came tomorrow.

He was trembling even before he led her forward, knowing that the nod would fall on her; knowing too that his frustrated rage would overmaster his fear and his wisdom both.

"Good," Da Fo said, leaning forward on his stool to see more closely. "Very good. The girl is yours?"

"She is, Excellence, my daughter—but she is not, she is not free."

"If she is married," said softly, "where is the husband, and why do you show her to me?"

"Not married, Excellence, no. But she is promised, promised this very day..."

"Ah, today? How inconvenient."

"The Emperor himself would not ask me to break such a promise."

"No, indeed. To whom was this promise made?"

A pause, a short one, while the village drew slow breath; then one of her suitors, fastest or boldest or most stupid, he stepped forward.

"To me, Excellence, the promise is to me."

Da Fo gestured quietly with his left hand. Two soldiers ran forward to seize the man and thrust him to his knees. Forward came another striding, a big man with a bigger sword, the Emperor's headsman.

Where there are no words, there can be no arguments. The air hissed, where the blade cut it; there was a thicker, wetter noise, and then the thud of a weight falling to earth.

"She is not promised now," Da Fo observed. "I made two girls orphan yesterday, before they were given as they should be. Must I do the same here?"

"No, no, Excellence. Now there is no promise, no, take her and welcome, my duty, my honour..."

"Indeed. Is this all?"

"There are no more girls suitable, I regret, Excellence," the headman stammered at his back.

"Very well. I am hungry now. We will eat, and sleep the night here. These hills make slow travelling; it will be some weeks before I reach the end of my mission, and can return to take the girl. In the meantime, I will leave one of my servants to watch over her."

To be sure her father didn't hide or steal her away, he meant—though that would mean death to half the village, and we were not fools enough to allow it. We would watch her ourselves, and watch him too.

IN the morning they left to a muted pulse of drumming, the rhythm of their trotting feet, no trumpets now. They left us hungrier than we had been, and more afraid; they left one man to be buried, another bereft, several with their hopes in ashes; and they left one more, one of their own, a lad called Lin. He was a eunuch, of course, he had to be, half guard and half body servant. He took Mei Mei out of her father's hut, and had the men repair an old shack at the further end of the river meadow where the two of them could live isolated from the village until his master should return to claim them.

Isolated from the village, not from me. I was a woman, and I had been *kuei jên* twenty years in the Garden of Felicity, where nothing ever changes. That was longer than he had been alive. I knew more than Mei Mei could learn from him if he had her for as long again. To his credit, he understood that, and allowed that I should live out those weeks with them. I could cook and clean, play servant, teach Mei Mei to be waited on; between us we could begin to teach her how to offer pleasure to an Emperor.

SHE was young so she was foolish, but she was no fool. She learned quickly. In the first days she was frightened, as she should be; she had the blind resilience of youth, though, and had never been afraid of me. No one could fear the gentle Lin. By the end of one week she was easy in this brief new world, between one life and another. By the end of two, it seemed too short for her. We all three slept together in the hut's one room, and every day she woke earlier, more eager for her lessons. At night, often and often I would rouse to hear murmurs in the darkness, her soft tones and his.

In daylight she was discreet, or tried to be. She hid her smiles behind her hand as a modest girl ought, and spoke little when I was in hearing. Her eyes she could not hide, though. They said too much as they followed Lin, sometimes shy and secretive, sometimes challenging; when she and I were alone they would search for him, down at the river's bank or out across the meadow. To find him was a joy, transparent, shining.

At last, I had to speak myself. I said, "You are a fool to dream, girl, and he a cruel fool to encourage you. That is no man, nor even a boy; he is a eunuch, and he belongs to the Emperor."

"And I to him."

"No, foolish; you also to the Emperor. And if you were free, both of you free, he would still be a eunuch. I should have him show you that."

"I have seen."

"Have you indeed?" With her fingers, she must mean, in the darkness while I slept. "Then why carry the sky in your eyes over such a scantling? You know you can never belong to him."

"I can be with him. That is all I want."

"If that is true, be easy. He can serve you all your life in the Garden, if you ask it; and if you are sent away as I was, he may be sent with you if you beg. Enough of touching, though, enough whispers in the night. You are not wise enough to hide from me; how can you hope to keep a secret from the Son of Heaven?"

"Ma Yi, there must be women in the Garden who have loved like this…"

"Hopelessly, absurdly? Yes, of course." So many women, and the Emperor so scarce—how not? How not to love even half a man, a hollow man, a shadow?

"How do they survive it?"

"By patience, day by day and every day. To love, yes, that is permitted; that is a nothing. Never to touch, though, never to play at man and woman. For that, he dies quickly; you more slowly. I have seen."

She shuddered, but not I thought for fear of the torture. Fear of not touching, more likely. Fear of burying love for a lifetime while she saw him daily, while he attended her while a thousand eyes were watching.

"I do not, I cannot bear…"

"Child, of course you can. We are women, you and I. We can bear anything that men may bring us, and more besides. They are stones, and we are water; they break, where we endure."

"But Lin—"

"Lin is not a man, either. He will not break."

"I do not want to live that way."

"Mei Mei, your only choice would be to die, and to see him die first. One is dead already over you; two more deaths would disturb no one's sleep, beyond this valley."

"We could run away."

"You could; and they would hunt you down, and find you, and kill you then."

"I think I would rather die, than live as you have told me."

"Would you? That is your childhood speaking, when death was a beautiful dream you knew from stories. You saw it truly this last winter, when you helped me wash Xiao-Yueh's boy-child that died of the cold; you saw it just weeks ago, when Da Mien was executed for your father's lie. You walked through death to meet this Lin, it was puddled in the blood around your feet. Death is a hard and an ugly thing, Mei Mei. Better to let love smother and live as you are told to."

She had no words to answer me; but those eyes, as ever her eyes spoke for her. Sorrowful, desperate, yearning—I did not trust those eyes, neither the mind behind them.

LIN was worse. Mostly he would only shake his head and smile, while his thin fingers stroked his shaven skull. When he did speak, what he said was useless.

"I have been ten years in the clouds, Ma Yi, and she has lifted me above. She is my moon and stars."

"You will be ten thousand years in the ground, and no stone to say that you are there. We will root rice between your ribs."

"That would not be so bad. We could feed all your village, she and I."

"You could kill all my village, before you kill yourselves. You have seen death, Lin—"

"Too much to think that it can matter. And perhaps not enough love, Ma Yi. It does not flourish, in the Emperor's gardens."

"Faugh! Another dreamer. Better for you, better for all of us if it withers here also. There is nothing, else."

He held his hands out, to show that they were empty. "What need more?"

"Mei Mei might need more. What if she wants what a eunuch cannot give her?"

"There are always babies their parents do not want or cannot feed. We will raise girl-children, and be thanked for it."

"And how will you feed them? How will you feed yourselves, where will you live? Where do you think you can hide, from the Son of Heaven or from his soldiers?"

He shrugged, he smiled, he stroked his skull; he looked around for Mei Mei.

ONE morning in the third week, I left him teaching her the Imperial flowers and their perfumes, what was fit for *kuei jên* to wear. I went into the village to find what food there was, and to hear any word of the chief eunuch's returning.

No message, the headman said, but there was meat; the men had slain a farrowing sow in the forest. They gave me a piglet, baked in clay. I carried that in triumph to our little hut, to find it empty.

Perhaps Lin had taken the girl into the forest, to show her the flowers and how they were scented; but what did he know of forests, who had only lived in a garden? She would be wiser than him, out there. And not wise enough, the two of them together did not have the wisdom of the idiot Gao, who at least knew to go where he was taken and to stay where he was left.

I was not idiot enough to go after them. Let anyone find me searching, hear me call, and all the village would know that they were gone. I could not save them then, I could not save myself.

The first day, the first night I hoped they might return. Even the old can be foolish, can be hopeful; even the young can find hunger and fear and rain too much to bear in the long night. I let a light burn late behind the door, but no one came.

The second day I sat in the hut and ate cold suckling pig: not waiting now but only thinking, and sometimes not thinking either.

On the third day, I took my old broom and went out into the forest myself, but not to search.

THE track is steep, up to the dragon king's shrine. That day, the rain trickled down it like a gutter. I took it slowly, using my broom as a crutch. When I came under his roof I stood there gasping, no more breath in my body than I had offerings in my hands. I showed him that, stretching them wide and empty; then I knocked over the little table before him, where old cakes had dried beneath his glare. His paint might be cracked and peeling, but his glare seemed ever fresh.

I glared back, and looked from him to the roadway, a long fall below. I could not carry him so far; likely I could not carry him at all. I might push and roll him over, but he would only tangle in some green creeper, beyond hope of my retrieval.

Instead I stood and railed at him, like a scolding bird. I turned the broom in my hands and began to strike upwards, knocking out the tiles of his roof so that they slid down and fell heavily into the mud. Where they fell on each other, they split and flindered.

Some days a voice is swallowed altogether by the forest; sometimes it is hurled up and down the valley, and out into the hills. That day, that voice, my shrill and furious voice was heard everywhere. Hunters came from the trees, women came from the paddy, children came from where they had been grubbing for roots and insects in the mud.

They stood and stared at me; some moaned and hugged themselves for fear of my madness. At last the headman came. He said, "Ma Yi, what are you doing?"

"You should ask him," I gasped, "the dragon king, what is he doing? Help me carry him down to the roadway, let the rain have him, he shows no care of us…"

"This is foolishness. It should rain now, and it is raining; why do you complain? Why do you break his house, where he is watching us?"

"Because he is not watching. A leaking roof will wake anyone, a little cold rain in the night will stir his heart, perhaps, if you will not help me put him in the flood."

"We have no need to wake him; you will only make him angry. Are you mad?"

"No," I said, knowing that he would not believe me.

"Then get you back to Mei Mei and the eunuch, you should be serving them, not making a noise like a screech-monkey on the mountain. Someone see her down the hill, and chase her home. We will patch his roof with fronds, until fresh tiles can be shaped and baked…"

WELL, they might try. It was raining; it would rain harder. We had all tried to live under forest thatch when the typhoon took our good roofs away. The god was wet, and would be getting wetter. Good.

I suffered my escorts down to the meadow, then scared them off with dreadful hints of what Lin might be teaching Mei Mei, and how specific the Emperor's vengeance would be if they spied on his concubine at her lessons. Left alone, I sat over my pot of pork and plotted, much like the mad old woman they thought me.

In the afternoon I gathered greens where they were sprouting by the river. Someone would be watching me; they should have something to report. Besides, too much meat is heavy on the stomach.

Heavy on the mind, also: it was surely that which kept me wakeful all the night, and not worry about two children out in the darkness, in the rain. I was only angry with them, heedless and headstrong as they were. Love is not blind but blindfold, and lovers bind their own eyes, not each other's.

Tired to the bone of me, I was up before the sun and trudging up to that same shrine again, bowed beneath the rain in my old wide hat and cape. The track was more stream than gutter now; I had my broom again, and needed it.

When I reached him, I found the old god sat clean beneath a drip, where it struck his forehead every few moments and ran down into his eyes.

"Well, that should have your attention. Here…" The broom knocked away the rough thatch above his head, where I had made a hole before. Rain came in, of course, more than before, but I thought that might be better than a drip. "Now listen," I said, and talked to him as I used to, long ago.

He sat and listened, I think he listened while the birds and small creatures sang the dawn around us, while the smells of sodden forest rose to greet us, while his ancient paintwork glistened wetly in the coming light.

Then I turned and looked down at the road and further down, down to the roofs of the village and further still, the little hut in the meadow and the running river, the far bank and the rising valley and all the high hills beyond. The light was grey and wet, no sun this dawn but something was on its way there from the east, pushing over the hills, running almost to find us.

It was a shadow against the sky, no solid shape or substance: a squall of rain, perhaps, some stray finger of a storm, but it moved against the wind and with a certain purpose. I knew what, I knew who it was. I could see him in its shifts, constant as himself is constant, ever-changing and always there: some momentary figure of a man at speed, a reared horse but then a hint of wings, of flame in all that wind and water, just a glimpse of dragon.

And yet it was still wind and water, a pocketful of storm. It hit the valley with the voice of its own thunder, its noise overflowed us; it ripped a path across the valley floor, leaving a trail of gouged earth and splintered trees. It broke our paddy walls, our careful terracing, because there is always a price to be paid.

When it had destroyed the paddy, it tore through the water meadow and destroyed our little shack; then came back to the river, and dissolved. The river had been running high and muddy in any case. Now it burst its dykes, overran the meadow, washed all traces of the hut away. It must be lapping around the village too, but we knew its sudden tempers; all our houses there were built on legs.

I was trembling a little on my own legs, but I had strength enough and manners enough to turn and bow my thanks to him where he sat there, under his roof, in his own rain. Later I would weave him garlands of spring flowers; all summer I would bring him rice-cakes and palm wine. And perhaps go on, high into the hills with rice-cakes and wine, to see how far I could go and whom I could find on the way.

THE chief eunuch came down the road that same day, with half a dozen hill-girls in his long train. He could not come into the village, there was too much water yet; but the headman showed where the shack had stood, and told how men were searching downstream for the bodies. Da Fo grunted, but did not condemn. He was perhaps content with my treasures, that he took as our gift to the Emperor; one girl and a eunuch boy were no great loss between them, and it was always wiser not to tread on the gods' sensitivities.

THE people of the village are stranger with me now. Not rougher, but more wary. They think I am an old mad woman, only that. They think what they know is the only thing to be known, that dragon kings are gods for them to worship, gods of tides and seasons and great moment. Which they are, but love too has its season and its strength. Love is a rain, a tempest, a dissolution; and rain, rain is the province of the dragon king.

FOR KICKS

A MYSTERY STORY

N OT DIFFICULT TO TRACE HER PATH across gravel and grass, to read the story of her passing. Not difficult, no—but God, it was hard.

Hard just to stand and look, to do it privately in his head. Harder still to do it all aloud, to make it real for others as it was already far too real for him.

To say, *Look, here is where she was kicked the first time. Kicked and kicked, just here.* And, *See this, see? This is where she crawled to, before he came back and kicked her again.*

God knows why she didn't die, he said, *she was meant to. But oh, she's tough,* too tough, he thought, *brilliant girl, she hung on somehow. Look, see, here she grabbed the railing, hauled herself up. Forgot where she was, maybe. Saw the river and just droppped back, though,* and who could blame her? No blame if she'd wriggled under the railing and gone head first into the water. *When she moved again she went the other way, up onto the bank there, you can see the trail she left,* blood and bent grass and the red stone deeply stained. *That's where *we found her,* unconscious, seven or eight hours after she'd first been kicked; and she hadn't woken up since and wasn't likely to, the doctors said, amazing that she was still alive at all. Only their machines to keep her so, to do her breathing for her.

And she was seventeen years old, and that was the story of her night out, as far as they could piece it together from the waymarks that she'd left; and Christ, but it was hard to tell it.

HE sent them off then, these young constables, to make their enquiries door-to-door; and one word of advice he sent with them. "Don't make a mystery out of this," he said. "Don't expect it to come out like the books. It won't. Nothing clever, no smart boys wanted. It's drudge-work will solve this one. The better you do it, the quicker we can wrap this up and get warm again."

Oh, he was cold and getting colder: exposed now, with the youngsters dispersed and the forensics team peeling off their coveralls and packing up their sheeting, giving back the land. He stood and watched them drive away, and thought he should be going too. Nothing useful he could do here, plenty to do elsewhere. But the wind's bite couldn't move him yet.

Someone had set a sculpture here, between the housing estate and the river: a sandstone archaeology, inherent with contradictions. It was a ruin recently made, the broken eroded shell of an old house to set against the hard finished angles of the new. This was where the girl had crawled to. Looking to find help, perhaps, all she'd found was some thin shelter from the weather, not enough.

Once there'd been shipyards all along this bank. That's what he remembered. Cranes' shadows stretched further than height and sun would suggest; the hooter's blast still echoed in his head at least, though the last of the yards was gone.

History was important. You couldn't escape history, and you couldn't defy it. There'd been housing here before the shipyards were ever built; one demolition followed another, and none of them mattered in the long run. What goes around, comes around. History moves in cycles. Pointless, even wishing to frustrate an inevitable machine...

As he rubbed with his thumb at a sandstone picture on a sandstone mantelpiece, a little piece flaked and fell away. He snatched back his guilty hand, absurdly feeling that it was history itself he was diminishing here; and was almost glad to let his eyes find that darker stain again, where the girl had bled on the stone.

THE father sat at the bedside, hunched and trembling. His skin was grey, his eyes watered; his hand reached constantly towards his daughter, reached and reached and never quite made it. Shaking fingers rested on the sheet just an inch short of her, too afraid to touch.

A restless tide had carried the mother over to the window, then ebbed and left her stranded. Narrow hips perched on the narrow sill, she stared out through the blind, not to see again what an ungentle world had made of her only child.

Better for them if she'd died outright, he thought as he watched them, as he watched the damage happen. Better that than this, waiting endlessly for an end to hope, far too long delayed.

Pulling up a chair beside the father, playing detective, he said, "One thing, if we could just get this sorted. The doctors say she's got other marks on her, older, five or six days old. Wouldn't know how she got those, would you?"

"Marks?"

"Bruises, mostly. Been knocked about a bit, she has."

"You want to ask her boyfriend about that."

"I'm asking you."

The father turned his head then, looked at him, looked away. "You want to ask the boyfriend."

The mother said nothing at all.

ALWAYS come back to what you've got, they used to tell him. So here he was, walking the riverside again. The wind had changed; it was at his back now, pushing and nudging but cold still, bitter still. *Plus ça change,* he thought wearily. Here it came again, that feeling of inevitability. Enough to make anyone cold, the sense of being only a fleeting ghost in the machine, too quickly gone and changing nothing.

Still, as well to make his body work a little. He wouldn't like to have things too easy, here where it had gone so hard with her.

Down in the dock, yachts rubbed keels with fishing boats, and he wondered how much damage a man could do with a pair of deck shoes. Not enough, at a guess. They were talking boots here, they were surely talking boots. What did fishermen wear on their feet?

Past the dock, past the housing estate was an office development with clever gates, whimsical gates designed to look open when they were shut and locked. They should have been shut and locked well before the girl went out looking for kicks, but that needed checking. If someone had been working late—some young man, say, with fashionable boots—then someone else would know.

He looped back around the unfinished estate, where some houses were only breeze-block shells with bricks growing up for cover, red to hide the grey; and grey was the colour of her father's face and red was the colour of her blood, and could it have been the father did this thing? Fathers had done worse before. Maybe that's why he was shaking.

No constable on guard now, no gawking civilians, no one to show where they'd found her. Nor any need. She'd made these stones her own, signed them with more courage than blood. And she was only a little thing, and he admired her so much; and couldn't say so, he could only hold it as a secret, a private pride in a client who had done marvellously better than anyone had any right to expect.

He tried to think of her coming along here alone and in the dark, and couldn't do it. Few enough reasons for a hard-booted stranger to be doing that, none at all for her. So she'd come with someone. Statistically likely candidates, father or boyfriend: and boyfriend surely more likely, a girl didn't often go out walking with her father. Not at night, not at seventeen.

THE boyfriend was all cropped hair and tattoos, no surprise; and the father must have looked just the same when he was younger.

"Knock her about a bit, did you, lad? Last week, I mean, not last night?"

"Nah, not me."

"Someone did."

"That'll be her dad," he said. "On her all the time, her dad. But so what, anyway? What about the bastard did her over, that's your job."

I think all you bastards did her over. Over and over, that's how I think you did her...

TALKING to a girlfriend:

"Yeah, they did, they beat her up. Both of 'em. Not together, like, but they both did it."

"Why did she put up with it?"

"Nowhere else to go, was there? Home's home."

"She could have stopped seeing her boyfriend."

"Aye, she said that. She said she was going to finish with him, maybe."

"Uh-huh," and another motive, another reason to get kicked, if she wanted to kick him. If she told him. "Have anyone else in mind, did she?"

"There was this lad, yeah. Don't know if she ever went out with him, like, but she wanted to..."

NOT hard, to find the other lad. The girlfriend had his name. Feed that into the computer, and bingo: an address, a record, a brand-new theory.

And a sad sigh, a shake of the head, *Oh, lass, lass. Why did you keep doing this to yourself? Why do it over and over again?*

Because she was seventeen, of course, and she thought she would always heal. She thought she was immortal. Didn't they all?

The record said here was another guy who knew how to use his feet, all the way from common assault to GBH. Nine months in prison for that one, and he'd only been out for three; and the address was a flat just over the road from the new estate, only five minutes' walk from where they'd found her.

SO a hard knocking, fist on wood, and then a foot in the door as soon as it opened; and because he was watching his feet, he saw this lad's feet as well.

Saw big shiny paratrooper boots, excellent for kicking but not a scuff, not a mark on them; and swore silently as he flashed his ID.

The lad bridled without conviction, flexed his tattoos uncertainly.

"Nice boots, son. New, are they?"

"Yeah. Yeah, they are. Got 'em in the market. Good, eh?" And he wasn't challenging, he wasn't confrontational, he wasn't right at all.

"Terrific. So what have you done with the old ones, then? Have a look at them, can I?"

"Nah, they're gone. Put 'em out with the rubbish, like…"

Uh-huh. That meant a happy day or two for a vanload of constables, sifting through shit on the council dump. And all a waste of time, because those boots wouldn't be there, they'd be in the river. If they went in at the right time, just at the turn, they'd be halfway to Norway by now.

HE took the lad in anyway, on general principles and utter personal certainty. No charge of charging him without a confession, and no real chance of that; but a man could dream. And he had it in his dreams that if by some fluke this ever did come to court, he'd want to say to the judge something that judges had all too often, all too outrageously said for themselves:

She was asking for it, your honour, he'd want to say, and would never have the chance. *That's why she got herself into this. For kicks, for the kickings. It's all she knew, you see, it's the only way she had to measure affection. Everyone who ought to love her beat her up. That's what love was, what it meant. So the worse she caught it, the better she was doing. The more the bastard loved her, do you see?*

TAKING a break from the interview room, from the sound of his own voice hammering against a sullen silence, he walked through the story one more time. The wind threw a hard rain against big signs as he passed, *Development Corporation* and *European Funds*, all the machinery that kept a battered city breathing against the odds.

What goes around comes around, he thought, like bad music snagged in the head, repeating and repeating. History marches with its boots on, and always in circles. Why kick against it?

Walking in circles, he came to that sculpture again, red stone more deeply stained with red. Weather would see to that, he thought, no need for scrubbing brushes. Weather was time's tool, and irresistible. Some day too soon there'd be nothing left of her bar the husk of her body in a hospital bed, maintained by vigilant machines.

And one of these days—when it was politic, when it was advisable—they were going to turn off the machines.

PARTING SHOTS

WHEN YOU'RE BURYING A MAN, YOU can give a lot of time to what he wears, how he looks, what he takes with him. That last, especially. You don't have to get all Ancient Egyptian on his ass, he's probably not Tutankhamun, but—well, it's a thing. You can do it.

US, we stood around his bed and cracked a litre of Stolichnaya. Shot-glasses straight from the freezer, the way he'd taught us all to drink it: we drank him a toast of parting shots, wetted his forehead, opened his wardrobes and set to work. Dressing Miss Daisy, Micky called it.

We'd already washed and shaved him, we were good at that; it was routine, we'd been doing it a year already. I would've liked to have his hair cut, but none of us was competent with scissors and who can you ask, to do that? We were sending him on shaggy, then—but we did touch up his roots, not to let him go greyly.

Underwear was simple, a pair of his favourite Calvins; he'd seen a banned advert once, dissolved into hysterical lust and never wore anything else after. Clean black jeans and a silk shirt, the Issey Miyake jacket with the mandarin collar that he loved, all of that was straightforward.

We argued over footwear, because he hated his smart shoes. For preference he went around in sandals and socks, and we all hated that and always had. He'd have been thrilled, to know that we were still fighting over his feet. In the end, we decided he could go barefoot. Clouds are fluffy, and the road to hell is notoriously well-paved; he'd be fine, either way.

We crossed his legs for comfort—"sorted for ease," Sally said—and because we were all settling in to make a night of it, and because he'd always been a crusader. We laid his hands across his belly, fingers linked, because he used to do that when he was drunk or tired or bored enough, when he was just sitting back and listening while we bickered and flirted and debated great matters all around him, and you'd think we did it entirely for his amusement. Likely we did.

Then it was all about decoration. His favourite rings, that had grown too heavy for his fingers: they could go back on now, the jet and the jade and the skull-knuckle silver ring. They were too loose, but that didn't matter any more. He wouldn't be flinging his hands around to make his points again, his stillness did that for him.

No watch—he used to say there never was that much hurry, that a man had to carry the time on his person; and I never knew him late, though it was odd how often the rest of us turned out to be early—but we plaited leather thongs around his wrist, and each of us tied a knot in the trailing ends to hold them.

Around his throat, what he liked to call his giveaway: "I'm a creature of the seventies," he used to say, "medallion man to the core." Only his medallion hung on a fine silver chain and was silver itself, a moon in crescent, the bulk of its disc black and secret, with just that sliver shining. He loved that.

A silver Bajoran cuff on his right ear, with the finest imaginable chain linking it to the sleeper in the lobe. In his left, a stud of white gold, which was all the gold he ever had or wanted: one of a pair, and these days Gerard wore the other. Gerard wasn't there. He'd given this to us to do, which was either acutely generous or an acute surrender, and I wasn't sure which.

We'd already ruled out a post-mortem tattoo, even if we could have found someone to ink it. We had discussed it, though. He'd have liked that.

Nothing left, then, bar what went into his pockets or into the coffin with him. Much of that was standard, those things he always used to carry in his jeans when he was still able for it, when he was up and about: his purse with all his credit cards in case he needed money, house keys in case he wanted to come home. A corkscrew, a toothpick. Loose change. He liked to jingle a little as he went.

In his right-hand outer jacket pocket, a fresh pack of Winstons and a lighter, because he hadn't been able to smoke for a long time now and he'd want that; left-hand outer pocket, a flask of Lagavulin. The last thing he drank in this life, first drink in the next.

Left-hand inner pocket, a wallet of photographs: his mum, his sister, us. Some of us individually or in twos and threes, the ones he'd taken himself; and then the team photo, all of us together at the foot of his bed on the day he came home from hospital, the day we started nursing him ourselves. All of us bar him. He took photographs, he didn't appear in them. He used to say he wasn't interested in how he looked to other people, only in how they looked to him. It wasn't true, of course, which is why he found it necessary to invent.

Right-hand inner pocket, his passport. We'd renewed that for him just six months ago, when he was long past leaving his bed. He'd need it now, wherever he was going.

In the same pocket, because every journey involves longeurs, he'd want a book. We gave him—no, we let him keep his copy of *Religio Medici,* a slim Victorian edition with the leather long since worn to a butter softness. That'd see him through.

Tucked under his arm, of course, a cuddly toy. How not, when it would infuriate him to find her there? Besides, she had a function: this was Vespa, the vast fluffy wasp we'd bought him years back and hung on the back of his door to remind him never to go out without his epinephrine.

THAT, of course, was the moment that Alix yelped, and scurried out of the room; and came back a minute later, blushing and laughing, with his EpiPen in her hand. We'd almost sent him off without it.

SO that went into his jacket pocket with the fags, because there was nothing he liked better than a smoke after a crisis; and then we were done. The vodka was gone, but hey, there's always another bottle. And this was a wake and a houseparty and, what, did anybody imagine we were going to *bed* tonight…?

AT some uncertain time during that long night, when the others were all out in the kitchen, concocting some witches'-brew punch to welcome Gerard home, I slipped into the front room—laughingly renamed the parlour, just for the occasion, because that's what he would have done—and I added one little memento of my own, slipping it into his pocket with the rest of his loose change. My lucky silver dollar, that I'd been carrying since I was thirteen, since my astronomer-uncle sent it to me from Mount Palomar: the design showed an eagle with an olive-branch in its claws, descending on the moon. It was a sharp counterpoint to his own moon-medallion, and I wanted him to have something that would hurt one of us, at least.

LATER we gave Gerard some time with him alone, while we went out walking in the dawn mist and the chill of it, climbing a hill and passing a bottle from hand to hand, drinking one more toast on the summit. And then—at last, too soon, whichever, both—it was properly tomorrow, and we had to let him go. See him off. We had to be good in public, dress as sober as he was and act as quiet in church and at the graveside and over sandwiches and squash in the church hall after. His sister presided, while his mother sat quiet and proud and miserable in her wheelchair at a table in the corner. One by one we all went over to do the dutiful by him as well as her, listening to her and failing utterly to recognise her son in anything she said.

And when that was over, we could go home and there could be wine in plenty or whisky for those that wanted it, the rest of that bottle of Lagavulin; and it turned out that I was the only one who wanted it, so I did that, I applied myself to what I wanted most.

Then Tig started rolling joints and sending them around, clockwise and anticlockwise each in turn, so I got them coming and going; and eventually between the whisky and the dope it was me that was going, losing contact, drifting hard.

AND when I was roused, when Gerard roused me everyone else had gone, seemingly; and he said, "Not so much a wake, more a sleep, eh? Bed for you, sweets. I've made up the spare, so shift yourself."

So I did that, I shifted myself upstairs: through the bathroom on auto-pilot, toothbrush and towel, and so to the little boxroom where I must have dossed a hundred times when we were sharing shifts, while he was slowly slowly dying in the room below, breathing no more than a leaf breathes, heedless and fractional.

I tumbled into bed and slept, or passed out if you're not polite; and woke in the deep dark, to a terrible sense of presence.

I hadn't thought to pull the curtains, and I could see him, almost, as a shadow against the stars; I hadn't closed the window either, and I could smell him like rain on the road outside, like the risen roots of matter.

I lay very still and didn't speak, didn't breathe; felt watched, watched over, not free after all. As though there were still expectations, and I had better not disappoint.

And then he was gone and I could breathe again, like a child at Christmas who has been desperate not to let his father guess that he was still awake, not to spoil an adult's pleasure in a supposed secret; and I was still dizzy unless I was dizzy again, and I went spinning away again into incoherent dreaming, and didn't wake again till it was full day.

AND when I did, when I roused and sat up and fumbled for my glasses on the bedside cabinet, the first thing I found was my lucky silver dollar, laid gently down for my fingers to discover, clean and cool and misted with the breath of leaves.

A FOLD IN THE HEART

"I DON'T UNDERSTAND," SHE SAID, GAZING DISCONTENT-EDLY around the churchyard, "why we always want to hold on to everything, regardless. We don't even let our dead go, for God's sake."

I said nothing, I who had spent a long year trying to hold on to the living, and failing badly. I had an urn full of ashes in my wardrobe and no idea, none, what to do with it: only that I couldn't let it go.

Rowan was—well, sometimes I called her my favourite niece, sometimes my goddaughter. Neither was actually true, but she was the first child of old friends and she mattered to me more than blood, far more than belief.

She said, "I want a woodland burial, a woven wicker coffin, no marker. Just stick a tree on top of me and forget which one it was."

"I could bury you at sea," I said cheerfully. "Sewn into a hammock, with cannonballs at your feet to hold you down."

"Hey. Can you actually do that?"

"Sure. I'd need a licence, and I was joking about the hammock, you have to have a coffin weighted with steel and concrete, but it's doable if you want it."

She thought about it, as we clambered over the stile into the ninety-acre field; then she shook her head. "Nah. I never did like boats that much. Or fish. Sorry, I know I'm a disappointment."

"You are that. Trees it is, then. I can't promise to forget where we plant you, but I'll make sure your parents don't put in a rowan."

"That would be tacky," she agreed. "Something to grow old and bent and hoary, please. No good for building boats. I don't want you cutting me down for parts."

"Pity. You'd make excellent planking: long and straight and lissome."

I stuck my elbow out, as I used to do. Obligingly, she slipped her arm through mine as we plodged through heavy wet turf in patproof wellies. There was no beaten path between the stile and the sea-cliff. This was cow-pasture; we took a different route every time, veering around new pats and high-stepping over old ones. Even in wellingtons. Even so, there was a mid-point, a waymarker that was hard to avoid. From the stile to the sheepfold, from the fold to the sea: it was native, inherent, absolute. A given.

When she was little, the fold meant a break in our journey, a necessary pause while she clambered over dry stone walls and played king-of-the-castle on top of its walls, hide-and-seek within them, while we made up stories about wizards snared in lonely towers and the brave princesses who came to rescue them. In later years she'd join local kids and visitors in rowdy games of tag or kiss-chase where the fold was always home, safe ground.

Now that she was grown, now that I was far beyond rescuing and she wouldn't dream of running from a kiss, she laid a hand on the upper coursework and said, "Someone's been working on this." Almost accusatory, as though it should properly have been left in the state of half-collapse that she remembered.

A sheepfold in a cow-pasture has no obvious purpose, and more enemies than time; but even so. "People do," I said mildly. "Every now and then a lad gets interested, wants to know how to wall. There's always a farmer willing to teach him. This is where they learn. Cows are always rubbing their arses on it, knocking stones off. Sometimes they bring down a whole corner, over time. Well, you know; you've seen it at its worst. Then it's a job of work to put it back up again. But it does get done." There hadn't been sheep on this land for a hundred years or more, but the fold was here yet, blunt grey walls in a green field.

She grunted, a little sceptical, and leaned her own arse against a hip-high wall as if tempted to give it a nudge, see if she could knock off a coping-stone.

Her eyes on the horizon, she said, "Tell me about Bruce."

"Tell you what about Bruce? You knew him all your life."

She said, "Yeah, but I was a kid and he was an old man, and—well, you know. Not at all grandfatherly. He really didn't want me in the yard, where I had to be watched all the time because of the tools, and—"

"And that took my eye off him and my mind off the work, and he didn't like either of those, no. And he didn't want you in the cottage either, because you were too loud and again, my eye off him. It wasn't you as such, just kids in general. Just anyone in general, he didn't much like me having friends around either."

"Right. I didn't really get that when I was little, but later I did. When I was a teen, I mean, and he still didn't want me there."

"And you still came, so bless you for that."

And she came to his funeral too, by herself, which might almost have been her first truly adult act; and I might have seized the moment to say so, except that she pre-empted me. "It was toxic, though, wasn't it? He was just controlling your life, and I don't see how you could let him do that."

Of course she didn't. She was twenty, and free in ways that I had never been; and his being dead didn't change a thing. I said, "Toxic maybe—but people say that about tomatoes, potatoes, just because they're the same family as nightshade. Poison is as poison does; whole civilisations have been built on potatoes. Bruce was never easy, but he took a feral kid at risk of growing into pond scum, and he made something decent out of me. By his lights, and my own," which in fairness were entirely of his making, indistinguishable. He'd trained me in more than joinery and sailcraft.

"Oh, you're better than decent. You are. But even so. You shouldn't ever have let him dominate you that way."

"Sweetheart, I'm not even going to pretend I had a choice. That's how dominance works; you don't elect it, you don't get to vote it down. And I remain grateful. Best thing that ever happened to me."

"The only thing that ever happened to you, more like. You lived the life he chose, and you still do. His boatyard, his business. His cottage."

"Mine, now. He took over my life, sure—when it wasn't worth anything, except to him. He gave it value. He gave me everything; which is fair trade, it seems to me, for everything he took."

She sniffed. "I still think he groomed you."

"Of course he did. I was fifteen when he took me in. Nothing but clay, ready to be made into whatever he wanted. He was forty," and the strength in his hands, in his will—I could shudder yet, just at the memory. "Twenty-five years, love, it's a lethal distance. I never stood a chance."

"That's the distance between you and Josh," she said, eyeing me a little sideways.

"It is—and between you and me, that too. But you were never clay. We took care of that. By the time you were fifteen, you were sharpened steel. As for Josh, well. I didn't know him at fifteen. He came to me fully formed." All of twenty, like herself: which was why she'd swallow the lie, because she believed it wholeheartedly of herself.

She nodded and stood up, ready to go on. Holding her hand out, not ready to go on without me.

"Not yet," I said, smiling. Leaning on the wall of the fold. "Dusk is coming. Things are about to get noisy."

She blinked, looking up a little wildly into the empty sky. "Oh—are they still here?"

"Not all of them; but Easter's early this year, and they haven't all gone. Still enough left to make a noise."

"Oh, lovely…"

She perched again beside me and we watched the sky, the sea, the boats, the horizon until they came.

From October through April, the starlings gather in great roosts along the cliffs and inland, on church roofs and pub window-ledges, on every tree that offers. In daylight they scatter, to forage in smaller flocks all across the parish and further yet; as the sun sets they all converge, to wheel and dance and display in extravagant, astonishing flights that write patterns in the air. The world calls it a murmuration. *The noisy sky*, Rowan had called it once when she was little. That worked for us: noise in three dimensions, figured by forces far beyond the random. White noise loosed into the world, given shape and substance and a name.

We watched it happen, we saw the sky fold itself in sheets and curves and angles, in blasts of sound and shadow that gave momentary solidity to the wind, as though they outlined all its fluid edges.

There's a native human urge to see patterns in what's random, to give significance to what is incidental. We have a word for it, even. We see shapes in clouds and call it pareidolia, as though we understood it. As though there were anything to understand.

If I saw faces, one face, making itself again and again and again—well, nobody could blame me. Besides, I didn't need to say what I was seeing, so long as I didn't ask her.

At last the light began to fail and the birds spread themselves more thinly, diving this way and that, tearing themselves out of all coherence. We stirred, gathered each other silently and tromped on arm in arm again, and here came the cliff-edge.

"Careful now," I said, pulling free and guiding her behind me. "The council's done nothing to make this path any safer, and the cliff-face is still crumbling."

"Of course it is. It's not going to stop, just because a parish council finds it inconvenient. Or expensive. I'll step where you step." She put both hands on my shoulders, to be sure. When she was small we'd go down just like this, except the other way around: I'd set her in front and steer her slender frame, keep fast hold and think how fragile she was, and how robust. She could outlive any boat that left the yard, and I knew exactly how well those were put together.

Down and down, winding back and forth until we came to where the path splays out onto the beach. It is, in honesty, not much of a beach. More rock-pool than sand, and more simple rock than either one; at high tide there's a bare margin between sea and cliff, at spring tides none at all. Tourists head to the other side of the bay, to the wide sprawling spaces and the cafés and the tat. Ramblers following the coast find their way down sometimes, if they're serious, but mostly not.

Which suited me, because at the end of the beach, in that marginal questionable territory where the river runs into the sea, just on the point there was my yard. Formal access came from the other direction, along the riverbank. Approach from this side and all you saw was a wall of timber and corrugated iron, reaching from cliff to water. In fact there was a gate, but you might not spot it, first thing: like the whole stretch of wall, it was compounded of wood and iron, painted with pitch against the actions of storm and sea. Black on black, salt-stained and discreet.

There was no more an established path down here than there was in the ninety-acre; what the cows achieved above, surf and tide worked to match below. Pools and puddles shifted, new weed was laid down while old was washed away. Even I stepped somewhat differently from sand to rock to sand again, every time I crossed the strand. Rowan hopped and cursed and giggled, slipped and shrieked and drew her foot up sans boot, leaving it stuck in a crevice. Batted me away when I went to the rescue, then grabbed for me again; couldn't decide whether to cling to my side or hold my hand more distantly or spurn me altogether.

"Piggyback?" I offered neutrally.

"Uh, yes. Please..."

First I rescued her waterlogged boot while she balanced stork-like on one leg, then I bent my back so that she could climb aboard. With her legs jutting forward at waist-height, I used her feet as a battering-ram to knock the gate ajar, and carried her through like a queen.

WE built our boats in wood, with handheld tools. Nevertheless, noise was no stranger to the boatyard, echoing off the cliff and out across the water.

Nevertheless, the racket that evening was exceptional. One boy, one mallet and a heavy copper sheet: he'd laid an old folded tarpaulin between sheet and concrete, and even so. Sixteen square feet of copper will sing, when it's beaten.

So also will a boy sing, when he's thumping something in rhythm. At least until he looks up, to see that he's no longer alone.

The Japanese are a quiet folk, by and large, with a yen for quiet art, low-cal, static. A solitary flower in a *wabi-sabi* vase, three characters in slow ink with a swift brush, a garden of raked gravel. A single square of paper folded whole— uncut, untorn—into a formal stylised figure: a crane, a unicorn, a frog. A boat.

There was nothing Japanese about Josh, and nothing quiet. Rather it was a restless energy that had led him to origami, simply to give him something to do with his hands. All through our first interview—in the pub, which doubled as my office—his swift neat fingers had transformed sheets of coloured paper into a little line of figures: Darth Vader and R2D2, two copulating unicorns, a cat in a box. Classic technique married to pop culture in a crisp and reckless style as inappropriate as it was charming. Mix that with tools, materials, and the space to scale up; the result had proved robust. Noisy. Origami unleashed.

The Boat of Going Nowhere was a yacht flying a jib and a mainsail, folded from four-by-four copper rather than paper. It had cost me one sheet already as proof-of-concept, a practice piece to learn how to fold and crease metal sharply; now he was working on the thing itself. Technically in his spare time, outside working hours—but my young apprentice shared not only my yard and my home, but also my casual approach to timekeeping. Sometimes we'd be up half the night, working under arc lights until the task was done; some days we'd start at noon or quit at three or never reach the yard at all. Just now I couldn't have turned his mind away from the Boat of Going Nowhere if I'd tried.

Rowan was unsure how to feel about Josh, the idea of him or the boy himself. In other circumstances I could have been amused by her wary detachment, her inability to figure out which of us was the more vulnerable, who was exploiting whom. She saw me replicating what Bruce had done—for me, with me, to me—and so forging one more link in a chain I might have broken. She could disapprove of that quite thoroughly. At the same time she could thoroughly distrust the motives of a young man latching onto an older in his grief, at his time of least resistance. She loved me, was protective of me, knew what was best for me far better—of course!—than I did; and that best did not include a boy her age, less than half of mine.

And now she was here, face to face with the reality of him, in the cottage and in the yard. Angular beauty and heedless charm, the relentless driving energy and the sudden slamming walls: she might have been his next conquest, or he hers, if it wasn't that he occupied that unexpected, unnegotiated space, the bed that Bruce built.

She was quite bewildered what to feel. And I hated to see her in such a muddle, so confused where she ought to have felt most comfortable; and I could think of no resolution except to do as Bruce had done, live with the boy for the rest of my life and see if that was some kind of reassurance to her.

JUST now, I set her down on an upturned cable drum and handed her lost boot back to her with a courtly bow. Knowing, as she knew, that Josh was watching, mallet poised, work suspended.

"Hey, Cinders," he called. "Aren't you supposed to leave the slipper and run away?"

"Yeah, well. I can't get anything right. He's not even my Prince Charming." Slight emphasis on the *my*, and none at all otherwise: bless her, she was really trying. She might disapprove of both of us concurrently and consecutively, but she'd do her best not to let it show. At least to him.

Freshly shod, she walked over to view his progress and admire the crispness of his creases. "But will it float, when it's finished? We learned how to fold boats at school one time, but they were different, more like barges. Those floated. And you could load them up with cargo, beads and stuff. Until you overloaded them, and they sank."

"I guess this would float," he said. "You can make boats out of concrete, so copper ought to work. I think she'd turn turtle, though, first thing. The sails make her top-lofty, see, and there's not enough keel to counter that. Unless you load the hull with ballast, but then I guess she'd sink anyway."

"Just as well it won't be going to sea, then. Or going anywhere."

"Aye that."

He left his model lying on its tarp, rose and stretched—slowly, fastidiously, like a roused cat reaching back into itself—and smiled across the yard at me. All physicality, all purpose: wickedly deliberate. Rubbing her nose in it, but that was incidental. If he knew how she was feeling, he didn't let it trouble him. Or stop him.

Oh dear God, but he reminded me of me, sometimes so much. Sometimes too much. Young man aware of his own power and reckless with it, heedless with it, willing to give it away. Willing to give it all away, in exchange for— what? A life, a companion, a craft, a home. Everything I had from Bruce, I was handing on wholesale, the complete package. Unless the thing existed separate from ourselves, and we merely inhabited the roles for a while, each in turn. It could feel that way sometimes, that we were groomed by some force outside ourselves, shaped to fit and held in place by a nameless inevitability. I had been him; he would be me. We would both of us be Bruce in the end, ashes in an urn. Lessons learned; lessons passed on. Someone else's duty.

Something stirred in the sky. At first I thought it was one more late flight of starlings, turning in unison towards a cliffside roost, their wings catching some fugitive final glimpse of light from the sunken sun. The other two hadn't noticed, intent as they were on building some kind of awkward *detente* on sand sodden with resentment and distrust. I had the words in my throat before I saw more, they were out before I could swallow them down: "Hey, look, look up—"

They turned, lifting their heads just at the moment when I would have called them back, when I would have said *No, don't look, don't see that...*

In the dark of the sky was his face again, impossibly, irresistibly. No matter if it was only scudding cloud lit from beneath, each of us saw the same thing. Pareidolia. And each of us knew whose face that was. Two of us had known the man himself; Josh knew him only from photographs, but that was enough to put a bewildered certainty into his voice.

"That was, that was…" It was a sentence that couldn't end, certainty notwithstanding; so he ducked it. "Was that awesome, or what? The way that looked like Bruce?"

He was at my elbow, though I hadn't seen him come; and Rowan was just as sudden on my other side, taking my arm and clinging tight, no hint of adult irony. "It did," she said. "Didn't it?"

It did; and no, it was not awesome. A portrait like a sidelong glance, painted with twilight and cloud and suggestion—but not randomly, and not in our heads. If Josh was sure, who'd never met the man; if Rowan was sure, who'd known him and disliked him; how much more sure was I, who had known him and loved him and lived with him for thirty years? All three of us stared up and saw clouds shred into the wind, saw the first pale stars in the looming gloom, saw no hint of any face at all, and even so.

"Come on, kids. You know he never took his eye off me. Why should death make any difference?"

Jocularity struck a jarringly false note, but what could I do? Give one·last lingering, anxious glance upward, then grip each of them by the shoulder and turn them bodily. Sometimes the inexplicable is too great for challenge, for question, for curiosity. You have simply to stand under the reality of what's numinous, and then to walk away.

It's hard to turn your back on the sky, but we could at least set the sea behind us. And a bare dozen paces ahead lay the workshop, with a light already burning and the side-door set ajar.

Far more than the cottage, this was home and shelter to me, since I was that feral teenage boy. I used to sleep down here more often than not, curled in a nest of blankets, my dreams scented with wood shavings and diesel; and wake to brew coffee on the paraffin stove and sharpen yesterday's tools on the oilstone and call greetings across the water to friends on the day-boats as they chugged out in pursuit of shoaling mackerel or pilchard. All with one eye on the cliff-path, waiting for the day's first sight of Bruce, a distant potent figure headed down.

There was electricity in the building now, a new floor beneath a new roof and proper plumbing, a real bed for Josh or me or both of us together, those nights we never made it home. Even so, it was still essentially the same place, imbued with the same long history. Even the paraffin-smell still lingered. Perhaps that was only in my mind, like fugitive glimpses of that same distant figure with that same familiar stride. I could almost find a comfort in those moments, that he still kept watch over me. Especially when I turned my head and looked more closely and of course he wasn't there. He was still dead, and I was still dealing; and what better comfort could he give me, than these occasional reminders that I really could get by without him?

No comfort now. Here I was moving beyond mourning and with my own apprentice, this sudden shift, a turning away that could seem quite like abandonment; and here was Rowan too, ever a thorn, a trouble, a wall between us where nothing should ever have come; and now his face was in the sky, and no comfort meant. Something else, something more, some expression of fury or claim of possession and death apparently not a factor.

But here we were, all three of us under my roof—mine now, mine!—and cut off from the sky's glare, his. The workshop had no view out to the slipway and the sea; that wall was all door. The window looked onto the river and the road.

Just as I steered them both inside, Josh glanced back and yiked, ducking free of my grip and slithering outside again. I half-turned to follow and felt myself seized by indecision, there in the doorway with her on one side and him the other. Chase or stay, him or her? It wasn't possible—and then thank God it wasn't necessary, because Josh was no sooner gone than he was coming back.

With the Boat of Going Nowhere snatched up from the concrete apron, tucked securely under his arm.

"In case it means a storm, that sky," he said, laughing, shrugging. "I'm not leaving her out there for some stupid flood tide to take away."

People think that way. We all do. It's what makes me a blue-water sailor, why I want a hundred miles between myself and any land when weather's on the way: because danger lies in that liminal space where the ocean meets the shore. It comes from the deep and hits the land and God help you if you lie between the hammer and the anvil. It's why we stand and look outward, why lighthouses and foghorns, barriers and sea-walls and defences.

Sometimes we should look the other way. Inland, where everything is fixed, reliable, coherent: where structures have weight and certainty, where the variable moon harbours no influence, where wind and rain together must work hard and hard to achieve a little local damage. Where it's all too easy to forget how everything from peak to valley bottom is designed to channel trouble to the sea.

Water finds its own level, they say. That would be here, where the rushing river meets the rising tide.

PERHAPS there was a natural dam high up on the moor somewhere: a fallen tree, accumulated blockage, no one to notice. Perhaps there was a freak of weather, rain beyond measure just where a lake could build and build. Or perhaps water is somehow an expression of malevolence, or of will, or of endurance. Perhaps he could just make water happen. All at once, in flood.

It started as a rumour, a distant rumbling, something ripping deep in the fabric of the world. The kids looked to me for reassurance, enlightenment, anything; I had nothing to offer except a mirror for their own blank questioning stares. I shook my head at them, and turned to the window.

It was dark out there, not dark enough. I could see what was coming, all too well. The village upstream gave me a horizon of light, a beacon that drew us nightly to pub, to cottage, to dinner, to bed. This night I saw half those lights go out, almost all at once. Those that survived on higher ground served only to frame that darkness. Everything happens at the margins;

that lit edge here was a churning chaos, a moving roiling wall in silhouette, sound made solid, that growing growling roar...

"Get out," I said. "Out now. Not that way," as Rowan turned hesitantly towards the door we'd come in by. That way lay my truck, the gateway, the road and the village and the world; but half the village was gone, heading our way in all its shattered pieces. It was breaking the road to ruin as it came.

"The river's in flood," I said, as mild a way as I could find to say *It's over, that world you knew; death is coming, and it's meant for us.* "We'll go along the beach and up the cliff. Keep together and we'll stay safe."

Quick as I was to herd them out, I was almost already too slow. Floods should lose their power as their reach broadens, as a narrow valley river-bed opens to the sea—but this one met a wind and tide that should never have come together, that neither clock nor calendar was ready for. We were a week past springs and three hours before the full, and even so: here was the tide racing up the slipway as I heaved open the workshop door, too high and too soon. And the wind that battered me, that tried to force me all the way back inside: a storm-wind was out of season and unforecast, implausible, as close to impossible as any weather ever.

The wind held up that rushing wall of river; the tide thrust underneath and lifted it higher yet, the water and the rubble that it swept along, half the village in its seize. I stood on the slipway and saw it hurtling towards my gate, my truck, my workshop—towards *us,* head-high and lethal with rocks and beams and filth and sheer force.

Sheer force of will, but I didn't want to think about that.

I snatched for Rowan's hand and Josh's too, where they stood mesmerised and struggling to stand in the blast. I tugged each, and they each came with me, grimly step by step. It was a hard slog just to reach the side-gate, even with the impetus of what was following, that brute blunt fear to drive us on.

The gate still stood open. The wind was slamming it back against its hinges, slam and slam again; something in me wanted to stop and pull it shut, give it a chance of surviving the night.

But nothing here would survive the flood when it hit, and I had no free hand in any case. My true interest lay in their survival, the two youngsters who clung and hauled alongside me as we made a difficult panicked passage over the rocks of the beach with tidewater swirling about our feet, and behind us the dreadful sounds of destruction as the flood took my gateway, my truck, my workshop in strict order.

A sudden wave took us from behind, soaking us waist-high and floating Rowan off her feet for a moment. After that she clung closer. I ploughed on doggedly, letting Josh foray forwards while I trod more or less in his footsteps, making myself the anchor of our trio. That wave must have been the flood's last gasp. But we still had wind and tide to face, not out of the water yet.

And something more. Perhaps.

"SINGLE file," I yelled above the wind's howl as we reached the foot of the cliff-path, "hand in hand, slow and careful. Keep tight against the rock. Josh, you first," and me in the middle, keeping a grip on them both. The path might give way before us or behind us, or underneath all three; but if we went, we would all three go together.

Mostly I kept my eyes on my own feet, for what little good that did, and my back flat against the cliff to give the wind least possible purchase. Rowan copied me with care; but Josh was leading, looking ahead, inclined to step out to see better. Each time, the movement of his feet snagged the corner of my eye, pulling my head up in anxiety, having me tug at his hand to draw him back into the rock wall's mockery of safety.

Maybe he was getting confident, thinking the worst was behind us; maybe he could see the end of the path, the top of the cliff. At last he didn't let me do that; this time he tugged back teasingly, tried to draw me forward into his body's better shelter.

I was distracted, not ready, taken aback. Just for a moment I went with him, took a step too far, lost my place as the body-bridge between him and Rowan.

I broke my grip on her hand. She was too far behind, she couldn't stretch that far, I felt her fingers slip between mine and away.

And flailed blindly to recapture them, before my head could whip around to see; and felt a strong hand close with mine again.

Strong and wet and bitter chill, compounded of salt and wind and water, and so very very much not Rowan's hand.

Familiar none the less. Not Rowan, and not supposed to be there. Anywhere.

We always want to hold on to everything. We don't even let our dead go.

Sometimes, the dead don't let us.

Now I looked.

I couldn't see Rowan at all, through the dark and the wind and the figure that stood between us. Broad-chested, raw-boned, standing four-square on the path; known, integral, unmistakable. Dead. Holding my hand.

I took a second, I needed that one second just to stand there, to be back, to be sheltered and watched over and held.

Then I plunged: straight through whatever there was of him contained within that shaping, the seaspray and the wind and all, a great stillness made of movement as we all are, as all things are.

I hurled myself recklessly and blindly through, to reach Rowan.

Doing that, I had to let go of Josh.

Every story is about betrayal, in the end. We lucky ones, we're allowed maybe to choose who we betray.

If the briefest breathless moment can truly be forever, then I honestly never thought I'd find her. I thought she'd be gone: over the edge, or the path collapsed beneath her, or just not there, not anywhere.

But I hurtled into her very physical self, and for a moment we clung, almost going over; and then we scrambled to some awkward mutual desperate balance, and if that was some kind of Sophie's choice, apparently I'd made it.

Made it and couldn't conceivably regret it, when she was right there wrapped around me, damp and chill and trembling; and even so. Already it rived me, that I had let Josh slip. I gazed yearningly back over her head, thinking that Bruce must have taken what I had abandoned, sure that I would never see the boy again—and suddenly there he was, plunging out of a darkness deeper than the night, just as I had.

Again we teetered, again we didn't fall. And now I had them both within the circle of my arms, and Bruce had lost his advantage. Whatever choice I'd made, there were others free and able to make choices too.

"All together or not at all," I said; and this time I set Rowan before me, with my hands on her shoulders as they used to be long since, as they always should be. Josh took his cue from me, without being told or asked: set young strong fingers on each of my shoulders, stood close enough behind me that I could feel his breath on my neck, even in that wind; was young enough to brush a kiss against my nape, even in that danger.

I nudged Rowan forward, and that's how we climbed the last of the path: caterpillar-style, stepping all together and gripping tight. I suppose I was still making the same choice, Rowan the one I gave my strength to, only trusting Josh to hold to me; but now it didn't feel like betrayal. Recognition, rather. Something new between us, a shift of state, that I lay within his compass as much as he in mine.

Up and up, step by step; and here we were at the top and the wind was almost helpful now, blowing inland, pushing us to greater safety, away from the cliff-edge. It was hard even now to believe that I had lost neither one on the path below, when I'd thought to lose them both. And now I could fling an arm around each and march them forward, laughing almost in the teeth of the night. Bruce had had his chance, I thought, and missed his mark, and—

AND of course that's when he came again, in that moment of stupid confidence, when we thought the worst behind us. He'd always had a knack for catching me off-guard, keeping me off-balance, so that I'd forever be falling into him, needing him to catch me once again.

Again he was a stormshadow, woven from dark and wind and water. He shaped himself out of nowhere, and stood before us, undeniable as death—and then he walked away, across the ninety-acre, as though he were a guide in the night.

Towards the sheepfold, where of course we had been headed anyway: somewhere to pause, to catch our breath, to huddle in an angle of the walls and let the wind batter itself against stone while we wrapped our heads around what we had just survived.

He led us and we followed, because what else could we do, where else go? There was no path to better safety, no path at all. If we had him in sight, at least we knew where he stood.

Besides, the wind hustled us neatly at his heels. I leaned back against it, tried to drag my feet, to act as a brake for all three of us. Even so, I could barely keep us from catching him up. We dogged him, and he led us exactly where we had all meant to be. Every step felt inevitable, preordained, irresistible.

The sheepfold has a gateway, though no gate. He brought us there and paused, and turned—I want to say to face us, although the weathermask he wore offered no suggestion of a face.

We came to a halt, all three of us together. Even the wind seemed to pause for that breathless confrontation, until he moved again. Reshaped himself. Made a frame around the gateway, like an open invitation, *come on in.*

Like a lych-gate, a threat as much as promise.

Not wide enough for three of us abreast, however close we huddled. He wanted to force me into choice again, and this time there would be no reprieve. Whoever I left outside, he would take. And he had tested me once already, and he knew—we all knew—which way that decision fell.

Maybe he wanted a new apprentice.

Not this time.

I could feel Josh stiffening at my side, seeing what I saw, leaping to the same conclusions. Waiting to feel me pull away.

Not this time.

This time, I made a different choice.

I stepped away from both of them at once, one brisk pace back. I took a wrist of each, before they could protest it, and locked their two hands together; then I gripped them by the neck, one in each hand, and propelled them forwards.

The young cling by instinct. If either of them knew what I was doing, if they understood, they had no time to overcome that instinct and unlatch. I pushed them by main force through the opening in the fold's wall, through the gatemouth Bruce had made.

He didn't touch them; I don't believe he could. The fold was home, safe ground, always had been. Even the wind couldn't reach them, I thought, in there.

And now I was alone out here, my choice made, and I didn't even try to follow them in. That wasn't in the rules, and it wasn't in the contract.

Instead—well. Hand in hand and two by two, that's the way we choose to go.

I reached out my hand to touch the nebulous near column of that strange shimmering gateway.

And felt my hand seized again, by the same strong frigid fingers as before; and there he was again in almost-human form, his own size, his own shape.

If he had all the powers of wind and water, he chose not to use them. Perhaps bonding himself into an almost-body, as near as he could come, gave him only that body's strength. The memory of mortality, with all its limits implied.

At any rate, I could pit my own body's strength against his and not make a mockery of myself. I could tug him, indeed, against the wind's shove, back towards the cliff-edge and the path. It may be that he was willing to be tugged. Denied what he'd expected, the cruel choice, one child or the other, he might be bewildered now; he might be intrigued. If he was capable of either one, or capable of anything but malice. I couldn't tell: was he a ghost, was he himself remade with all his old attributes and antagonisms, was he only a memory or a lingering aspect somehow cut off from death, cut off by death and left behind?

It didn't matter. Nothing mattered except this moment, this determination: to take him away from the kids, away from the world if I could.

Young or otherwise, the human instinct is to cling. *We always want to hold on. We don't even let our dead go.*

I was gambling, I suppose, that I could hold on to him now, and take him with me one last time. That he wouldn't have the strength or else the will to leave me.

I was almost running now. And hauling him along, and if he thought anything at all—if he was capable of thinking—he must have thought I was headed for the path and trusting him to keep me safe in a foolish, hectic descent.

Not I. I ran him clean off the edge of the cliff.

THAT was all I had. My way to save the kids, if it could work: to keep him bound to me and end myself. I had no time for regrets, for second thoughts, for fond farewells. Just straight to the edge and over.

Hurling myself and him too into that wind, almost rising before we could start to fall; hoping he would, what, disintegrate perhaps? Lose coherence and fray away into the air that he was made from? I'd had no time for analysis either, or I might have thought myself foolish, hopeless, illogical. Lost.

I thought I was lost anyway. Dead myself and not reckoning to come back, malevolently or otherwise.

I leaped, almost flew, almost fell—and didn't, quite.

He had always had the saving of me, in his hands. Always been the saving of me, always made that choice.

Now, one more time—who knows why?—he did that again.

I was such a man in my pride, in my strength, mature and responsible and knowing. Now suddenly I was a child again, while a grown-up swung me by one arm.

That grip I had, I'd thought I had; turned out to be his grip after all, his on me, as ever. He swung me high and hurled me, back to the land again.

I hit hard, and couldn't breathe for a while. And couldn't see for a while after that, because of the wind and the night. The wind died, though, in time. Then I could stand, and see that there was nothing to see; and walk to the fold, and find Josh and Rowan still huddling there.

DID he linger, did he depart, did he dissipate? I had no way of knowing: only that he seemed not to be there any longer.

Nor was the yard there when I went down, when I could. Nor the bulk of the workshop. The roof and doors were gone; some walls survived, but none worth keeping. There was nothing in me, no will to build again. It had been his, and barely mine before he took it back; and the village was in ruin, and my life there.

Besides, I had insurance. His insurance, transferred to my name just before he died; he always had been careful of everything that was his. Me not excluded. That money bought me a yacht: none so fine as those we used to build, but good enough. Blue-water worthy.

The cottage I gifted to Rowan, if she should decide to want it. If not, to Josh; if not, then to the distress fund for the village, all my friends and neighbours.

From the cottage, I took nothing but Bruce's ashes; from the wreckage of the yard, nothing but the wreck of Josh's copper origami, the Boat of Going Nowhere. Crushed and mangled as it was, no kind of seaworthy, I would take it out, far and far; and pour the ashes into its deepest crevice, give them to the ocean, watch it drink them down.

And then—well, not come back. Not yet, not now. Let the winds have me for a while, winds and blue water.

WINTER JOURNEY

THERE IS NOTHING QUITE SO WICKED as a young girl catching first sight of her womanhood to come. I know this to be true. I had it from my mother.

In other matters, I am less certain. Less certain now. Stories shift in the telling. Narrative is no man's land; we share no common ground. Here, though, I may—I must!—hold fast. Otherwise...

No. There is no otherwise. There cannot be. This is the tale of one girl's wickedness, and nothing more.

BUT let me tell it straightly, where I can.

It was the third winter after the Great War. In the cities, we had heard, spirits and hemlines both were rising fast. Not so in the country, where fields still lay fallow for lack of men to work them. Like a blinded man's bandage, those blank patches in the plough told over what was lost, in every valley another reckoning of sorrow. Absence lay upon us, inescapable.

In a sober season, at a rectory tea, I found myself unexpectedly invited to escort two small people on a melancholy pilgrimage.

"Their father was reported missing after Loos in '15," the curate said. "Their mother was prostrate for a long time, and is still not strong, though I hope to see her better soon, now that she's moved to the parish. Our good air and God's good grace, working hand in hand…

"However. She heard last month that her husband's remains have been located at last. Of course he's been reburied over there, and she cannot visit his resting-place; even if she had the strength to make the journey, her spirit could never sustain it. She is anxious, though, that her children at least should see where their father lies.

"Which brings me to you, dear lady. I know you've been across several times, on your own behalf and others'. Everyone here thinks you quite intrepid. Which is why I make so bold as to ask if you'll be bolder yet. Would you consider shepherding the children, there and back again? They are a girl and a boy, thirteen and nine. Quiet creatures, nicely raised and nicely mannered. I think a figure of womanly authority would answer better than any man we might find willing. And far better than the housemaid, who was their mother's first proposal."

It seemed strange to me, that a woman who could not face a thing should set her children to it in her stead; that she should depend on narrow shoulders to bear what she could not. It was unnatural, to lay such a load on such young ones.

But everything in our lives was unnatural, in those years. More than once I had seen women in the fields draw a plough, where there were no men nor horses. When the world turns so coarse, it should be no surprise if healthy adults take to their beds or to the road or to the bottle, if the youngest must bear most.

Those of us who are still strong, it falls to us to lend a hand where we may. Why else would I have been across so often? I take my camera, I take commissions. I go because others cannot.

If I must go hand in hand with two children, well. That I could do. I had two hands.

I said that, or something like it. The curate beamed behind his whiskers. "Will you come tomorrow, to meet the bairns?"

Again, I thought that oddly expressed. Should I not meet the mother first? The curate's imprimatur was all very well, but even so...

But I said yes, of course; and the next day found me striding side by side with him up a muddy lane in boots fit for the occasion.

The Beeches stood well back above the lane, behind a veil of the trees that it was named for. I knew where to find it, but had never called before. This was my first true sight of the place, and I thought it both bleak and shocking. Someone in the old queen's time had taken a plain, severe frontage and decorated it with ridiculous stonework, all castellations and gargoyles. Small wonder if later occupants planted so many trees between the lane and their embarrassment.

The curate was eyeing me, waiting for a judgement. "It looks," I said, "like an old man playing bawdy with a harlot's paints."

He laughed unexpectedly, explosively. "Yes," he said, "it does rather. That's very well put, and possibly the best thing to be said about it."

He seemed to find the house funny. I thought it both foreboding and false, like the booth of a fairground fortune-teller. Artificial wickedness, the pretence of sin: which is a sin in itself, in my book. "Does the interior—?"

"Match? I'm afraid it does, in terms of Gothic imitation. I believe the children enjoy it."

No doubt they did. I couldn't help but be concerned. Two imaginative children could make what they liked from such a setting; what worried me was what it might make of them.

Perhaps it was foolish in me, to be so anxious before I had even crossed the threshold. Perhaps it was a moment of insight, a genuine foretelling. Who can say? Retrospect brands us all, in the name of guilt.

The curate led me not to the studded oak of the front door, but around the side of the house where the gravelled drive must lead back to the stable yard and the kitchens.

I balked, a little. "Should we not...?" My hand finished the question for me, indicating the door implying the bell, the housemaid, the enquiry: all the ritual of a morning call, implied with a pause and a gesture. Synecdoche, metonymy, *pars pro toto*: my tutor in rhetoric would have been proud.

"No, no. The children are under the servants' care. I always come to the back."

Even now, were we not to interview their mother?

Apparently not. We trooped around to the rear, and let ourselves into the house without knocking. The curate halloo'd instead, his voice echoing past pantry and stillroom to the heat and noise of a busy kitchen.

He was answered by the brisk patter of light feet, and, "Hullo, Dr Walrus." A short, slight boy manifested before us, vividly blond and visibly pleased.

His sister—taller, darker, older—was swift behind him, and swift to rebuke. "Joe, you mustn't call him that! I told you what Mother said."

The boy scowled over his shoulder, as he should, and then straightened into a sudden schoolroom formality. "I beg your pardon, sir. Dr Wilcock. But," his youth breaking through his manners again, "you did say we might—"

"In private, was what Dr Wilcock said! Not in company...!"

Inevitably, his eyes and hers both moved to me. Her voice died, and she bobbed an awkward resentful curtsey, all angles and no grace.

I laughed. "Oh, I hardly think I count as company, do I? Slipping in the back way, in the curate's shadow? If I were company, I'd come to the front door and ring the bell and ask if your mother was receiving."

The girl hesitated, those sharp eyes of hers coming to her brother: who said stoutly, "Mamma's resting."

Following orders, was he? *If anyone asks, Mamma's resting. That's all you say.* Her sigh of relief was almost inaudible, her nodding head overdone. I wondered quite what "resting" might mean in this house: rendered incapable by drink? Or by laudanum? Perhaps it was only nerves, as the curate had amiably suggested. Whatever the truth, the girl thought it ought to be a secret, and she didn't quite trust the boy to keep it so.

"Well, in that case," I said, "why don't we go out into the garden, where we won't disturb her nor get under Cook's feet? Your shoes look up to the task, and the rain has stopped at last. My name's Miss Alcott, but you can call me Auntie Win."

They exchanged glances, in that uncomfortable way that siblings do: exchanges impossible to eavesdrop, except that children have such revealing faces. When do we learn to hide what lies beneath?

She said, "I'm Alice Northolt, and this is my brother Joe. Joseph," with a little quirk of her lips, remembering to speak properly to strangers. "But I suppose you know that already," because they knew already that grown-ups talked about them behind their backs. It was a privilege of adulthood to breach all the laws of decency and honour.

"Actually not," I said comfortably. "Alice and Joe, is it? Come, show me around outside," and I held out my hand boldly for the boy's.

He stood firm. "You have mud on your hem," he said.

"I have, I know; and you're quite clean. I don't suppose that will last, though. Will it?"

There was wickedness suddenly in my invitation, in my open hand. His eyes sparked; his sister's narrowed. She might have held her breath, against a budding protest; it's another privilege of adulthood, to lead the young astray.

It was already quite clear to me, the degree of dominance that Alice held over her brother. I supposed it inevitable. She was the elder, the taller, no doubt the wiser too. Of course he would look to her for guidance; of course she would expect it. Assume it. And act accordingly, half nursemaid and half tutor: keep him clean and orderly, teach him what she knew of the world, make a path for his feet to follow.

Personally I thought him a little too clean, a little too orderly. Small boys should be harum-scarum. I recognised her influence, approved it even, and nevertheless: I would still subvert it where I could.

Their garden is their territory, to any child. Far more so than the house, where walls and rules stand rigidly in place, where doors can be open or closed or locked against small fingers. Where servants can be stricter than family, and less kind. Open air is good for more than healthful exercise; nature and weather compound with the imagination, to offer shifting boundaries and a wealth of possibility. A boy beneath an oak stands on his own ground, in a way he never can in bedroom or schoolroom or nursery.

Also, where the boundaries are looser or wilder or less ruthless, children may be more inclined to share. They took me all over, from the regimented rows of the vegetable garden to the reckless tangle of the hawthorn-brake and the stream beyond; and before we were done out there, matters were already settled in my head.

Even so, "Really," I said to the curate privately, while the boy was showing me just how he scrambled up the apple tree, while the girl bore silent witness to the ruin of his stockings, "I must speak to their mother. Without her absolute approval, this can go no further."

"But dear lady, I told you, this whole adventure was her idea. Her insistence, indeed. I shouldn't have broached it else."

"Her approval of me, I mean." It was starting to feel peculiar, that I had not yet so much as set eyes on her. Ahead of us lay a journey of some days and some difficulty, with an emotional weight I could not measure on two young souls I had only newly met. The less keen the mother seemed to speak with me, the more determined I was that she should do so.

Dr Wilcock sighed and said, "Very well. Of course. Come this way. Children, go in now, and change your shoes. Cook will give you bread-and-dripping, I expect, if you ask nicely and have clean hands to show her."

The boy was quick; he said again, "Mamma's resting."

"Even so. Miss Alcott needs to speak with her. Grown-ups must sometimes stir themselves, for their children's sake."

Joe hung by his knees from an apple-branch and watched us invertedly away—but it was his sister's gaze that I felt, silent and fierce, burning between my shoulder blades. The boy was simply and swiftly protective; the girl was… something other. Something more complicated, and less charming. I couldn't fathom it, quite, but I could feel it.

Dr Wilcock brought me to the cook; the cook summoned the housemaid; the housemaid led us through to the front. Nothing in that was unusual, and it still felt a deliberate process, a distancing, a succession of curtains in place between the children and their mother. I was more accustomed to small people bursting through the layers of propriety like a cricket ball through a drawing-room window, *Mummy, Mummy, come and see!*

Not here. If even her youngest was so careful of her, if even the curate followed protocol from one servant to the next, then the green baize door was more than a physical reality. Mrs Northolt was hardly the first parent to leave her children's care to the staff, of course. If her health were uncertain, it might seem as reasonable as it was commonplace. From outside the house, it might indeed.

Inside, the transition from linoleum to parquet, from bare plastered walls to linenfold panelling and heavy fabrics, from clear sun to cool dim shade, everything served to underscore the division, and nothing about it seemed healthy to me. On this side, light and sound both were intentionally smothered; the air itself felt dense and textured.

The housemaid opened a door and sidled through ahead of us, bobbed a curtsey in the murk beyond and said, "Dr Wilcock and a lady to see you, if you please, ma'am."

The murmur that came back was weak and inaudible to me, through the thickness of the door. If hardly a welcome, it was at least not a refusal; the maid opened the door wider to admit us, closed it behind us as she left.

Mrs Northolt lay on a day-bed in the glow of a shaded lamp, with a rug across her knees. Her setting, her pose seemed designed to declare her an invalid even before she spoke; her thin, querulous voice could only confirm it.

She said, "And who is this you have brought me, Father? Miss Alcott, is it, who will take my poor orphaned children to mourn their dear Papa at his graveside, where alas I may not go myself?"

"Oh come, my dear Mrs Northolt, they are hardly—"

"I call my children orphans, you see, Miss Alcott," she went on, irrepressible as the weak so often are, "because I cannot be a proper mother to them. I don't have the strength to keep up, and my doctors say I must seek quiet above all things. Quiet and rest, however much it runs against my better instincts."

I was not quite sure I believed in her better instincts—but that was surely uncharitable in me, and presumptuous besides. I bowed my head as much in remorse as acknowledgement, and took the seat she indicated.

"The good Father tells me that you have taken that mournful journey many times, Miss Alcott, to where our heroes lie in foreign soil."

"It is my privilege," I murmured, "to be free to travel, where others are not." Her language seemed to me as overblown as her surroundings; perhaps Gothic arches encouraged a Gothic turn of phrase. Or turn of mind. But I was bordering on the unkind again. I squashed that sardonic inner voice, and let her murmur on.

"I only wish that I could go myself; but my health, my nerves… It would be an impossible journey. I am not robust, as you are." People have used other words, less generous. I have a sturdy frame. "The children can be my eyes and legs, go for me, see where their father lies, my dear Rodney. Say that you will take them, do."

In honesty, I thought I was committed already. If I had doubts, it was now: not on sight of the children, but rather their mother. If I wanted to change my mind—well. That is a matter for me alone. My conscience can take the weight of it. What's harder to bear is what I said then, instead of a simple *Yes*. Until that moment, I had not known myself cruel. I said, "Let's have the children in, and ask them if they're willing. A total stranger, after all, and we'd be a week away."

For the first time, I saw genuine emotion on her face: what in hindsight I believe I had been pushing for.

Naked fear was what she showed to me.

She ought never to have been so exposed.

After a moment, "I hardly think we need consult the children," Dr Wilcock said behind me. "They are well-trained little creatures, obedient as they should be. We here can decide what's best for them, and no doubt they will accept it."

No doubt they would: as we all did, as we already had. In the meantime, his intervention cut through the room's tension like a blade through an overstrained cable. In sheer relief, the woman was suddenly babbling. "...When I'm stronger, perhaps we can all go, as a family and you to speak for us and guide us, Miss Alcott, yes, our dragoman, if you don't dislike the word..."

Of course I disliked it. What Christian woman would not? Fortunately, I was too busy disbelieving her to take offence. Hers was an opium daydream, nothing more; false prophets should try harder. If she wouldn't willingly keep company with her children for an hour, there was no prospect of a week's travel together—and certainly not together with me, no. I was too wise to find myself so embroiled.

I didn't say so. I let my silence speak for me, until the curate felt obliged to intervene. "The term is unfortunate, but the office is an honest one. I believe the Sublime Porte ranked its dragomans very highly. Still. We will not look that far to the future, nor impose further on Miss Alcott's goodwill. A trip to Belgium, yes, with the two little ones in hand; and the best hotels, of course, and all found, all expenses covered..."

If one of us played dragoman that day, it was he: oil on turbulent waters, greasing the wheels, interpreting her silences and my own with a steady good humour that refused to buckle under strain. I thought he stood in loco parentis—*for their father,* I thought she would say, where I thought the truth was that he stood in for her—whether or not he quite realised it himself.

ALL proper adventures start at the railway station amid all that noise and bustle, jostling figures in the fog of escaping steam. This was where I met them, case in hand. My companions-to-be were scrubbed and sober-suited, solemn to match their dress and the occasion. Dr Wilcock held each by the hand, while a porter followed with the baggage. Of course their mother had not come.

"Here you are, Miss Alcott. Splendid. And a fine forecast for tomorrow's crossing, too: cold but crisp, the sea should be as smooth as a pressed handkerchief. I'd half a mind to come with you as far as Dover, but the young people wouldn't have it. Can't wait to be out from under, eh, Joe?"

"You should stay with Mamma," the boy said, soft but clear even in all the hubbub of raised voices and slamming carriage doors.

"Well, I do have other duties in the parish—but I shall call, certainly. Tell her that I've seen you safe away. She'll be concerned."

"She'll be relieved." In contrast to her brother, Alice was barely audible, muttering into the collar of her coat. I was standing close, though, and my hearing is excellent.

Still: there was an empty compartment to be found and claimed, the cases to be heaved aboard and the porter tipped two warm pennies that Joe had been clutching all this time, primed for the duty but still needing his sister's elbow to nudge him into it. It's hard to be nine and the man of the family, and the youngest.

Perhaps I should encourage Alice to lay more little burdens on him. The more we expected of him, day to day, the less he might dwell on what this journey meant, for now and for the future. If I was reading her correctly, though, she was a domineering little miss already. There had almost been a squabble over seats, certainly a silent clash of wills; the boy subsided gracelessly with a have-it-your-own-way gesture that looked all too ingrained. The girl's frown seemed to promise retribution in any case.

Of course they had the window seats. I'd have faced them both forward if I could, let them see and share our headlong plunge into the future. As it was, his seat could show him only where we were coming from, land traversed, a vanishing-point of home. I hoped there was no message, no meaning in that. We are all too prone to backward-looking, in these days of a terrible recovery.

Coming or going, the onrush of a train will silence any child for a while. I let them sit and stare as long as they would: valley and viaduct, tunnels that wrapped us about in smoke, the cramping soot-black city and then open countryside once more, a winding river that we bridged and bridged again.

Even the swiftest locomotive will seem to crawl eventually, though. Horizons drew back and nothing changed, nothing out there drew the eye or held it.

"Miss Alcott?"

"Yes, Joe?" There was no *Auntie Win* after all; not here, not now. Not yet.

"Why did we not take the boat train? It would have been much quicker, and we needn't leave Mamma so long…"

Perhaps your mother wanted a respite from the pair of you—with any other children I might have said that, and seen them smile comfortably in response. With these two, it was all too dreadfully true, or I thought so. Instead I told another truth. "There's no guarantee that the boat train will actually meet the boat. They can't hold the steam packet indefinitely, if the train's delayed; it carries the mails, you know. Besides, you've never seen the crush when the boat train comes in. Everyone dashing, luggage being left behind, children lost… We will have a good night's rest, and enjoy our breakfast and a stroll about the town before we board tomorrow, ahead of the crowd."

Besides, it gave me an extra day in England, a day to change my mind if the children turned out to be impossible. There was always the chance of that. None of us had said it, but we allowed for it regardless.

"Uncle Walrus—I mean, Dr Wilcock said it would stop us getting over-tired, if we take the journey one step at a time, with bed in between."

"Dr Wilcock is a wise man. He's very careful of you two, isn't he? You three, I should say. He clearly cares deeply for your mother as well."

"He can't have her."

As God is my witness, I had no intention then or ever of discussing their mother's affairs with her children. I might have a private opinion about the curate's intentions, but I meant that to remain private. Still, I cocked an eyebrow at Alice and said, "Do you mean *can't,* or *shan't?*"

She only shrugged sourly, and turned back to the window. I thought the comment had been stung out of her, before she'd had the chance to swallow it. I also thought that I was right, that she would do whatever she could to obstruct a courtship. She was hardly the first adolescent girl to resent the notion of a stepfather. No doubt she ruled the roost at home, with her mother in retirement, a little brother to bully and the servants trained to twist around her finger on command. No doubt she planned to go on doing so. She might run wild entirely, with no man to oversee her. She might intend just that; she was a forward-thinking creature, I was sure.

Now I had a better reason to take the children away. If I was right about Dr Wilcock, and he was wise enough to take advantage, his suit might prosper more in this single week than in the months thus far.

Time drags, always, towards the end of a journey. To forestall their sniping at each other, I raised the subject of pilgrimage: in a general way at first, allowing them to make the connection with themselves, this journey, us. Soon enough, as I'd intended, Joe stepped cautiously over the bounds of propriety, to ask the obvious question.

"Dr Wilcock said that you'd been over and over, Miss Alcott." His sister kicked his ankle quite noticeably, but he shook his head at her and soldiered on. "Why do you keep going back? Is there someone out there who was yours...?"

"My brother," I said simply. "And our parents are dead, so there's no one to remember him but me. But really, it's not that. Not that alone. It's what I was saying about duty. My poor Michael has only me to go; how many others have no one at all? How many people are there on this side, the elderly and the infirm, who would go but are not able? I can take that duty for them, be there on their behalf. I will take photographs for those who want them, and leave flowers and messages, and bring back perhaps a little of the soil from the grave: whatever I'm asked to do."

"Like taking us," he said, nodding, "when Mamma's not well enough."

"Yes. Exactly like that. I'm very glad to do it. I hope I can make it as easy as possible for both of you," *and give your mother an easy time for a week at least. Take the strain off, let Dr Wilcock have his chance, if he's willing to take it...*

I ought to stop thinking that way. It was impertinent. Besides, I was afraid the girl might read my mind. She had a way of watching me, head cocked, considering. Only a child, and even so; not mine, I barely knew her, and even so. Already I found her unnerving.

THE notion of "the best hotels" had drifted away like smoke on a breeze: unhurried, lingering, but not to be detained. I could see the horses of extravagance reined sharply in, and feel the grit of economy beneath the heels of my shoes. Sooner than be disappointed, I said myself that I'd prefer less luxury and more familiarity, places I knew, where I was known.

On my own, I would have walked from the railway station to Mrs Morgan's boarding-house. With two tired and fractious children in tow, I took a cab. Better the expense of a few shillings than to find ourselves halfway and the boy unable to manage his case, the girl unwilling to be doubly burdened.

Alice might not like it, but the children of course would share a room. If there'd been one with three beds, I would have taken that and kept us all together. Instead, I would sleep across the landing. I watched as Joseph forestalled another losing argument by resignedly claiming the bed furthest from the window; I saw them through supper and a brisk evening toilet; I heard their prayers and tucked them up and left them to it.

Herding children is wearisome work, and they were unlikely to sleep late. I was not far behind them with my own night-time rituals and sliding gratefully between the coarse, worn, well-ironed sheets.

Standing as I did *in loco parentis,* I slept with one ear open for trouble, and trouble dutifully came. Perhaps it was the faintest possible tap on the door that roused me; perhaps I had been roused already, by hissing whispers on the landing or just an impending sense of what's awry.

"Come!"

What came was a small, unhappy boy in damp nightwear, with his sister looming behind him. Nudging him when he faltered, making him speak for himself.

"Please, Miss Alcott, I'm terribly sorry, but I… I'm afraid I wet the bed."

At nine years old? Well, it was possible. A fatherless boy with a neuraesthenic mother, finding himself in a strange bed far from home at the dawn of a disturbing journey: perhaps it was even likely.

"Well, never mind, dear. Let's find you some dry pyjamas, first of all... No, Alice, he doesn't need you standing over him. Trot along to the bathroom, Joe, and clean yourself up. Alice and I will strip your bed and see what's what. Quietly now, both of you; try not to wake the house."

First impressions linger in the mind's eye. I might otherwise only have seen the rumpled bed, the wet sheets, the mattress stained dark beneath. The sister's tight-lipped silence might have worked as it was meant to, her sidelong glances might have been enough to nudge me where she wanted me to go. But something in me was reluctant to take any of this at face value. I thought they were both deceiving me, the girl and the boy together in conspiracy: she driving it, he acceding, as the victim always does. We bully by consent, or not at all.

So I looked, yes, and saw what I was looking for; and at last—when we had folded the sheets and hung them over the back of a chair, humped up the mattress to let the air beneath—I said, "Now, Alice. I think there's another story here, isn't there? Do you want to tell it me, or shall I tell it you?"

She just gazed at me, mute and hostile. I sighed. "Very well, then. There's a chamber-pot beneath the dress-stand." I bent to slide it out: cream earthenware, damp inside. Yes. "I think you used it, didn't you? While your brother slept. Little boys sleep deeply. Deeply enough that you could peel back his blankets, up-end the pot, even perhaps cover him up again before you woke him. Does he even know? He won't say, of course, he's too much the gentleman; but does he actually believe this farrago, or is he covering up for you? You won't say? Very well. I expect he covers up for you a lot at home, doesn't he, when you play tricks like this to put him in trouble...?

"So what was the idea here," I went on, remorseless against her stubborn silence, "is it just original sin, or was there a greater end in mind? Did you think I'd leave him behind, perhaps? Not send him home to Mother, I couldn't do that and you wouldn't want me to; you wouldn't want them to have a week alone, to build an alliance against you in your absence. Here, though: we could leave him here, under Mrs Morgan's eye. She'd keep him, and he could skivvy for her, was that your thought? You'd enjoy that, travelling abroad with me while your brother stayed behind to carry coal and scrub floors in disgrace, not worthy to come with us...

"Well, miss, it won't be happening that way. You're quite right, of course, about Mrs Morgan. I think I know her well enough to say so. But if either one of you stays behind to skivvy, it won't be little Joe. Think on that tonight, and in the morning. I'll tell you my decision before we sail."

Joe came back from the bathroom then, clean and dry and subdued. I took him into my room, my bed for what remained of the night, leaving Alice to find what sleep she could in the fug and stink that she had raised herself, poetic justice. Come morning, the boy and I enjoyed our wander in the town, while his sister washed bedsheets and scrubbed a mattress under Mrs Morgan's scrupulous eye.

I decided that was justice enough, and as much warning as she needed. She knew my eye was on her now. All three of us climbed the gangplank, onto the steam-packet *Curraghmore*; all three of us made an easy crossing to Ostend. I kept the children on deck, to let the sea-air work what good it could. The boy stayed close to me, while the girl flung her defiant face into the wind and let it whip her hair into Medusa-snakes as she stared forward. Dreaming of romantic adventures in far foreign lands, I guessed, free of pesky brothers and domineering adults both.

She would come to no such adventures under my charge. I didn't need her love to ensure that, only her obedience, and so I told her. I told them both: "Stay close to me, guard your tongues and guard your manners. You represent your country now, and more. This is a solemn undertaking we are on, a sacred pilgrimage. Wear these," a black armband, one for each, "and everyone will know why we have come. Every step you take, remember that. Walk as though you followed your father's coffin all the way; in a very real sense, you do."

I fell into conversation, as one does, with the woman who set up her deckchair beside mine. She was older than me, a widow making her first trip across, emboldened by the companionship of her Pekinese. "Of course," she murmured confidentially, "one is not strictly allowed to take dogs to and fro, not even little pets like Frou-Frou. Those draconian quarantine laws… That's why we're sailing this line, when Calais would actually land me closer. The captain is…known to be sympathetic. I was put in touch with him by the son of an old friend, a Tommy whose squad had adopted a dog in the trenches. Our captain commanded the troopship that brought them all home, and— well. The dog came with them.

"Keep it to yourself, dear, but he has quite the little business going now. One of the sailors smuggled Frou-Frou aboard for me, and he'll take him ashore the other side. It's such a small dishonesty, and it lets me do this big thing, that I never could manage without him."

Her face was intimately, bitterly familiar to me, though she herself was a stranger. We have a common look to us, we who cross the water to minister to the dead. There was never any need to ask *who?* or *how?;* we spoke rather of where he lay, and what best way to reach him, and which hotels to room in on the way, while the boy sat on the deck at my feet and made friends with Frou-Frou.

I was sorry that my advice to her was mostly warnings, the sourness of experience, *don't trust the natives,* but it was true. There was a new breed of men that battened on the grieving, presenting themselves as guides and help-meets, out actually to skin us of everything they could. I had met women abandoned, stranded, penniless and bereft.

In her turn, my new acquaintance offered her own words to the wise: "Keep the children close. That girl, especially. A boy is neither here nor there at that age, but she: oh, she thinks she's ready for the world. Don't let her find it."

"You echo my own thoughts," I murmured, as we watched her posing in the prow. "I might not have taken her, but that their mother can't. And she is the elder; I couldn't favour her brother over her."

"No, of course not—but do watch, she will bear the watching. One hears so much that's so disquieting: the unsavoury characters you speak of and more, and worse. There are so many girls left without home or family, refugees, adrift; of course they attract the worst of the species. Agents of the

White Slave trade, I have heard, young girls bought and sold like cattle. You keep your eye on that one."

"Well, I will," I said faintly, thinking that she read too much in the halfpenny papers, and wishing that she might not regurgitate her reading quite so freely. Little boys are all ears, especially when they ought not to be listening.

I sent Joe off to take the Peke for a circuit of the deck, and resolved to hope that he hadn't understood. He was not my worry, in any case.

His sister saw him go, and stood watching through the wind-torn veil of her hair. The intensity of her stare quite made me shiver. I thought I would not be that little boy for all the tea in China. Never mind what he might have overheard; the male youth is flibbertigibbet, in at one ear and out at the other. A girl poised on the brink of women's mystery keeps everything, and keeps it close. This one said little, but she watched on her own account, and plotted mischief. That much I knew. That she might fall into someone else's mischief... Well. I had not thought. It was proper, perhaps, that I should. White Slavers might be a phantasm of what our American cousins call the yellow press, but no doubt Mrs Bellham was right, that there were dramas in wait for any girl, irrespective of her own nature.

There is no drama in the approach to Ostend harbour. On a misty day, the low land can barely distinguish itself from the grey sea. By the time the spires of the town proper impinged upon my consciousness, we were close enough to hurry me.

"Alice! Alice, go seek your brother and chase him back with Mrs Bellham's little dog. I must just run and see about our bags. It's hopeless wishing for a porter in such a scrum. I'll make myself quite plain at the head of the gangway, you can't possibly miss me..."

Nor they could, but it was Joe alone who came first, sans dog or sister, slipping his little hand into mine in a way that seemed trusting and anxious both at once.

"Did you deliver Frou-Frou safely back? And what have you done with Alice? I assume she found you."

He nodded his head, and shook his head, and I wasn't sure at all what he meant until he lifted his head and softly said, "She's coming."

That was apparently all he had to tell me, or all he wanted to. He turned to avoid my gaze, perhaps, or else just to try to spot his sister. I craned my neck to do the same, as the throng thickened around us; and there she was at last, breathing hard and wild-eyed, just as the gangplank was rattled down to the quay.

Something had happened, that was clear. But the crowd around us was already beginnng to sweep forward, and threatening to sweep us along with it. This was no place for an inquest. With two children and three suitcases to marshal, to steer and contain, I could spare small attention for anything else as we marched down to *terra firma*. I was aware, distantly, of a woman's voice raised in shrieking horror; glancing despite myself up the sheer cliff of the ship's flank, I saw a man in the white uniform of a company officer lean perilously over the rail with a boat-hook in his hand, trying to snag something that hung swaying on a cord. A muff, I thought, most likely: unseasonable, some bizarrerie of fashion casually treated and almost lost overboard in the excitement of arrival, surely no occasion for such fuss.

The children might have lingered, as children do, staring upward; I shooed them on towards another indulgent taxi and a short ride to the Continental. It was not where we were staying tonight—I preferred a smaller hotel on the outskirts, cheaper, less smart and less busy—but some traditions are paramount. Any Englishwoman making our melancholy journey will stop at the Continental, if only for a pot of tea and a quiet word with a sister in misfortune. Sometimes we form travelling-parties of a dozen or more, all headed to the same destination. The staff and management are used to us; in their off-season, they possibly depend on us. Mourning makes its own season, bereft of calendars.

At this time of year, all the ballroom is made over to tea-tables. We sat in a corner, fenced in by luggage, and I treated the children to hot chocolate and cakes. It was a bribe, and they knew it: whether to elicit their story or simply to buy their ongoing silence, we were none of us quite certain. I had not known myself a coward before this, but truth is a predator sometimes, a fox in the hen-house.

In the event, fate pre-empted me. I had excused myself to the lavatory, and coming out, I found myself face to face with Mrs Bellham.

Who drew breath, as it seemed to scream at the sight of me; and in that shocking moment, all came clear to me like a cascade of falling dominoes.

"Your little dog," I said hastily, "is he, is he…?"

"He is being cared for," she gasped, apparently needing all that breath simply to speak at all. "He, he is not despaired of. But oh, he is terribly ill, choked half to death and terrified the remainder; and you, your children, that *girl*… Oh, she you should despair of. She should be *whipped*…"

I wished that I could say *she shall be*—but that was not my office, nor my right. All that I could offer—the apologies, the promises, the gratitude for her forbearance—was nothing like enough, and we both knew that too.

At length I made my way back to the children, relieved only not to have her at my side.

Either they had seen her accost me, or else they saw my knowing in my face. The girl already had her petulant glower in place, and tried to forestall the accusation.

"He bit Joseph, so—"

"Did he so? Show me."

The boy flinched a little from my voice, but bent obediently to roll up his trouser-leg and down his sock. He had certainly been bitten, though the skin was barely marked. There was no blood.

"I see. And for that, for *that* you appointed yourself judge and jury and executioner too? You took the dog from your brother, and flung it overboard?"

She said nothing more. What more was there?

I had half a mind to march the children straight back to the harbour and take them home. This kind of wickedness was too much. But to go back now would render the whole expedition pointless at best, and perhaps harmful. I ought not to inhibit the curate's chances; and besides, I had brought them on a promise to God, as much as to either of the adults. I was determined yet to fulfil that promise. They should stand by their father's grave, and we would see if the dreadful solemnity of that moment might have an impact.

And besides again, an immediate return would mean another trip on the *Curraghmore*, before the infamy of what she'd done had any chance to fade in the memory of officers or the gossip of the crew. Again I was surprised by my own timidity, but—well. I preferred not to set foot on the vessel quite so soon.

"Very well, Alice. Clearly, you are not to be trusted out of my sight; from now on, you will not leave it. You will share my room at night; you will dog my heels in the day, when we are out and about. It will be pleasant for neither one of us, but needs must. As soon as we reach our boarding-house, you will go straight to bed and I shall lock you in while your brother and I take supper. You should use this opportunity to consider your behaviour, and how to mend it."

The little sinner had much to ponder. At least she wasn't argumentative; I would have abominated a shouting-match. Her sullen silence made her tolerably easy to control. It was tiresome, having to restrict my own movements and feeling her dark angry gaze constantly on me, but a glower never did any harm beyond bringing a headache to the glowerer. I bore up.

The next day we took a train to Hagenzeele. Our hotel was right beside the railway station; after lunch, a brisk walk brought us to the gates of the cemetery still known as Hagenzeele Three.

I had been many times to the neighbouring cemetery, now called the Sucrerie; it was where my brother lay. I had taken my trusty Kodak to Hagenzeele One and Two, on commission for others; I knew them well. It was only happenstance that I'd never come to Three until this trip.

Veteran though I was, the state of it quite shocked me. Years on from the Armistice, I no longer expected rough raw earth and hand-numbered wooden crosses. The Imperial War Graves Commission had done so much elsewhere to make these places restful; long lines of regular white stones amid green grass can be almost comforting. Not this, where rude clods of broken ground spoke more of shell-holes and trenches than the peace of long sleep until the honoured dead shall rise.

The children were both quiet by nature, albeit for different reasons. What in Joseph was a wary care coupled to an appealing shyness, in Alice was a character flaw. Nevertheless: their first exposure to the awful residue of war silenced them utterly. Joe's hand slipped hesitantly into mine as we passed the gate. His sister hung back, until a glance from me had her tossing her head and stalking forward to join us.

It was a threshold as symbolic as it was actual. Within lay death, undisguised, unmitigated. They were too young, of course. One always is.

I had a map: not to guide their faltering feet through the realities of loss and the privilege of mourning, but at least to their father's graveside. That much, I could surely manage.

I should have managed. I had a map. But the simple geometric paper plot held no tangible relationship to the reality of this blasted land, where mud paths wound seemingly at random between the mounds of earth in their close-packed melancholy rows, directionless and dizzying. I struck out confidently enough, but there was no guidance on the ground, and no way to distinguish one section from another.

Soon I was utterly bewildered. The children knew it; they followed me in single file, trying to kick sticky mud from their boots, gathering round me as I faltered and gazing up with cynical, distrustful eyes.

"Perhaps we came in at the wrong gate…?" I muttered helplessly, fatally, trying once more to relate the map I held to the bleak and dreary landscape that seemed to shift about me, leading us further and further astray, out of all knowing. The sky overhead was thick and grey and lowering, threatening to engulf us in fog; my imagination filled with smoke, with shell-blasts and the screaming of horses, the screaming of men…

When he rose up beside us, I might have screamed myself. I know I gasped at the shock of it, a man seeming to materialise out of mud and nothing.

But he had earth on his fingers and a trug at his side, tools and green sprouts laid ready to be planted. I took him for a gardener.

God forgive me, I took him for a gardener.

He said, "May I help you find who you are looking for?"

"Oh, please," I gabbled, "could you? I'm usually so good at this, but…"

"Tell me what you know."

I told him the name and the number, I showed him the map; he led us directly to Captain Northolt's grave.

His name, he said, was Haiter. He was a slim, indeterminate man, with an accent I couldn't quite identify. His soft hat and pencil moustache suggested one origin, his worn English tweeds another, his olive skin perhaps a third. The War had left Europe aswill with such mongrels, refugee from one state or another, settling where they might.

He had nice manners, standing back to let the three of us be private at the graveside. I spoke somewhat to the children, then stepped back in my turn; they should have a period alone with their father and their memories.

Which left me with Mr Haiter. I had half expected him to vanish like a good angel, but he stood fast.

"Their father," he said softly, "but not I think your husband?"

"No, indeed. I am playing usher"—I almost said *dragoman,* almost didn't mind it here and now, with him—"on behalf of a lady not fit to travel."

"Ah. I too have led solemn children to the edge of sorrow. It is work that we must do, who can. You have your own shadow, though, as well as theirs."

"Of course. Who does not?"

"Indeed. But you knew the way, until this last."

"Yes. My brother lies in the Sucrerie."

"I have planted hedges," he said, "in the Sucrerie."

I thanked him for that, though it embarrassed him to listen. I want to think we both recognised the same instinct to service, albeit mine was rendered to the living, his to the dead.

I still had that word *dragoman* in my head, and I was glad now that I hadn't used it; he might actually be Turkish. Or Austrian, or Algerian French. I really couldn't say, and it really didn't matter. He was here. With Flanders mud beneath his nails, and an intimate knowledge of the graves he tended. It was enough.

When I called the children away, it was somehow no surprise to hear him say, "I can show you an excellent place to take your lunch: cheap and nourishing, and accustomed to the English. And afterwards I could bring you to places of some interest, if Miss Alcott doesn't mind it...?"

This was not a sightseeing holiday, but even so: young Joe had so much hope in his eyes, I couldn't play the strict nursemaid now. Even Alice asked quite prettily for leave to look around. They had had their solemn moment, and wanted to be children once again.

"Do you not need to return to your work, Mr Haiter?"

"Ah. No one pays me, for what I do in the gardens of the dead. It is a service," my own word, that I had not used aloud, "for the fallen and their families. My time is my own, and I am a lenient employer. Come. I have heard that the English are not afraid of walking?"

"Certainly not. Lead on, and we are with you."

TO Mr Haiter's mind, at least, a tour of the town meant a running account of the battles that had rolled back and forth across these wretched levels. To be fair to him, there was little else to be seen, perhaps little more to be said about the place; and Joseph at least was eyebright and eager to be shown the ruins of the mediaeval guild-hall bombed by Zeppelin, and the trenches that had been British and then German and then British again, all during three terrible weeks in '16. Apparently there was already talk of preserving one or the other, in some kind of perverse monument to slaughter. Myself, I felt that we had monuments enough, in our hearts and in our cemeteries.

Alice seemed to agree with me. At any rate, we were a more reluctant audience for Mr Haiter's eloquence. It may have been the first time we shared a common purpose, falling into step behind the males of our party and distracting each other with the tracery in a church window where some ancient glass yet clung, the Roman stones reworked by later masons, the determined baker working from a cart before the ruin of his shop.

Accordingly, I was a few paces back and in no position to intervene when Joseph asked—of course!—the exact question that he of course should not:

"What did you do in the war, Mr Haiter?"

His sister's hand made an abortive movement towards him, as if to catch his mouth and hold the words back by main force. Again, I found myself unexpectedly but entirely in sympathy with her intent, approving of her instincts.

"Ah, well, you see, Joe, I was not anywhere near this front. Not in this country at all, as it happens. My struggle was elsewhere."

He was a clever man, or at least a swift talker. Without ever quite spelling it out, he gave the boy an impression of undercover work, risks run and secrets traded far away. I might credit the risks and the secrets, but not the implied official sanction, from our side or the other. The more I considered Mr Haiter, the more shady he seemed. At home I should have avoided him altogether. Here he seemed all of a piece with the blast-pocked, uncertain town and its shifting, shiftless population. He might have come from anywhere and I doubted that he'd stay, but even so. He had already brought great help to me, to us; and whatever else he might have been, on whatever side of the law or the war, he was doing good work now. I believe wholeheartedly in redemption; we are called to do so, surely. The alternative is unthinkable, for any of us. For me.

Deliberately, I let Joe and Mr Haiter draw ahead, just far enough that their soft voices grew inaudible. The girl was more properly my concern, and here was my chance to speak to her in ways her mother never would or could.

It was a surprise, rather, to find myself speaking of my schooldays; a greater surprise to see her emerge from the sullens and seem almost keen. She had been raised with a governess, and had known no taste of school; to listen to her now, one would have thought it her greatest wish to be sent away. Perhaps it was. I did think it might be the saving of her.

In rare accord, then, we came back to the hotel and invited Mr Haiter to tea. He and Joe were well away, quite lost to us. With sugar-bowl and cruet, they reenacted some vital engagement on the tablecloth. Mr Haiter added his pocket-watch, winding the chain back and forth for trenches, to the greater danger of our sandwiches. At length Alice and I were obliged to retreat to a settee by the fireplace, ceding the entire table to their enthusiasm.

We passed the time with more tales out of school, well-beloved mistresses and dormitory adventures. If I exaggerated at all, it was no more than she encouraged in me; and I kept a careful eye on my other charge. He and Mr Haiter sat heads-together, far longer than I'd have thought any shy young boy could bear with a near-stranger. But any boy can tap a depth of focus when you speak to his fascination; and what boy would not be fascinated by a war that he has watched from far away, when he stands in the very places of its happening?

We left them to it, Alice and I—and it was suddenly *Alice and I,* two souls united, I thought it a victory achieved—until supper-time and bedtime intervened. I had warmed far enough towards the girl that when her brother pleaded for her, I lifted my former ukase and let her stay with him. Being clear of course that it was for his sake and not for hers, that she was still disgraced in my eyes and had a long way to go to mend that. Good discipline has a long memory, and cannot be wheedled into humour in an afternoon. She would do well to learn it before there was any prospect of school, and so I told her.

PERHAPS it was that which did the harm, after so much good. I have no way of telling. And a conscience, of course, and no way to appease it except to remind myself again that there is nothing quite so wicked as a girl.

I was not far behind the children, settling into my own room with a sense of comfort at the end of a day well spent. I was glad enough to have that time to myself, without a sulky girl's dark eyes burning at my back; glad to settle into bed and into sleep in short order, feeling that a Rubicon had been crossed, that the watershed was behind us, that muddled metaphor should nevertheless mean easier days ahead.

I was roused again, in the dark again, by a tentative knocking on my door.

My first thought, I confess, was *What has she done this time?*

Never in my darkest imaginings... Well.

I called "Come," and the door opened, and there was Joe once more in his pyjamas, but this time on his own.

Perhaps I had a premonition. Perhaps only his stance, his solitude was enough to tell me. Certainly he seemed to have no words, until I prompted him—and not by asking what the trouble was, how I might help, what he needed. None of that.

"Where's your sister, Joe?"

Perhaps it was only my subconscious seeking the course of logic, as water flows downhill. What could bring him to my door, but something of his sister?

He shook his head, mute but not of malice, only struggling to speak of the enormity. Even at his age, he knew how dreadful this was.

"She is...gone," he managed at last.

"Gone? What do you mean, gone?"

"Run away," he said, familiar with the idea no doubt from story-books.

"Oh, dear Lord..."

"With Mr Haiter."

That was an idea that had come from no story-book. I stopped in the act of reaching for my slippers, and stared at him. "What nonsense, child! What are you thinking?"

"There's a note," he said simply.

THERE was a note. Not from her to me, no. From Haiter to her: written on a page torn from a notebook, folded so small that it might be slipped surreptitiously from one hand to another when he bent to kiss her fingers in what I had thought a mockery of formal manners; a hasty scrawl of such passion and desire that I blushed to think of Joseph reading this.

It might have drawn any girl who wanted to believe it, who craved another life than that she had. It was an open door, and an act of wanton wickedness to step across the threshold. That would never stop her, of course; it might spur her on. The child was bad to the bone. She might not know what she was walking into, but she knew what she was doing to her family, how she disgraced them all. And yet she went. I almost wrote *And so she went.* It did feel that deliberate, a slap in the face to all that was honourable and English and upright. She even chose to leave the note, that we should know exactly of her choice.

I knew, I *knew* what she was, or something of it; and even so. I had let myself be mollified, be woo'd, led by the hand down the paths of self-deception. I saw what I had so wanted to see, what she had so carefully shown me, first signs of reformation. Dormitory feasts and kindly mistresses, oh dear Lord, while all the time…

I roused the hotel, of course; knowing it was too late, of course. She and Haiter were long gone. He had a motor-car; they might be anywhere in the Low Countries, if Alice had sneaked out as soon as Joe was well asleep. The night-porter denied all knowledge, insisting that no girl had come by him. Perhaps it was even true. Perhaps not—morals were slippery in those times, probity as broken as the stonework, and who would not take bribes if he could get them?—but the hotel was old and, yes, broken, and badly patched. There might be half a dozen ways for a lithe and nimble girl to slither out unnoticed.

We interviewed the police, of course, but they were frankly little interested in the sins of a foreign girl. The notion of a marriageable age was still new enough that they wanted just to shrug at the English termagant and say "Let her go."

Which I felt almost that I would have done, had she been my own. Almost. She had made her bed, now let her lie in it.

But of course she was not my own, and I made all the fuss that was owing, and more besides. And it availed me nothing, of course, it did not find Alice at the border nor summon her back in penitence; and after several futile days I did at last have to return Joseph to England. He needed the reassurance of his home and his mother; I could do no more good here, or for him.

Cables, of course, had gone ahead of us, to warn his mother and the curate too. Only a cad would have looked in their responses for any hint of relief, that I was not bringing the girl safe back.

It was on the boat going home that I experienced my first qualm, a kind of mental sea-sickness, a lurch of whatever solid ground was left me.

We were on deck with the good sea breeze in our faces, sniffing as it were for the first scent of home; and the boy was playing with something, holding it close, running its chain through his fingers.

"Joe, what do you have there?"

He showed me, nothing loth; I think perhaps he had meant for me to see.

It was a gentleman's pocket-watch, a rather fine one, and I had seen it before.

"How did you come by that?"

"Mr Haiter gave it me, after tea. He said I might keep it. He said the world was all awash with watches."

Perhaps that was true, at least of Haiter's world. Even so, men of that bent do not give away gold half-hunters on a whim. Even in that moment, the first dim suspicion touched my mind.

It was too late, of course. I could hardly make him return the watch to its owner; and besides, I was very afraid that he had earned it. *"Hear nothing, Joe, as your sister leaves the room. Say nothing until after midnight, buy us some time; this watch will tell it to you, and then it is yours if you're a good boy, if you help us both..."*

And why shouldn't he want his sister gone, she who terrorised him and his mother both? He would have let her go regardless; of course he took the watch, in compensation for what he wanted most to lose. Boys are always acquisitive, regardless.

THAT was my first thought: shocked, but not surprised. Arguing a logic, albeit a child's logic, to what he had done. What he might have done.

Later, in bed in Mrs Morgan's house, I couldn't sleep; and so of course my mind ran on into fancy, constructing a whole new interpretation, a whole new world of horror.

How if the boy had been no innocent in this, how if he had sold not his silence but his sister?

"Take this watch in fee, and be like the monkeys: see no evil, hear no evil. Say nothing, when I come. I will take the girl, and leave you free. And leave this note, to tell another story altogether…"

If he came with chloroform, one man might take a sleeping girl with ease. And carry her out past the complaisant, well-paid porter; and carry her off to who knew what evil?

And Joseph… Well. Joseph had a watch.

It wasn't possible, no. It couldn't be. No boy his age could be so thoroughly wicked as my imagination was trying to paint him now. He would need to have deceived me utterly, and to have so subdued his sister that she would bow her head and take the blame for anything—for Mrs Bellham's dog, for anything—rather than call him a liar. She would need to have seen him believed so often and so long that she had quite given up protesting her innocence or his guilt.

I had thought I knew how cruelly unfair the world could be, a middle-aged spinster with no wealth and no beauty—but I could take lessons from that girl, if I was right.

But no, of course I was not right. It was a night-time farrago of distress and fantasy compounded with guilt. Nothing more.

No.

NEXT morning, as we waited for the train, he glanced up and said, "My mother will be so lonely in the house now, with no female companionship; and you must be lonely too, Auntie Win, all on your own in your little cottage there. I think you should come to live with us. I think I will suggest it, to my mother."

And I shuddered as he said it, and saw it all, all come to pass.

THERMODYNAMICS AND/OR THE REMITTANCE MEN

*A*LEXANDRIA IS WHERE WE GO; CAIRO *is what we come back to.*
There's a truth in there, a resonance deeper than the simple facts of travel, of journey and return. Alexandria, city of poets and exiles, stranger in a strange land, in exile itself from its own proper country: of course we'd want to go there. How not?

Cairo, though: Cairo is where we belong, what we belong to. What we were made for, made from. Both. And made by, that too. Cairo is the blood and the stink and the bone of us; Alexandria can only ever be the dream and the hope and the yearning. Cairo is a state of being, where Alexandria is merely a state of mind.

CAIRO is the colonial city, the very expression of empire. The British—I should say *we British,* of course, but I will not—stroll about with their swagger-sticks and their bristling moustaches, their uniforms of serge or crumpled linen or crisp white cotton duck, their parasols and their pets. Dogs and monkeys and mocking clinging birds, the British will make a pet of anything that moves. And take fond possession of anything that does not. Except Alexandria, perhaps. It lies within their ambit, beneath their aegis, under their control and yet never quite within their reach or understanding.

Here in Cairo, they press an alien order into the heart of the city. Streets and structures, steam lines and railway lines, queues and currency and church parade on Sundays, ten thousand little British days played out under a Cairene sun.

GOD be thanked, I never was a part of that great enterprise. I can look the part and act the part, but it has only ever been a performance. I can don the skin of the Englishman abroad, and doff it just as easily. Underneath—well, I am still and always irredeemably an Englishman, and still and always irrefutably abroad, and yet. Not one of them.

Sometimes I wonder if that isn't true of us all. Stand on any street corner in what we laughingly call the British Quarter and see the nursemaids go to and fro with their charges, the corporals and the memsahibs, the schoolboys and the bankers, the bureaucrats from the Colonial Office: perhaps every one of them wears their label as superficially as I would. Inside, perhaps they all know they're playing a role in this grand absurd theatre that we call an Empire, and ours.

Nothing here is truly ours, any more than we are truly us.

THE Voyagers' Club might have been lifted wholesale from Pall Mall and deposited discreetly just off Soliman Pasha Square. Down a side-street so narrow it's an alley by another name the club stands, behind its classic Georgian façade and its curtained windows. If gentlemen have to abandon their steam-fiacres in the square and walk fifty yards to the door, so be it. The club servants keep the path swept clean and the gas-lamps lit above the door, and tip a street-boy to chase off the inevitable stray dogs. Stray cats, of course, are as welcome as anyone.

More welcome than we ever were, I and my kind: strays ourselves, who have the right of entry by virtue of our birth, and but few rights else. Few virtues else, that too.

This particular night, I came light-footed up the steps from the street, to be greeted by the doorman with his usual resentful nod.

"All well, Barrows?"

"As well as might be expected, sir." *Not very well at all, so long as the true gentlemen continue to tolerate your sort.* Not that he actually said so, of course; he liked his job too well for honesty. Like any London club, the Voyagers' offers its members and their guests all the comforts of Home: British food and drink, British newspapers in the library, British beds in narrow rooms, and British servants to judge you where even God would not.

My friends and I were born to this, to all of this, but we seldom ascended to the penetralia of the Voyagers'. Members in good standing we might be; unwelcome none the less. One grows tired of sidelong glances in the dining hall, the disapproving rustle of papers in the library, the sudden heavy silence in the billiard room.

Still we came, for stubbornness and convenience and an excellent port. For the most part we chose to congregate in the basement, and keep the servants trotting up and down those narrow stairs all night.

Properly, we met in the Silence Room, which was meant for study and private contemplation. We had long since turned out the scholars, though, and made over the room to our own desires and designs. A rug and easy chairs, convenient low tables, coals for the fire—a weapon against damp as much as chill, with the Nile such a very close neighbour—and a bell to bring those sullen servants down.

This day, I opened the door to the Silence Room and was met by a fug of smoke and a buzz of quarrelsome voices. Bellaire's pipe, I diagnosed, two rival cigars and a cigarette; Creighton's voice and Mallenby's, with inter-jections from one Smith or the other, both. Smith Major would be one of the cigars; Smith Minor—no relation—was careful of his wind, and didn't smoke. Creighton was the cigarette, certainly. I recognised the sulphur of his hand-rolled street tobacco. Which meant that either Mallenby was smoking tonight, not likely where the possibility of port came into play, or—

"Tattersall, man—the handle stands by you, sir! In God's name, use the thing. I can hear Minor's wheezing from here, and I can see nothing at all."

"To be strictly accurate," came his voice from the miasma, "I stand by the handle; but I take your meaning. One moment."

I heard a metallic cranking, backed by the swift busy rasp of a ratchet imparting load to a spring. After that came a soft, scrupulous ticking, some-where within the walls, and the air began to clear in short order. Being subterranean, of course we have no window; Bellaire had fashioned an inge-nious mechanical flue in lieu. He called it his aerator, and spoke of a patent application. That would never happen. Bellaire's inventions all tended the same way: a working prototype that he would fiddle into convenient usabil-ity, and then no more. His own house was a wondrous engine, devices of every sort all powered by a steam-driven clock, but it was also a premature museum, a monument to unrecognised endeavour.

At least we could all enjoy the effects of his aerator—so long as someone remembered to pump the handle every hour or so. Tattersall applied himself to the task, then looked me up and down and said, "My dear Chapman, I rejoice in your good news."

"I have shared no news," I said bluntly, irritated. It was none of his business, and besides: how could he know?

"Your very clothes betray you. All last week you were walking here, those dreary miles from your digs. Today you have no dust in your turn-ups, no camel-dung on your Oxford brogues. Indeed, you are quite nattily turned out; from which I deduce a recent pleasant call upon your banker, followed by your arrival here in the fiacre you haven't been able to afford for a month or more. In short, sir, you have received your quarterly subvention, and are in funds."

"Damn your eyes, Tattersall!" I took swift rein on my temper, and went on more moderately, "Are you always right?"

He shrugged elegantly, and I felt briefly envious of his tailoring.

"Detective tricks," came a growl from the wing-chair. "Chose the wrong path in life, didn't you, Tatters?"

"Not noticeably," Tattersall murmured, shooting his very expensive cuffs. Perhaps my envy was not so much brief as ongoing. If clothes make the man, he was very much the better-made. "I do know what a detective earns. I have made…significantly more. And don't need to pester my banker every quarter-day to learn if my distant and disgusted relatives have kept their word once more."

"I'm hardly the only one here who has taken money to leave his country for his country's good," I said, as mildly as I could manage. "Indeed, you might be the only one who has not. Though I hear you were barely a step ahead of Scotland Yard when you took your own departure."

"There but for the grace of God, old boy. We all have our histories, that drove or dragged us here." His gaze strayed idly around the room, and mine followed as by nature, as he meant it to. The debtor, the runaway bridegroom, the defrocked priest, the cashiered cavalry captain: England allows so little leeway to its disreputable. Happily, the colonies are less nice.

On a table beside the hearth, bottle and soda-syphon stood waiting, alongside a jug of beer. I filled a glass with whisky and seltzer-water, and looked about more purposefully. I was last of the likely arrivals; everyone had a drink; I lifted mine and said, "A toast, then. I give you the Remittance Men—and long may our families continue to remit."

We were a club within a club, and disliked for that as much as for our individual reprehensible pasts, our current seedy, shady tenancy and our likely future shame.

Still, no one on the committee had ever offered to blackball us. Provisions were made; we had our bolt-hole here, we had our drinks and licence to wander upstairs when we must. I sank into my place on the ottoman beside Smith Minor, touched my glass against his beer mug in a quiet, private toast, then gazed more closely at the boy.

"You're looking a little peaky, old lad. How's the chest?"

"Nothing to worry about," he said stoutly. "It's this beastly weather, that's all."

Last month, it had been *this beastly heat*. The first rains had already broken that excuse.

I said, "Dr Murchison is safe to be upstairs at this hour. I could hale him down, to have a look at you."

He pulled a face, like the child he almost still was. "Not tonight." Children always seek to bargain with the inevitable. "I'll see him tomorrow, when I don't have to do it in the club."

"You'd rather go to that clinic he runs by the souk?" Murchison was a genuinely good man, which was why we rarely saw him in the Silence Room. Definitively, not one of us.

"Frankly, yes."

"He'll charge you the same. And say the same, and send the same nurse to see you follow orders."

"Nevertheless."

Nevertheless, he'd rather wait among the dispossessed in the noise and dust of the market than make an exhibition of himself under the members' eyes. Of course he would.

"All right, but I'll come with you. Just to be sure that you do."

He shrugged, smiled. We left it at that.

"I'll tell you what, Bellaire," Tattersall said, speaking supposedly to one but actually to us all. "I've a curio here I picked up, which I think might tickle your fancy. Yours too, Padre."

Creighton looked aggrieved, as he always did when we used that title; but we were fond of it. And a man may lose his living, but not the curiosity that cost it him. Of course he rose and came to see what Tattersall had laid down on the sideboard. So did Bellaire, and so did we all.

"A scarab, surely?" Creighton said. "In the style of the heart scarabs of the New Kingdom, but—"

"Contemporary," from Bellaire. "Unquestionably. Brass, largely, with steel banding. Cast, not carved. Fine work, too: not a tool-mark to be seen, and these coloured patinas are not easy to—I say!"

His startlement was echoed in all of us, gasps and cries and more. I think we all took a step back, except of course for Tattersall. Then—reassured, perhaps, by his stillness—we pressed forward again, to see just what this thing was doing.

It was a toy, a mechanism, the simulacrum of a scarab beetle. It had opened its wing-cases when Bellaire poked at it; the sudden movement and the sharp buzzing sound were wholly unexpected and disturbingly lifelike. Not one of us thought the thing an actual living creature, but if devices could harbour life, it would have been utterly persuasive.

It fluttered those enamelled wing-cases at us, and rose up on needle staccato legs, and scuttled about on the mahogany. Something in it could seemingly sense an edge; its movements seemed quite random, but it never fell off the sideboard. Nor, when we laid obstacles in its path, did it run into them. Those jewelled eyes could not possibly see, but something greater than the laws of chance was turning it away from trouble.

"Is it clockwork?" Creighton breathed. I think we were all moved by the beauty and the mystery of the thing, but that would never stop us seeking to anatomise it. Taking things apart was what we did.

"Oh, surely," Bellaire said. "How else would you motivate it? The workings must be a marvel, though: so complex, so delicate, and silent too."

In motion, the thing was anything but silent. Its dagger-feet clicked on the varnish, its wing-cases rattled aggressively, I thought some tiny bellows-action was giving it a voice, a hint of whistle. But there was no resolute ticking of a clock-action in its interior.

Bellaire was our man of science, though, our ingenious engineer; we took his word for it unquestioningly. Tattersall said not a word, he only held up one finger: *wait*.

Every clockwork toy has a cycle that it runs through, before it runs down. This had one trick more to show us. It stood abruptly still, so that we'd have thought it done if not for Tattersall's alert anticipation; and then it unfolded wings of tender filigree, the finest gold and silver wire. They trembled so credibly in the still air, I do believe we all expected to see it lift and fly.

Of course it did no such thing. It stretched those wings and agitated them, as if to hint of more; and then it put them away again and closed its shell, folded its legs beneath it and was still.

"May I...?"

In response to Tattersall's nod, Bellaire snatched the gadget up and examined it minutely. Baffled, he said, "I can find no hole for a key."

"There is none," Tattersall replied. "No hole, no key. I had it up till dawn, running through its little repertoire over and over; and then again a dozen times today. It has had small rest and no refreshment, and yet it is as bright and busy as it ever was, no sign of depletion in its energies. I thought that might be a matter of some interest."

"Indeed, indeed. It's not powered by steam, clearly; so if not clockwork, then what? I can find no screws either, that might allow access to its interior." Bellaire screwed a jeweller's loupe into his eye and continued to turn the thing over in his hands, seeking and seeking, unrewarded. He muttered to himself as he peered, repeating the laws of thermodynamics and conservation of energy, "heat is work, and yet it's not even warm to the touch..."

We knew all about the laws of thermodynamics. I ignored him. "Tattersall? Whence came this trinket?"

"I told you, I picked it up."

"Yes, but in whose house?"

"Shepheard's," he said nonchalantly.

"They still let you through the door?"

He raised an eloquent eyebrow. "My dear man! I have the entrée to some of the most exclusive salons on the Continent. I hardly think the doorman of a busy hotel is going to bar my way. Nor the manager issue a ukase against me. As it happens, I am *persona grata* with the staff of Shepheard's at every level; they won't hear a word against me."

"Just as well, in the circumstances," Smith Major growled. Minor snickered softly, where he was hanging over my shoulder, hoping for another sight of the wonder.

"Be that as it may," Creighton said, with not a note of censure in his voice. "You were let into Shepheard's on the nod; you let yourself into some other man's room, and helped yourself to this—I am going to call it a puzzle, because I am not sure what words else to use—among other goods, no doubt."

"No doubt," Tattersall agreed dryly.

"Very well, then. The question remains, whose room? Who had possession of this before you, and how did he come by it, and where?"

"It didn't exactly come with a provenance attached," Tattersall murmured. "I did look about quite carefully"—I believe we all felt sure of that already—"and I found nothing else remotely like it. Nor the tools and templates of a craftsman, the designs of a draftsman. He's no more an artificer in secret, an amateur of the craft, than he is in public."

"Perhaps he leaves all that behind him," Minor suggested, "in his workshop at home. Do you travel with your lockpicks and safebreaking tools?"

For answer, Tattersall simply shook his jacket pocket. The resultant rattle was enough to leave Minor gasping and wheezing—it was never good to make him laugh, when his chest was bad—and holding his hands up in apology, abashed.

"You still haven't put a name to him," Mallenby observed.

"No. There is that within me which would prefer not to do so, even now. I no more choose to boast my activities here, than I do to apologise for them. However," he went on swiftly to stem our rising protest, "tonight—well, tonight the man himself has taken that choice out of my hands. His name is Sir Edward Bolsover."

Possibly that name meant something to each of us, except perhaps to Smith Minor, who's a heedless young devil. In the digestive silence after Tattersall let drop the name, Creighton said, "Sir Edward Bolsover has a room in the club here tonight, at my invitation."

"I know it," said Tattersall. "That's why I couldn't keep him anonymous, and why the choice is no longer mine to make. You know the man, Padre. What can you tell us, beyond what we read in the newspapers and hear in the tap-room?"

"Well, for one thing, you're right that he could not have made this, nor anything like it. He no more has the skill in his fingers than he has the understanding in his head, or the invention in his soul. He could not conceive of such a thing; if he were given the conception, he could not design it; if he were given the designs, he could not achieve it. No, if this was found in his possession, the kindest thought I have is that he bought it. More likely— well, I will not say. It's still possible that he's an honest man."

"Padre?" Mallenby spoke for us all. "How do you come to know the Great Wen?"

"Oh, don't call him that, it's too ridiculous—and we were at school and university together. Five years at Rugby and then Oxford after, though I was Keble, of course, and he was Magdalen."

"Why do you call him the Great Wen?" Minor asked, all innocence. "I thought that was London?"

"And so it is—but Bolsover owns great swathes from the City to the East End, and so I suppose the name stuck."

"Come, Padre, you're too good to the man. He's a grotesque swelling on the face of humanity, Minor, and *so* the name stuck." That was Smith Major, making even Creighton smile, albeit reluctantly.

"Well. He is a boor, certainly. A loud boor, and a bully. I tried to see less of him at Oxford, and he wouldn't stand for that. If any man was ever bullied into a social circle, that man would be myself. Sounds absurd, doesn't it? But I believe he liked to show me off, as though my credentials could add to his credibility. So long as he had such a great intellectual in his train, in his *eager* train, then no one could accuse him of vapidity or worse, do you see?"

"Oh, I think we see," Tattersall said, smiling. "Truth now, Padre—just how eager were you?"

"Well, the food at Keble was particularly diabolical in my time, so..." The end of that sentence was lost in a shout of sympathetic laughter

"So, Padre." Smith Major again, determined. "Vapidity, or worse? What *would* you accuse him of?"

"Oh, worse. Far worse, since he's been loosed on the world. I hesitate to speak ill of my alma maters—almae matres, I suppose that should be—but neither Rugby nor Oxford did him any good at all. He inherited money, too much and too young; he's made much more since, by means I prefer not to think about. If he's in Egypt now, it's because he's found some way to exploit a new country."

"Oh, be fair, Padre," Mallenby said, only half joking, "we all do that. Even those of us who only live here because we're not wanted at home. We exploit that distance, and the opportunity it gives us to live our own little mockery of English life without penalty of English law. It's shameful, really."

"It is shameful, but the weather's better." That was Minor, trying to lighten the mood.

"It is shameful," Creighton went on, "and we are the least of it, the least worst of all the Empire means and does. Britannia wouldn't believe it, but it's true. Her rule is...not benign, for any of the native peoples. We see that best, perhaps, who live here on the margins of empire, less engaged with it; disinterested observers, if you like, merely taking advantage. Bolsover is the other thing, deeply invested and cruelly disposed. He owns diamond mines on the other side of the continent, and he treats his people barbarously. Barbarously. I would fear for the *fellahin,* if he saw and seized an opportunity here."

"Well," I said, "and this is the man you have invited in among us? I'm hurt, Padre. We might count as members more by default than acclamation, but nevertheless. Do you despise us so very much?"

"Don't be absurd. You can't imagine that I want him here. He sent a boy with a note this morning, saying that his hotel room had been burgled"— with a pause to glower at Tattersall—"and he no longer felt his property or his person safe at Shepheard's. He has a berth on the airship tomorrow, but in the meantime could I recommend him somewhere? I was his only friend in Cairo, and he didn't at all trust the men who had enticed him here, etc etc. It was all nonsense, of course—he is no kind of milksop, to be alarmed by an intruder, nor yet by the shady creatures he does business with—but he will have enjoyed tracking me down and obliging me to offer assistance. If I'd ignored the note, he'd have turned up himself, and—well, you know my domestic situation."

We did. The last thing poor Creighton could ever want to see on his doorstep would be a wealthy acquaintance from his former life. Not that he actually had a doorstep. He barely had a door to call his own, sharing his quarters with an excommunicate Copt and a Jain who had somehow wandered here from Portuguese India. We called them the Three Seekers. They occupied a grim hut at the desert's edge and pooled all their resources, funds from England and alms from the charitable and letter-writing fees from the illiterate. Some nights, I knew, they went to bed hungry and called it a fast.

"The club was the best I could think of," Creighton went on. "Where he could be answered, accommodated, and evaded, all at once. I wrote that I was unable to join him for dinner, due to a previous engagement. He'll be upstairs right now, I expect, making some other member's life a misery, thank God." He lifted his glass to us, his previous engagement, and tried to look suitably ashamed of himself.

"He is," Tattersall confirmed. "He's found himself a table of cronies already. I'll give him this much, the man's a fast worker. Happily, so am I."

He looked at us meaningfully; we gazed back at him, a little aghast. He was impossible to misunderstand, and almost impossible to credit. It was the laws of thermodynamics that had kept us friends—or his interpretation of those laws, rather, a particular sense of honour that transmuted them into laws of hospitality. *The virtuous thief does not steal from those poorer than himself.* That was the Second Law, and the one that allowed his welcome into our variously shabby homes. The First Law stated that *The virtuous thief does not steal from his host;* any roof that offered him shelter was safe from his depradations.

That had always included the Voyagers'. Until, apparently, tonight.

"Gentlemen—does any man among you believe that he came by this… trinket…honestly or honourably?"

Silence.

"No. Well, then: we have one last chance to learn whence he had it, and what else he had. I've already taken as much as I want of his wealth; this is a quest for information. If you can be quick and quiet, you are welcome to assist."

That was unprecedented. Tattersall did his work alone, and never discussed it. We had all respected that discretion—which is not to say that we were incurious. At first mention of this opportunity, we rose to our feet *en masse.*

"What, all of you? Well, so be it. Mob-handed it is. Quick and quiet, mind. Do as I tell you, and touch nothing until I say. Bring your smokes, by all means; leave your glasses here."

BARROWS must have been startled to see us troop up from the basement, file through his demesne and head on into the club proper. As a servant of the house, he was owed no explanation; nevertheless, Tattersall tossed him a glance as we passed. "Villeforte using his telescope this evening, d'ye know, Barrows?"

"I believe Sir Marcus is at dinner, sir."

"Is he? Splendid. Then he won't mind if we spend an hour peering at the native beauties, will he?"

"Sir Marcus did give me to understand, sir, that he was…increasingly frustrated to find that his instrument had been meddled with in his absence."

"Gave you to understand, did he? Well, well. Did he give you two bob at the same time?"

"Sir, I cannot—"

"No. No, of course not. But I can. Tuppence is more in his line, I believe. Tell you what, Barrows: here's half a sovereign," and a flicker of gold passed between them, barely appearing in the one hand before it had vanished into the other. "That's to make up for all those times we've kept you running up and down the stairs, above and beyond the call of duty. All serene?"

"That is very generous, sir." The man's face was a mask, professional to the core. No device known to man would have been adequate to measure the depth of his surprise. Still, we knew: and it was certain sure that if, as a result of our activities tonight, some unholy detective were to interrogate him about the members' doings, he would remember only that we six had been playing with another man's property, turning the magnificent astronomical telescope on the roof to more mundane pursuits, hoping to focus those highly polished lenses on heavenly bodies somewhat closer to hand.

We proceeded in single file up the stairs, Tattersall keeping the rear like a sheepdog herding an unwieldy flock. Past the first floor, library and billiard-room and dining hall, the steady buzz-and-clatter of a male congregation at the trough; past the second floor, members' bedrooms and bathrooms. Minor was somehow in the lead, and he led us all the way up through the attics—servants' bedrooms, boxrooms and the like—to a narrow door out onto the flat roof.

We gathered there in the air and the lowering dusk, and he said, "I thought, if we'd said we were coming up here, we probably should."

He sounded uncertain, but Tattersall clapped him on the shoulder and said, "Quite right. Always establish an alibi first. We said we'd make a nuisance of ourselves with Villeforte's precious telescope; let us nuise. Is that a word? Never mind. Take five minutes, gentlemen. Stroll about, scatter your ash widely, enjoy the view and leave your cigar stubs in inappropriate places. That'll confirm our occupation here, if matters should come so far. And meanwhile…"

He stripped the oilcloth cover from Villeforte's magnificent brass tube, dropping that carelessly at the foot of a chimney. The telescope was pointed at the heavens; he twisted it about and tilted it crudely downwards, towards the low rooftops where young Cairene women were accustomed to take their evening baths, their voices shrill as crickets as they called to each other through the gloaming.

The lens caps followed the oilcloth into obscurity, in a gesture guaranteed to enrage Sir Marcus. There were no other guarantees. When men such as we turn to downright larceny, we cross a border that we have no more than stalked before. That side of the line was *terra incognita* to all of us, bar Tattersall.

He took me by the elbow now and drew me to the parapet. "I love to watch the city as the sun sets," he murmured. "It's like a change of master, or at least of oversight. The light goes, the Empire salutes the flag as it comes down, soldiers are confined to barracks and the night city marches in to reclaim its own."

It was happening as he spoke, eerily as it seemed in response to his words. Hazelights in the streets, more traditional lamps showing through windows and on rooftops and the vicious furnace flare of ironworks, the smudged glow of smokestacks and steamships on the river, locomotives oozing like fireworms through and through the city, the slow drift of bright-lit airships overhead, and all backed by the uncanny unlight that invested the pyramids on our horizon, on every horizon, so that those three stolen tombs stood out even more boldly after dark than they did throughout the day: even with so many and so varied lights all about, they served only to herald and enforce the dark as it closed in upon us, as it transposed our Cairo from one reality to another.

We are creatures of the margin, we Remittance Men, belonging not quite anywhere. Which was another way to say that Tattersall was really not quite one of us, because he held himself a full subject of both worlds, light and shadow. The idle companionable sardonic man-about-town slipped away with the sun, and standing beside me in his place was the Tattersall I'd never seen till now, brisk and businesslike, competent, experienced and careful. He gathered us all with a whistle and a jerk of his head, and led us across the roof to another doorway, another staircase down.

Of course he had prospected this route ahead of time. Down two floors, along a corridor to one numbered door among a dozen such; a brisk tap, a brief pause, and he drew a sinister set of steel hooks from his pocket.

"Are those…?"

"Yes. Be quiet."

Minor subsided, abashed. I touched his shoulder for comfort, won myself a sidelong smile that warmed my heart for a moment before we both turned back to watch Tattersall at work.

There was little enough to see. Perhaps he'd practised this too, on this very door; perhaps he had tested himself against every door, every lock in the club, just in case. He slipped one shaft into the keyhole, fiddled briefly, followed it with a second, a third. There was no fuss or drama, only a sudden anticlimactic click and the door was open.

He withdrew his instruments and oiled his way inside, staying us with a gesture. I don't suppose I was the only one to wonder what we'd say if someone came along the corridor now, or which one of us would be bold enough to say it.

It can't honestly have been more than a few seconds, though it seemed so very much longer, before he appeared again in the doorway.

"All serene," he said in a murmur. "Even so: don't speak unless you have to, and keep your voices down. Try not to touch anything. Just hover. When I need you, I'll let you know."

So we stood in a cluster in the middle of the rug, and watched him go to work. Creighton might have murmured a prayer, to a god that none of us was quite sure he believed in; Minor might have slipped his arm through mine and rested his chin upon my shoulder, wheezing softly into my ear. That boy never could keep still or quiet, without drawing on someone else's strength. His captaincy was purchased, never earned; a less military soul would be hard to imagine. Though I'm sure he looked a picture in his uniform, on his horse.

It had not occurred to me hitherto that there might be an art to burglary. A science, of course: Tattersall's speed and skill with the picklocks was impressive, but not really surprising. But he went around that room with a particular grace that spoke to a deep understanding of the human psyche, the very work we commonly look to art to provide.

From hat-boxes to shoe-trees, he looked at everything with swift fingers and sharp eyes. Through the wardrobe, through the drawers of the dressing table, through the suitcases—two, and both quite empty, which had him pausing for a moment, gazing towards the door, unexpectedly thoughtful and out of his rhythm—before he said, "Very well, then. I was hoping for something, anything physical that might have yielded a clue as to the scarab's provenance. Even if it only served to deepen the mystery, to confirm that we're looking in the right place." Another glance at the mute and unrevealing door. "Lacking that—and I've looked twice and found nothing—then here's where you come in, gentlemen. I'm afraid it's noses to the grindstone and devil take the hindmost. Devil take us all, if we're caught here before the hindmost is done with his reading."

So saying, he hauled a leather case out from under the bed, deposited it on the covers and flipped open the lid. Papers spilled out, and he distributed them by the handful.

"Quick as you can," he said crisply. "If we learn what his business is here, where he's been and who he's been dealing with, we'll have a better chance of tracking this thing down to its source."

Honestly, I thought he was clutching at straws now, and we were all of us men of straw. Other men made a go of colonial life, made fortunes indeed; we merely floated in increasing anxiety from one grudging payment to the next. Tattersall was the only one among us who took his living from the teeming city that we called our home.

Still: Remittance Men know when to pull together, before the world entire pulls apart. That thing in Tattersall's pocket gave me a chill deep in my bones, where all of Egypt's heat could never penetrate. We of the modern world are used to wonders, be they clockwork or steam-driven or more arcane yet. This, though—this was something other. It came from somewhere other, I was sure; no mortal hand—or at least, no human hand—had made it. There was no such science known to man. If it baffled the Empire, it baffled us all; and between us, creatures of shadow though we were, we could more or less represent the Empire. Or at least her sum of knowledge. Bellaire spoke for science and engineering, Creighton for philosophy and religion. Smith Major was somehow a poor gambler but a fine mathematician; he said that he could calculate probabilities, but that luck always forsook him in the end. Mallenby was our linguist, a school usher before love betrayed him. And I?— Well, I had my uses. If you needed a précis of any novel within the Oxford syllabus, or a more thoughtful essay on the effect of the Romantic poets on the English landscape—or vice versa—I was your man. No good asking me to write a poem—never seek me in Alexandria, for you will always find me here—but if a critic's what you're after, look no further.

I flicked through the sheaf of notes that Tattersall had handed me, and was first to hand them back. "Bills, notes of tender, notes of hand," I said briskly. "He seems to be mounting an expedition. And paying for everything in advance, which is…unusual."

"'Unprecedented' would be closer to the mark," Tattersall said. "He must be very confident. Not only of discoveries, but market value. Major, would you care to cast your eye across these, in case there's something hidden in the numbers?"

"No need," Smith Major rasped. "I've numbers here of my own. I can tell you this, it's not a expedition he's outfitting, it's a small army. Whatever he thinks he's on to, he intends to take it by force. Likely a place, not an artefact; this manifest is enough to stock a siegetown for the winter."

"Or a campsite," Minor murmured, "that he thinks he'll need to defend all season long, while they dig out whatever artefact he's after. I've names here that I recognise, from regimental gossip. Old soldiers, cashiered for worse sins than my own."

"Does anyone have a map?"

No. No one had a map.

"Very well. All the papers back in the case, please, gentlemen. Don't worry about original order; that had been disturbed already, for I tipped everything out haphazardly on my first incursion. And found the scarab buried beneath, for what that's worth. We have what we came for, more or less. Bolsover knows something, the whereabouts of something, or believes that he does. We have learned no more of the location than we have of the target; either he knows neither himself yet, or else he's holding those secret in his head. It's a fair guess that the scarab is connected, but not a certainty. We—"

We all turned our heads as one, at the sound of a key in the door.

HAD Tattersall locked it again behind us? It didn't matter, either way. A moment's delay for us, a moment's warning for the new arrival: the door was going to open in any case, and there was neither time nor room to hide. We stood where we were, six men grouped around the bed. I felt Minor's hand on the small of my back, firm and reassuring. Perhaps he drew strength from the touch, just as I did: the whole maybe greater than the sum of its parts, though that too would be a breach in the laws of thermodynamics.

A figure, a man stood in the doorway, momentarily still, gazing at us each in turn, it seemed; then he took a slow, careful pace into the room, and closed the door equally carefully behind him. "There is no need for that, sir."

I was briefly puzzled, till I saw Tattersall put away the revolver I had not seen him draw. His dinner jacket must be remarkably well-cut, to conceal such a weight. Once more I envied him his tailor.

The man before us was far more modestly dressed, and most certainly not the man whose secrets we were here to burgle. He was thin, sallow, almost nondescript in his clean but faded linen suit.

"We forget," Tattersall said slowly into the silence, "we who live this life in exile from the norms of society—but of course a gentleman travelling abroad would have a man to attend him. I knew it, the moment I saw that he was unpacked here, for just the one night's stay. He would never have done so much himself. And of course you'd use the dinner hour to lay out his night-things and see that all was as he liked it. However, I do have to say, you don't look much like an Englishman's valet."

"No, sir. Sir Edward's own man was…unable to continue in his service, after falling ill last week. I was the local contact, acting as dragoman so long as Sir Edward remained in Egypt; I said I would be happy to attend to his personal needs also. I am not inexperienced in these matters."

"No, I daresay not." Smith Major gave him the once-over with an impeccably jaundiced eye. "Dismissed—for what, for drinking, was it? or for petty thieving?—well, no matter. No more a gentleman's gentleman, anyway. So you make shift as best you can, eh? And find your way to Cairo because this is where all the dregs of Empire wash up at the last."

"Indeed, sir." His voice was bland, his gaze was indirect; his insolence was absolute, and absolutely telling. Remittance men all, we had not a word to say in our own defence. "And now, if I may ask…?"

"Oh, I don't think you need to ask, do you?" Tattersall was the coolest of us all. "You know very well why we're here. In fact, you know better than we do. Why don't you explain it to us?"

"Sir?"

"Oh, come. His valet didn't fall so conveniently ill without help, did he? With you so handily situated to stand in? My guess is, your masters had you in place from the beginning just to keep an eye on Bolsover because he's dangerous; then you saw what he had, or what he meant, and acted straight away. With the valet out of the picture and you to substitute, you could—well, what? Disrupt his plans or share them, steal his fame or his achievement, what?"

"No, we would steal nothing," the man said, open at last in the face of openness. "Stop him, rather, from stealing what he has no right to."

"Yes, I thought that might be the case. But what? Something to do with this?"

Tattersall took the scarab from his pocket, and tossed it casually onto the bed.

The hiss of air through the man's teeth was answer enough. The device itself lay inert on the coverlet, as though it had no thought of movement.

"I never should have thought it his, now should I?" Tattersall went on musingly. "Master and man: when you're travelling, the boundaries get rubbed away.

In a hotel like Shepheard's, you share the same quarters, more or less. I didn't bother to search the connecting valet's room, while I was robbing Sir Edward. It's a point of principle with me," *the honourable thief does not steal from those poorer than himself.* "Perhaps I should have forgone that principle, just for once."

"You would have found nothing worth your attention," the man said bitterly. "Sir Edward had found it already. I do not know what right he had, to be rootling among my things."

"Perhaps the same right you had," Creighton suggested, "to be insinuating yourself into his service, in lieu of the valet you had—what, suborned? Poisoned? Abducted?"

"Oh, nothing grievous. A little ipecac in his dinner, followed by a doctor of our own; the man believes himself far sicker than actually we made him. He is taking a slow recuperative sea-voyage home, with the promise on arrival of a place in a household less…abrasive than Sir Edward's. You're right, of course, it was a liberty or worse, to be playing games with someone else's life, even if he comes out of it better than before—but Sir Edward plays a different kind of game, and really cannot be allowed at the table. We felt that he bore watching."

"Who is 'we', sir, in this argument? Whom do you represent?"

The man smiled thinly. "Men such as yourselves, sir: a caste apart, who look at the world a little differently and perhaps see more than our neighbours do. Men who can see the danger of a Sir Edward Bolsover, and are prepared to take risks to forestall that danger."

"Wait," Bellaire said, sounding bewildered. "What in the world can you know of us?"

"Obviously, we know that Mr Tattersall rifled Sir Edward's rooms at Shepheard's, and came away with more than a comfortable profit." His eyes moved inexorably to the scarab, seemingly against his own intent. "In fact, though, we know a good deal about each one of you. The work of the Remittance Men is…not entirely unnoticed in this city."

"Well." He spoke softly, almost in a drawl, and I may never have heard Tattersall sound more dangerous. "You have the advantage of us, seemingly.

Despite our best endeavours. So what's next, will you make us known to your principals?"

"I will not. I don't have that authority."

"Ah, yes. Just a lowly dragoman, I remember: and not above standing in as a body-servant, where required."

"Just so, sir. I am a dragoman; I have been a valet. I can probably never go home. To be fair, I don't know that I would want to. The life suits me, I find—and here I can be of service to more than the occasional needy gentleman, or a party of sightseers. Here I can do work that counts for something."

"And that is—?"

This time it wasn't only his eyes that moved. He stepped towards the bed, somehow contriving to seem small and self-effacing and yet purposeful, all at once.

We made room, watchfully. This time I think we were all aware—the newcomer included—that Tattersall's hand was in his pocket again. At least he kept the revolver out of sight this time. It was Minor unexpectedly who stalled the man, however briefly. "May we know your name? Sir?"

The man hesitated. "My name?—Yes, I suppose so. My name is Hegarty."

"I expect that's the name of Sir Edward's supposed dragoman, isn't it?" I had not known Minor so perceptive, nor so stubborn. "I was asking for your own name. As you claim to be privy to all of ours."

The man might have been twice Minor's age. His mouth quirked a little at the corner; then, quite straightforwardly, he said, "As you wish, Captain Smith. My own name is Parsons, Melchior Parsons. Though I'm not sure how well you will find it serve you. It is...very little known, here in Cairo."

"No matter for that. It's known to us, now. Don't worry, we'll treat it kindly." Minor stepped back—conveniently into my embrace, as he knew full well—to allow Parsons to go that last yard.

He stepped, he reached, he lifted the scarab from the coverlet. He was almost reverential, holding it cupped in the palm of his hand, touching its back lightly with a finger. The wing-cases seemed to shiver, but it lay static otherwise.

"Will you tell us what it is?" That was Creighton, one enquiring mind speaking for us all.

"Come. I will show you."

The room was small and narrow, but even so: french windows led out to a tiny balcony. There was just room for Parsons to stand out in the air and set the scarab on the balustrade, while the rest of us massed in the opening.

Then his hand dipped into his pocket, and emerged with something that gleamed darkly, that lay heavy in his hand, that matched our scarab exactly when he laid them side by side.

He barely had time to take his hand away before the two of them were moving: rising up on those needle legs, rattling their wing-cases at each other, extending their fragile wings.

I thought at first that they would fight like crickets, that this after all was the point of them: mechanical gladiators, the one pointless and purposeless without the other. But all they did was mop and mow like two disdainful courtiers, fluttering wings and bobbing up and down on spindly limbs, waving antennae in complex patterns.

"What are they doing?" Minor asked softly.

"Talking." The man was succinct, so matter-of-fact we could almost take it unquestioned. "Or we think it may be more like dictation, an exchange of information, so that each learns what the other has registered. Bring any two together, they will do this. And in greater numbers, too. They pair off with one after another until their observations have been shared by all. At least, that's what we believe."

"How many of them are there?" Major asked.

"Untold. We know of...many. In our keeping, and kept elsewhere, and abroad, on their own occasions."

"But what are they for?"

"For this. For data-gathering, and sharing, and reporting in. Wait. Watch now."

Night or day, the light in Cairo is not like light anywhere else in the known world. Night or day, the human eye can't help but turn towards the pyramids and what nests within them, leaking its effluence into the sordid air. Even under the baked glare of a Cairo noon it can be seen, something like a shimmer if shadow shimmered, if an incomprehensible overcast beneath a clear sky could somehow disperse its own corruption of what light is, if it could spread a luminous kind of darkness through the day. Night is its true time, though. Under a blaze of stars in a perennially cloudless sky, the pyramids radiate black light against a black background: visible, almost tangible, a pulse from otherwhere.

It ran over the scarabs' shells like tidal water, lapping, reaching, claiming. When they were done with each other, whatever strange form of mechanical communication that was, they turned as one to face the source of that unlight, the jutting peaks on our horizon that loom over all the city and all our lives. They raised their wing-cases again, unfurled their wings again and now squatted motionless on bent legs, almost like worshippers at a shrine.

No one had to ask; Parsons knew well enough what was in our minds. "They all do this," he said, "whenever they have clear line of sight. It is in our minds again that they are communicating, reporting to their masters, and perhaps receiving new instructions. If those wings were wireless aerials of some kind, if they could transmit and receive like miniature mobile Marconi stations..."

"Yes," Bellaire murmured, "but how? In so small a device: how is it energised, how engineered? Communicate what, and by what means, what code, what intelligence? And to whom?"

"Such questions are our stock-in-trade," Parsons said, with a sad smile. "As to the energy, we theorise that they draw it somehow from the pyramids, that they are doing so now: that those wings act as collectors also, for some storage-battery within. Certainly, those gone far abroad lose their speed first, then any movement at all, while these do not. As to the rest, to the best of our belief, the pharaohs' tombs have been parasitised by creatures from another world. Cuckoos have nested in the pyramids, and these are their servants, gathering what information their masters might require. Before they emerge, perhaps? Reborn, perhaps? It may be that the pyramids play the role of a chrysalis, sheltering the invader through its metamorphosis into a creature that can survive this world. Or it may be that they are a tomb again, that the invaders are dead and that all this is mechanical residue, service to a long-lost lord. Faith and guesswork, these are all we have to offer, where answers are impossible to come by."

"Say faith and deduction, rather," Creighton intervened, "employed within a theoretical framework. Many an answer can be found—has been found, indeed—with such an approach."

"Mr Creighton, yes—but how are we to know when we are right? If we are ever right? Faith is all very well, but it will not actually move mountains. Neither open them."

A soft chime came from Parsons' pocket. He glanced at his watch, flipped a switch, then put it away again. "Sir Edward is a man of regular habits. He will be moving now from the dining hall to the library, from claret to port—but unless his company is congenial, he won't stay above one glass and a smoke."

I could hear the sound of Mallenby's blink, I swear, in the silence that we left ready for him. I daresay we all could; certainly I felt Minor's delight, his indrawn breath and the quiver of anticipation that coursed all through his body.

"The port here is…exceptional," Mallenby said carefully. "Surely he will not smoke?"

"Ah, but he will, Mr Mallenby. He will smoke, and orate—and he will recruit. It's a coarse kind of charisma, but effective."

"Tell us, then, swiftly: what is he recruiting for? An expedition of some sort, clearly—and nothing to do with our pyramids. He could be there in an hour, but he's budgeting for months. I take it those plans have not changed, despite our colleague's infiltration yesternight?"

"I'm afraid not. He had plans to visit London anyway, for business reasons. He always intended to return to Egypt after the rains, with everything in place for an immediate departure into the desert. I see no hope of those plans being altered. Even the loss of the scarab has not really shifted him, it only makes his arguments more difficult to establish."

"And his arguments—and his intentions—are—?"

"Are my fault, largely." He suppressed a smile, and then a sigh; and went on, "In truth, I found this scarab through a rumour in the bazaar. It is known that they are looked for, and will be paid for. We usually hear indirectly, when another turns up in the city. I was sent to track this one down; I found my way to an elderly widow, whose husband had dug it up and was afraid of it, thinking it possessed by the spirit of a djinni, and so sealed it in a pot. With him dead, she was keen to sell. That's all the story, but I was already engaged by Sir Edward, and had no time to take it to my masters. I thought it would be safe among my things, for true darkness always keeps them quiescent. I thought I could pursue my other responsibility, to keep a watchful eye on a figure known to be dangerous and keep him perhaps from doing too much harm, or growing too interested in places we have protected, with cause, for a long time now.

"It was a mistake, of course. I underestimated his coarseness, or his curiosity. Or else I did something to arouse his suspicions, that I might be more than I seemed: what employer goes through his valet's bags as a matter of course? At any rate, he did it, and found the scarab. And kept it, and interrogated me at length, and threatened me with dire consequences if I didn't reveal its provenance. He didn't ask me about its meaning; what could I know? He called me a greasy sponger, a half-caste, all kinds of names. He threatened my person, my family, my future.

"I resisted long enough to be credible, I hope; then I told him what he most wanted to hear, a fantastical tale about an oasis in the desert, a people unknown to the Empire, discoveries unknown—or long lost—to science. I hinted at a lost tribe of Israel."

"And he fell for this farrago? Even under this—corpselight," with a broad wave towards the pyramids, "where any sensible man's inquiry would first turn?" If Bellaire was outraged, it was at this obvious neglect of scientific principles and the rule of Occam's Razor.

"Hook, line and sinker," Parsons confirmed, not without a note of pride at having carried off such a conceit. "Nothing would satisfy him but to plan an expedition, which as you have noted reads more like an invasion force. He is leaving me in charge of implementing his plans, while he flies back to London."

"He's not worried that you'll just vanish in his absence?" God knew, there would be opportunity aplenty: upriver, or to Alexandria, or simply into the city's slums where a man like Parsons could find shelter that a man like Bolsover would never breach.

"He's not, because he thinks he knows too many ways to hurt me, even in my absence. And in fact I won't, because left to himself, raging through the city with tales of lost toys, he might blunder into worse trouble than he's made already. No, I will submissively follow his orders, and have his people ready to march on his return. I will guide them into the high desert, and…"

"And leave him there?" Minor suggested, with an edge of hopeful cruelty that always surprised me when it showed itself. One forgets, perhaps, how savage the young can be. I quieted him with a touch, as Parsons shook his head.

"I dare not; he'll have men with him who could bring him safely out again. And there would be too many questions asked, in any case. No, I thought I'd just lead him in circles as long as I can, and then admit that I have no idea where the blessed oasis can be found. Let him do with me as he will; with any luck, he'll spend his time, his fortune and his life on a wild goose chase, far and far beyond any chance of harm."

"Except to yourself. And your family thereby, if they depend on you or hope for your safe return." That was Creighton, inevitably concerned for the man, for the individual soul.

"Yes, sir. I've a wife and child here, and parents still back home, and nevertheless. I see no way, otherwise. The issue is too important. My responsibility—"

His sense of responsibility was breaking him, seemingly. We none of us thought that he could see his project through, even if any of us had thought that he ought to.

"Oh," said Tattersall, "I think we can take that responsibility from you. How say you, fellows?"

"Least we can do," grunted Smith Major.

"Best we can do," chimed in Minor.

"It may be the most we can do," said Mallenby, "but it'll have to be enough. Padre?"

"My guest," said Creighton firmly, "my responsibility. We'll take it from here, Mr Parsons. You do your work for Sir Edward tonight. Tomorrow, deal with the scarabs as your conscience and your duty require, and have an eye to your family. Leave the rest to us."

"I don't think I can do that, sir. With all respect. I am sworn to—"

"I think you are sworn to many things, Mr Parsons. Too many things, and they are tearing you apart. We can shift some of that burden from your shoulders. This…will not be the first time. Do you tidy up here and lay out your master's pyjamas; by the time he comes to bed, you should have no more than that to concern you. Just lend us those scarabs for an hour, though. You shall have them back after your valeting is done, my word on it."

IT was a tall order, but not one beyond our reach. This was our city, our tribe—in the final analysis, our club, however unwelcome we might be within its purlieus.

Nor was this the first time we had rallied in defence of something nebulous, out of our reach, perhaps beyond our understanding. We are citizens of no mean or quotidian city; here where East meets West, where science and more ancient lore lean hard upon each other, where the boot of Empire presses into soft river-mud and barely leaves a mark that lasts. There may be nothing new under the sun, but there is much in Cairo that is very old indeed, and we modern folk must struggle constantly to keep it down, or else keep others from disturbing it.

We trooped out of the room, along the corridor and down the stairs, almost without discussion. On the first floor, we divided our forces, this way and that. Minor clattered off down the servants' stairs to the nether regions, kitchen and scullery; Creighton stepped into the card-room, empty at this hour, for a moment's private reflection that he preferred not to call a prayer. Tattersall vanished, as is his wont.

Mallenby stood back, in a niche that held a group portrait of the Voyagers' founding spirits. He'd wait for the padre, but not join him. Mallenby wasn't much of a joiner; really it was a surprise that we Remittance Men had managed to catch and keep hold of him.

Myself, I thrust open the library doors and held them wide for Smith Major. I was already talking.

We call it the library, and it is shelved as is traditional with many and many a book that's never read; but in honesty, it's far more a tale of easy chairs and lamplight and firelight in season, of brandy-snifters and cigars and that legendary port, with a club servant ever on call to bring you more. It's not at all the sort of library where people hush you for speaking out; that's what the Silence Room is for.

Used to be for, before we annexed it for our very own, our club-within-a-club.

"...SO here, sit yourself down and I'll show you, it really is the most extraordinary thing..."

Library or not, it's still a place for quiet after-dinner converse, mulling over your preferred glass and your smokes, in your preferred company. My voice deliberately shattered that calm, turning every head.

I did try not to look, I tried to be oblivious, but even so: there was a group of half a dozen in the most favoured seats around the fireplace, and I recognised all the faces bar one in that brief glimpse that I couldn't quite restrain.

I guided Major to a lamp-lit alcove and a table for two, where we could sit hunched and mysterious about our doings. Not too close to the fire, not too far away: I could pitch my voice to be heard across the silence of broken conversations, while still seeming to speak privately to Major alone.

"Take a pew. The boy'll be over in a minute with the decanter, they know what I like hereabouts. Light up if you want to smoke, that's the way. But look, here's what I meant to show you. I call it my magic beetle. No need to wind it up, no need to stoke it, d'ye see? It just runs and runs, and stretches out those pretty wings, and waves its whatchamacallits, its feelers, and never ever topples over the edge of the table…"

I had set the scarab between us, and nudged it into life. It was running through all its repertoire of party tricks, with all their unfathomable purpose; I fancied even the clicking of its feet on polished wood must be carrying to my intended audience.

True enough. I was still warming to my patter when a heavy hand closed crushingly on my shoulder, and a voice thick with fury said, "Sir, how do you come by my property?"

"I beg your pardon?" For sheer fastidious contempt, there's nothing to touch a prefect at an English public school, faced with an impertinent junior. I put all my remembered lessons into effect, rising to meet him face to face, giving him the benefit of my finest supercilious eyebrow and the coldest, crispest accent at my command.

Inwardly, I might perhaps have felt a little daunted, if I'd been in truth the solitary swindler that I seemed. Even with my cohort at hand, he was a hard man to face: half a head taller than I, bull-necked and bull-tempered, the shadow of his beard already darkening his jaw though I knew Parsons would have shaved him before dinner.

"That," he said, pointing at the scarab with one huge hand, while the other still kept a grip on my shoulder, "belongs to me. And was stolen from my room just yesterday. Are you a thief, sir, or do you merely consort with thieves?"

"Oh, here, I say!" That was Mallenby, escorting Creighton in with exquisite timing. "You can't sling words like that about in here. Not to members. It's just not on, old man."

"You mind your own business," Bolsover snarled, "and leave me to mind mine."

"Well, but you're making it everybody's business, if you start a dust-up in the library. What's it all about, anyway, what's Farrant done to have you accuse him like this?" Somehow, Mallenby managed to say *what's Farrant done?* and make it sound like *what's Farrant done now?,* which was just right for the occasion.

"That's mine," Bolsover said unequivocally, pointing again at the scuttling scarab. "It was taken from my room at Shepheard's last night, along with a quantity of cash and cufflinks and such—but it was this I valued most. And now I find him playing with it here, trying to sell it to this customer," a gesture at Smith Major, "unless I miss my guess."

"Well, that would be in character," Mallenby confirmed—a little maliciously, I thought—speaking over Major's spluttered protest that no one had mentioned money, it was just a curio he was being shown for interest's sake. "But, oh lord, sir—Sir Edward, isn't it? I heard you were to be our guest tonight—don't you know what you have there?"

"I know it to be a mystery of the highest order, and a precursor of great discoveries to come."

"Oh, dear. I am sorry, Sir Edward, I shouldn't laugh—but truly, it's just a gimcrack bazaar toy, designed to catch the eye and the pocket of the gullible. Heavens, you carry one yourself, don't you, Padre?"

"I do indeed," Creighton confirmed, pulling Parsons' second scarab from his pocket and setting it down beside the first. "I had it from a beggar for a broken sixpence. I use it to amuse the children in the poor ward, and sometimes as an object lesson in hollowness and show. These trinkets seem mysterious and wonderful, but in the end they don't actually amount to anything."

Our two on the table there were conducting their courtly dance, like two dowagers bringing each other up to date on the latest happenings in Society. Which—if Parsons and his masters were right—was a tolerably accurate summation, I supposed.

I had no leisure then to wonder about the devices' makers, or by what science they were powered and instructed, or by what means or language they communicated with each other or with the pyramids. Here in Cairo, we grow used to unanswered questions and permeable borders between what is or can be known and what lies entirely beyond our reach, even when it sits in the palm of our hand. Strangers to our city have more rigid attitudes and expectations. Sometimes our task is merely to distract them; sometimes actually, actively to deceive.

I said, "I really must protest—" but I said it softly, like a man already exposed, and Creighton simply talked right over me. I suppose possession of a pulpit in a draughty church teaches the clergy all the gifts of oratory; certainly for a quiet and self-effacing man he has a hidden power in his voice.

"I was curious to learn where they came from," he said, "there are so many cropping up all across the city. I asked questions in the bazaar, and made myself quite unpopular among the trading classes; but in the end I tracked the source down to a warehouse full of Chinese coolies. It's quite wonderful, in a way, watching how they work. Each man has a specific task, and the skills and tools required for that and that alone. It's the opposite of craftsman work; no one man made either of these, or any. Still, they turn them out by the crateload. Many go straight onto ships, bound for every port in the Empire; more are sold at the door to any beggar or street dealer with a few piastres in hand and a plausible manner. I'm sorry to see a gentleman engaged in the trade, though—or the club being used in such a way. It is all rather sordid. Especially living where we do, in the light of something legitimately esoteric. These things are mere fribble, but the unethical amongst us have been known to use them as bait for worse deceptions. Whole expeditions have been financed and their funds misappropriated; or the principals have been led directly into the hands of bandits and held for ransom—"

"Oh, no, really, that's too much!" I expostulated, unconvincingly. "I have this charming little artefact, which I wanted to show off to my new friend here, and suddenly I'm accused of banditry and peculation and all sorts!"

"Well, it's hardly the first time, is it, Farrant? I believe the Chief of Police has been in here asking questions about you, more than once." That was Mallenby, being as insinuating as he knew how.

"He is a member, after all," I murmured vaguely, looking about as though for rescue—and instead finding Tattersall, as brisk to appear as he often is to vanish, with the club's president in tow.

"Again, Mr Farrant?" Parfitt rules the Voyagers' with a will of steel, wrapped in a voice of silk. "What is it this time, a case of simple fraud? Well, as I believe I heard you mention on my way in, that really is too much. If we'd only known you better, you should have been blackballed from the start. As it is—well, I can do that *post facto, ex parte* and *ex officio.* The rules allow it, and I believe the occasion insists. Remove yourself, if you please, and don't trouble to return."

"I'll do no such thing!" I protested vehemently.

"No? Then I must have you removed. If you would, Smith…"

Smith Major, still the gullible victim, startled at the mention of his name, but didn't move else. There was no need. I felt strong young hands close upon my person, and a bare glance behind showed me Smith Minor, now in the get-up of a club servant, complete with apron buttoned over his waistcoat.

"This way, sir. *If* you please…"

I struggled, partly for show and partly for the pleasure of being man-handled by a lean and wiry youth who was enjoying it as much as I. We're not often licensed to sport in public, but we made a splendid spectacle of ourselves, all the way out of the library and down the staircase.

Assured that Parfitt had detained Bolsover above—with apologies, certainly, and alcohol no doubt—we unhanded each other in the hallway and pulled our clothing straight, all under Barrows' disapproving eye. Disapproving, but experienced: this was hardly the first time we'd played out this scene, or others like it.

"I have to say, I do quite like you in uniform," I murmured, reaching out to tweak Minor's collar straight.

"You say that every time. And its corollary."

"Well, both are equally true. I do quite like you out of uniform as well."

Minor snorted, and pushed me towards the basement stairs. Barrows looked on, the very embodiment of distaste. He loved none of us, but Minor and me he loved the least of all.

Alas for him, we thrived under his antipathy. Ensconced once more in the Silence Room, we poured ourselves glasses of port—I refrained from smoking, in deference to Minor's sensitivities, though of course he asserted it was rather in deference to Mallenby's: "You care more about his opinions than you do about my lungs, and that's all there is to it"—and settled back to wait for the others.

One by one, they manifested. I had already set the aerator in motion, in anticipation of Major's cigar; he nodded at me, and stood courteously by the flue with his pint of ale. Creighton and Mallenby were full of the joys of deception; Tattersall came in last and late, with the president still in tow.

"Gentlemen. I am to suppose that tonight's—theatre—had a purpose behind it, yes?"

"Yes, sir." Smith Major was taciturn as ever; the others were too elevated to make sense. It fell to me to be the rational one, and make our case. "Bolsover was indeed planning an expedition, on the basis of one scarab. He…had been misled, and it would have availed him nothing; but he was out to recruit, and he would have dragged club members and the club's good name into quicksand before he was done. We deemed it better to intervene early, and discourage him from the start."

"Well, that much you've done. He's still headed home in the morning, and he says he won't be back. These fly-by-night entrepreneurs are quick to see an advantage, but quick too to revoke under pressure. In the club's interest, gentlemen, I believe I have to thank you once again. Despite certain disruptions in the even progress of our ways."

We apologised for that, profusely; and insisted that he share a glass of his own port with us, and kept him amused with tales that fell barely the right side of decency, until he took his decent departure and left us to our revels.

Almost as soon as he was gone, Parsons slipped in. Tattersall dipped hands into pockets, and restored two scarabs to the man.

"All serene," he said blithely. "He was so upset at being so nearly taken for a fool, I don't believe he even noticed these had vanished again. That was well done, by the way, Padre, leaving your own as if it were of no account."

"Oh—in honesty, I just forgot it in all the kerfuffle. Still, if that helped…"

"We all helped, I believe. It was a splendid caper, one and all. We have one bully fewer to trouble the country, and one secret more to tackle— because you do understand, Parsons, that we shall be prying under every rock until we can find out just who your mysterious masters are, and what exactly they intend? Cairo is our city of choice, for all that we talk so much about Alexandria; the instinct to defend her is strong within us all."

"Oh, sir, I understand you perfectly. And I wish you joy of the hunt." Parsons smiled knowingly, slipped the scarabs into his own pockets and departed, very much with the air of a man who never expected to be troubled with us again.

"Alexandria sounds good to me," I murmured into Minor's ear. "Maybe I could set up as a poet after all, at least for a month or two."

"You'd never stick it," he said sorrowfully. "You'd be wanting to come back in a week, just to take soundings in the club here, just to check that nothing newly awful was going on and you not here to mend it."

And he was right, of course: which is why we are and will remain tolerated at the Voyagers', at least until the pyramids crank open to give up their unlawful dead.

FREECELL

A bomb is an act of beauty.
A body is a flower, yet to open.
Blossom falls in the beckoning wind.

A bomb is an act of beauty:

WE WATCHED IT FROM ABOVE, FROM behind, from a dozen different viewpoints. Witness was important. Besides, who wouldn't want to see?

Shami had chosen the space herself—a high-grade mall, perfect for her who was a terminal low-grade shopper, perfect for us because these places are so busy, so core, and so carefully supervised—and Tux cut us into ParaSec. We were crushed into a storeroom that day, squeezed between cartons of new hardware for the livebars, the four of us and Tux who takes up no space physically, only all the mental space there is. On a normal day, that is, he takes up all the space. Today—well, today there was Shami. The five of us and Shami, so many images of her, and another on every monitor we could unpack. We pulled them from the cartons, powered them up, linked them in; Tux filled them. He filled our eyes with her, she filled that crowded room.

The boys had brought stills, hardcopy captures from all the times they'd had with her: parties and sex sessions, chill sessions, X-ports. And shopping, eating, talking, all the things she simply did when she wasn't doing anything else. Sleeping. I was surprised, how many shots there were of Shami sleeping. Probably I shouldn't be; the boys did like to share, and whatever they shared together they always wanted to share with the world after.

So many caps, bright memories of Shami in her pomp, in her clothes, in her skin. And suited up outside the habitat, Shami at play in her sky-pinks, drifting off beneath a lightrider or leading a scramble from the dead pitted mouths of the ramjets to the bright windows of the Bridge. That was Shami to the core, Shami at her best, racing and gambling and breaking whatever she could, records and rules and safety codes and more, snapping off the odd antenna as she leaped for a handhold here, dishing the occasional dish there as her boot scrabbled for purchase. Wherever she went, whatever she did, she always left a trail, detritus in her wake. Broken hearts, broken bones, as many broken devices as she could manage. She'd have been brigged for that if they'd ever caught up, wastage is the one true offence Upside, the core of all law; but of course they never did.

After today, after we were gone they'd find this room enshrined to her, the walls bedecked with her still image, and all these screens replaying what she did today. Then they might catch on, but still they'd never catch up. We ride the leading wave; they push us forward, even as they chase.

SHAMI was everywhere, and she'd never looked more beautiful than she did on the monitors today. We'd fixed her make-up for her with the tattoo-gun, to be sure it didn't smudge.

Blood rose in full thorn: this wasn't her native mall, and she should have been triggering every alarm ParaSec has, simply by being there and looking like she did. Tux was covering that, though, filtering what the system picked up or else blocking its reaction, so that she could have her day her way. All those lenses were turned on her, but there was only us to see: us and the people shopping all around her, clean and corporate, an exercise in contrast.

Her hair was a crimson crest, and that same colour—selfsame, the tattoo-gun had matched it—was dragged down like leakage from her hair-line, as if the dye had oozed and stained her skin. As if. Off her brow, it dripped and streaked like tears down her cheeks; but the heart of chaos is certainty, and down the jawline it turned fractal, dominant, a little scary.

The backs of her hands we'd done like traditional henna patterning, but still in that rich crimson, like blood against her nut-butter skin.

Generally she had more skin on show, but face and hands was it today. For the rest, she was in clothes. Remarkable clothes, clothes that told a story. It was a lie, or at least a fiction, but that was legit; she lacked the body to sustain the lie, so she couldn't even pretend to be faking it. She was dressed that way for herself and for us, and for the moment.

What she wore was miners' gear from the Downside bubble colony: rockboots and padded trousers, hippohide jacket hanging down over her knees. The shoulder seams reached halfway to her elbows. If we hadn't rigged straps to hold them rolled back double on themselves, the sleeves would have swallowed her hands and never given them up again. Then no one would have seen the pretty patterns.

She looked tiny, in those clothes. Well, she was tiny, but she looked absurd, a little kid playing dress-up in her daddy's gear. It was all old stuff well used, the real thing, no kitsch fashion copies with designer stitching and live logos; she'd insisted on that. Ripped seams, scuffed toes, patches on the elbows, the smells of dust and sweat and machine-oil spilled in the dark.

She looked tiny and vulnerable and utterly lost, adrift in that high-status mall and dressed in someone else's dirt. People glanced at her in that way that says *Where's security, why hasn't she been lifted yet? She belongs Downside, if she belongs anywhere. Or lurking in the flea-markets, perhaps. With the other fleas. Not here.*

They gave her room, but never room enough. What's to be afraid of, in a badly-dressed girl? They didn't need to shun her; she was beneath their shunning. If she was in their way, they stepped around her. That was all.

Besides, that little-girl-lost look was unutterably sexy. Here, where the clientele was as brightly polished as the floor, her simple presence was like finding a brothel suddenly open in the lobby of a chapel: shocking and compulsive, attractive on a gravitational scale. She drew men towards her, and women too. We could have boosted that with a pheromone spray, but she said no; she knew we wouldn't need to. Shami always knew.

They came close, they peeped or glanced or stared openly; they swerved around her and moved on, and most of them looked back. Some of them, the young ones, lingered; they murmured between themselves, paused by a display, made large and positive gestures to each other, *I'm sure there was something better back that way* and so somehow happened to end up going the same way that Shami was.

She was a comet with a tail, our Shami, dragging the less committed in her unheeding wake. She knew.

UPSIDE there are malls for the likes of us, malls for the likes of them, malls for those who are unlike anything you've ever seen. But never mind the grav settings and never mind the air, never mind the company, the credit or the clientele: they all follow the same configuration, they're all bent around the same arc of orbital wall and they cling to all the old ways of real-time shopping. There are long galleries for the boutiques or stores or market stalls, extended five ways from a central hub; half a dozen access points, then, but one node, one place to meet, to eat—if eating's what you do—and talk, show & tell, compare & contrast, do everything that's shoppy that you don't actually need to do in a shop.

Shami headed for the hub, and so did half the folk who saw her, and why not? They had nothing better to do with their time; in that echelon, even wastage was let by, even something that couldn't be recycled.

Shami had something exact to do with her time, and she'd chosen it as carefully as she had the space. This was mid-shift; to be shopping now was a statement, an expression of wealth. If you were in the mall, you were not, by any definition, working. By any definition, then, you didn't need to work.

By some definitions, that made you waste, in and of yourself. Here, of course, that didn't matter.

This high in society, to be seen was as important as seeing for yourself. They shopped, they paraded, they forgathered; the hub was crowded, even before Shami erupted into it with her entourage.

Her shriek of hair, above her hopelessly inappropriate clothes and the sense she gave of almost slipping out of them at every step; her entranced pursuit, half the glitteryouth of Upside sauntering so casually at her heels, just hoping to see who she was and what she did, what she was doing here; small wonder if heads turned at her arrival, conversations faltered.

Oh, she knew what she was doing. She walked solidly, determinedly to the heart of the hub, where there was just never quite enough seating; she blinked at all those busy tables, all those curious and bewildered faces; she glanced behind her at her captive, captivated audience; and then she looked at us.

She'd researched this, all of it, so well. She knew just where the lenses were. She found one, no hesitation, no casting about. And lifted her hands to her neck, and one by one set all her fingers just where they ought to be, under the jawline there, on the nodes we'd tattooed in last night.

A moment before the last finger touched home, she smiled at us all and said, "Contact." Tux caught the sound from somewhere and piped it through to us, one last touch of her voice, and half a breath of wasted air, and—

CONNECTIVITY is all.

Power was in her fingertips, the implants that we'd set there earlier this morning. The tattoos were conductive, her skin beneath her clothes a minutely detailed circuit-board, a chart of binary instruction. Those instructions followed intricate paths, and learned, and passed the word along; and the word was *finish*, unless it was *begin*.

Every cell in her body below the neck heard that word, and for once in her life she was obedient. She let go, or they did: all the energy inherent in a biomass was released on the instant.

And was contained, briefly, by that so-carefully-chosen clothing; and that was her achievement, to make herself a bomb.

Half the security lenses went dark, a moment after. We lost all our near views; kinder souls might have been grateful. We were jubilant, celebrating, loving our friend and her success and ourselves too for being her friends, but we still wanted to see; there was a chorus of appeals to Tux, to find some closer feed.

The miners in that bubble Downside wear steel mesh inforcements as standard, against the certainty of being slammed around by tremors, flesh into rock. Wrap that around an explosion—a human bomb, a biombe—and every ripped-open link is a flechette. The boots were steel-lined, for a weightier shrapnel. In an open, unprotected space, Shami in her clothes was simply lethal.

The long views that we had just showed us bodies, wreckage, everything overturned that wasn't torn apart. The display cases in the walls were armoured plass, and even those were smashed.

From distance, all we could see of the bodies was how they lay, broken and thrown. We called that urban sprawl. And giggled, and thought ourselves so clever, and longed for close-ups. Light reflected oddly, darkly all around them; we could intuit, we could understand but we wanted to see. Witness was important. We didn't only want to count the dead, it's not a numbers game, we had to clock the damage.

It's not just a numbers game. Numbers of course are important. There may be no glamour in them, but impact, yes, they do have impact. So long as they're big. These days, you really need three figures if you want the news 'cast anywhere beyond the orbital.

We had that, all of that and more. Shami had that. This was her day, and it was a triumph.

THERE were figures—the other sort of figures, wet ones—moving among the fallen, of course there were. You never do get all your dead together, all at once. Some of these might even survive—though the heavy metals and other tox that clung to the miners' gear would tend to work against that, in the run. Might be the long run, if they were lucky. But if they were lucky, they wouldn't be here, now, in that condition. Barbed.

There was movement on the edges, around the walls of the hub. Movement away, the walking wounded and the truly, amazingly lucky, the untouched; we didn't care about that. They were witnesses, they mattered, but only generically. What we wanted was movement towards, help on its way—and here it came, magnificently just too late.

Tux must have tipped them off, the Corps, just that calculated little time before the blast. He's good like that.

So in they came, helmets and body-armour and weapons at the ready, just in case; and every helmet had a lens, and every lens was uplinked to ParaSec, so Tux could suck on their feed and give it all to us.

The monitors gave us everything they saw and everything they sent, the whole heads-up display. That's what we used to call them, Heads-Up, HU for short when we were kids and always in a hurry, spraying or breaking something and running away. You'd think it would be hard to run Upside, when you can't get off-station and there are lenses everywhere, but there's always some corner to hide in when you're little and squirmy and not scared of the dark. And that was before we had Tux on our side, fouling signals and fudging records, hiding us in a whole new dimension of concealment.

They—the Corps, HU, and the Council too, all our good governance—thought they knew all about us, but they didn't know about Tux. They thought we were over, finished, dead. And so we were, in any way that mattered; but—well, they didn't know about Tux. Nobody did. They may have suspected something, but it was probably a human hand they thought at work, sabotaging and subverting their precious system. They purged it anyway, at regular intervals and on general principles, but for Tux too—unreadable, unknowable Esparantux, coded in a language no one spoke, he said—there was always somewhere to hide.

THEIR own safety is their prime concern, when the Corps moves in. Heavily Underwritten, Tux says. I wouldn't know about that, but heavy-handed, that's for sure. Best not to be a bystander. These people didn't know that. Survivors and onlookers, the walking wounded and the simply stunned: they lacked the wit to melt away, and so they found themselves staring into the bellmouth of a piezol, hearing the traditional, thoroughly unofficial warning, *all I need to do is close my fist...*

That was old to us, listening in from our cupboard, we'd heard it all our lives. To them it was shocking, and they were shocked already; this was the kicker, to see their rescue & protection come and have it turn on them, find themselves the wrong side of the weapon.

We saw their fear, their bewilderment close-to, through the helmet lenses. Outrage would come later, no doubt. For now there was only one more unexpected terror to endure, an unfamiliar obedience to authority that till now they had thought belonged to them. They fumbled for ID when it was demanded, they backed off at the wave of a piezol, they stood where they were told and stammered answers: no, they didn't know what had happened here; a girl, they thought, perhaps, and an explosion; no, she hadn't seemed to have a partner; no, there had been no threats, no speeches, no warning of any kind; no, this blood that spattered them, they didn't think it was their own...

For some of them, of course, it was their own. Some hadn't realised until they looked down, saw it, suddenly felt the pain.

No matter; they were walking wounded, they could look after themselves or each other. The Corps didn't do concern. Once they were sure of no second biombe, no sniper in the aisles, no ambush, those helmet-heads all turned away from the margins, back towards the heart, what we most wanted to see.

Close-to, there was nothing leisurely, nothing relaxed about those sprawly bodies. Even those that were still relatively whole carried Shami's eruptive message, writ large in how awkwardly they lay, posed by a brutalising hand; writ small all over, where the spray of shattered steel wire had ripped flesh to the bone.

I could never have imagined so much blood. It had nowhere to pool on the marblised flooring, quicksilver-smooth; it just flowed in search of a drain that wasn't there, sucked this way and that by fluctuations in the artificial gravity. It made a dark mirror that underlay every view we looked at.

People still moved, in every view we looked at. That was the Corps' first role, always, to find the living in among the dead. Once found, there was a quick triage, a rapid assessment of their chances; but the Corps is not medically trained, except in a swift despatch. And wastage is still the ultimate crime, and who would waste air—who among the electors would vote to waste air—or other resources on someone who would certainly be an expensive dependent hereafter? Anyone who hasn't got to their feet and at least tried to get out of there before the Heads-Up come, anyone who can't do more than just lift their head up in hope—well, lifting their head only makes it easier, is all.

The mercy-chord is a neat white plastic box that adheres to the temple when it's put there, it clings to the skin until the HU presses a button. Then it unleashes a disharmonic pulse, a chord that simply undoes the human brain, disrupts its sequencing, makes every separate synapse miss fire all at once, and there's an end of it.

We watched this, over and over. People were alive, and then they were not, and we could see it happen. Shami had achieved the same thing, but not been able to watch; we did it for her, as much as for ourselves.

Tux says the chord is inductive, it resonates through the skull and inward, so the operator is entirely safe. We wouldn't have trusted the device ourselves, we agreed that, but the Corps is trained to be without imagination; Highly Unresponsive, Tux says, when he isn't calling them the Hitler eUth.

Then all the monitors changed to the one image, the one man's work, as he turned from his latest execution and took up another role.

Many of the dead were frankly in pieces, where shrapnel had disarticulated them. Someone had to pick up all those pieces, and the Corps was ready to do that, in the interest of gathering evidence. This man maybe didn't know it as he did it, but he'd just found Shami's head.

That had been her one stipulation, that she wanted to leave her head intact. For evidence's sake, for DNA certainty, *I did this*; but also for the art of it, the style, the statement. *See, my body is my weapon, as it always was—but my face is my own, and will outlive me.*

He picked it up, and for a moment she was there in his hands and we could see her, and oh, but she was beautiful.

A body is a flower, yet to open:

The boys went to the game, of course, together. It's good to share.

TASH and I didn't need to lurk in some unseen space to watch this; the game was out there, public, all but compulsory. Every livebar showed it live on every screen. We got to party while we kept an eye on what our friends were up to. We couldn't talk to Tux, of course, directly; but we knew he was watching us as well, we knew he'd be listening in, he'd find some way to get a message to us if he had to.

We were being perhaps a little more careful than before. The Corps, the Council, they had all thought we were dead before. Ourselves, our cause, our struggle, all finished with, over. Most of us were, indeed. And the cause, for sure. We were the remnant: pitiful probably, hopeless certainly, doomed undeniably.

And yet, they had shrugged us off too soon and we had punished them for it, and that was a victory, no doubt; and tonight was another already. Even before we saw the boys inside the stadium, we'd won. ParaSec was everywhere: scanning, searching, questioning. The start of the game had been delayed, because they were so slow to pass the audience through. The Council would be hating that, every aspect of it; if they could hear the conversation in our bar—and they could, for sure, if they asked to—they'd hate it more. Ridicule is the hardest thing to bear, in the face of failure. They'd declared us beaten, and Shami had shown them oh so wrong in that; and now their hard arm had to underline it, a guard on every corner and no leeway, no grace. Every glance an interrogation: *identify yourself, explain yourself, persuade me.* People talked of nothing else. They were scared, twice scared, of us and of the Corps, and so they mocked us both and the Council too. We didn't care; every laugh was a score for us, a loss for the Council, joy.

Tonight we were joyful beyond measure, because the screen commentary was suddenly turned up loud, just as if someone wanted to drown out all those little conversations all through the orbital, and had given orders that it should be so—but even the commentators at the game were talking about security, because they had nothing else just yet to talk about.

They noted ParaSec everywhere, they couldn't not, and the screens followed their words to emphasise all those helmets, gloves, batons, the inherent threat of power and the manifest failure of the Council to keep the people safe. That would have been enough for us, on any other night. Tonight there was more, so much more. There was a special section in the stands, they said, finest views and so close to the Council's own box, set aside for victims of the outrage at the mall. Not many of them, of course, the mercy-chords had seen to that; but there were a dozen survivors in seats and another half-dozen on wheeled gurneys, improvised—the commentators told us—in lieu of the normal powerchairs for security reasons, because a powerchair meant a fuel cell, which might so easily be rigged by terrorists. Better to be safe, and have these unfortunates fetched in by the Corps, happy to be seen to do their part in serving the community…

They were probably not happy, to be wheeling cripples through the station under the lenses' eyes. We were delighted, because two of those cripples were our own best boys, Tanner and Maxie.

Tux had faked their credentials, giving them a whole history of regular Upside life before they were so unluckily caught up in the catastrophe at the mall. Between us, Tash and I with Tux advising, we had done things to their legs that were not fake at all. They did need those gurneys now. On the outside, they sported all the scars and dressings of major surgery, just as all their fellow victims did; and they were of an age, and if the Corps did not remember letting quite so many of the badly wounded live, well, their own records proved them wrong, and there was an end of it.

Soon, there would be an end to it. I wasn't sure that either of the boys could wait for the game to start. We'd done what we could with neural blocks, but Tash and I were like the Corps, not medically trained except in ways of killing; there was abiding pain, however much we all pretended. And more than pain, because we couldn't use the tattoo-gun again, anyone with tats was simply taken. We'd needed to be cruder and more clever, and no body was made to endure what we'd done to those poor boys. They were numbed on the one hand and drugged up on the other, and it left them feeling sick and sore all through, they said. They weren't sure quite how long they could bear it. Kick-off would be good, we all agreed, but if not—well, no matter.

They'd waited for the Council, that at least. There were fanfares and announcements, speeches and entrances, iron-haired men and women dressed to rule and acknowledging the crowd. Tanner and Maxie were below and to the side, a little, but really very close. That hadn't been our aim, but it was a gleeful bonus.

There would be a show, parades and music before the game began. It was too much to ask. Tux found a view that focused on our boys, and that was good enough; that was plenty. He cut it suddenly into every screen in the livebar, likely every screen on the station. People yelled in protest, but they went on watching; there was nothing else to look at.

We saw the boys holding hands, gurney to gurney; we saw them haul each other up, lean in.

We saw them kiss.

THIS was a truecast camera we were watching through, not a hidden speck of short-range security lens. It must have been right across the other side of the stadium, to see all this and not lose a moment of its image.

We saw the kiss, Tash and I, and held hands ourselves beneath the table.

The boys were each other's catalysts—"as we always have been," they'd said, loving it, wanting no other solution—and their saliva was the vector. The bones of their legs were reservoirs, the marrow all sucked out and replaced with tox, two separate cocktails, harmful on their own, explosive in combination. The moulded plass that made a protective shield for the boys' poor wounded bodies, covering them from the waist down—clear plass, to show the Heads-Up that there was nothing but damaged flesh and bone beneath—was made to shatter, to shard like steel.

We saw them go in a flare of light, a great disintegration. We whooped stupidly into that suddenly silent bar; but Tux was ahead of us, as ever, dialling up the volume even as we shrieked. Not much he could do to disguise our leaping up, and we did that too; but then there was so much swearing, shoving, rushing about in such a small space, no one was likely to remember two kids who were a fraction premature in their reaction, who seemed more celebratory than shocked.

Tux fed the Corps' audio channel all through the station, to let everyone know just how panicked they were, how out of control. No one else would have noticed his own voice among so many, though to us it was sharp and clear, cutting through the hubbub in the livebar and telling us to get out of there, where to go, what route to take.

We did what we were told. Perhaps we skipped it where we should have walked, danced instead of running; but that was all tribute to the boys, Tux must have known that, and he could hide it from any authoritative eyes who might come scanning, now or later.

As we went, we heard news all the way, reports from the bewildered Corps still echoing down every corridor. Half the Council was down, by the sound of it. Headless Uproar, Tash suggested, but just for a moment there, I didn't want to laugh. A year ago, when we were a Movement, that would have been a triumph; it might even have led to real measurable victory, the whole system down and a new dispensation. Now it was only incidental, a distraction even, not the point at all. Who would stop to think about the thing itself, the achieve of it, if all they did was number and name the dead?

Tux sent us to a public baths, empty, out of use according to the panel by the door. It opened at our approach, though, and locked again behind us. Nobody showers, Upside; water is heavy but energy is cheap, and a little steam goes a long way. Tux gave us as much steam as we could bear, till the walls ran with condensation and there were conspicuously wasteful puddles on the floor, another petty blow for freedom.

I wished aloud that the boys had been the other end of the stadium, away from the elite. It would have kept the action pure, I said, save it looking political. When there's nothing left to fight for, I said, it's a shame to have people misunderstand the fight. They'd pass us off as helpless, hopeless: bitter failures who couldn't recognise their own defeat.

Tash said no. She said it didn't matter what they thought, what they said, what they wanted. She came and lay beside me, warm and wet, a skinful of content; she said this was what mattered, this and this, her body and my own. Beauty is what you do, she said, not how you're interpreted. It's an absolute, she said, it has to be. That's what this is all about, she said; if we can't set our people free, then fuck it, let's outshine 'em.

You know all this, she said, you do. And she was right, of course, I did. So I kissed her and nestled close; and was it Tash or was it me who asked Tux to rerun all that coverage on the screens in the bath-house there, so that we had Maxie and Tanner erupting silently, vastly, continually on every wall, giving a reflective glory of gas-giant colours to the billowing steam…?

Blossom falls in the beckoning wind:

We're ambitious, Tash and I. When we go—soon now, soon—we want it to be effulgent; but it needs to be on a human scale too. No warnings, though, no statements, no messages of any kind. We agreed that after Conclave was betrayed, we last half-dozen shabby survivors watching the bulk of us, the best of us displayed in triumph every hour on the hour while commentators endlessly debated our destruction. From then on, what we did had to speak for itself, these brief parting glances, little glimpses of a waking world. Shami has spoken, and the boys, magnificently so; what else is said comes down to us, and what we can achieve together.

It has to be together. We need to help each other, physically and otherwise. Tux will do what he can, of course, but he has limits and he has his own concerns, which he can't or won't share with us. A rebel program, a ghost in the machine: how could we hope to understand him?

I'm fairly sure he understands us very well. Sometimes I think he made us—not in his image, exactly, but surely to his design. History asserts that the Movement came first, but history can be wrong. Or faked, to give us faith in ourselves. Perhaps he lurked, guiding the early pioneers discreetly from the shadows, and only revealed himself later; or—sudden inspiration!—perhaps he only ever revealed himself to us, his last few surviving children. Those who recruited us, they never spoke of him; he came later, after the betrayal, seeking us out in our solitude, in our couples, in our bewilderment. He brought us together and gave us this last and beautiful purpose, to assert the power of what we do, *sui generis*, whole unto itself.

We don't need to declare our cause; why would we? They know who we are and what we stand for, what we used to fight for. They have the lists of our demands; all that is known ground, quarrelled over, unconceded. They have the lists of our dead, just as we do theirs. We at least will not parade our own, to their shame and our own.

What we will do, we will parade ourselves. Here's joy: the Council—what's left of the Council—has so lost touch, lost confidence, lost control, they've gifted us the only victory we want now. They're 'casting an appeal, to us directly: to Tash, to Tux, to me, though I don't suppose they know our names or number. "To the last pitiful remnant of the insurgency" is what they say—see, I said we were pitiful—but even that's a capitulation. They want us to stop killing innocents, our brothers and sisters of the Upside; they appeal to our intelligence, to our humanity, to realise that it achieves nothing. We note that they made no such appeal until we'd killed a few of them, and no doubt others—the human, the intelligent—will note it too. No matter. They ask what we can hope to win, and never understand that in their question is our reply. Just the asking cedes the ground to us.

As an afterthought, a gesture, they invite us to surrender.

That's what we'll do, then, Tash and I. Publicly, in one last arena.

We're not naïve, we don't imagine for a moment that we'll get anywhere near the people who matter. ParaSec will interpose the bodies of the Corps as a kind of insulation, Heavily Upgraded. What they don't understand, what they'll never understand, is that we don't care.

No more multideaths, but so what? It never was about the numbers. Everyone—station-wide, system-wide—absolutely everyone will be watching. Tux will make sure of that. We'll march into whatever space has been agreed, we'll gaze around at whatever cordon sanitaire they've dared to risk themselves behind—and we'll smile at each other, and whisper to each other because there is no point in shouting now, and the words we say will trigger each other's little, little packages, and we'll go off *pouf!* under the bright and fascinated gaze of every lens that could squeeze or argue, bully or smuggle its way in.

Just the two of us, together, that's enough. That's a statement of intent.

I don't know what mess they'll be left with, to clear up after. How much damage can two people do? Two more deaths, numerically that shouldn't matter. Politically, they can try to spin it as their victory, the end of the insurgency, security restored; there's not a chance of that. Who would believe them, or us? Lambs to the slaughter, we're going to look like, two scapegoats sent out as cover, nothing more. Tash and I, we could never be convincing. They're looking for masterminds, Machiavellian corruptors; all we have to offer them is us, young and sweet and hopeful.

Maybe the station will rise up in disgust against the overlords, when it sees us give our pretty lives away.

MAYBE not. It hasn't yet, so why would it now? We're not that hopeful, truly.

Truly, what I'm guessing, I think Tux will finish what we started. Once that 'cast goes out, once the message spreads, I think he'll wait till things settle down again, until they think we really are defeated, dead, no more—and then he'll blow the station. All of it. I think he can do that. *Fiat lux.*

I'm sure he'll have cameras beyond the orbital, to see it happen and send the images on. Hey, he's Tux; he'll wait till there are people out there playing X-ports, with lenses on their lightriders. They'll see it, they'll record it; and then that photon-wave will send them riding far, far out into the dark, and they should be glad of that because they'll be surfing ahead of the worse radiation, our own manufacture of solar wind, and just maybe someone will come and find them before their air runs out. If not, someone's sure to come and find their bodies, with their records, what they saw as witness. That's important.

A TERRIBLE PROSPECT OF BRIDGES

I DON'T THINK THERE'S EVEN A WORD, for what I've got. There are other words, of course, people offer me those, but mostly they don't come close. Hydrophobia, for instance, that's a favourite; but that's different, that's rabies, that way madness lies.

It's not water I'm afraid of, no. I'll drink it, wash in it, I'll even go swimming if it's an old-fashioned pool with no wave-machine and preferably no crowds, no happy families splashing in the shallows. But count me among the witches and the spirits, we can none of us cross running water. I can't bear to walk across a bridge.

THERE are currently eight bridges over the Tyne at Newcastle, eight and counting. Six I can see from my window.

IF you drove west from here—I don't, I don't drive; but if you do, if you did—you could go some way without ever crossing a bridge. You could go quite far enough, at any rate: to where two villages have almost the same name, and are divided only by a wooded valley, and a stream.

You could park in either one, it doesn't matter. There should be plenty of space for cars, there used to be; and both have good pubs, or used to.

But the pub would be for later, after the walk. You'd go on a Sunday, if you had any sense; go nice and easy and relaxed, no hurry. There really isn't any hurry now.

So you'd go, you'd park, you'd lock the car because that's your habit, even in the heart of the country; then you'd look for the footpath that takes you down into the valley, into the wood. At one end it starts in a churchyard, at the other by a barn. But it's still the same path, it would still get you there, whichever way you came.

Fields and stiles, cowpats and mud: you've walked in the country before, you'd know what to expect. You'd wear good boots. A little of that, and then the trees and the path plunging steeply between them. Down you'd go, being careful not to slip; wouldn't want a fall down here, wouldn't want to start a landslide.

Believe me, you wouldn't. Never know what you might uncover.

Finally you'd come to the stream, and the settlement; and this would be what you'd come for, maybe. If you'd heard the story.

You'd cross the stream if you were on the wrong side of it, if that was the way you'd come; and you'd notice that there used to be a bridge over, and that there isn't any more. These days, you have to use the stones. It wouldn't be a problem, probably; most people don't find it hard. But even so, you might glance at the wooden uprights still standing firm in the bed of the stream, you might wonder what happened to the bridge across, and why it hasn't been rebuilt.

But then you'd be on the other side, safely over and not even a wet foot to show for it, the stones are solid as any bridge and almost as easy to walk on. And then, all about you, you'd see the settlement.

It was abandoned, of course, a long time ago, and no doubt it shows. Myself, I haven't been back in twenty years; things will be different now. Someone might even have rebuilt the bridge, though I wouldn't have thought so. I wouldn't have thought they would dare.

Anyway, what you'd see is the relics, the remains of a community that built itself around one man's vision, sustained itself as long as that vision lasted and died when the vision died. Twenty years ago it died, and what you'd see is the bones, only the bones.

Skeletal huts you'd see, for sure: rotting wooden walls, fallen roofs. Hearths and chimneys still surviving, perhaps, where they were stone-built, left to point like accusing fingers at the uninterested sky. Some were more ambitious, proper houses, you couldn't call them huts; but they were wood too, they needed their upkeep and won't have received it, they'll be gone like the meanest hovel. Some fallen to the weather, one or two burnt out, I imagine, by accident or design.

I imagine it quite often, how that clearing must look now. Sometimes I think that I may be the only one left who remembers it as it was, in its last casual and heedless days of life; and how I envy the others, all those fortunates whom I suppose to have forgotten, to have trained their minds not to recall it. I try to train mine by picturing the bones, only the bones with no life in them.

And I fail, again and again I fail. Reality is not so easy to cast out.

THESE days I live freelance and alone and always moving, but never moving far. At the moment my flat overlooks the Tyne, but it might as easily be the Tees or the Wear, or any smaller river. I have to gaze at water, that I dare not stand above.

I am a musician and an artist, occasionally a writer. I have been other things: a baker, a cook, partner in a vegetarian cafe, sole proprietor of a wholefood shop. Always on the side of the angels, you'll notice, never in the pocket of the establishment. And, of course, always moving on. But never far.

I am known now as Thomas Woodson, but that is not my name. I think it a clever, if a bitter choice. This much at least you can say for certain about my haphazard life: that the man I am, the man I have become was born in that hidden clearing, among the trees and the secrets of that wood.

THE Thomas of those days, who was not called Woodson—the man I still long, I still yearn to be—was a tall and vigorous man, often solemn and as often laughing. He saw visions and dreamed dreams, and he believed passionately that what was dreamed could be made real by faith and works together, by intellectual rigour and the body's dedicated labour.

You could call him a messiah, I suppose, on a small scale. A kitchen ecclesiast. He had all the qualifications: he had charisma and he had disciples, both something to say and a way to make people listen. Above all he had the will, the drive, the urge to evangelise. He saw the world very clearly as it was, and he wanted to change it.

In his own way, though, as with everything; he wanted to do it all his own way.

"I'm not going to preach on street corners," he said time and time again, till he was weary of saying it. "We've built our mousetrap, and it's better than anyone else's; let the world come to us. Just let them see what we've done, and then we'll trap 'em." With a grin and a resounding clap of the hands, perhaps a glance around at his little, hopeful paradise.

Because what he'd done, of course, was just what all messiahs mean to do, on whatever scale they can manage.

He'd set his people free.

I find it hard now, impossibly hard to explain how it was in those days, how it felt. New friends always ask: "Thomas," they say, "I don't understand. How could you do that? How could you just lead thirty people off into the wilderness that way, why would they go? What were you all trying to achieve?"

I don't have an answer, there never was any answer except the thing itself, the settlement as it was; but the settlement is dead now, and so there is no answer any more.

In those days, of course, it was the question that didn't seem to make sense. We knew who we were and what we had; and when journalists asked us where the settlement was going, what we were aiming at, there was nothing to do but laugh. We weren't going anywhere, we were here, we'd arrived. This was forever, our little company in the woods.

People are more cynical today, they have to be, it's the spirit of the age; but I don't think we were naïve even then, it's only cynicism that says so. We had hope, that was all, we had dreams. That was the fashion, that was the culture, the milieu we moved in; and one must needs be fashionable, then as now.

THOMAS (and I must, I will still write of him in that way, as someone separated from myself; there's been a lot of water under the bridge since then, and I am not he), Thomas had two women at the settlement, to share his house and his bed and his dreams. Two wives, in all honesty, though there were no certificates of marriage and not a wedding-ring between them.

Two wives, but only one child: a curious, amiable little boy who probably didn't know which his mother was and certainly showed no signs of caring. He was quite happy to share himself between them.

There were other post-hippy colonies, of course, in other places, and most of those were teeming with children; but not this one. Thomas said children were to be cherished when they came, but not hungered for. Human greed, he said, was the one great danger to this planet; and greed for children was the worst, the most immoral and the most dangerous. We were breeding ourselves out of existence, he said. We all had a responsibility to the future;

moderation couldn't be legislated for, it had to be an individual decision individually policed.

He and his household were the example, the living precept, and his disciples were all responsible people, or they wouldn't have been there. A couple of the older men had families from an earlier existence, pre-Thomas; but they'd left wives and children both, to live this enclosed and responsible life. So little Paul found himself the only child in a community of tender adults, flourished under their mutual care and no doubt thought the entire world like that.

And never had the chance to learn otherwise; because that was a bridge to cross when he came to it, and Paul never got that far.

I only have new friends, so they're always asking questions; and the questions are always more or less the same. Couched in other language, perhaps, or the emphasis alters, but that's all the difference. One of the favourites might come as, "The rest of your community, Thomas—what happened to them, are you still in touch?" or it might be, "How can you bear it, being alone with so much to carry? How do you survive that?"

It's still the same question, underneath; and it's usually the young who ask it, having no experience or understanding of solitude, seeing perhaps the first possibility of it in my own great change from that to this, and being afraid.

I tell them no, I'm not in touch with any of the others. A few must be dead by now, and the rest are scattered. Returned to the world or else still in flight from it, dancing to a different drummer; and no, I don't worry about them, how could I? I barely wonder. We can only ever truly care about our own lives, about what touches us; and they are gone from me.

Or I answer the other way, if that's how they ask it. There are some things, I tell them, that it's easier to carry alone.

SO Thomas had two wives, one son and a community of seekers. But he had a brother, too. He had Stephen; and Stephen was there from the start, Stephen built the houses.

He was the practical one, converting vision to reality. *A community,* his brother said, *somewhere among trees. A long walk from the city,* Thomas said; and Stephen found the place. *Shelter,* Thomas said, standing in the clearing, looking round. *We'll need shelter, more than tents. We've got a baby coming, and the summer's on the turn.* So Stephen lived there first, alone in a bender while he built the first rough shelters. After that he had help, Thomas and the disciples working willingly under his direction as he got more ambitious on their behalf, and his huts turned to houses; but he was still very much the builder, the man who could make things happen. A man of his hands, always.

So Stephen gave them shelter, and Thomas gave them hope; and they all lived happily ever after, until the end came and all hope died, all shelter proved itself illusion.

But who were they, these communards, these settlers? These disciples?

Well, there were the inevitable hippies, left over from their golden age. There were men and women who'd had one life already, and failed with it. Among the younger people there were student drop-outs and druggies and graduates who weren't ready to tackle the unlimited world, who still wanted to live within someone else's definition.

They were a mixed bag, in other words, a curious assortment. But they all had this much in common, that they believed in Thomas. He wrote their gospels for them, he paved their path to heaven—and they were all prepared to work, to keep it so.

ANOTHER of those questions that people always ask came up again last week. I've been teaching an art class for the WEA, and I had a few of them back for drinks afterwards, my newest circle of friends; and one of the lads, he's barely in his twenties yet, he said, "So you had them two girls,

Thomas—but what about the others? Was it all like that, was it, what did they use to call it, free love, was it, like that?"

I smiled, and told him love was never free. He'd learn, I said. But then I answered his question. Why not?

We had everything, I told him. Take a small community of healthy, active people trying to build a new way of life; then tell them to lose their inhibitions, tell them there aren't any rules and demonstrate by example. You're not going to get a rerun of the Victorians, are you? We had singles and couples, straights and gays; more than one plural marriage, and more than one divorce. We were always shuffling people from house to house or bringing an old abandoned hut back into service, to accommodate a new grouping who wanted to be together or an established partnership who wanted to split.

STEPHEN was that rare thing, a singleton who really wanted to be alone. He built himself a hut on the fringes of the settlement, and never shared it in all the years the colony survived. Mostly, people thought he was doing it to prove a point that already didn't need proving, that he and his brother were poles apart.

There was always some question why Stephen was there at all; he made the settlement happen, but he never made himself a part of it. They murmured about him often, in groups over a communal fire or more privately in bed at night, and mostly they came up with the same answer again. If he hadn't been constantly there, constantly setting himself against Thomas for all to see the difference, people might have assumed that Thomas' brother was cast in the same mould as Thomas himself. Hard enough to live in that man's shadow, people said, worse still to be taken for his shadow. No, they said, Stephen stays because it's important to assert his independence, his separateness; and to do that he has to be here, where it can clearly be seen.

Or, less thoughtfully, they said, "He's a bolshie little bugger, that Stephen. Place'd go to pot without him, but Christ, he's hard sometimes. The way he sneers at Thomas, well, I wouldn't stand for it myself. You'd never know they were brothers, would you? I mean, would you?"

"Oh, yes," someone else might say. "Yes, I think they'd have to be. They couldn't be like that, else. I mean, Thomas just stands there and takes it; and I know he's a saint, but even so, I don't think even he would take that from anyone except a brother..."

If Stephen truly loved anyone in the settlement, it would have to be little Paul, his nephew. He used to walk the baby through the woods for hours, when he was colicky and wouldn't sleep; and later they would walk together, as far as Paul's stumpy legs would carry him. The boy would come back from these adventures riding on his uncle's shoulders, or else asleep in his arms; and would be full of tales afterwards of red squirrels and deer seen, of foxes' tracks and badgers visited who were too sleepy to come to the doors of their setts when Stephen knocked. Paul was the one member of the community whom Stephen was always easy with, always patient; and the reverse was true too, or seemed to be, that if there was any one person that Paul loved more than equally, that person might be Stephen.

THEY ask me about fights and disputes in a society without rules, of course they do. Who adjudicated, they want to know, who was the policeman?

Sometimes I say no one and there wasn't one, sometimes I say we all did, we all were. Both answers are true, but neither satisfies. So then I sidetrack, I take issue with their assumptions. Who says there weren't any rules? I ask. Of course there were rules, I tell them. It's only that they were so obvious, so taken for granted that they never needed writing down, they barely needed mentioning.

Everything was shared, everything was common, that was the primary rule: whatever came in came to us, whatever went out went from us. We did everything together: we worked and played, raised a child, ate and talked and slept together. Put at its simplest, we lived all for one and one for all; or rather, we should have done. In practice, it never quite worked out that way.

In practice what we had, how we lived was all for one and one for all, and Stephen.

SEVEN years the settlement lasted, all told. There was never any real trouble with the locals, and even the landowner was glad to have them there for the simple forestry and conservation work they did, logging fallen trees and keeping the stream clear, mending walls and watching for summer fires.

Seven years; and it ended in a single rainy night, when the wood was filled with screaming, and more than one life died too soon.

It had been building for a long time, of course, months or perhaps even years; and Stephen it was who built it, he was always the builder. Stephen it was who sat restless at the fire many nights that summer, digging his knife into the earth and glowering at Thomas through the flames, making strange demands.

"Tell them you're not a saint," he said one time, with a contemptuous gesture at the listening disciples. "Go on, tell them."

"I'm not a saint," Thomas said obligingly, smiling, *anything you want, Stephen. You're not heavy, you're my brother.*

"Now say it like you mean it. Go on, try. Try and believe it, why don't you?"

"I never say anything I don't mean," Thomas said, and meant it. "Stephen, I don't understand. What's all this in aid of?"

"You're not leaving me any room," in a vicious mutter, while his knife slashed and slashed. "You're not leaving me any *choices*, Thomas."

"I'm sorry, I don't understand that. You've got the same choices that any of us have."

"No. No, that's not true. The rest of you don't have to live my life. Because if you're a saint, Thomas," riding over the sighs and the strong denials, "if you're a saint, then what the hell does that leave me? What does that *make* me?"

"Human, at a guess," Thomas suggested, still smiling.

"I've tried that," Stephen said, with a wild shake of the head. "I've tried it, and it doesn't *work*."

"Oh, come on, Stephen. Look around you. Of course it works, it's what we're best at. It's working pretty well here, isn't it? Wouldn't you say?"

"Oh, for you it works," bitter and angry now. "It works for *you,* that's what I'm saying. Doesn't work for me, though, does it? Does it?" And Thomas looked at him, and for once didn't answer a question directly; because he wouldn't lie, he didn't know how to, and the truth was plain to see.

"You don't have to stay," he said instead, gentle and understanding and unhappy. "You can always leave, if you don't feel comfortable here. We'd be desperately sorry to lose you, you've given us so much; but…"

"I can't go," Stephen said, with all his masks fallen away except perhaps one, except perhaps the last. "I can't go, and leave all this behind me. I'm *invested* here. And you're not giving me any *choice.*"

And Stephen left the fire and walked away into the night, as he had done so often that summer. He left the company and the conversation brighter by his absence, even the firelight seemed brighter with him gone; but even so there were little shivers, there were goose pimples to be rubbed down and lovers to be silently reassured. Because if Thomas was a saint—and no one doubted it except the man himself, his one blind spot, his failing—and Stephen was the opposite of his brother, if Stephen was working so hard to achieve that, then what *did* that make him, exactly? What was he working towards, where would it end?

WHERE it ended, of course, was that night of rain and screaming, and an unbridgeable gulf torn between brother and brother.

I make a point of telling new friends about it. I tell them everything, except my true name. As far as that goes, Thomas Woodson will do, but I conceal nothing else. No one can share my burden, but I think it important that they at least understand where it came from.

Mostly they are quiet afterwards, caught awkwardly between sympathy and horror, nowhere that can be fitted easily into a package of words. After that, they're usually frightened to ask questions, for a while; but they get there in the end, they're driven to it. That's when they ask about the others, and however do I manage on my own—and eventually, inevitably, someone will ask about Stephen, what happened to him.

And I tell them, I tell them even that. Why not? It's a pitiless world, let them learn.

IT was a child's scream that split the wet night's noises, clean and tight as glass, and as fragile.

There was no communal fire that night, and seemingly no community; everyone was in their own house or hut, most in their own rooms, their own beds by now. It was early yet, but they lived a daylight life in any case, and the rain was a spoiler.

Even the ones who were sleeping heard the scream. And woke, and knew who made it even though they'd never heard it before, not like that. Even while they were talking of animals, a howling dog perhaps, they were sitting up and frantically scrabbling in darkness for their clothes.

Then he screamed again, and no talking now, they came tumbling from their houses into the rain. They ran to Thomas, and found him in the doorway of his house; and in his hand a note, a scrap of paper.

"This was on Paul's pillow," he said. "It's Stephen, he says, he says he's taken Paul to meet the badgers."

Because it's not the sort of thing you'd think of, the note didn't say. *One last proof* it didn't say, it didn't need to.

Again Paul screamed, somewhere on the valley's slope, high above their heads; and this time there were words in it, but they were confused by distance and blurred by rain, and even his father could make no sense of them.

"Where are they?" Thomas demanded. "Badgers, what does he mean, what's he *doing?*"

Silence, frantic looks and shrugs and shaking heads. Stephen was the one who knew about badgers, where the setts were and which were occupied. Others had seen holes in the ground, to be sure, and guessed their origin; but to find them again, in the dark, in the rain, in a panic?

"We'll just have to, have to follow the noise," someone said. "And call, let him know we're coming."

"And pray he keeps screaming," another voice. "Sorry, Thomas, but it's the only way we'll find him."

Everyone went to search. They shared this, as they shared it all; and not one would stay behind, not one was willing to be separated from their mutual terror.

"The more of us there are, the more ground we can cover," they said. "They're out there somewhere, we've just got to find them, that's what counts."

So they started up the hill in a long file, taking sticks to help them on the muddy slopes; but they ended up finding another use for them, because Paul's screams did stop too soon. They were all but helpless then, in the dark and the rain and the fear, the confusion of it all. They used the sticks to beat the bushes, but it was frustration more than method; fury, almost, seeking to thrash an answer out of the silent wood.

And they shouted, they called Paul's name and Stephen's, and heard nothing but each other and their own muddled fancies, woven from hope and desperation mixed: "Quiet, I thought I heard something then, will you be *quiet...*"

They found the badger's sett at last, and beside it a deep, steep-sided pit; but though Thomas jumped straight into it and felt with his hands in the muddy water collected at the bottom, he found nothing except deep furrows in the stony earth where it seemed an animal had scratched at it, or a child worked his fingers to the bone.

It was someone else who found Paul's clothes, kicked under a bush a few yards distant.

They searched on for an hour, for two hours, for three; and at last, sick and filthy and exhausted, one by one they turned back to the settlement again. Some were limping, some were in tears; the first to go were merely furtive, betraying their trust, sharing nothing any longer.

Someone took Paul's two mothers back eventually, dragged them almost, the last to give up; but Thomas stayed out. All night he stayed, walking and searching for as long as he had the strength, calling his son; and even when his legs and heart failed him, still he wouldn't go in. He dared not admit that his son was lost, for fear of making it true by his own acceptance; so he stood at the valley's heart, on the bridge that spanned the rising stream. He stood unmoving for hours, his big hands clenched around the rail and his head tipped back in the rain, straining for any sound that might be his son discovered.

And he heard nothing but the rain and the stream and the pebbles in the stream-bed rolling, until the morning came; and the first new thing he heard in the morning was the sound of his own voice screaming.

His head had fallen by now and his shoulders were bowed at last, though the rain had stopped; and his eyes could see something in the water below his feet, even before there was light enough to make out what it was.

Not even thinking by now, far too far gone to guess or wonder, he could only look at it until the light was better. Then he saw that there was a rope tied around the central upright, and a sack tied to the rope: a sack too large for its light contents, bobbing and tugging in the greedy water.

Thomas stood staring for a long time longer, before he vaulted the rail and plunged waist-deep into the bitter stream. Now he was urgent, now he didn't have time to fight the sodden, swollen knots and the rope was too short to reach the bank; so he lifted the sack onto the bridge, and drew himself up after. Sat on the worn wet planks and fumbled with the rope, where it was tied around the sack's mouth; and still couldn't deal with the knots, so he took hold of the sack in two great handfuls, and heaved.

And even as the seam ripped apart, if he was thinking at all he must have been thinking *No,* thinking *It's too small, too light, if there's anything dead in here it'll be a badger, that's all. I don't know what game Stephen's playing but it's not that, at least it's not Paul...*

And even as the seam ripped, even as he thought his child safe—if he were thinking at all—he must have seen that he was wrong.

Badgers have savage teeth, and will fight viciously in a trap; but badger-bites were the least of what was done to Paul. That was just the start of it, when Stephen baited the badger with the boy for bait.

After that he used his knife. From the look of it in the weak morning sun, he'd done that work on the bridge, while the settlers searched the woods above. Even all the rain they'd had wasn't enough to hide new chips and gouges in the old wood, too darkly stained too soon.

And then Paul had gone in the sack and the sack had gone in the stream, tied where it could be neatly found in the morning; and the real sweet gift from Stephen to Thomas, brother to brother, was the knowledge that Paul might still have been alive when he went in the sack. Might still have been bleeding to death or slowly drowning, might still have been fighting for life while Thomas stood only a foot higher and a yard away, on the bridge in the deep dark of a cloudy country night.

I told them this story last week because they asked, they wanted to know what happened to end the settlement. It was right that they should know, and so I told them; and after the usual silence, the shifting around, the hunt for words that don't exist to express what cannot and should not be expressed, someone asked the question I'd been waiting for.

"Thomas, what, what happened to Stephen?"

"Nothing," I said. "Nothing happened to Stephen. He'd proved his point and gone, and that was all. He disappeared."

"But surely, the police, surely they could find him..."

I shook my head. "No police. They were never told. The colony must have been scattered long before they even heard rumours; and no one left a forwarding address. So they had no witnesses, no body, even the bridge was gone by then, no evidence there—nothing they could do, really, except file and forget. Journalists the same. They still catch hints of it, they ask questions; but I won't talk to journalists and they don't know where else to turn. No handle, no story. File and forget."

THAT must have been the last communal decision they made: that even in desolation, even in their final days they had to cling to the dream. The evil was theirs to be shared among them, and the outer world had no claim. So they dealt with Paul's body in their own way, and then they left. Not together, they could never do anything together any more; but in ones and twos they went, walking or hitching or catching a bus, barely saying goodbye and leaving almost everything behind them.

In a week the settlement was empty, but for Thomas. He stayed a few days on his own, one wife gone south and the other west, talking of America; then he too was gone one morning, the bridge burned behind him and he never came back.

THAT'S the story as I tell it, as I told it to my art class. Privileged information, I told them, keep it to yourselves. And they did, I think, generally they do. It's too terrible for common gossip.

But last night I was drinking on the Quayside a few minutes' walk from my flat, when one of my pupils came in with a much older woman.

Ailie saw me, and waved, and brought her companion over.

"Thomas," she said, "meet my friend Kate. Kate, this is Thomas, he teaches that art class I go to."

But, "Oh, no," Kate said, staring at me, twenty years unmasked on her face. "No," she said, "oh, no. That isn't Thomas," she said, "that's Stephen."

I should be teaching my class tonight, but I don't think I'll go. If I did go, I don't think there would be anybody there.

I believe my brother is dead. I think he must be; I cannot see how he could have lived this long, or why he would have wanted to, or where he could have gone.

So I live his life for him, as best I can. This is the final irony, if you like: that having shown myself so different, having given so much to prove it, I must now come as close as I am able. I am not a saint, of course, but I wear his name, and try to keep on the side of the angels now. They were right not to pursue me, with their own justice or other people's. It would have been quite wasted.

I am Thomas for a few months here and a few months there, as long as I can bear it in any one place. I make friends, I work, and I tell his story. They deserve that much from me, he and Paul both.

I don't know what they did with Paul, I wasn't there to see. Perhaps they buried him in the pit beside the badgers, it would have been convenient; perhaps elsewhere in the wood. Perhaps they fed him to the badgers, I don't know.

I loved that boy. I had to, or I couldn't have done what I did. It wouldn't have been right, done without love.

I wish I knew where he was buried, I'd like to visit him; but having once got away, I cannot go back to the wood.

I live with bridges always in my view, inescapable as water; but I cannot bear, I cannot *bear* to walk across a bridge.

WHITE SKIES

W E LIVE IN THE WORLD WE made, and it doesn't matter.

These are the lessons of the skies, says 'Mester Truman. They are white by day and fit to be written on, fit for the hand of man, just as the hand of man has made them; and at day's end red and rotten, the sun-sink like the promise of a bloody closure. Every day the same promise, whatever the weather, and nothing we can say to that. We can do as we like, says 'Mester Truman, because in the end there's nothing we can do.

Maybe you get to be cynical—or realist, pragmatist, whatever he would call himself—when you must sail from township to distant township, a semester here and a semester there, never let stay a full year together. Never let in.

Maybe something else happens, something worse. That's what Dad says. He says all that exposure, staring at the skies and sleeping under them, he says it makes you unsteady in the world, it snaps your keel. He says you can turn turtle. Turtle Truman we called the 'mester for a while after that, Mish and me. It didn't catch on, but wouldn't matter if it had. No one else would understand it, only us.

My dad's a keelman, he likes to make out he sees us all in terms of hulls and sails. At the world's mercy, needing skill to survive. Luck and skill together, but skill mostly. By his reckoning your hull and keel are nature and nurture both, they are what you're given but you have to take care of them or the sea will get you sooner or later, worm or rot or that sudden snap in a storm. Your sailing skills are nurture all the way, the ways you're taught to get by.

I don't think motors have much place in his metaphor. If they did—well, the guys with motors would be the streaky ones, high-powered, top deck. Not like us.

Definitely not like 'Mester Truman. A 'mester isn't bilge, no, far from that. True 'mesters are almost legendary in the schoolrooms and in our parents' talk, but even so. Folks like us, Dad says, we're at the mercy of the wind, except for how we learn to use it; he says that and he means it, but I think even more he means folks like the 'mester. Metaphorically he means it, and literally too. He likes that, when something he says strikes absolutely true.

'MESTER Truman's sailboat measures five metres, stem to stern. He had us down to measure her and map her in the dock, the whole class of us together.

"My kind are not so common any more," he said, "that you should miss this chance. You might not see another. Another like me, I mean," tall and lean, we thought he meant, with his long black hair caught back in a silver ring, "a sea-gypsy with knowledge to trade. I know every township does exchanges, you swap teachers regularly and call them 'mesters too, but that's a different thing."

Oh, it was, a very different thing. Teachers are teachers, but he was a wild man, dark and dangerous and bold. Someone to love, and we thought we half loved him already, Mish and I. How not, when he sailed this tiny fragile cockleshell craft ocean-free, out of sight of land and townships both? On his own under the dreadful blank of the sky, into the dreadful blank of an empty future that he would have to write for himself, find a 'ship willing to sign him, willing to let him stay one semester for the sake of their young generation. He'd need to be persuasive. Persuasive first, and then good. And even then, good as he was, as he proved to be, he'd still be sent free again at year's end, sailing off again, untrusted, unretained.

He took us aboard to let us chart his boat, in twos and threes together. There wasn't room for more. Waiting our turn, Mish and I sat on the wharf and kicked our heels above the water and said, "It's so *small...*" And the world so big, we meant, and the sea's temper so swift to turn. Mish and I rarely needed to say so much aloud. We lived in each other's pockets, almost in each other's minds; in each other's hands and trust entirely.

Maybe everyone needs someone they can trust, just the one? I had Mish and he had me and we were sufficient together, against all the caution and doubt of the edifice that is a township, through all the turbulence and question of a shared adolescence.

Maybe 'Mester Truman was still looking for his one to trust. Or maybe he was sufficient unto himself, content to lay his trust where he could see it, hold it close. For sure he must trust his own abilities, from basic maintenance to higher navigation. The sea has a thousand ways to threaten a man alone. His simple survival was a testament to his skills; he hardly needed a reference else.

"You two, is it?" he said as we stepped aboard, last of the class, magnificent in our patience. We'd actually waved other kids ahead, to be sure of this final slot. There might be advantage in it. He'd sent the others away once their time was over, not to have them hanging around on the docks annoying the grown-ups; with no pressure and no one waiting, now that we had him to ourselves perhaps he'd let us linger, ask questions, slip curious fingers beneath the skin of him. We'd bury our romantic hearts within his blood-beat, maybe. If there was profit in it. "Are you actually inseparable, or does it just seem that way?"

"Oh, totally," we assured him. "There are rumours that the world will end, if anyone ever contrives to separate us. Like splitting the atom, only more so: all the energy there is, released in one great vengeful cataclysm. It's all right, though, we're very careful. Always have been. No one gets between us. Our parents will confirm."

"I'm sure. Nevertheless, I'm going to put this sail between you. There's only room for one at a time at the winch. This boat's designed that way, optimised for my life, a man alone."

Nevertheless he was glad to have us there, I thought: two bright boys pliable and attentive, swift to learn and eager to please. Devoted, almost, very much his slaves for the hour. Not practical slaves, as there was nowhere actually to go and no work to do, but welcome none the less. We rattled sails up and down and flung the tiller to and fro in response to his commands, to various imagined winds and sets of sea, storm and calm and steady swell, while this isolated pool actually stirred hardly at all beneath us.

He had to duck through the hatchway to the cramp of the cabin below. Neither Mish nor I was tall enough to worry, but we both ducked anyway, in possessive imitation. "Now," he said. "With the stars and planets hidden as they are, how do you imagine I find my way from one township to another?"

"GPS, of course," we chorused, with a flourish at the bank of electronica, all dark here in dock, all silent but still blackly gleaming with potential, the promise of data. We loved data.

"What, would you trust your life to satellites not under your control?"

That brought us up short. No, of course we wouldn't. They could be switched off at any moment; they could be sabotaged. Worse, they could be corrupted, they could corrupt their own data, feed us misinformation, lose us in an ocean of lies.

He told us about the old ways, ready reckoning, which sounded to us little better than blind guesswork and nothing to chance your life on; he told us about new ways that were more reassuring, alternate data, the salinity of ocean currents and flux in the magnetic field, mappable through time, fluid but secure. If anything could ever be secure, out at sea.

We asked the right questions, expressed a proper admiration, flattered his ego and his boat together. He did brew chai, and he did let us squirm among his wiring, turning this on and testing that, taking the backs off his boxes to learn how they were linked, what languages they spoke, what they said to each other and to him.

We didn't leave until he chased us out. What we really wanted, of course, was what all the class had wanted, a trip out of the dock into open water. Teach us to sail, why not, when he was teaching us so much? We did ask, but that turned out to be the wrong question at last.

"I can't do that," he said. "Not without your parents' consent," which he knew and we knew that he would not get. Dad with his talk of white skies and how they unsettle a man, falling down to the horizon like a solid wall ahead; and the township churning away from us towards that wall, and only the various wind to fetch us back if it ever could get us up to speed again? No chance.

He told us to forget pleasure-jaunts and learn from his life, the truth of him, his solitude. Without that, he said, we'd never understand the 'Mester Truman that we saw, nor what he tried to teach us. Then he sent us away.

We kicked along the dockside, looking at all the other boats, the tenders and speedboats and barges that never get to sail while the township's moving, and yes. Of course we were both thinking the same thing, talking about the one thing, how we could sneak down here some evening and take the 'mester's boat out by ourselves, now that we'd learned the ropes.

And how we couldn't, because the dock doors are locked up tight when we're in motion, there's no way out without a pass key and a code. Which kids don't get, of course, and would they give them to a transitory 'mester? We didn't know. All that talk about our parents might be bluff. He might be locked up too, as tight as any of us, no way off until his strict term ends.

So then we shrugged off dreaming and compared treasures, actuality: the little things we'd contrived to filch, one of us helping himself while the other held 'Mester Truman distracted. Fuses, cables; chips and tools. Mostly taken from his box of spares, nothing he would miss until he needed it, nothing he would need aboard the township.

THEY used to call us seedships, because we made the oceans bloom. Maybe they still do, back in the dry. I wouldn't know. Would anyone? We don't talk much any more, the dryfolk and us.

We do still seed the oceans with iron, we do cultivate the algae, we do our bit. Welcome or otherwise.

That's what they tell us, that's what we're taught: that what we do is right, regardless of what other nations think. Someone had to do something. So we cast iron dust into the sea where the plankton it spawns will sequester the carbon dioxide they munch on, and drag it down into the deeps. They tell us it's a mission. Mission-critical, they say.

"Plankton" comes from the Greek and means "wandering", that's what 'Mester Truman told us. Which is what we do: we wander the oceans and spread the dust and tend the algal blooms, harvest the fish that feed on them. It's what he does too, he says. He wanders the ocean and spreads the knowledge that he carries, and tends the young minds that grow on it. That's us. The township harvests our future, he said, his metaphor breaking down around him but never mind.

These days townships names us better. We grew around the seeding, and we do still seed, but that's not what we are any more. We grew. The ships grew into argosies, because why go back and forth sowing iron dust and doing nothing else when we could be bigger, carry goods, offer services to ports and provinces and nations? Ports, provinces, even nations that might see little traffic else by the time we'd finished growing, by the time we'd eaten all the small fry?

And then the argosies grew into manufactories, because why buy goods when we had power and raw materials and personnel, everything we needed to turn them out ourselves?

And the manufactories made weapons, first thing they did make, because there's always a demand and we demanded them ourselves, we had to defend the 'ship. We'd been hated from the first, because we soured the oceans and some people, some *peoples* could never settle to that; and now we were taking trade from the mercantile lines and they loved us not for that either. And there were regular pirates too, who might have thought us easy—bloated wealth, the softest of targets—if we weren't so conspicuously otherwise.

History. Old history, mostly. People don't touch us now. Not us, nor any of our sisters. The townships are a nation, and we protect each other.

Still make weapons, though, and sometimes it seems like half the township is barracks, half the folk aboard are soldiers when we come to land. Everyone has another job at sea, which matters more; but why sell weapons when you can hire them out with the personnel trained to use them, a strike-force ready made? We don't linger for long wars, but mercenary missions are just one of the services we offer. In and out, and no one left behind.

They double-check on that, the drysiders, that no one's been left behind. Of course they do. Paranoia is the fuel that runs us all, so says 'Mester Truman, since oil came up short. They count us off the 'ship, and count us on again. We do the same. And guard our flanks as carefully at sea, let few folk aboard at all and fewer stay. No one looks kindly on strangers any more; they might too easily turn out to be spies and saboteurs.

That's why we take teachers for a term, a semester, no longer. How can you trust an itinerant? They see too much, they go too far, they might have come from anywhere.

Cross-fertilisation is good, everyone knows that. New tech, new insights come from all over, and 'mesters spread them around. It's all about control, though: we let them on, we do not take them in.

Mostly we take them from other townships, known quantities, already tried and tested. Still not trusted. We are a nation but not entirely one people, never quite at ease even with each other. Paranoia sits too deep, 'Mester Truman says. Every township sets its own course, listens to its own counsel, never lets a stranger be alone and unwatched anywhere that matters.

"I guess we don't matter, then," Mish said later, after we'd talked it through in class. "Nobody watches the 'mesters while they teach."

We'd come up high like good boys, to spend an hour standing an unofficial and redundant watch in our favourite spot just forward of the main bridge, just where we could be best seen to do it. The 'ship has electronica, of course, to scan seas and skies and far horizons—but tech can always be superseded, machines can be subverted. Watchfulness is an unshakable tradition, deep-laid: *don't waste the good years, while your eyes are sharp. If you've nothing else to look at, look out.* It was our own creed, our common sense that added *be visible about it,* not to waste the effort, or the credit that ensued.

"Don't be dry," I said, grinning at him sideways, just to catch his profile against the muted glare of sun behind the sky. We stood under the shelter of an overhang, always, but the skies fall like curtains, all the way to the water. "We all do, the whole class of us."

"Oh. Yeah…"

Chagrin: it's a beautiful thing. We think so much the same, Mish and I, we each of us hate it when the other one thinks ahead, is faster or sharper or better prepared.

Either our parents and governors trust us entirely, individually—the 'ship is ours, after all, our life today and our floating future: how could any of us ever wish it harm?—or else they trust us collectively, practically. If any 'mester ever tried to subvert us, someone among us would be sure to report it; which being true, of course we would all report it, because who wants to be singled out as the one who didn't? The slowest, the driest-thinking of us could see the danger in that. We'd fight to be first. And be watched ourselves thereafter, of course, for fear we'd been subverted anyway; and submit to it with a careful grace, because we knew the alternatives. One way or the other, our elders could be sure of us. Thought they could be sure.

And of course the 'mesters know that too, every detail of that, and so would never try to subvert us, not in class.

Even so, 'Mester Truman took us out of the classroom when he could, up on deck when the weather let him. On deck and not in shelter, under the sky, white sky. He was used to it, I suppose.

So were we all, used to living beneath it; but our way kept us below as much as possible, taught us to eye it askance and distrust what it concealed.

We seed the oceans and some people hate us for it, teach against us, declare boycotts and threaten what sabotage they can.

Other people seed the skies.

It's an evil, but what can we do? We can't even see them at it, let alone come at them. There were raids once, 'ship to shore, but now they build their airfields far inland, beyond our reach.

They strew sulphates into the atmosphere, to turn back the sun's rays, they say: to raise our albedo, and so cool us all down. We should all of us be grateful, they say.

We've heard them, Mish and I, on the propaganda channels. We're not supposed to listen, but we do. We built our own receiver, three semesters back.

They say their plan is better, they're not poisoning the planet the way we are. It isn't true, of course; we're not fool enough to believe them. We know what harm they do, we've been taught it, year on year. Besides, we can see: or rather we can't, because it was them who turned the skies white, so we can't even see their planes as they fly overhead.

'Mester Truman says it doesn't matter. They do what they do, and we do what we do, and neither one of us can save the other. Or ourselves, or anyone else. It's gone too far, and the world will kill us all in the end, soon now, sooner than we think. So he says. So it really doesn't matter what we do.

MISH and I, we pretty much do what we like outside of school. Our parents are working, neither of us has sibs and everyone knows who we are. We're good boys; we've been very careful about that. No wild stuff that anyone might notice, no bad reps, no public trouble.

We have places to go, people to be seen with, pictures of innocence. Schoolkids aren't allowed to work, but we work anyway: fetching and carry-ing mostly, a bucket of chai to the engine room, bento boxes to the bridge. If you want to know the 'ship, work from the galley outwards; if you want the 'ship to know you, start with the junior officers and let your reps trickle up. The commodore knows our faces, the engineer knows our names. We know everyone. And everything. How safe the pile is, how many years'-worth of fuel is stored in lead-lined bunkers deep, deep in the hull; how much is stowed secretly on distant rocks far from any shore. Where we're due to sail next, where after that. Who's up for promotion, who's going the other way, who's not trusted at all.

It's all currency, it's negotiable, though mostly we just hoard it. Spend wisely, and always have more in reserve; never tell everything you know. People think we're strictly small-scale, just kids, barely understand the use they make of us; they think they pay us in sweets and baubles and petty cash, they think we're content with that.

They have no idea. No *idea* what we know, how much there is of it, how it makes a webwork of information from mast to keel, from wind to lee and stem to stern.

Once, just once we did spend big. We tipped a woman off that she had been listed as subversive. She wasn't a 'mester, not an incomer at all, she was born on board and we liked her, rather; we didn't want to see her go. She put her name down to trans'ship at once, of course. If you're quick, if you're lucky—if they can't prove anything against you, if it's only suspicion that they have—you can start again with a clean record on another hull. No new captain would believe whatever record came with you, anyway. How could they trust another 'ship's judgement? It might be unreliable, dishonest, subversive itself, any of a hundred ways of wrong.

She left, swift and sudden, as people tend to do. Properly, her cabin should have been reassigned, but there's always more space than crew. Too many solo berths, and who likes to sleep alone? Couples sometimes look for privacy, that may be only natural; what's truly natural is to draw together, to bunk together in dormitories and barracks, look never to be left alone. Never to be caught alone. Common sense goes hand in hand with nature: if people see you acting solitary, holding yourself apart, how can they help but be suspicious?

That was her trouble, perhaps, or the start of it, that she'd taken a single cabin. She actually took it to bundle in, someone she wasn't meant to be bundling—we knew!—but of course that wasn't on the record. Of course people would look at her askance, when she moved out of the common dorm and set up on her own. And wasn't around, wasn't available for her old friends in the way she used to be. Perhaps they heard she had a secret lover—but lovers have been used before, as excuse for espionage. Sabotage, even, the unforgivable sin.

So she left, just ahead of the rising wave, because we tipped her off. Perhaps she was glad to go, glad to leave the lover with all the other trouble at her back. We were sorry, but still: there was profit in it.

We were known quantities, people thought they had the measure of us. If we offered to spend half a shift helping in the purser's office, doing routine admin, they assumed we were storing up treasure in heaven, accumulating credit to be cashed in later. We did it all the time. Nothing different now, except for letting one minor call on the system—the availability of an undesirable single cabin, say—be slipped aside all unheeded, action taken, never mind.

So we had our own space, with our own doorcode, so buried that no one official would ever dig it up. Nor anyone unofficial, by any chance that we could reasonably guard against. If people saw us in that corridor, anywhere on that hull, we always had a reason to be there. It was usually visible in our hands: we were fetching supplies up from the hold, running an errand to the commissariat, bringing a mop to a pool of vomit, something. Someone else's vomit, obviously. We would be conspicuously acquiring merit, and very likely dodging school. People liked to see that written so clear on our transparent, innocently guilty faces; they found it obscurely reassuring. The world was as it was, and boys were being boys. School was being dodged. All was well.

No one ever, ever saw us going in and out of the cabin. We were scrupulously careful about that. First thing, we tapped a line into the 'ship's security, so that we could watch the corridor and be sure.

Second thing, we diverted that camera's feed only to our own monitor, so no one else could catch us by unhappy accident or random check.

We had our space, securely; then we had to fill it. The bunk was built-in, but we weren't there to bundle. We did our courting in the common rooms like wise boys, transparent, innocently carnal. The mattress went out and in came furniture, as much as we could fit: two hard chairs and a table. The stripped bunk made more and better surface-space. The door came off the closet and went for recycling, which made those shelves more handily available for servers, comms units and the like.

Everything we had was cannibalised or reclaimed, almost all of it hand-built with our own tender hands, but that's just the way a township works. Everything gets used and used again, nothing is ever wasted or thrown away. It's cool to be in school: chips, cables, redundant circuitboards and sockets find their way to the classroom playbox, for science lessons and experiments. We could take what we wanted, Mish and I. We left a few builds big and obvious in the labs, and never mind if they didn't actually work; teachers need something to criticise, something to misunderstand besides their actual pupils. What we actually wanted was smuggled back to our own place where it was repurposed, conjoined with whatever fresher tech we could beg or more likely steal, and so incorporated into the masterwork.

If you'd asked us what it was, that masterwork, what we were eventually making, I don't believe either one of us could have told you. It grew as we did, day by day. It had no name. Our old receiver was a part of it, that mattered, that it could listen to the world; now there was a transmitter too, we could talk back to the world, if we'd only had anything to say. That was still only an aspect, only a functionality of something far broader and deeper.

We thought it was deep, at least. We thought it was art, as much as engineering. We loved it, almost as much as we loved ourselves for making it, for the achievement of the thing. It was a way to say—in code and electronics, in solid matter and transient current and immeasurable ideation—how we felt about the world and our place within it. It was a machine that started from the same place every day, that couldn't be reprogrammed; but it could reach out into the world, it could listen and learn and reply in kind. We had made it, we could use it, and it wasn't us but very much itself, the perfect spy: alert to others, honest to itself.

It wasn't us, but it was ours and we were mighty proud.

DID we give ourselves away in some kind of rash joint enterprise, not quite oblique enough, or did we say something directly, one of us? I don't know, Mish says he doesn't either. I guess I can believe that. We're made of the same stuff, Mish and I. Unique together. We've been told so all our lives. Uniquely sinful, is what they usually say. We like that.

Uniquely exposed, once 'Mester Truman knew our secret.

It had to be him, of course; we'd have wanted it to be him. Which is why I wonder if either or both of us let something slip deliberately, or halfway that. Half wishing that he knew, so letting it happen, letting him learn.

Anyway. It was just our careful secret, and then suddenly it wasn't. One way or another, he knew.

"Show me," he said, "show me what you boys have done."

We didn't really have the choice. Once that was true, of course, we wanted to show it off, every detail: our fabulous network of links and inter-links, all the subtle coding, the engineering hard and soft, the sneaky attack modes and sneakier defences...

WE'VE never seen it since.

Next we knew, men came and took us out of our beds, middle of the night, nightmare time. Our parents wept and shouted, which did them no good at all. At least, our mothers wept, in fear or fury or helplessness, all three. Mish's father, he shouted. I could hear that, clean down the corridor. My own father looked at me silently, watched me taken away, wondered I think what tangle I had in my lines, whether my hull was breached. Had my keel snapped?

If I'd said this storm was none of my own making, he would have shrugged and waited, to see if I said true. A fit vessel and good seamanship would survive whatever honest weather came, he would be sure of that. He must be. He needed it. If I sank and was lost, it must necessarily be my own fault.

As it was, of course, but I didn't mean to sink.

They wouldn't let Mish and me see each other, except for one glimpse in the corridor, so that we both knew the other was taken too. They wouldn't let us speak at all.

No matter. I could trust him. I thought I could trust him. I had to; that was my own need this night.

All I needed. Everything else was ready.

THEY said, *this system that you've built with stolen parts, tell us of its purpose, what it does.*

I said, "It taps into the township, quiet as a cat. It listens, it reads, it measures. It remembers everything."

And it talks, too?

"Yes, of course. It could talk to the world, and you'd never hear it: microbursts on frequencies that shift according to a shifting algorithm."

The innocence of youth, doubled up with arrogance. It's hard to overplay it, when that's just exactly what they're looking for.

And to whom have you been talking, lad, who has this precious algorithm? Who's listening to all our secrets?

"Why, no one, of course. No one except 'Mester Truman. He promised that. This was just a test, he said, a project, see if we were as smart as we thought we were, could we subvert the 'ship's security, like that…"

DID he think, did he really think we wouldn't have defences in place, beyond whatever we'd shown him? Not protect ourselves, in all our youth and arrogance?

If township life has taught us one thing, *one*, it is to watch our own backs, and each other's.

IF he'd spent more than a semester on this 'ship or any other, he'd have learned that too. It seeps into your bones, but not I guess when you're always shifting, always moving on.

He hadn't thought to check, hadn't stopped to wonder who we might have set up for the fall, if that fall ever came. He just betrayed us, handed us over like the hired servant that he was.

Perhaps he thought it might win him citizenship, see him invited in.

I took them down to the dock and showed them the receiver on his boat, with its clever little patch that knew our algorithm and could listen in to everything we sent. I let them look further on their own account, didn't even try to point them to the equally clever little patch on his transmitter, that could shuffle all our data into other people's codes and send it on, still in those undetectable bursts. Now I'd brought them this far, they would find it.

That, and more. They'd find the data hidden in the class computers, everything he might have sent already, stored behind our own most obvious passwords that we would never have been so stupid as to use for such a purpose. A transient 'mester trying to cover his own back, though, thinking himself almost caught and so throwing his own pupils to the wolves to cover his escape, he might easily be so clumsy…

They'd find a stolen passkey and its codes on board his boat, ready for a swift illegal leaving if it came to that.

Best, worst, they'd find his sabotage, and all the records of it.

WHAT boy doesn't like to make explosions?

He'd had us making bombs, his hidden records said: so much of this chemical, so much of that, all requisitioned for lab lessons, just with the two of us. Pipes and welding gear, electronics.

"Of course," I said, when they asked me; just as Mish would be saying, when they asked him too. "'Mester Truman wanted to put on a display before he left, I think maybe he was hoping to persuade you to let him stay? Sort of fireworks, he said, only with a serious intent. He wanted to float targets in our wake and blow them up, sort of a *son et lumière...*"

A township isn't quite one ship, it isn't quite a dozen. At one time, I suppose it used to be a fleet. Now—well, you can still find records of the separate hulls under their separate names, there are charts and our lovely spy-thing will have captured them, but nobody thinks that way. It's not a unit, it's a unity.

Someone sometime understood that if they bound the fleet together, they'd have the bonus of guaranteed, chained loyalty—no one ship could go sliding away in the night, bearing secrets to the dry or to another fleet—and the bonus too of stability: with more breadth, they could build higher superstructures and never risk a capsize.

Catamarans, trimarans can be stiff, but not us, we cover acreages: all our links will flex when they need to. Still, we are one thing of many parts. And have reasons, yes, more than one reason to fear sabotage. Nobody could sink us, but cut those links at crucial nodes and half the township would be suddenly unseaworthy, turning turtle.

Turtle Truman's bombs, that we had made him—we had told them that nickname by now, we told them everything, how not?—would be found at all those crucial nodes, live and ready, waiting only the electronic order to erupt.

THEY'D find him guilty, and us not. That was written. We had written it.

US? We're just boys, foolish boys: foolish but loyal, demonstrably loyal. We gave him up as soon as we understood what he'd done, what he'd had us doing. We'd be watched more carefully, that's all. We'd learn.

We'd learn to be more careful. Trust no one but each other. Watchfully.

HIM? He's a saboteur. All the evidence is there. He is all the proof they need, why we can never trust a 'mester. Or any stranger else.

They'll snap the mast of his boat, cut all the sheets and crack the keel. Short out the electrics, jam the winches, shred the sails; leave him helpless and adrift in our determined wake. No food, no water, no succour, no hope.

HE'LL be a lesson to us all, a dot against the glare, lost soon enough as we churn on under white skies into a red sunset.

THIS is the world we made, and it doesn't matter. He taught us that.

WHEN JOHNNY COMES MARCHING HOME

T HE WAR WAS A TERROR, BUT it was the peace that terrified. Like the vast bleak mysteries of adulthood—so much space and empty yet, quiet yet, unmarked by anything of ours—after the battlefield that was school. Like school, the war was none of our doing, it had simply happened to us and was always obviously survivable. Now we had somehow to make things happen on our own account, with no idea what would happen if we failed.

The aliens didn't help—but that was the point, rather. They weren't here to help. None of us understood them, quite. Not an invasion or an occupying force—because of course we hadn't lost the war, exactly—they might have been ambassadors or tourists, traders or artisans or thieves. Or weapons inspectors, because if we hadn't quite managed to lose the war we had most certainly not won it.

They might have been weapons. It was very hard to tell, and the government wasn't telling. The government gave a fine impression of knowing very little more than we did.

The aliens didn't really matter, though, day to day. They were a mystery and could stay that way, an expression of faith; we saw very little of them, day to day.

Our own soldiers were another matter. The survivors, that is. They were everywhere, inescapable, returned.

The wounded we could deal with. Some we could even treat. The psychologically scarred, those too; that was old science, albeit faced with new hurts.

But then there were the others, those who came back altered in ways we didn't understand. Enhanced, some people said. Or cursed, or corrupted. Betrayed, or betraying—some called them traitors, spies, dishonoured.

Some called them gods.

I had one who sat below my window, day and night. She didn't beg or steal, she took nothing from the government or anyone else; so far as I could tell, she neither ate nor excreted. Nor slept. Whenever I looked—and sometimes I would spend days, nights, just watching her—she was exactly there, exactly where she had been, sitting cross-legged and playing with light. Running little balls of it up and down her arms, drawing lines of it in the dust, weaving patterns between her hands in a vivid and complex cat's cradle. Perhaps she lived on light now; perhaps she drew nourishment from the glowing air that engulfed her. Perhaps she was beyond feeding, as she was beyond sleep.

Some returnees were studied, of course, but there were too many and nowhere to house them; in honesty, nowhere that seemed safe, so many people so strangely changed and all together. Perhaps they were a danger after all?

So they leaked back into the world, and talked or did not talk, and were not understood either way. Not all could play with light. Some could shape sound, make an obscure sculpture of it, a new art that seemed to baffle them as much as us. Some were physically altered; I met a slipskin once, who could never quite be touched, as though he were magnetised to the same polarity as the world around. He was naked, necessarily, and there was a measurable distance between his feet and the floor. It seemed not to inhibit him, and not to be any kind of use.

Generally they seemed to have small use for us, or for any life that we could offer. Their eyes were turned to another horizon. Mostly they were patient, but not all, or not without limits. My own lightweaver: one night she stood and drew herself a framework as high and wide as she could reach, lines of light that burned in the air; then she stepped through it and was gone before those lines had faded.

Some slipskins went too, as though neither gravity nor love could hold them any longer, as though there was nothing they could cling to. They needed no bright gateway; their own condition took them away, at an angle that could be neither described nor recorded.

We looked more closely then at those who remained, those who would let us look. There was no breakthough, more the slow dawn of a consensus. These weren't victims, any more than they were accidents. They were templates, rather. Armatures. Design specs.

There was a phase-shift out there, waiting to be found: an alternate way to be, or to go. No wonder the aliens had proved unreachable; no wonder our war had fizzled out in mutual helplessness, where neither side could entirely reach the other. But these people, salvaged prisoners of that war, they were our guides into crossing the border. Or they could be, as soon as we had solved the equations of light and skin and absence. Monkey see, monkey do: knowing that it was possible, we could do this.

WE can do this. Not yet, but we'll get there. And then we'll get—somewhere else. Which is terrifying, true, but probably essential. It is what's waiting for us now. What these people have been altered for: skeleton keys to an uncertain lock. A gesture, a gift, an introduction. A helping hand.

There are still those who call them traitors, fifth-columnists, Trojans within the walls.

I call them Marshalls. With all that that implies.

WHERE IT ROOTS, HOW IT FRUITS

"**H**IGHWAY 61. WHOO, BOY. A ROAD that roots down below the Big Easy, fruits Bob Dylan 'way up on Lake Superior, near in Canada. God's truth. Robert Allen Zimmerman, born Duluth, Minnesota. On 61. Are you *getting* this?"

Oh, I'm getting it. New Orleans behind us, the road glinting dark under our wheels; Duluth, Minnesota, who knows how far ahead?

"Long way, you're thinking. Am I right? From the root to the fruit, a *long* way for that sap to rise. But it ain't sap we're talking here. It ain't sap. And it don't have to rise. It just runs."

Runs as the road runs, perhaps, as the wheels run, smooth and easy all the way. From there to here, from here to there.

"See how the highway *shines,* boy? How it gleams in the lights, how they *reflect?* Now you do me a courtesy, you reflect on that a while."

"The road's wet," I say unthinkingly, "that's all."

"Oh, is that all, is it? Is that all? Yup, the road's wet. The boy is right, the road is wet. Smart, these boys from England. But you don't think that's *rain,* do you, you don't think it's been *raining?*"

Damn. He's got a point. This is hot country, and it hasn't rained since Baton.

"NOW passing through Leland, Mississippi. The only thing to do. But I'll tell you what's safe, son, I'll tell you what's certain sure. One of these shacks, one of these tarpaper-and-shit little huts with the steps broken and the screen door hanging loose and the frame all splitting in the sun, there's a man dying inside. It's what Leland's for, can you see it? Can you *see* this? An old bluesman, used to sing about the road, Route 61, whoo yeah; but he never got it right, and now he's dying. Call it TB, call it cancer; a boy like you, you could call it AIDS. It don't matter what you call it. What it is, he's just dying of the wrong damn song. Had this tune in his head all his life, lived on the goddamn *road* all his life, and his hands won't play it no more and his voice is gone but it's still there, he can still hear it, and he's still got it wrong and it's killing him. Now you tell me true, boy, ain't that the saddest thing?"

Laughing, slapping his vast thigh, leaving a smear of sweaty palm-print on his tight white cotton pants.

"BESSIE Smith. Whoo. She got herself killed about here. Just about, right... *here*. Whoo, yeah. She didn't *die* here, mind. You don't know the story? Jeez. Don't know nothing, do you, boy? That's sad, that's wrong. You so poor and all, you all spent out, you should be smarter. Won't get nowhere, poor *and* dumb. You could stay on 61 for *ever*.

"All torn open, Bessie was. Argued with a truck, and that motherfucker ripped her right apart. World's greatest singer and you could see how her insides worked, you could try and find her voice in all that mess, hold it in your hand if you could find it.

"So they haul ass to the hospital—only she's black, right? Under all that blood, she's still black. Don't even need to clean her up, you can see that much. So she gets turned away. Ain't that right, ain't it sweet? World's greatest singer, she's leaking blood on the leather and she gets turned away.

"Bled to death in a cheap hotel, did Bessie.

"Clarksdale, Mississippi. My kind of town. Whoo, *yeah.*"

"MEMPHIS, Tennessee. Forget Elvis, who gives a shit about Elvis? Martin Luther King, that's your man. April fourth, 1968. James Earl Ray, one shot, bang. *My* man.

"Or maybe not, could be he didn't even do it. The man says he didn't do it. Who gives a shit? I'll tell you what counts, what's important. I'll tell you what route Ray took, to get out of town.

"No. No, you tell me. Go on, chance your arm. Give it your best shot, white boy."

"Highway 61," I say. *Revisited,* I want to add, except we've never left it; and are we going to drive all night?

"Highway 61," echoed in high delight. "The man is right. Highway 61.

"Shit," he says, "I *love* this road."

HIGHWAY 61, love it or leave it; but we leave it at last, or pretend to. Still south of St Louis and the sky bruising up with greys and blues, first promise of dawn, he twitches the wheel and we run off the road. The tyres grumble over gravel and dust and this is not a motel we're pulling up outside, joining a line of Chevys and Oldsmobiles and Jesus *Christ* is that a Ford *Edsel* up the end there?

Not a motel, no. Nothing so fresh, so attractive.

It's a big place, mansion-high, faking ante-bellum; but it's not that old. Not by fifty years. Just a roadside hotel, clapboard with pretensions; surely it can't ever have been the right size for its trade. Even on 61, road of dreams in a country of dreamers, there can't have been the traffic to feed something this big.

And now the paint is peeling and shutters are banging in the wind, it feels like a movie and it looks right too, all the colour burnt off by the sun or leached away in the dark so it's monochrome right now, it's almost black and white. Another for Norman Bates, you might think if you saw a picture. One dead hotel, heart-dead, soul-shrunken.

Except that this isn't a picture, and there are cars parked in a line and light in the windows, music pulsing through the open door: dark, rolling piano from a man who knows what his left hand's for.

"This place got a name, then?"

He smirks at me, he says, "You got a name?"

I shrug, and follow him inside.

THE hat-check girl's topless in her little hatchway, between the outer and the inner doors. This doesn't look like the sort of place, but there she is. More than topless, near naked, only a spangly G-string and stilettos.

Oh, and a scattering of bruises.

She's too damn young for this; but she smiles professionally enough, works her gum to one side and says hi there, says welcome, hopes we had a good drive up.

We don't have hats or anything else to check, but he tips her anyway, a torn dollar bill, just to leer as she tucks it inside her G-string with a big, *big* smile to show how grateful she is.

He cups her cheek with his fat hand and even her muddy brown eyes barely flinch, she's such a pro, she's so very good at this. His fingers dig into her hair, he rocks her head side to side, chuckling at her; and her tongue slips out to lick at the base of his thumb, just where brown fades into pink.

Just for a second, her tongue looks longer than it ought to be.

BUT everything's wry here, none of it looks quite right. It couldn't, with an Edsel parked out front.

He leaves the girl at last, takes me through the inner doors with a roll of his round head.

The air's heavy with smoke and beer and sweat, it stings the eyes; the music's louder than the voices, but not much. It's a big room and not too busy—one car, one customer; this is Highway 61, nobody *walks*—but everyone here is working their presence hard. Opinions spiked on adrenalin, hard laughter; hands drumming separate beats on bar or table-top; a squeal in the shadows, urgent encouragement, a dog's sharp bark.

There's a girl dancing naked in a cage, hung from a chain above the bar. The cage twists in the eddying smoke; the girl stares at nothing, grinds her body out of time with any rhythm I can hear.

More girls behind the bar, and scurrying with trays between the tables. G-strings and heels, bleached hair and big earrings, some tattoos.

Boys, too; but the boys are unlucky, they don't get the stilettos. One lad comes up to us with a tray on a ribbon round his neck; this is all he's wearing, bar a black *cache-sexe* and a fine gold ring in one nipple. He looks younger than I am.

"Cigarettes, sir? Cigar, chewing tobacco?"

He's not talking to me.

My driver, my lift, my host Elias Crawshaw takes his time selecting a thick cigar, cutting it, lighting up. Then he pulls a handful of crumpled notes from his pocket, drops a fin into the boy's tray.

The boy still stands there, biting his lip: not dismissed, not finished with.

Elias lifts a hand, slips his pinkie through that nipple-ring, pulls and twists. Flesh stretches further than you'd think, is slower to find its own shape again. Hurts more, too, maybe; but not a sound from the boy, only a sudden bead of blood on his lip where his teeth have caught it.

Elias chuckles wheezingly, sends him on his way with a casual waft of the hand.

The boy has butterflies on his buttocks, coloured blue, brown and yellow: bruises, from some heavy pinching. Livid welts on his back, too, but I don't want to think about those.

ELIAS makes a grand tour of the crowded tables, pressing the flesh, swapping sweat with his cronies. I'm right there at his heels, nowhere else to go; but he doesn't do introductions, doesn't acknowledge me at all. Neither do his friends.

That's okay. Friends of Elias are no friends of mine. I make like I'm no more interested in them, looking around me, taking in the room and the shadows, only half an eye on Elias to be ready to move when he does. Tagging along like a dog, to be sure I'm there if he wants me.

Over by the entrance, stairs lead up to a gallery that runs all the way around. Plenty of doors up there, not much light. Just about perfect.

Four slow fans stir the rising smoke, the girl gyrates numbly in her sway-ing cage; and there's the pianoman, driving his music hard. Around him a couple of card schools, six and eight to a table and playing with real bills, no chips. Naturally not, in a place like this. Who'd trust the manager?

We don't go into the corners on this unhurried processional, but in one of them as we pass I can see a man sitting with a girl down between his legs. He's bending her backwards, hand in her hair, while he tips his glass to run a steady stream of beer over her body, over her belly and breasts.

While his dog swarms all over her, hot breath and long tongue, licking and licking; while its claws raise scratches on her skin, and it licks those too when the blood comes.

His dog's a pit bull, and it's getting excited.

Can't hear a sound from the girl; but even above the dog's yelps and the music and the voices' ebb and run, I can hear the building rumble of traffic on 61.

A pitcher of beer on the table, two mugs and I drink when he pours me some, when he remembers. He has bourbon chasers, his shot glass refilled every time he taps it. The service here is great.

The service here is *incredible.*

A woman comes from upstairs; she's not the only one in the joint, there are women in the poker schools and a fair few at the tables, but she may be the only one that counts. If I had any money, any money at all, I'd take odds that she's the owner. Tall, narrow, dressed like Dietrich, cigarette-holder and all: a black Marlene, cool in this hotel of heat. And the music shifts to match her, and the mood follows the music.

She comes down the stairs, takes the holder from her mouth; a boy goes running over, but not with an ashtray, no. He's only got his hand, to make a cup with.

She taps ash into his palm, looks at the cigarette, changes her mind. Decides she's had enough.

Takes it from the holder, stubs it out.

Doesn't so much as glance at the boy, she just crushes the glowing butt into his hand and walks away.

From the other side of the room, I can see how hard the boy is breathing, not to cry aloud.

"JESUS, Elias. Where do you *find* these kids?"

"Find them? Oh, that's easy, son. White trash, we just pick 'em up. Anywhere on 61, there's always trash. Just pick it up, bring it on home."

And he looks at me, and he's laughing; and yes, he picked me up on 61. Where else?

HE whistles, crooks a summoning finger. The boy comes trotting over, still pale, his hand still cupped around the pain, cradled against his chest.

Elias takes the wrist, draws the hand down onto the table, forces the bunched fingers open, flat and wide.

Already the boy's palm has come up in a great blister, fierce red around a scabby black brand, still scattered with ash.

Elias grins at the boy, grins at me—and brings his fat thumb down, hard into the heart of that blister.

If anyone cries out, it's me. I'm not sure; I catch myself only halfway out of my chair, might have caught the cry too like a stone in my throat. Certainly it's hard to swallow, after.

All the boy does is whimper, though I can see his other hand clench hard below the table.

Elias flicks a brief glance at me, turns his attention back to where his thumb is working, rubbing and rubbing at the boy's swollen palm.

Rubbing and rubbing.

The boy shivers and sweats; his arm jerks, though I'm sure that's only instinct, no intent. In any case Elias has his wrist clamped hard to the table, no pulling away.

And dark thumb works pink palm like plasticine almost, kneading away there, moulding and shaping; and I can't see that black crater any more, where the cigarette had burned deep into the flesh. Even the angry blush of it is fading, and Elias is giggling, fat man playing games, pushing the last of the blister around like an air-bubble under the skin.

And now he lifts his hand and brings it slapping down flat, palm to palm against the boy's; and when he raises it again there's nothing left to see, no damage except maybe in the boy's head, surely in mine.

The boy stammers his thanks; Elias sends him away with a cuff round the ear and a demand for beer and Jim Beam.

And then he turns to me, chuckling. His heavy hand falls on my shoulder, that thumb presses deep; I can feel my bones begin to soften.

WHEN the pianoman finally breaks, it's like he cuts the strings on the caged girl's dancing. She slumps, one arm dangling through the bars, sweat running down and dripping from her fingers into the rings of spilt beer on the bar.

A boy wipes those rings away when he's not serving, wipes away the sweat, never glances up.

The pianoman sits at the bar, drinking beer after beer: keg to mug, straight down his throat in one long swallow and come right back for more.

When he's had his ration, he wipes his mouth on a handkerchief, belches loudly; stands up, reaches a long arm above his head, grips the girl's elbow and tugs.

Christ, no, I think urgently. Can't see how the girl got in there, I can't see a door; but those bars, they're too close-set, she could barely get her shoulder through if she squirmed for it, he's not going to, he couldn't possibly...

The pianoman's not listening. Neither's the girl. He stands there and pulls at her, and she comes to him, no resistance. She slithers out of her cage, boneless and impossible, and tumbles down onto the bar. She looks crazy-tall as she lies there, too long and too narrow and a skull stretched like a horse's skull, squeezed all out of shape to get through.

The pianoman throws her over his shoulder and carries her up the stairs with her hair dragging in sodden strings behind them, leaving a trail of wet on the floor.

END of the music, seemingly the end of the night. For some, at least. The poker's going strong yet, both tables, and there are men still drinking in a loose knot around the boss lady, Marlene of the darklight.

But other groups are splitting up, people are leaving; or else they're climbing the stairs, keys in one hand and nightcap in the other. As often as not, those who go upstairs have a weary girl at their heels, unless they have a boy.

Elias heaves to his feet, his brow glistening in the lights as the road had glistened under our wheels, but at least this time it's only sweat that's doing it, nothing more dangerous.

Not that I'm thinking *safe,* or anything like. Given the choice, his sweat is almost the last thing I'd be bathing in tonight.

But there are degrees of danger; and choice costs money, here more than anywhere. I'm all out of choosing.

So he heaves to his feet and I follow him up the stairs, just one more white kid in a black house, ready to melt in the heat. Better dressed, a little, shorts and sandals and a dirty shirt; just as weary.

Head of the stairs, there's a window. I look out. Don't stop moving, just look, eyes left for a moment as I pass.

Out there in the world, the sun still hasn't risen.

A hot, deep bed and I'm sinking, clutching at the edge of the mattress just for something to cling to, some way to hold myself together: *here I am, this is me, those are my fingers and the rest's still attached, see? See?*

He's asleep. Even with my mind so focused on my fingers'-ends, I can hear his snoring.

Eventually, at last, I loosen my neck—*my own neck, there it is, right under my skull where it's supposed to be and under my own charge too, see it move?*— just enough, turn it just a little.

Now I can see him. Now I can watch how the sweat runs from him even as he lies sprawled naked under the ceiling fan: how it gathers on chest and belly, pools together and dribbles down to soak the stained sheet and the mattress underneath.

Now I can see how deep asleep he is, how far from me.

SLOWLY, slowly, cat-cautious but afraid like no cat ever was, I reclaim all my body and make it move to my own desire now, make it slide slowly off the mattress and down to the dusty floor.

Breathing hard, sobbing almost even as I struggle to mask it, I bundle my things together, shorts and shirt and sandals, and crawl towards the door. There's money in his trousers, and I need money; but I won't touch his.

I've seen what happens to the kids who take their money. I took his drink, and I know what he bought with that: all the aches and uncertainties in me, a lien on my own flesh, temporary possession. Take his money, he'd see it as a contract. He'd take me.

FLOORBOARDS creak under my weight, the bed-springs creak behind me, the door creaks as I ease it open, still bare-assed on my hands and knees, too scared to stand.

I freeze at every creak, but nothing disturbs his snoring.

So I scuttle out, all my concentration on closing the door again behind me, soft as a feather falling, no noise, no *noise*—and only when that's done, only as I gasp my first good lungful of air that's not sodden with Elias, only then do I catch the murmur of voices down below me, see the light coming up.

I'm out on the balcony here, and there are people still in the bar.

Floors above me, stairs going up; but no more going down, that I can see. No other way out. There must be back stairs somewhere, a back door for the staff, but I'm not searching blind. God knows what I might find, before I found the door.

No. I'm scrambling into my shorts, flat on my back on the dirty carpet; then T-shirt over my head, sandals on, not to look like one of their boys—not to look so fucking *pliable*—and then it's stand up straight, walk down the stairs, walk right out of this place.

Don't run. Walk.

Yes.

BUT it takes a while, takes a hell of a time just to get me moving; and even then I'm crouched over, I'm *creeping* down those stairs, trying not to disturb the least mote of dust.

I didn't look through the balcony rails before I started down, didn't want to know who was here, what was going on. Not any more, I was all out of curiosity. Educated out.

But I'm looking now. Halfway down the stairs I'm stopping, looking. This isn't curiosity, it's caution. I need to know how many they are, and how engrossed.

Too many is the answer, and not enough.

Half a dozen of them there, either side of the bar; and they're not so tangled up, they haven't got their hands in so far they're not going to notice me leaving. And okay, they're old or fat or both, I could outrun them easy, and it's not so far: just the stairs and then five paces to the door, shoulder down and charge it.

But the boss lady's there as well, blowing dark smoke; and I can't run, no chance. Even if I wanted to. One glance from her, my legs wouldn't carry me.

I'm not sure they're going to anyway. From up here, I can see what the men have got on the bar there, what their hands are busy with; and already I'm backed up against the wall, my own hands are clinging to the dado, maybe all that holds me up right now.

It's an object-lesson, is what it is; and the hat-check girl's the object. I think it's her, I think I recognise the face. Hard to be sure, though. Might be any of them, really.

Doesn't matter, really. Makes no difference to me, probably makes little difference to them.

SHE'S still inside her skin, she's still together in some sense, still *contained*. Don't get me wrong. They haven't cut her, to open her up this way. They don't need to. Believe me, I know. I've repaid Elias tonight.

Skin's elastic, skin *stretches;* and all the more so, after they get their hot hands on it. And bones can bend and shift and dislocate, bones can hinge if you know which way to turn them; and she looks like a lesson in anatomy, opened out like a flower, or like a fish for smoking.

Her arms and legs are nothing now, dangling bags with bones in. Nothing connects.

Her hips still stand proud, two peaks above a plain spread too wide, too flat. But her chest, oh Christ…

Her ribs reach out instead of curling over, like fingers spread apart instead of linked; and in the bowl they've made I can see her lungs working like fat, flabby parasites, right under the skin there. I can see her heart, the meaty lump of it pulsing hard and fast and regular, doing its traitor job, keeping her going.

Keeping her there when she should be long gone, she should be dead and *gone,* the things they've done to her.

AND me, I sidle down that wall, step after step and my hands still clinging, won't let go; and I think maybe I won't be seen after all, they're all so busy playing, touching fingers to a tendon's tautness just to see what twitches.

But as I set foot on the floor, only those five running paces to go now, maybe twenty shuffling little sideways steps, my midnight Marlene looks up, looks straight at me, knew I was there all the time.

Says, "This is what it is, boy, this is the bargain. Take it or leave it."

No talk of love here, no *love it or leave it.* Love isn't a factor. What she's offering is pain and fear, blood and sweat and possession; but it's shelter too, in a world where the sun doesn't rise until you're ready for it.

Maybe Elias would have offered me the same choice, come morning.

Maybe all these kids, they're only staying till they've saved their tips awhile, they've got cash to face that other world again.

Maybe they think it's worth it. Maybe it is.

Maybe.

BUT I slide to the door, all their eyes on me now; and the girl's watching too, one more pair of eyes I could well have lived without, she doesn't have to do that. She doesn't have to make me leave like this, eye to eye with what I'm running out on.

A man's slipped his finger into her mouth, drawn out her tongue; he's playing it between his fingers, rolling and stretching, longer and longer and she's still watching me. He can do what he likes; of course, he can do what he likes. It's me that betrays, that her eyes accuse. It's me that leaves while she coils her tongue around his forearm, reaching for his elbow, anything to please.

My back to the inner doors now, I press hard and feel one give, feel it swing open. Edge through and let it close again—and it's still not over, quite. There's a boy in the lobby here, curled naked in the corner, sobbing quietly.

He might be next for that bar-top vivisection, or he might have been there already, maybe they've put him back together and it's only the memory hurts him now.

Tomorrow or yesterday, whatever. He's crying now; and he looks up as I walk to the main door, he smears a cocktail of snot and tears together with the back of his hand as I pull it open.

"Come on, then," I say, door held wide, an open invitation. If I get the choice, they all do.

But he's made it already, or he makes it again. He shakes his head longingly, still snivelling; I give him a moment more, and then I'm out of there and the door's banging shut behind me, him inside.

NOW I can run, with a door closed between us; and if it's more stagger than run, who the hell cares? Just to get away, that's the point: to be gone before they change their minds, or before Elias wakes and comes looking, or throws open a window and whistles. I might still go back for a whistle, my quisling feet might take me, too scared to say no: still held in his soft, shaping hands, still trapped in this long, long night.

Over the gravel forecourt, past the cars; and suddenly there's the road, and all the traffic rolling.

I'M not hitching, though. Not yet. Not while the tarmac still feels sticky under my feet, while it gleams in the passing lights.

I don't know what this is that clings to the soles of my sandals, whether it's the memory of too much blood or else time's bones dissolved in acid, spilt and never washed away; but I'm not sticking my thumb out, I'm not sticking my neck out till the road's dry and dusty underfoot, till the craven sun comes up to show me.

I'm too scared of what might stop. All the cars are the wrong shape; and who knows, maybe there's a gunman in one of them, heading for Canada with his rifle hot on the seat beside him. Or maybe there's a black woman bleeding, dying on the back seat and all her songs dying with her.

61 *remembers.*

Do it once, do it forever.

Everything that happens never stops, on 61.

HIGHWAY 61, it could run and run.

From the roots to the fruits.

Whoo, yeah.

2 PI TO LIVE

HE WAS FAMOUS ONCE, A PRODIGY, a child on the TV. I've seen the clips: small boy in a big chair, chanting numbers. His eyes looked overwhelmed, always, but not by the studio and never by the host. What was overwhelming, what carried him away was what he found in his own head, I thought: what he was finding, moment by moment, every predetermined unpredicted step of it. He teetered on the edge of awe just at the way his thoughts stalked ahead of him, in pursuit of this ever-unreeling number.

Those early clips, he had his mother with him: nervous but proud, as she felt she ought to be, reaching to ruffle her son's hair because that was what proud mothers did with their incomprehensible children. She could never ruffle the contents of his mind. His voice rang on, clear and incantatory. Digit by digit, the infant phenomenon reciting the value of pi.

Later on, it's his father who sits beside. No one mentions the mother now. He's a teenage wunderkind, and everyone asks about college. His father shrugs and shakes his head; what does a boy like this need with college?

What can anyone teach him that would make it worth interrupting this thing he does, what keeps him famous, this record string, this pi?

His father, clearly, is taking a slice of pi. There's a living in it, boasting up his boy. It's not that the lad has memorised unheard-of quantities of others' calculations; these numbers are coming fresh, he's working the math in his head there, monotonous as clockwork. That's worth paying for. These days there's a machine to check him, a screen ticking off the proper digits behind his head where he has no sight of them, to prove he isn't cheating. It also says how far he's got since he started this extraordinary sum. Pi to a hundred and thirty million places, the last clip I saw, still going strong.

BUT that was then and this is now. Novelty expires; so does childhood. Computers, of course, outraced him long ago. Universities lost interest in his mind, and so too did the TV. Just an *idiot savant*, got plenty of those, no thanks.

WHEN Johnny found him, when he dragged me down to see, the prodigious child was a man of middle age: thin of body, thin of hair, as though he wore himself to a nub with the effort of calculation. His voice too, ground down after decades of whispering pi for public entertainment.

He really wasn't very entertaining any more. Johnny had turned him up as a carnival sideshow. He was lucky, in a way, I guess. It was that kind of travelling show where you just pay once at the gate, all-day pass, see everything. No one had to bark for Simple Simon, and just as well: who would turn out their pockets, after all, to hear a man chant a string of numbers in a tent? Never mind what the computer said beside him, nearly half a billion digits now; it was astonishing, perhaps, but nobody cared. Nobody could care. He should be grateful, someone was willing to keep him fed and clothed and cared for. She was a woman, who owned the carnival; perhaps that made a difference. Perhaps not. Perhaps she just had a fondness for numbers, even outside her own bottom line.

Anyway, there he sat, an ageing man in an empty tent. Though it wasn't empty, of course, because we were in it. Johnny had paid again to come again, to bring me.

Simon—and his name really was Simon: coincidence or else his parents had changed it very early on, to make the pi-man connection long before he ever was a man—didn't speak to us, or acknowledge us at all. His eyes looked blankly, as though all his gaze were inward, at the whiteboard of his mind where he worked that dreadful sum. His voice never faltered; it was a pendulum fully wound, metronomic, pulsing to the rhythm of his brain. It frightened me, almost, but I still sat half an hour while shadows came and went in the doorway, puzzled adults and curious children hesitating on the threshold of wonder, deciding against.

AT last it was Johnny—necessarily—who tugged us out of there, tugged me with his fingers clenched in my shirt, I was that hard to get moving.

Out in the neon and the noise, I was bewildered for a while, all structure snatched away: how could the world be anything other than number, how did these people *live?*

When Johnny let me stand still, we were in the shadow of a trailer, in the smell of oil and onions, among the taut angled guys of another tent.

"Mind your feet," he said, and, "Here, eat," pressing something round and warm and flabby into my hand, a burger I hadn't seen him buy. "I knew you'd be like this," he said. "Bite, chew, swallow. In that order."

Sometimes, it's easier just to follow orders. I tasted nothing, but familiar process—*bite, chew, swallow*—brought me back, at least a little way. When my hand was empty, when the food was gone I took a breath, opened my mouth and was forestalled; he drew a can from a pocket, popped the tab and passed it to me, chill and damp.

"Sugar rush," he said. "Tilt, swallow. Try not to choke."

The foaming bite of it in my mouth, bitter cold and sweet as sin, cutting through grease and lingering nastiness: I swallowed, gasped, tilted and swallowed again.

"Right," said Johnny. "Now. Questions."

"What happens," I said, "what *happens* when he stops?"

"The stars go out. Obviously."

"No, but seriously. Every night. He has to stop, he has to eat and sleep. What does he *do?*"

I had this nightmare image of the numbers still ticking on in his head, relentless in his dreams.

"I don't know. If we wait, maybe we can ask him. Maybe we can see. Next question."

Johnny knows me too well. Of course there was another question. Now that I was out from the hypnotic beat of it, all I had was questions. First you see the thing itself, then you try to see all the way around it, define its borders, find the ground that's safe.

"Why does he do it? When there isn't a solution, when there can't be any end..." One nightmare breeds another: now I saw him as an old man, old and sick, restless with calculation, digits ticking over like time made manifest and himself caught in the fever of it, picking at his bedclothes with fingers like needles, as if he could tattoo his chant of figures physically into the world. Leave us marked with number, his number, his own. Pi to the power of Simon.

"Maybe it's just too hard to stop. Maybe he believes in what he's doing. Maybe one man has to do this, so that all the rest of us live free. We can ask."

Johnny has this ruthlessness, he never offers comfort; or else it's just that he's ruthless with me, because I need that. Because I deserve it. Whatever. He fielded my questions and tossed them back unresolved, leaving me still uneasy with speculation.

We lingered, then, and walked the carnival: in and out of booths, true freakshow under the shrieks and clatter of the rides. At last the crowds thinned, the glee faded; as if in response lights flickered in warning, voices called from one end of the ground to the other, "Closing now, shutting down, make your way to the gate please and go home."

No one enforced that call, no one tried to chivvy us out. All day could mean all night, for all that anyone cared; the carnies' wagons were inside the fence, and not all of them would be sleeping alone or with each other. Not all of them would be sleeping at all.

I still needed to see, to know how Simon slept, if he slept, if the numbers let him. How do you pause a human calculation?

We made our way back to his tent and there he was, still chanting: but on his feet now, bending over the laptop on a table by his chair. Working to the rhythm of his own voice. Glancing up at us this time, seeing us, surprised: still not faltering in his count, though, not until he had pressed a key sequence and closed the lid on the laptop.

The screen display vanished. At the same time, his voice fell silent. It was like a death, the little death of number. It staggered me; I wanted to clutch at something, at the tent-pole or at Johnny's arm, just to reassure myself that there was still solidity in the world, that fabric was not fraying into that sudden absence.

Simon struggled, it seemed, to speak, to find anything to say that was not an expression of pi. In the end he had to, though; neither one of us had any words to offer, here in his territory, at the heart of his calculation.

Bending his voice around all the awkwardnesses of words and meanings, he said, "Did you want me?"

In honesty, not. There was nothing of him, without that string of numbers: nothing left to want. Except that he had answers, maybe, some.

I said, "I'm sorry, I do have to ask. What's happening in your head, right now? Are you still working the math, ticking off the numbers?"

He smiled, with that weariness that some mistake for wisdom. I'm not original, I never imagined myself to be so; of course he had been asked before, how not? Likely the TV stations cut his answer, went to sponsors and their messages, not wanting to disappoint with banality. "No, no. I know the next calculation, I remember that but I don't work it through. It can wait. Thirty thousand a day, that's my ration."

"Exactly?"

"Yes. Why not?"

"No reason." He had to stop somewhere; why not there? But, "Does the computer ping you at the total, or…?"

"I count," he said. "The computer is just showmanship: for your benefit, not mine. I don't use it."

I don't need it, he meant. Alongside working pi, he was counting digits, just as his software did. This man was beginning to terrify me. I might understand intellectually about the ordered mind, the quantified life, but in the flesh it was another thing. Wet brain-matter ought not to function this way.

Even so: order and purpose are not the same, and I did still have to ask. I was hesitant—if heroes have feet of clay, who knows what muck might hide below a layer of perfect clarity? I was terrified to find that he was mad in any sort, a believer, an enthusiast, a missionary.

Still. Had to ask. "Why do you do it, though, this thing? What's the point?"

He shrugged. "It's a living."

I looked around the empty tent, poverty made manifest. "Hardly that. With a mind like yours—well. You ought to be in college. Teaching math, researching…"

"Not this, you mean? Not debasing myself with a performance no one cares about in a tent where no one's listening?"

"Yes," I said, "exactly that," though in fact I thought it was perhaps number that he debased, more than himself.

He said, "If a tree falls in the forest, does it matter whether anyone hears it? It's down, it's gone."

Was he saying that he didn't know how to stop, or else that he didn't dare? After such a life, a man might be frightened to find himself a hollow thing, dead from the inside, if he didn't rise every day to the sap of pi. I could see that, but, "You must know more about pi than any man alive. You don't have to abandon it, just…not do this. You don't need to be doing this. Surely?"

"Someone does," he said, and there it was, a glimpse behind the curtain, where mania dwells.

Had to ask. "Why?"

"Because numbers matter, they're entitled. Pi is a road, it needs someone to walk it."

"There are computers," Johnny said, jumping in at first sight of my face. "They can do that, faster and farther than any human in a lifetime..."

"Unmanned missions," Simon said. "Mars rovers, space probes, sure. It's not the same. We're an exploring species; we do need actually to go there. Someone has to follow pi, see where it leads, what's out there."

"You can't," Johnny protested, still watching me. "No one can."

"It is in the nature of the journey," he said, "that we should die on the way. Still moving, still going forward. That much is...written. It's in the math."

"Even so..."

"So you pass it on," he said. "It's a relay. Someone else can pick up where I leave off."

"There isn't anyone else. Who's like you?"

"People can learn. They can go slowly. Thirty a day, if they have to, not thirty thousand. Just as long as they take the baton and go on, keep it moving. Footprints in the dust. It's important."

He was right, it was. Oh, the world would go on turning if we left it. We could let the machines have all the numbers and nothing would fall down, nothing would crumble. We could turn our backs to the infinite and focus on what was small and within reach, capable to our hands. But what we lost would be something of ourselves, that mattered more than all the reaches of the universe.

Johnny knew. He might not be following Simon all the way, but he was following me. Everything I wasn't saying, I could see it all reflected right there in his eyes, in his appalled understanding.

Inside my head, I was just dipping my toe in, testing the water.

3.141592653589...

CH-CH-CHANGES

all art aspires
to the condition of music

THE RULES ARE FEW, AT PARRY'S. Indeed, they're barely rules at all, so much as customs observed—but they are scrupulously observed, and they can be rigorously enforced at need. Don't make that necessary. That's Rule One.

Rule Two? Don't call it a bar. Parry's quite clear about that; it's an establishment.

Don't let that stop you paying for your drinks. He's quite clear about that, too.

If you must kick up a ruckus, keep it quieter than the pilots'. They're privileged; you're not. And whatever else you do, don't approach the pilots. If one of them brings you in, that's fine: join their table, cling close, and welcome. If they beckon you over, the same applies. But always, always wait to be invited. Don't ever try to push in.

Actually, that's what most of the rules boil down to. It's the pilots' place of choice, and Parry means to keep it that way. Which means they get to do what they want, and you don't. That's it.

TO be fair, that's more or less the rule all over the Margin, all along the Limb, all through human space. With them so few and the need so great, who's ever going to say no to a pilot? Whoever they are, whatever they ask? Pilots are the new black: they are always in order and may never be debated.

Actually, that last is a joke, mostly. Pilots make a disordered crew by definition, and they'll cheerfully debate with each other or with anyone, if 'debate' means argue stubbornly or viciously or relentlessly, up to the very edge of fighting. Pilots don't fight each other, and you never, ever fight with a pilot. Not in Parry's, certainly, but not actually anywhere.

Actually, maybe that's Rule One. Maybe that's all the rules there are, all over. Let pilots be, let them find their own ways to damnation.

Trust me, they'll do that. They will.

TONIGHT, they're being peaceable enough. Parry's all but slumbers under the dead weight of their sobriety. That's literal, more or less—pilots don't drink, don't smoke, don't drug when they're in port: they're trying to come down, to remember what it's like to live with all the limits of a body and claim it as their own, to stop at the inside of their skin—but it's also situational. Out beyond Parry's door lie the lights and noise and reckless abandonment of the Margin, every twisted thing that humans find or do for fun compressed into a mile or two of sheetwalk, into a few thousand urgent transient bodies. Pilots are all about the body, this side of n-space: they'll do most of what's available out there. And then they'll come in here, because Parry's is quiet and comfortable, a place to catch their breath and touch base with their inner selves in the company of colleagues.

They come in here a *lot*. Which is why anybody else comes too, why everybody else looks in: just to drink where pilots are and watch how pilots sit, listen to the murmur—or the yelling—of their voices and breathe a little of their rarefied air. Nothing rubs off and no one would want it to, and even so. This is still the place to be, and here they are.

Not all, of course. Not most, for human space is a skein stretched fine and far; not even most of those you might have hoped to see hereabouts, if you were that kind of fan, if hope was still a thing for you. By definition, pilots are a fly-by-night crew, here and gone, always in demand. Some like the long haul, one end of the Limb to the other; they might not show their faces in Parry's from one year's end to the next. Some are in and out, barely flitting outside this system before they're back, barely pausing before they're off again, barely worth the effort and the risk.

And n-space is another variable, as whimsical as they are. Some times, some places—if there's a difference, if you could ever confidently divide time from space and say which was which—it may be slick as oil, squeezing ships through, spitting them out; or else it can be thick as porridge, clinging, close to impassable. And some pilots are cautious by nature, taking it slow and sweating all the way, while some are devil-may-care, slapdash, heroic in the worst way. Not noticeably dead yet, but even so. Mostly those get the cargo runs; passengers would sooner wait for someone steadier. Relatively steadier.

SO, yes: Parry's is quiet just now. Some of the regulars are out. Mercy Mercy and Ferrel have been gone so long, people are starting to think them lost, adrift in n-space. Irrecoverable. No surprise in Ferrel's case, but Mercy would be a real loss. Everyone loves Mercy Mercy; she's the acceptable face, the people's pilot, the single splendid example you can point to.

Could point to. Maybe. They've not been gone long enough to be certain, but the question's in the air now, whether they're ever coming back. The strangest thing, of course, is that they went together in the first place. Pilots never do that. They're too rare to risk, and if one gets into trouble the other can't get them out of it. Navigation isn't a science. It isn't even an art: it's an embedding, an act of faith written in the body, inherently individual. Impossible to repeat, almost—almost!—impossible to survive.

Which of course is why and how pilots are what they are, and why we put up with them.

THIS night—it's always night on the Margin, if "night" means "time to be out on the sheetwalk, looking for trouble," which it always, always does—there's the one settled table in Parry's, as so often, with the onlookers coming and going, staring and pretending not to stare, never quite daring to cross that gap that pilots create and Parry enforces, that narrow space between one table and the next, that unbridgeable gulf.

You want to cross that gulf, you'll need to fly. Unless you're lifted over.

This is Brone's table, by custom and practice and—well, by mere occupation. Brone the Shutterself entity, the pilot who never flies, who almost never leaves Parry's. It migrates in a slow shuffle between a room in the back and a table, this table, its table out here in the front where everyone can see, for values of seeing that include being baffled by layers of swaddling drab duffel. It has a head by courtesy, by inference alone, that hooded peak that's narrower than what might be its shoulders. It has a drinking tube of sorts, that emerges to suck at whatever's in its glass. Some people think that's a finger. Hollow and translucent and plumbed in, but a finger none the less.

None the less: Brone is as human as any of them, these pilots that we've made by luck and guesswork, great endeavour and great sacrifice. So many have been lost in n-space, lost to us, despite our need; none has ever—quite—lost their humanity, despite the changes bred into them, the wild experimentation, the slow gestation over generations. Despite random mutation and surgical intervention, despite mind-altering treatments and mind-altering drugs, despite it all. They're still human, if only because we say so. Because we could not bear for them to give that up, or because we could not bear to be the ones who made them or named them something other, or because we could not trust them after.

"BODIES like ships like buildings, machines for living in," says Ferenor who has never seen a building, who was bred in a bottle and hatched in orbit, cultivated for this life she leads. One of the rare successes, a design for a pilot that actually worked. Once, it worked once. All her litter-mates died or grew strange, strange as she, without the benefit of her ability. An unreproducible result; an experimental method recorded, remembered, not to be repeated. You can't call it science, if it never works again.

As usual, Brone says nothing. Does it even listen? Who can, who could possibly say? There's no standard measure for a pilot, any pilot; but whatever concept you have of what it means to be a pilot—or what it means to be human—the Shutterself entities are far and far beyond that. Far and far.

Ferenor wears her body as lightly and as fleetingly as she does her opinions—unless that's the other way around—whereas everything in Brone is slow and fixed and solid. If it knows change, that could only be on a geologic scale. Ferenor is air, limitless and uncontained, a breeze across Brone's mountain. Here and gone. Perhaps that's what it cherishes in her. Perhaps it likes them fickle, transient, departed.

Perhaps that's why it stays.

"Living is incidental." So says Ten Barry, the devolved clone. His—brother? twin? simulacrum?—who answers to the same name is for once absent from his side. They're doing their bewildering double act solo, perhaps simply to mystify twice as many people at once. One thing for sure, he won't be flying a ship alone. It takes them both: that much we know. Not much more, for some pilots are open and some have been thoroughly exposed, but the clone gestalt holds its secrets close. Are there ten? Were there ten? No one has ever seen more than two abroad, and they're believed to be the same two, though how would you, how would anyone know? And are they a single distributed individual, or a family? Or worse? And above all, of course, how does the flying happen, what's the methodology, how is it achieved?

They—or he—won't say, and there is no power and no law that might compel them. Dozens, perhaps hundreds of such laws exist in draft, all through human space; no jurisdiction has ever dared enact them. Of course it would be for the greater good, we could learn so much, enhance our chances of making another generation of pilots—but what if this generation responded with a blockade, an absolute refusal to fly into that region of space? No government could survive that, however strong or secure their grip. The hold that pilots have on their privacy is so much stronger, it has never been tested. They've never even needed to threaten such a blockade. A politician's imagination is enough. More than enough. Pilots get what they want, here as everywhere. In Ten Barry's case, that means he—or they, or what you will—can be oblique, obstructive and infuriatingly unforthcoming, to their dual hearts' content.

"How incidental?" Ferenor asks.

"A ship is a machine, yes—not built for living in, no. Built to journey, to endure n-space, to come out elsewhere, with goods or passengers or war or what you will. The same is true of us: built to journey, built to survive, built to be going somewhere else. If they could make machines instead, they would do that, and do without us gladly. The living are inconvenient, and not at all to the purpose."

It's true enough, and hardly a new argument. In honesty, it's hardly an argument at all. No autopilot yet attempted has even found a way into n-space, never mind emerging otherwise. Those that have been taken into n-space by human pilots and triggered there have never found their way out, despite the best of planning. Either the pilot has abandoned the experiment and taken control again, or else the ship has been lost entirely, to our great cost. One pilot down, each time. Very few such experiments occur. We can't afford them.

But if Ten Barry's not speaking metaphorically, at least he's told us something about his own origins. *Built to journey,* he said. If that's to say the devolved clone was created to pilot a ship, if this is someone's private and successful experiment—well, that's something we didn't know before. It might have been happenstance; many pilots are completely unprepared, unschooled, unexpected. Most, perhaps.

Perhaps that's why you rarely see Ten Barry—either Ten Barry, or any—without the other, or one other, at his side. Perhaps they act as a guard on each other's tongue, and here's this one free tonight, saying more than he meant, perhaps.

Saying it to pilots, though. There's no one else at Brone's table today, and no one close enough to overhear. Parry has a brisk way with eavesdroppers, be they human or mechanical or something other.

Pilots don't care, particularly. They're not big on origin stories from others, when they all have their own; nor are they particularly big on posterity, that relentless search for the next generation, for more and more reliable and better pilots, better controlled. They like themselves pretty much the way they are. For sure they like the life, the privilege, the freedom.

For sure, Maellelin was never built to be a pilot. If she had been, they'd have built her to a standard measure; she wouldn't need a booster-seat just to join the pilots' table. She had the gift of it, that feeling, a sense of n-space unfolding all about her; it wasn't enough, so she had herself rebuilt. Not to scale, no. Just everything she needed, to suit her particular vision. Eyes seven times the size, and so forth. It's said that there are other changes, less clear to be seen: at the molecular level, her brain and nerves rewired. She doesn't need drugs to ease her passage through n-space, nor devices to find her way about. She only has to look. That she comes with her own ship—bespoke again, with a cockpit tailored to her size—is just a bonus.

She's promised that scientists can have her blueprints, her biotech and her body, once she's gone. If they can figure out what she was or what she had to start with, and then the nature and scope of her alterations, see what she made of herself, maybe she'll be replicable. That's if she dies within reach, within our knowledge. If she doesn't lose herself out there somewhere, beyond recall or investigation. We speak of human space as though it were coherent and within bounds, as though we were secure in our holding and in our travelling back and forth, known roads swept free of danger, but none of that is true. Not many pilots die in their beds, in port, convenient for autopsy and study.

A lot of them may not be dead at all. Adrift in n-space, beyond all understanding—who knows, who can tell?

Just how late are Ferrel and Mercy Mercy, anyway?

They're not here, that's all we know. Not here now. Maybe they'll blow in tomorrow, all smiles and ease, full of news and more. A shipful of cargo and great expectations, a new route won, a new system discovered. Something.

Maybe not. Magical thinking is endemic, where pilots are concerned. Their whole process, their individual processes seem halfway to magic at least. People say that it's unlucky to wish them well: that the harder you struggle to believe they'll bring their ships in safe, the less likely that is to happen. Scientists say that. It's been measured. People try not to think about it, mostly.

Murun is here, has brought his ship in safe. To everyone's always surprise. Murun is really not what you'd look for, in a pilot. He does not inspire confidence. Really not. The best of Murun is his companion Telfer, always at his side, calm and cooling and engaged. Telfer's the one you'd want in control, except that Telfer is no pilot. Telfer's just the rock, the counterweight, ballast or reaction mass or whatever metaphor you like: what allows Murun to work, that's Telfer. Possibly also what keeps Murun sane, if sane he be. Pilots don't usually fly with a partner—come to that, pilots don't usually have a partner—but every one's exceptional in some way, and this is Murun's.

Also he's an asshole and no one knows why Telfer stays with him, but there it is. Here they are.

Here they all are, this tableful: extraordinary anywhere, vanishingly rare all along the Limb, quite commonplace at Parry's. What people come to see, except that he'll never, never make an exhibition of them.

Parry serves drinks relentlessly, distributes smokes and other intoxicants, passes food orders through to the kitchen, answers questions from customers and servers both, watches the door, helps stray tourists find what they're actually looking for as soon as it's clear that his place is not that—and never takes his eye off the pilots' table. There's a barrier between them and the rest of the room; it's immaterial but clear to be seen and widely acknowledged. Let anyone breach that—and people will: drunk or determined, with a question to ask or an axe to grind—and Parry is there, swifter than you'd have thought possible, to steer them aside or throw them out, whichever. He's not always proportionate. Hell, he's not always appropriate. But it's his name above the door, or at least his singular initial, and he gets to make the rules and interpret them too. And enforce them, at need.

Tonight, though—well, tonight here comes a stranger. Five score eyes check him through the door, and no one recognises him. That means he's not a pilot. If he'd brought a ship to Dock, he'd be known by now: new and hence intriguing, mysterious and hence more to be gossiped about than any of the stalwarts.

Nor does he seem to recognise anyone here, even Parry behind the bar. That means he's not local, he doesn't work anywhere in Dock or anywhere on Base, because everyone knows Parry. By the look of him, he's only come here because he was told about it; and there's only one reason why he might have listened, only one reason ever for people to talk about Parry's.

But he's not heading to the bar for a drink, he's not joining the relentless not-quite-staring of the gathered crowd. No, indeed. One look around, and he knows just exactly where he's going: straight to the pilots' table, because he like everyone here knows pilots by sight alone, or else he just sees that barrier of awareness, that do-not-cross, and makes up his mind to cross it—and Parry does nothing.

No, that's not true. Parry does nothing but watch. He knows what's happening, none better; and he makes no move to interfere.

That's unprecedented. He can't have been bribed; this is his place, and what could you possibly offer him that's worth more?

Unknown territory makes uncertain ground. There's a breathlessness all over, people watching Parry watching the newcomer as he steps up, as the pilots lift their heads from that odd little conversation they're having.

They look, and see that they don't know him, and for a moment that is oh so unexpected, they don't know what to do else. Then they remember, one by one but in rapid succession, that this is Brone's table. So all their heads turn its way, relieved of responsibility, curious to see what it will do in their stead.

Unhurried as ever, Brone extends a hand—at least, two visible fingertips emerging from a fold in its swathe of blankets—and a welcome with it, gesturing towards the vacant seat opposite.

Parry never comes to take orders at the table, never—but he comes tonight, and stands at the man's shoulder with that kind of patient submissive authority that demands the attention of those on whom it waits.

He looks so ordinary, this man: there's nothing to him, no reason for any of this.

No observable reason.

Until he speaks, until he says "I don't want a drink, I never drink in port—and I couldn't pay you anyway," which is more honest than many a proprietor would expect.

Parry takes it in his stride, or rather in his stillness. Quite comfortably, he says, "The first one's on the house, always. And no one at this table drinks alcohol in port."

All of which goes to say one thing, and one thing only: and Parry might be down on eavesdroppers, but somehow everyone in the place hears that one thing, as it goes entirely and graciously unsaid.

The newcomer's a pilot after all. For all that he came in without a ship.

First Ferrel goes off with Mercy Mercy, and now this. Someone must have brought him in—but why? Any pilot can always find a ship. We have too many lying idle, when there are always passengers to ferry and cargo to shift, one end of the Limb to the other. There are a dozen here in Dock right now, their owners bidding high for any pilot's time, desperate to see their craft in service. The same is true at every station, every port of call.

Here he is, though, a pilot who didn't fly here, who must have been no more than a passenger in someone else's journey. Parry knows. Maybe Brone knows too. Maybe there's something about a pilot, something detectable, known to others of their craft. And to Parry, obviously.

Maybe he's just been talked about between themselves. Maybe he was hot gossip from the moment he arrived, and they've all been waiting to see him show up. Sooner or later, every pilot in Dock steps off the Margin and into Parry's, if only just to catch their breath before they dive back in.

He asks for honeymint, which may be the humblest request any pilot has ever made in here. Parry nods, doesn't bat an eye, but there's a murmur all around. Maybe no one's conspicuously eavesdropping, but no one's talking either, they're trying to absorb the conversation by osmosis; and he seems keen to help. His voice is extraordinary: a baritone that holds its own music, that strikes pure through every syllable and resonates throughout the space, through people's heads as though it were their own proper note each time, entirely personal and entirely true.

Honeymint is good for the throat, but he really, really doesn't need it.

Except—well, is that a tremolo in his voice, or is it just a tremor? Certainly there's a tremor in his fingers, where he lays them so neatly, so carefully along the edge of the table. Here as elsewhere, every head is turned his way; here as elsewhere, every voice is hushed and waiting, leaving space for his. Maybe some of them only want to hear him speak again, and never mind the matter. Maybe. Pilots aren't usually so susceptible, but there's nothing usual happening here.

Brone gestures again, and this time maybe with an open hand, palm up. If it has palms, or hands. Nothing's certain, where there's almost nothing to be seen: a muffled movement within the fabric, perhaps another glimpse of fingers.

It's enough, seemingly. Or he was going to talk anyway, invited or otherwise. Just like he was going to approach anyway, he was going to push his way in. He has a seat, he has a drink on its way: both of those might be superfluous, might not have been needful at all. Not to the purpose. He might be all about the purpose.

He says, "My name is Almarine. I dislike to break in on you, but my need is urgent. I—I am a stranger to you, but…"

Even such a voice can lose its words, it seems, and die away, leaving a sense of absence that's both intolerable and insurmountable. No one is in a hurry to fill that vacancy, knowing how they must inevitably disappoint, however wisely they speak. Cadence should perhaps not matter so much, but sometimes—this time—yes, it truly does.

If anyone ever wants to tell you that pilots have no vanity, that they can't afford it—well. Laugh in the idiot's face. Even Almarine's silence has a mellow musicality to it, the attentive thrumming silence of a classic instrument, and not one of these wants to set their chicken-scratch voices against that, like an affront.

"You are a pilot."

Perhaps it had to be so, that Brone came forward at the last. Brone's table, after all; and Brone so seldom speaks, this wasn't so much an opportunity as a sucking vacuum. They hardly know what it sounds like, any of its cohort here; its voice is as much a shock as Almarine's, though for different reasons.

A figure so large, you'd expect it to boom hollowly, but it doesn't. There's a great deal of flesh in its voice, an unexpected wetness, a sense of marsh life where you'd think more of the high desert plains, as much of the dust and dry as you can imagine, who have never been to a Shutterself habitat.

"A pilot, yes." Almarine confirms it, and seems likely to go on, and then falls short of words again.

"Then whatever you need, in this place it is yours." And *this place* might mean Parry's establishment, or the Margin at large, or Dock or the whole station or the whole of human space: it's still a truth, plain and simple. It's not quite *carte blanche,* it's not *whatever you want*—but a pilot's need, any need, oh yes. If it's humanly possible, that will be met—and if it's not humanly possible, then it's not a need, by definition.

"I need a ship," he says—and then holds his hand up to stay them, to hold back the whole table. A little late: someone's laughing, someone's rolling their eyes, only Brone is showing no emotion at all. Brone's a rock. But

Almarine goes on, "I mean, I need a ride. On someone else's ship. I can't, I can't do this alone. Not again."

And now no one's laughing, though their degrees of puzzlement or denial are probably no easier to take. Once again they leave this in Brone's hands, as though it were dependable, a rock. It says, "What, that you will not do? Pilots fly."

That's the criterion, really, that everything turns upon. *Whatever you need,* yes—but you do have to fly. For preference you have to get where you're going, with more or less what you were given—the ship, the passengers, the cargo—in more or less working order. Within tolerances, at least, in all particulars. Pilots have come in to the wrong port with the ship and the people and the goods too strangely changed; but they flew, and they survived.

Rock bottom, if you're a pilot, you really do have to fly.

Unless you're Brone, of course. Brone's unique, which is why there can't be two.

"You don't have to fly alone," Murun says, sounding almost considerate for once. It's a matter that touches him deeply, of course; maybe that makes a difference. He curls a hand around Telfer's wrist, and smiles, and for that little moment he's almost not an asshole.

"I do," says Almarine, and it might almost be his tragedy; certainly it is his sorrow, if not its cause. "I have to be alone. I," and this is really no news, now that they've heard his speaking voice, "I sing my way through n-space. The music of the spheres is quite literal to me: from planet to planet, and from star to star. Someone else with me would...not be in tune."

Nods around the table. None of them could do that, or even understand it, but it makes perfect sense. They know a pilot who sees her path and draws it, a sequence of rapid sketches that somehow carries her and her craft along. If sketches, why not song? And if Murun needs Telfer, then of course another might need solitude.

"So," Maellelin says, "why can't you fly alone, if you have to be alone to fly?"

"I come from Reynmark's Star," he says slowly. "I grew up a planet-hopper, singing cargoes back and forth. I was happy there." More nods. Everyone knows

Reynmark's, it's a constant port of call. A dozen ports of call, more habitable planets than any other system in human space, and enough traffic between them to sustain its own small navy, its own coterie of pilots.

To sustain, of course, does not mean *to keep.*

"I was offered better ships and a better life, if I would only go further. I was happy, but. The music of the planets was extraordinary; what might, what must the music of the stars be like? I could only ever hear Reynmark's Star, in-system. I thought there must be more, they must all sing in chorus; I thought I could join that chorus. I thought I had to hear it. I thought I only had to hear it, to know it. I thought it was the song the Sirens sang…"

"So?"

"So I took an offer, I took a ship to go far and far, from one end of the Limb to the other. The further I went, the greater the music, you see? I wanted to hear all the galaxy sing to me…"

"And?"

"And I heard all the galaxy sing to me, and it was the most dreadful terrible thing in my life," and they know how that feels, none better, though none of them can ever hope to hear what he's heard. Each of them in their different ways has confronted n-space, and each of them has found it appalling, each and every time.

That's the other reason why they're treated very, very well. They go through hell out there, every time they go; we have to counter that with some little taste of heaven, every time they make it back, or why would they ever go?

Conversely, they do actually have to go, to justify their status. Everyone at this table—well, except for Brone, who is a law unto itself—does that, over and over. There's not much sympathy to be found here, for a man who won't.

"Aww, did it scare you, diddums?" Murun, being an asshole, as advertised.

Almarine looks at him, and something causes Murun to fall quiet, which may be the thing least expected in this most unexpected evening.

Parry brings Almarine's drink, and he sips it, holds it in his throat, almost seems to gargle it before he swallows. Must be a singer thing.

He says, "The planets around Reynmark's Star were like, like plainchant: organised, methodical, a unity. Anyone with an ear could sing with them. The star itself was grander, symphonic, still within my compass. I thought the stars at large would be like that. I thought I could reach them. I thought I could *aspire*." Even that magnificent voice can crack, seemingly. Another sip of honeymint, another pause. "I was wrong. I could barely survive the stars."

"And yet you did. We do." Maellelin, laying down the bare base fact of it like a card that could never be trumped.

"Not me. Not again. I came too far, I heard too much… I need to go home. In other people's ships, and small jumps. However long it takes. I can still hear them, even when I'm just a passenger. Not so, not so vividly, not inside me, blood and bone, but still. I hear them. And I can only stand so much."

He stares around the table, looking for contempt and finding that—Murun, yes, but not Murun alone: this isn't asshole territory, this is earned, the achievement of weakness, of broken oaths and neglected duty—and more, a kind of weary dismissal, *if you're choosing not to be a pilot, why are you sitting at our table?* Pilots have *noblesse oblige* written into their DNA—literally, in some instances—and they're very sensitive to betrayal.

"The stars leave their scars on us all." That's Brone again, saying more tonight than he might have said in a month before this.

"Not the stars," Almarine counters, and this, now: this is what he's here for. What he's here to say. Why he needs that ride so very, very much. Three short words, in that voice, with that emphasis: they were half turned away from him already, but now they're turning back as he goes on, "The others. The voices, singing their own way between the stars. They're out there, and I hear them."

"No." That's Ten Barry, and you could say that he's invested here. "No two pilots have ever worked n-space the same way," except themself, perhaps. If that's what happens when you clone. "We never heard of another pilot singing. We never heard of any pilot singing, until now."

"Not one of us," says Almarine, and this is what they were all listening for, what none of them wanted to hear. "Not human. Their voices, their chord-sequences, their tonality—nothing human. But singing, yes, and doing what I do, riding the music from star to star. I can't bear to hear them, but I am sure. They're everywhere, out there."

And that's the thing, there's the moment. You could call it first contact, except it's not. Just a footfall on the stair, the sound of someone else's passage. All this time, all this space, nothing but human traffic, they had almost begun to believe themselves alone; and here's this sole voice—this extraordinary voice, but never mind that—to tell them it's not so. To say there's some other culture, creature, civilisation out there. Doing what he does, but doing it routinely: training up pilots the way we train up doctors or managers or civil engineers. Or barkeeps.

Here's Parry, and if anyone actually eavesdrops here, that would be him, so it would hardly count. The world or life or the universe just changed, something just changed radically, human perspective, turning over on itself; and he's here taking orders for fresh drinks, offering snacks from the kitchen, saying, "So, will one of you be taking Almarine on, the next step, towards home?"

And they all look at each other, still swimming from the revelation; and of course it's Brone, because Brone is talkative tonight where they apparently cannot be, who says, "I will find a ship, and take Almarine home. All the way. With pauses, when he needs them."

Which is unprecedented, more than implausible; which would have broken their understanding of the very way things are, if that weren't already lying in shatters about their feet; and which none of them, not one of the pilots at the table there needs so much as a moment to understand, to acknowledge, to accept.

Because it's the human thing to do.

QUINQUEREME OF NINEVEH

BIRDS CARRY SEEDS, MERCHANTS CARRY WORD of other lives. Civilisations rise on trade, exchange, cargoes: it's all about the traffic.

As a little boy I loved to go for a family hike up the mountain, but what was best in the day came early and late, going up and coming down. Our path crossed a motorway, as we left the city; and what I would anticipate beforehand and remember after was standing with my hands clenched around the railings of the bridge, gazing down, seeing cars and trucks and coaches hurtle beneath me, this way and that. Uncounted strangers, unimaginable lives: all their individual errands and needs and urges dragging them into this common rush, this sense of progress, traffic.

I could have stood and watched them go for ever.

Apparently, I still can.

THIS particular night I should have been one among them, man in car, one pixel in the glow. It would have made far better sense. But no: I had to be a boy again this night, this one night, this world of waiting.

I was lucky, I suppose, that I could walk to work. Every time, it felt like walking into the future: from what had been my parents' house throughout my childhood—with a pause, a ritual pause on the footbridge, look down at the road, watch the traffic—and then up and over the mountain.

The bridge at night was more of a teenage memory, a cluster of us kicking our legs above the traffic, staying out as late as we dared, passing cigarettes and cans up and down the line and talking, talking. And always looking down.

Apparently, kids still do that. I passed a bunch of them rail-hugging like my own private ghosts and wanted to stop, wanted to say *look up, look up!*— but we never did, they never would and there was nothing to see yet in any case, against the light-stain of the city's glow.

Besides, they were no ghosts of mine. Their future was on a different track. Tonight more than ever I felt like a dead end, an evolutionary sideshow.

Pass them by, then, and never mind the whispers, the giggles at my back. I'd have giggled too.

Up the winding path, difficult in the dark but my feet remembered; and found it less steep than they remembered, that sudden shock of adulthood still lingering even in middle-age. You think you've made adjustments, fitted the world to your new scale, and you're still wrong.

There should have been crowds on the peak, whispers and hush, a lingering anticipation.

Two men there were, with a single boy between them. Telescopes and cameras, they had the works, and the amateur enthusiasm to go with: but still. I thought the night deserved better.

I bade them a soft good evening and went on by.

The other side of the mountain, all the broad sweep of the airfield lay below me: more lights, a lure, *duty calls*. Truly, though, all my work now was waiting, and I could do it just as well up here.

No telescope, no camera, but I had brought my binoculars, and I did know just where to look. There was old reliable Orion, there his belt and the sword of his belt; and there, what was that, a smudge on the scabbard, a new jewel, an adornment...?

Even then, I barely needed the binoculars. After an hour, they were swinging disregarded from my neck while I just looked. Not a new star, no. Not a supernova. Not a comet, not an asteroid inbound, nobody's calamity.

Traffic.

I stood there and watched it all the way in. By the time it was clearly a ship, a starship, alien and unique, there were people all over the mountainside at last, rowdy with alcohol or trainspotter-fussy about detail, where I thought they should all be hushed with respect.

Too much to ask. When the sun came up, when I went down, I was picking my way through a litter of discarded cans and burger-wraps, thinking *it should have been champagne and oysters, you owed them that at least...*

I should have been fighting my way through a scrum of press and public, and I wasn't. That was the worst of it, almost, that almost nobody cared.

Almost the worst.

WHEN everything had cooled enough, the ship's door finally cracked open and alien figures came stalking down a ramp. For them this was a great event, a culmination, the pursuit of many lifetimes; and waiting for them, what they found was me.

Greeting them impossibly in their own tongue.

Knowing their ancestries in detail, the long course of generations from their home star to ours.

"We are not the first?" they said, bereft. "We thought we were the first..."

"You were...overtaken." By information, by the speed of light: messages that could be translated, understood. Machines that could be built. Instantaneous transfer, across a terrible span.

Traffic.

What need ships, when we could send people, news, tech and luxuries across the galaxy at the touch of a button?

Isolated in their unreachable vessel, they didn't know and couldn't be told. On and on they had sailed, redundant already, their histories known and their trade goods long superseded.

People massed on the scorched tarmac at my back, and the newcomers tried to draw comfort from that. "These, who are they in their eagerness, in their want?"

"Oh," I said. "Those? Those are archaeologists."

THE ASTRAKHAN, THE HOMBURG AND THE RED RED COAL

"**P**ARIS? PARIS IS RUINED FOR ME, alas. It has become a haven for Americans—or should I say a heaven? When good Americans die, perhaps they really do go to Paris. That would explain the flood."

"What about the others, Mr Holland? The ones who aren't good?"

"Ah. Have you not heard? I thought that was common knowledge. When bad Americans die, they go to America. Which, again, would explain its huddled masses yearning to be free. But we were speaking of Paris. It was a good place to pause, to catch my breath. I never could have stayed there. If I had stayed in Paris, I should have died myself. The wallpaper alone would have seen to that."

"And what then, Mr Holland? Where do good Irishmen go when they die?"

"Hah." He made to fold his hands across a generous belly, as in the days of pomp—and found it not so generous after all, and lost for a moment the practised grace of his self-content. A man can forget the new truths of his own body, after a period of alteration. Truly Paris had a lot to answer for. Paris, and what had come before. What had made it necessary.

"This particular Irishman," he said, "is in hopes of seeing Cassini the crater-city on its lake, and finding his eternal rest in your own San Michele, within the sound of Thunder Fall. If I've only been good enough."

"And if not? Where do bad Irishmen go?"

It was the one question that should never have been asked. It came from the shadows behind our little circle; I disdained to turn around, to see what man had voiced it.

"Well," Mr Holland said, gazing about him with vivid horror painted expertly across his mobile face, "I seem to have found myself in Marsport. What did I ever do to deserve this?"

There was a common shout of laughter, but it was true all the same. Marsport at its best is not a place to wish upon anyone, virtuous or otherwise; and the Blue Dolphin is not the best of what we have. Far from it. Lying somewhat awkwardly between the honest hotels and the slummish boarding-houses, it was perhaps the place that met his purse halfway. Notoriety is notoriously mean in its rewards. He couldn't conceivably slum, but neither—I was guessing—could he live high on the hog. Even now it wasn't clear quite who had paid his way to Mars. The voyage out is subsidised by Authority, while those who want to go home again must pay through the nose for the privilege, but even so. He would not have travelled steerage, and the cost of a cabin on an aethership is…significant. Prohibitive, I should have said, for a man in exile from his own history, whose once success could only drag behind him now like Marley's chains, nothing but a burden. He might have assumed his children's name for public purposes, but he could not have joined the ship without offering his right one.

No matter. He was here now, with money enough for a room at the Dolphin and hopes of a journey on. We would sit at his feet meanwhile and be the audience he was accustomed to, attentive, admiring, if it would make him happy.

It was possible that nothing now could make him exactly happy. Still: who could treasure him more than we who made our home in a gateway city, an entrepôt, and found our company in the lobby of a cheap hotel?

"Marsport's not so dreadful," the same voice said. "It's the hub of the wheel, not the pit of hell. From here you can go anywhere you choose: by canal, by airship, by camel if you're hardy. Steam-camel, if you're foolhardy. On the face of it, I grant you, there's not much reason to stay—and yet, people do. Our kind."

"Our kind?"

There was a moment's pause, after Mr Holland had placed the question: so carefully, like a card laid down in invitation, or a token to seal the bet.

"Adventurers," the man said. "Those unafraid to stand where the light spills into darkness: who know that a threshold serves to hold two worlds apart, as much as it allows congress between them."

"Ah. I am afraid my adventuring days are behind me."

"Oh, nonsense, sir! Why, the journey to Mars is an adventure in itself!"

Now there was a voice I did recognise: Parringer, as fatuous a fool as the schools of Home were ever likely to produce. He was marginal even here, one of us only by courtesy. And thrusting himself forward, protesting jovially, trying to prove himself at the heart of the affair and showing only how very remote he was.

"Well, perhaps. Perhaps." Mr Holland could afford to be generous; he didn't have to live with the man. "If so, it has been my last. I am weary, gentlemen. And wounded and heart-sore and unwell, but weary above all. All I ask now is a place to settle. A fireside, a view, a little company: no more than that. No more adventuring."

"Time on Mars may yet restore your health and energy. It is what we are famous for." This was our unknown again, pressing again. "But you are not of an age to want or seek retirement, Mr... Holland. Great heavens, man, you can't be fifty yet! Besides, the adventure I propose will hardly tax your reserves. There's no need even to leave the hotel, if you will only shift with me into the conservatory. You may want your overcoats, gentlemen, and another round of drinks. No more than that. I've had a boy in there already to light the stove."

That was presumptuous. Manners inhibited me from twisting around and staring, but no one objects to a little honest subterfuge. I rose, took two paces towards the fire and pressed the bell by the mantelshelf.

"My shout, I think. Mr Holland, yours I know is gin and French. Gentlemen...?"

No one resists an open invitation; Marsporter gin is excellent, but imported drinks come dear. The boy needed his notebook to take down a swift flurry of orders.

"Thanks, Barley." I tucked half a sovereign into his rear pocket—unthinkable largesse, but we all had reasons to treat kindly with Barley—and turned to face my cohort.

On my feet and playing host, I could reasonably meet them all eye to eye, count them off like call-over at school. Hereth and Maskelyne, who were not friends but nevertheless arrived together and sat together, left together every time. Thomson who rarely spoke, who measured us all through his disguising spectacles and might have been a copper's nark, might have been here to betray us all except that circumstances had shown, time and time again, that he was not. Gribbin the engineer and van Heuren the boatman, Poole from the newspaper and the vacuous Parringer of course, and Mr Holland our guest for the occasion, and—

AND our unannounced visitor, the uninvited, the unknown. He was tall even for Mars, where the shortest of us would overtop the average Earthman. Mr Holland must have been a giant in his own generation, six foot three or thereabouts; here he was no more than commonplace. In his strength, in his pride I thought he would have resented that. Perhaps he still did. Years of detention and disgrace had diminished body and spirit both, but something must survive yet, unbroken, undismayed. He could never have made this journey else. Nor sat with us. Every felled tree holds a memory of the forest.

The stranger was in his middle years, an established man, confident in himself and his position. That he held authority in some kind was not, could not be in question. It was written in the way he stood, the way he waited; the way he had taken charge so effortlessly, making my own display seem feeble, sullen, nugatory.

Mr Holland apparently saw the same. He said, "I don't believe we were introduced, sir. If I were to venture a guess, I should say you had a look of the Guards about you." Or perhaps he said *the guards,* and meant something entirely different.

"I don't believe any of us have been introduced," I said, as rudely as I knew how. "You are...?"

Even his smile carried that same settled certainty. "Gregory Durand, late of the King's Own," with a little nod to Mr Holland: the one true regiment to any man of Mars, Guards in all but name, "and currently of the Colonial Service."

He didn't offer a title, nor even a department. Ordinarily, a civil servant is more punctilious. I tried to pin him down: "Meaning the police, I suppose?" It was a common career move, after the army.

"On occasion," he said. "Not tonight."

If that was meant to be reassuring, it fell short. By some distance. If we were casting about for our coats, half-inclined not to wait for those drinks, it was not because we were urgent to follow him into the conservatory. Rather, our eyes were on the door and the street beyond.

"Gentlemen," he said, "be easy." He was almost laughing at us. "Tonight I dress as you do," anonymous overcoat and hat, as good as a *nom de guerre* on such a man, an absolute announcement that this was not his real self, "and share everything and nothing, one great secret and nothing personal or private, nothing prejudicial. I will not say 'nothing perilous', but the peril is mutual and assured. We stand or fall together, if at all. Will you come? For the Queen Empress, if not for the Empire?"

The Empire had given us little enough reason to love it, which he knew. An appeal to the Widow, though, will always carry weight. There is something irresistible in that blend of decrepit sentimentality and strength beyond measure, endurance beyond imagination. Like all her subjects else, we had cried for her, we would die for her. We were on our feet almost before we knew it. I took that so much for granted, indeed, it needed a moment more for me to realise that Mr Holland was still struggling to rise. Unless he was simply slower to commit himself, he whose reasons—whose scars—were freshest on his body and raw yet on his soul.

Still. I reached down my hand to help him, and he took it resolutely. And then stepped out staunchly at my side, committed after all. We found ourselves already in chase of the pack; the others filed one by one through a door beside the hearth, that was almost always locked this time of year. Beyond lay the unshielded conservatory, an open invitation to the night.

An invitation that Mr Holland balked at, and rightly. He said, "You gentlemen are dressed for this, but I have a room here, and had not expected to need my coat tonight."

"You'll freeze without it. Perhaps you should stay in the warm." Perhaps we all should, but it was too late for that. Our company was following Durand like sheep, trusting where they should have been most wary. Tempted where they should have been resistant, yielding where they should have been most strong.

And yet, and yet. Dubious and resentful as I was, I too would give myself over to this man—for the mystery or for the adventure, something. For something to do that was different, original, unforeseen. I was weary of the same faces, the same drinks, the same conversations. We all were. Which was why Mr Holland had been so welcome, one reason why.

This, though—I thought he of all men should keep out of this. I thought I should keep him out, if I could.

Here came Durand to prevent me: stepping through the door again, reaching for his elbow, light and persuasive and yielding nothing.

"Here's the boy come handily now, just when we need him. I'll take that, lad," lifting Barley's tray of refreshments as though he had been host all along. "You run up to Mr Holland's room and fetch down his overcoat. And his hat too, we'll need to keep that great head warm. Meanwhile, Mr Holland, we've a chair for you hard by the stove…"

THE chairs were set out ready in a circle: stern and upright, uncushioned, claimed perhaps from the hotel servants' table. Our companions were milling, choosing, settling, in clouds of their own breath. The conservatory was all glass and lead, roof and walls together; in the dark of a Martian winter, the air was bitter indeed, despite the stove's best efforts. The chill pressed in from every side, as the night pressed against the lamplight. There was no comfort here to be found; there would be no warmth tonight.

On a table to one side stood a machine, a construction of wires and plates in a succession of steel frames with rubber insulation. One cable led out of it, to something that most resembled an inverted umbrella, or the skeleton of such a thing, bones of wind-stripped wire.

"What is that thing?"

"Let me come to that. If you gentlemen would take your seats…"

Whoever laid the chairs out knew our number. There was none for Durand; he stood apart, beside the machine. Once we were settled, drinks in hand—and most of us wishing we had sent for something warmer—he began.

"Nation shall speak peace unto nation—and for some of us, it is our task to see it happen. Notoriously, traditionally we go after this by sending in the army first and then the diplomats. Probably we have that backwards, but it's the system that builds empires. It's the system of the world.

"Worlds, I should say. Here on Mars, of course, it's the merlins that we need to hold in conversation. Mr Holland—"

"I am not a child, sir. Indeed, I have children of my own." Indeed, he travelled now under their name, the name they took at their mother's insistence; he could still acknowledge them, even if they were obliged to disown him. "I have exactly a child's understanding of your merlins: which is to say, what we were taught in my own schooldays. I know that you converse with them as you can, in each of their different stages: by sign language with the youngster, the nymph, and then by bubbling through pipes at the naiad in her depth, and watching the bubbles she spouts back. With the imago, when the creature takes to the air, I do not believe that you can speak at all."

"Just so, sir—and that is precisely the point of our gathering tonight."

In fact the point of our gathering had been ostensibly to celebrate and welcome Mr Holland, actually to fester in our own rank company while we displayed like bantam cocks before our guest. Durand had coopted it, and us, entirely. Possibly that was no bad thing. He had our interest, at least, if not our best interests at heart.

"It has long been believed," he said, "that the imagos—"

"—imagines—"

—to our shame that came as a chorus, essential pedantry—

"—that imagos," he went on firmly, having no truck with ridiculous Latin plurals, "have no language, no way to speak, perhaps no wit to speak with. As though the merlins slump into senescence in their third stage, or infantilism might say it better: as though they lose any rational ability, overwhelmed by the sexual imperative. They live decades, perhaps centuries in their slower stages here below, nymph and naiad; and then they pupate, and then they hatch a second time and the fire of youth overtakes them once more: they fly, they fight, they mate, they die. What need thought, or tongue?

"So our wise men said, at least. Now perhaps we are grown wiser. We believe they do indeed communicate, with each other and perhaps their water-based cousins too. It may be that nymphs or naiads or both have the capacity to hear them. We don't, because they do not use sound as we understand it. Rather, they have an organ in their heads that sends out electromagnetic pulses, closer to Hertzian waves than anything we have previously observed in nature. Hence this apparatus," with a mild gesture towards the table and its machinery. "With this, it is believed that we can not only hear the imagos, but speak back to them."

A moment's considerate pause, before Gribbin asked the obvious question. "And us? Why do you want to involve us?"

"Not want, so much as need. The device has existed for some time; it has been tried, and tried again. It does work, there is no question of that. Something is received, something transmitted."

"—But?"

"But the first man who tried it, its inventor occupies a private room—a locked room—in an asylum now, and may never be fit for release."

"And the second?"

"Was a military captain, the inventor's overseer. He has the room next door." There was no equivocation in this man, nothing but the blunt direct truth.

"And yet you come to us? You surely don't suppose that we are saner, healthier, more to be depended on...?"

"Nor more willing," Durand said, before one of us could get to it. "I do not. And yet I am here, and I have brought the machine. Will you listen?"

None of us trusted him, I think. Mr Holland had better reason than any to be wary, yet it was he whose hand sketched a gesture, *I am listening*. The rest of us—well, silence has ever been taken for consent.

"Thank you, gentlemen. What transpired from the tragedy—after a careful reading of the notes and as much interrogation of the victims as proved possible—was that the mind of an imago is simply too strange, too alien, for the mind of a man to encompass. A human brain under that kind of pressure can break, in distressing and irrecoverable ways."

"And yet," I said, "we speak to nymphs, to naiads." I had done it myself, indeed. I had bespoken nymphs on the great canals when I was younger, nimble-fingered, foolish and immortal. For all the good it had done me, I might as well have kept my hands in my pockets and my thoughts to myself, but nevertheless. I spoke, they replied; none of us ran mad.

"We do—and a poor shoddy helpless kind of speech it is. Finger-talk or bubble-talk, all we ever really manage to do is misunderstand each other almost entirely. That 'almost' has made the game just about worth the candle, for a hundred years and more—it brought us here and keeps us here in more or less safety, it ferries us back and forth—but this is different. When the imagos speak to each other, they speak mind-to-mind. It's not literally telepathy, but it is the closest thing we know. And when we contact them through this device, we encounter the very shape of their minds, almost from the inside; and our minds—our *individual* minds—cannot encompass that. No one man's intellect can stand up to the strain."

"And yet," again, "here we are. And here you are, and your maddening machine. I say again, why are we here?"

"Because you chose to be," and it was not at all clear whether his answer meant *in this room* or *in this hotel* or *in this situation*. "I am the only one here under orders. The rest of you are free to leave at any time, though you did at least agree to listen. And I did say 'one man's intellect'. Where one man alone cannot survive it without a kind of mental dislocation—in the wicked sense, a disjointment, his every mental limb pulled each from each—a group of men working together is a different case. It may be that the secret lies in strength, in mutual support; it may lie in flexibility. A group of officers made the endeavour, and none of them was harmed beyond exhaustion and a passing bewilderment, a lingering discomfort with each other. But neither did they make much headway. Enlisted men did better."

He paused, because the moment demanded it: because drama has its natural rhythms and he did after all have Mr Holland in his audience, the great dramatist of our age. We sat still, uncommitted, listening yet.

"The enlisted men did better, we believe, because their lives are more earthy, less refined. They live cheek by jowl, they sleep all together and bathe together, they share the same women in the same bawdy-houses. That seems to help."

"And so you come to us? To *us?*" Ah, Parringer. "Because you find us indistinguishable from common bloody Tommies?"

"No, because you are most precisely distinguishable. The Tommies were no great success either, but they pointed us a way to go. The more comfortable the men are with each other, physically and mentally, the better hope we have. Officers inhabit a bonded hierarchy, isolated from one another as they are from their men, like pockets of water in an Archimedes' screw. Cadets might have done better, but we went straight to the barracks. With, as I say, some success—but enlisted men are unsophisticated. Hence we turn to you, gentlemen. It is a bow drawn at a venture, no more: but you are familiar with, intimate with the bodies of other men, and we do believe that will help enormously; and yet you are educated beyond the aspiration of any Tommy Atkins—some of you beyond the aspiration of any mere soldier, up to and including the generals of my acquaintance—and that too can only prove to the good. With the one thing and the other, these two strengths in parallel, in harmony, we stand in high hopes of a successful outcome. At least, gentlemen, I can promise you that you won't be bored. Come, now: will you play?"

"Is that as much as you can promise?" Thomson raised his voice, querulous and demanding. "You ask a lot of us, to venture in the margins of madness; it seems to me you might offer more in return."

"I can offer you benign neglect," Durand said cheerfully. "Official inattention: no one watching you, no one pursuing. I can see that enshrined in policy, to carry over *ad infinitum*. If you're discreet, you can live untroubled hereafter; you, and the generations that follow you. This is a once-and-for-all offer, for services rendered."

There must be more wrapped up in this even than Durand suggested or we guessed. A way to speak to the imagines might prove only the gateway to further secrets and discoveries. If we could speak directly to the chrysalid pilots of the aetherships, humankind might even learn to fly ourselves between one planet and another, and lose all dependence on the merlins…

That surely would be worth a blind eye turned in perpetuity to our shady meeting-places, our shadier activities.

Mr Holland thought so, at least. "Say more, of how this process works. Not what you hope might come of it; we all have dreams. Some of us have followed them, somewhat. I am here, after all, among the stars," with a wave of his hand through glass to the bitter clarity of the Martian night sky. "How is it that you want us to work together? And how do we work with the machine, and why above all do we have to do it here, in this wicked cold?"

"To treat with the last first: Mr Heaviside has happily demonstrated here as well as on Earth, that aetheric waves carry further after dark. We don't know how far we need to reach, to find a receptive imago; we stand a better chance at night. Besides, you gentlemen tend to forgather in the evenings. I wasn't certain of finding you by daylight."

Someone chuckled, someone snorted. I said, "I have never seen an imago fly by night, though. I don't believe they can."

"Not fly, no: never that. But neither do they sleep, so far as we can tell. All we want to do—all we want you to do—is to touch the creature's mind, fit yourselves to the shape of it and find whether you can understand each other."

"I still don't see how you mean us to achieve that?"

"No. It's almost easier to have you do it, than to explain how it might be done. We're stepping into an area where words lose their value, against lived experience. It's one reason I was so particularly hoping to enlist your company, sir," with a nod to Mr Holland, "because who better to stand before the nondescript and find means to describe it? If anyone can pin this down with words, it will be you. If anyone can speak for us to an alien power—"

"Now that," he said, "I have been doing all my life."

The run of laughter he provoked seemed more obligatory than spontaneous, but came as a relief none the less. Durand joined in, briefly. As it tailed away, he said, "Very well—but there is of course more to it than one man's dexterity with language. Our wise men speak of the, ah, inversion of the generative principle, as a bonding-agent stronger than blood or shared danger or duty or sworn word—but again, there is more than that. You gentlemen may be a brotherhood, drawn from within and pressed close from without; we can make you something greater, a single purpose formed from all your parts. The wise men would have me flourish foreign words at you, *gestalt* or *phasis* or the like; but wise men are not always the most helpful.

"Let me rather say this, that you all have some experience of the demimonde. By choice or by instinct or necessity, your lives have led you into the shadows. This very hotel is a gateway to more disreputable ventures. There is an opium den behind the Turkish bath, a brothel two doors down. I do not say that any of you is a libertine at core: only that the life you lead draws you into contact and exchange with those who avoid the light for other reasons.

"I will be plain. Mr Holland, you have a known taste for absinthe and for opium cigarettes. Mr Parringer, laudanum is your poison; Mr Hereth, you stick to gin, but that jug of water at your elbow that you mix in so judiciously is actually more gin, and you will drink the entire jugful before the night is out. Mr Gribbin—but I don't need to go on, do I? You each have your weaknesses, your ways of setting yourselves a little adrift from the world.

"We need to take you out of yourselves more thoroughly in order to bind you into a single motive force, in order to create the mind-space wherein you might meet an imago and make some sense of it. I have brought an alchemical concoction, a kind of hatchis, more potent than any pill or pipe or potion that you have met before."

He laid it on a tray, on a table that he set centre-circle between us all: a silver pot containing something green and unctuous, an array of coffee-spoons beside.

"Something more from your wise men, Mr Durand?"

"Exactly so."

"I'm not sure how keen I am, actually, to swallow some hellbrew dreamed up in a government laboratory." Gribbin leaned forward and stirred it dubiously. There were gleams of oily gold amidst the green. "Does nobody remember *The Strange Case of Dr Jekyll and Mr Hyde?*"

"'Can anyone forget it?' should rather be your question," Mr Holland observed. "Stevenson was as much a master of delicate, fanciful prose as he was of a strong driving story. But he—or his character, rather, his creation: do we dare impute the motives of the dream unto the dreamer?—he certainly saw the merits of a man testing his own invention on himself, before bringing it to the public." Even huddled as he was against the ironwork of the stove, he could still exude a spark of knowing mischief.

Durand smiled. "I would be only too happy to swallow my own spoonful, to show you gentlemen the way—but alas, my duty is to the device, not to the *entente*. You will need me sober and attentive. Besides which, I am not of your persuasion. I should only hold you back. Let me stress, though, that senior officers and common troops both have trod this path before you, and not been harmed. Not by the drug. Think of the hatchis as grease to the engine, no more; it will ease your way there and back again. Now come: I promised you adventure, and this is the beginning. Who's first to chance the hazard?"

There is a self-destructive tendency in some men that falls only a little short of self-murder. We have it worse than most; something not quite terror, not quite exhilaration drives us higher, faster, farther than good sense ever could dictate. Some consider it a weakness, evidence of a disordered nature. I hope that it's a badge of courage acquired against the odds, that we will fling ourselves from the precipice in no certain knowledge of a rope to hold us, no faith in any net below.

Of course it was Mr Holland who reached first, to draw up a noble spoonful and slide it into his mouth. No tentative sips, no tasting: he was all or nothing, or rather simply all.

The surprise was Parringer, thrusting himself forward to do the same, gulping it down wholesale while Mr Holland still lingered, the spoon's stem jutting from between his full contented lips like a cherry-stem, like a child's lollipop.

Where Parringer plunged, who among us would choose to hold back? A little resentfully, and with a great many questions still unasked, we fell mob-handed on the spoons, the jar, the glistening oleaginous jelly.

IT was bitter on my tongue and something harsh, as though it breathed out fumes, catching at the back of my throat before it slithered down to soothe that same discomfort with a distraction of tastes behind a cool and melting kiss. Bitter and then sour and then sweet, layer beneath layer, and I couldn't decide whether its flavours were woven one into another or whether its very nature changed as it opened, as it bloomed within the warm wet of my mouth.

He was right, of course, Durand. Not one of us there was a stranger to the more louche pleasures of the twilit world. Myself, I was a smoker in those days: hashish or opium, anything to lift me out of the quotidian world for an hour or a night. In company or alone, sweating or shivering or serene, I would always, always look to rise. Skin becomes permeable, bodies lose their margins; dreams are welcome but not needful, where what I seek is always that sense of being uncontained, of reaching further than my strict self allows.

From what he said, I took Durand's potion to be one more path to that effect: slower for sure, because smoke is the very breath of fire and lifts as easily as it rises, while anything swallowed is dank and low-lying by its nature. I never had been an opium-eater, and hatchis was less than that, surely: a thinner draught, ale to spirits, tea to coffee. Sunshine to lightning. Something.

If I had the glare of lightning in my mind, it was only in the expectation of disappointment: rain, no storm. I never thought to ride it. Nor to find myself insidiously companion'd—in my own mind, yet—where before I had always gone alone.

Even in bed, even with a slick and willing accomplice in the throes of mutual excess, my melting boundaries had never pretended to melt me into another man's thoughts. Now, though: now suddenly I was aware of minds in parallel, rising entangled with mine, like smoke from separate cigarettes caught in the same eddy. Or burning coals in the same grate, fusing awkwardly together. Here was a mind cool and in command of itself, trying to sheer off at such exposure: that was Gribbin, finding nowhere to go, pressed in from every side at once. Here was one bold and fanciful and weary all at once, and that was surely Mr Holland, though it was hard to hold on to that ostensible name in this intimate revelation. Here was one tentative and blustering together, Parringer of course...

One by one, each one of us declared an identity, if not quite a location. We were this many and this various, neither a medley nor a synthesis, untuned: glimpsing one man's overweening physical arrogance and another's craven unsatisfied ambition, sharing the urge to seize both and achieve a high vaulting reach with them, beyond the imagination of either. Even without seeing a way to do that, even as we swarmed inconsequentially like elvers in a bucket, the notion was there already with flashes of the vision. Perhaps Durand was right to come to us.

Durand, now: Durand was no part of this. Walled off, separated, necessary: to us he was prosthetic, inert, a tool to be wielded. He stood by his machine, fiddling with knobs and wires, almost as mechanical himself.

Here was the boy Barley coming in, no part of anything, bringing the hat and overcoat he'd been sent for. At Durand's gesture he dressed Mr Holland like a doll, as though he were invalid or decrepit. Perhaps we all seemed so to him, huddled in our circle, unspeaking, seeming unaware. The truth was opposite; we were aware of everything, within the limits of our bodies' senses. We watched him crouch to feed the stove; we heard the slide and crunch of the redcoal tipping in, the softer sounds of ash falling through the grate beneath; we felt the sear of heat released, how it stirred the frigid air about us, how it rose towards the bitter glass.

"Enough now, lad. Leave us be until I call again."

"Yes, sir."

He picked up the tray from the table and bore it off towards the door, with a rattle of discarded spoons. Durand had already turned back to his machine. We watched avidly, aware of nothing more intently than the little silver pot and its gleaming residue. We knew it, when the boy hesitated just inside the door; we knew it when he glanced warily back at us, when he decided he was safe, when he scooped up a fingerful from the pot's rim and sucked it clean.

We knew; Durand did not.

Durand fired up his machine.

WE had the boy. Not one of us, not part of us, not yet: we were as unprepared for this as he was, and the more susceptible to his fear and bewilderment because we were each of us intimately familiar with his body, in ways not necessarily true of one another's.

Still: we had him among us, with us, this side of the wall. We had his nervous energy to draw on, like a flame to our black powder; we had his yearning, his curiosity. And more, we had that shared knowledge of him, common ground. Where we couldn't fit one to another, we could all of us fit around him: the core of the matrix, the unifying frame, the necessary element Durand had not foreseen.

DURAND fired up his machine while we were still adjusting, before we had nudged one another into any kind of order.

He really should have warned us, though I don't suppose he could. He hadn't been this way himself; all he had was secondhand reports from men more or less broken by the process. We could none of us truly have understood that, until now.

We weren't pioneers; he only hoped that we might be survivors. Still, we deserved some better warning than we had.

WE forget sometimes that names are not descriptions; that Mars is not Earth; that the merlins are no more native than ourselves. We call them Martians sometimes because our parents did, because their parents did before them, and so back all the way to Farmer George. More commonly we call them merlins because we think it's clever, because they seem to end their lives so backward, from long years of maturity in the depths to one brief adolescent lustful idiocy in the sky. When we call them imagos—or imagines—because they remind us of dragonflies back home, if dragonflies were built to the scale of biplanes.

Which they are not. The map is not the territory; the name is not the creature. Even redcoal is not coal, not carbon of any kind, for all that it is mined and burned alike. We forget that. We name artefacts after the places of their manufacture, or their first manufacture, or the myth of it; did the homburg hat in fact see first light in Bad Homburg, or is that only a story that we tell? Does anybody know? We let a man name himself after his children, after a country not relevant to any of them, not true to any story of their lives. We assert that names are changeable, assignable at whim, and then we attach unalterable value to them.

Durand had given no name to his machine. That was just as well, but not enough. He had given us a task to do, in words we thought we understood; he had laid the groundwork, given us an argument about the uses of debauchery and then a drug to prove it; then he flung us forth, all undefended.

He flung us, and we dragged poor Barley along, unwitting, unprepared.

IT started with a hum, as he connected electrical wires to a seething acid battery. Lamps glowed into dim flickering life. Sparks crackled ominously, intermittently, before settling to a steady mechanical pulse. A steel disc spun frantically inside a cage.

Nothing actually moved, except fixedly in place; and even so, everything about it was all rush and urgency, a sensation of swift decisive movement: *that* way, through the run of frames and wires to the umbrella-structure at the far end of the table. There was nothing to draw the eye except a certainty, logic married to something more, an intangible impulsion. *That* way: through and up and out into the night.

And none of us moved from our places, and yet, and yet. The machine hurled us forth, and forth we went.

If we had understood anything, we had understood that the machine would bring an imago's voice to us, and we would somehow speak back to it, if we could think of anything to say. That would have been Mr Holland's lot, surely; he was never short of things to say.

We had misunderstood, or else been misdirected. Unless the drug seduced us all into a mutual hallucination, and in plain truth our intelligences never left that room any more than our abandoned bodies did. But it seemed to us—to *all* of us, united—that we were shot out like a stone from a catapult; that we streaked over all the lights of Marsport and into the bleak dark of the desert beyond; that we hurtled thus directly into the static mind of an imago at rest.

NO creature's thoughts should be…architectural. Or vast. At first we thought we were fallen into halls of stone, or caverns water-worn. But we had found our shape by then, in the flight from there to here; we might fit poorly all together, but we all fitted well around Barley. And something in that resettling, that nudging into a new conformation, caused a shift in our perspective. A thought is just an echo of the mind-state it betrays, as an astrakhan overcoat is a memory of the lambs that died to make it.

Where we fancied that we stood, these grand and pillared spaces—this was an imago's notion of its night-time world, beyond all heat and passion, poised, expectant. A memory of the chrysalis, perhaps.

Expectant, but not expecting us. Not expecting anything until the sun, the bright and burning day, the vivid endeavour. We came like thieves into a mountain, to disturb the dragon's rest; we were alien, intrusive, self-aware. It knew us in the moment of our coming.

I have seen set-changes in the theatre where one scene glides inexplicably into another, defying expectation, almost defying the eye that saw it happen. I had never stood in a place and had that happen all about me; but we were there, we were recognised, and its awareness of us changed the shape of its thinking.

Even as we changed ourselves, that happened: as we slid and shifted, as we found our point of balance with Barley serving at the heart of all, as we arrayed ourselves about him. Even Mr Holland, who would need to speak for us, if anything could ever come to words here; even Parringer, whose motives were as insidious as his manner. There was an unbridgeable gulf between the imago as we had always understood it, flighty and maniacal, and this lofty habitation. A naiad in the depths might have such a ponderous mind, such chilly detachment, but not the frenzied imago, no. Surely not.

Save that the imago had been a naiad before; perhaps it retained that mind-set, in ways we had not expected or imagined. Perhaps it could be contemplative at night, while the sun burned off its intellect and lent it only heat?

It closed in upon us almost geometrically, like tiled walls, if tiles and walls could occupy more dimensions than a man can see, in shapes we have no words for. We should have felt threatened, perhaps, but Barley's curiosity was matched now by his tumbling delight, and what burns at the core reaches out all the way to the skin. We sheltered him and drew from him and leaned on him, all in equal measure; he linked us and leaned on us and drew from us, in ways for which there never could be words.

WITH so many names for our kind—leering, contemptuous, descriptive, dismissive—we know both the fallibility and the savage power of words. The map seeks to define the territory, to claim it, sometimes to contain it. Without a map, without a shared vocabulary, without a mode of thought in common—well, no wonder men alone went mad here. No wonder men together had achieved so little, beyond a mere survival. Mr Holland might have flung wit all night with no more effect than a monkey flinging dung against a cliff-face, if we had only been a group forgathered by circumstance, struggling to work together. With the drug to bond us, with each man contributing the heart's-blood of himself in this strange transfusion, there was no struggle and we found what we needed as the need came to us.

Whether we said what was needed, whether it needed to be said: that is some other kind of question. Did anyone suppose that the confluence of us all would be a diplomat?

The imago pressed us close, but that was an enquiry. There was pattern in the pressure: we could see it, we could read it almost, those of us with finger-talk or bubble-talk or both. *What lives, what choices? Swim or fly, drown or burn? Swallow or be swallowed?*

We knew, we thought, how to press back, how to pattern a reply. Mr Holland gave us what we lacked: content, poetry, response. Meaning more than words. Sometimes the map declares the territory.

For he who lives more lives than one
More deaths than one must die.

He would have turned the bitterness all against himself, but our collective consciousness couldn't sustain that. We all wanted our share, we all deserved it: all but Barley, who had no hidden other self, who'd had no time to grow one.

Suddenly he couldn't hold us together any longer. Fraying, we fled back to Durand, back to our waiting bodies—and the imago pursued, flying by sheer will in the dreadful night, wreaking havoc in its own frozen body. It followed us to the Dolphin and hurtled against the conservatory where we were anything but sheltered, battering at the windows like a moth at the chimney of a lamp, until the only abiding question was whether the glass would shatter first or the machine, or the creature, or ourselves.

THE INSOLENCE OF CANDLES AGAINST THE LIGHT'S DYING

"GOD, THAT'S SAD," QUIN SAID, STARING at the wall.

He didn't mean it nicely. Nice wasn't a thing that he did much any more; the thinner his voice became, the sharper it thrust. And it wasn't only his voice. The thinner he got all over, the edgier his relationship with the world. A razor-blade scratching down a mirror, was Quin in that last year we had together: doing no real damage—what could he hurt, after all? Not the image, certainly, and not the reality either, razors can't score glass—but trying hard none the less.

We were standing in the hallway of my uncle's house and both of us were staring at the wall, both feeling further even than we'd come, a very long way from anywhere that we understood.

My uncle Jarrold had been dead six months, so it shouldn't have been him who had marked the wall, the scratches looked too fresh; but what did I know? Maybe erosion worked more slowly up here than it did down south, or else the house had gone into mourning at his death. Maybe more than the clocks had been stopped.

Oh, it was sad, as Quin said, what some unseen hand had dug deep into the paintwork and the plaster; it was the work of some sad and sorry bastard, and it sure as hell sounded like my uncle.

He is gone, he is gone, I cannot find him. It was a cry from the heart, in letters two feet high; and I knew the sound of that bruised heart in all its grief, its stasis. I knew my uncle's voice as well as any, and sad though it was, though it always had been, I missed it still.

UNCLE Jarrold had lived and died in London, in a bijou little flat close to Parliament Square: a spinster of the Parish of Westminster, he used to call himself when he was in faux-jovial mood. He definitely wanted us to dispute that, to agree with his own unspoken view of himself, that he was a widow, the Widow of Westminster. We never did that even to his face, young and cruel as we were; behind his back we named him the biggest queen in Christendom.

He lived and died in London and was very much a Londoner, of that type that believes all civilization inheres in the capital; but he kept a house in the country also, like the Edwardian gentleman that he so earnestly aspired to be. It was the greatest sorrow of his life, that he had been born fifty years too late to wear a smoking-jacket and have his boots shined daily by the kitchen-boy.

No, it wasn't. That's a ridiculous thing to say. The greatest sorrow of his life was what defined his life, as so often it is; and though he made a good pretence of yearning for a bygone style and nothing more, he made it oh so clear that this was only a pretence, a diaphanous veil that he chose to lay across his heartache. He always took care to let us see the clear light of his pain, shining through that inadequate curtain.

I say us, but I don't mean Quin and me. Quin never met Uncle Jarrold. In those days, when I saw him often, I rarely had the same partner two visits running; he had the right perhaps to scorn me as he did. Even the first time, when he withered me: even then, with hindsight, he was dead on the money.

It wasn't the first time I'd met him, not by a distance. He'd been a constant Christmas presence throughout my life and an occasional visitor at other times, a fat and slightly foolish man who brought sweets more welcome than his kisses were. Smooth of voice and silky-smooth of cheek, smelling of bay rum and good tobacco, handing down boxes of chocolate and candied fruits: those were my childhood memories of Uncle Jarrold. Later, when I was adolescent, he was more interested in me; he'd take me off for the day and give me lunch in a country pub, making great play of seeking out a table in a discreet and shadowy corner where I could safely enjoy a couple of halves of ale. His words, repeated every time. He always used to claim that he'd taught me how to drink; I never bothered to disillusion him.

The first time I went to stay with him, though, the world had changed, or I had changed within it. I was a student then, and deeply snared in my first affair; I hadn't seen Jarrold for a couple of years, and it seemed such an obvious move. I wanted to show off my conquest, to glean approval. No hope of that from my parents, they'd have put us in separate rooms and scowled throughout. Not my uncle, though, or so I thought. I thought he'd rejoice in us, as we rejoiced in the wonder of ourselves.

How wrong can you be?

WE drove all the way from Cambridge, which was an adventure in itself: my first car, the classic student rattlemobile made of patchwork pieces and held together with string, kept going with prayer and overconfidence. Two hundred miles was a lot to ask, but we had that faith that flourishes in ignorance, and never thought twice about it.

Like his flat, like his life, my uncle's holiday cottage—his country house he called it, as we did not—was on an island, and largely cut off from the real world. Splendid isolation, he used to call it, though it was neither.

He'd told us about the tides, in the long letter of direction he'd sent me the week before, but we'd paid no attention to his warnings. We'd ignored the enclosed timetable, started later than we'd meant to and underestimated how long the journey would take; when we finally came to the causeway that should take us across, it was deep dark and our headlights showed us only surging water where the road was meant to be.

Never mind, not a problem. Not a problem in the least. We turned the car and drove a mile, back to the nearest pub. If the tide was high now, it had to be low by closing time, or low enough. Take enough beer on board, we could float across if need be; and there'd be no breathalysers out here. One major advantage of the rural life, though almost the only one we could think of just then.

We scrounged a couple of bacon sandwiches from the landlady, ate her out of crisps and pork scratchings, played a lot of pool and drank without rest; closing-time came and went, and it was near midnight before I thought to check the clock.

Then, too late, I thought we ought to have phoned Jarrold earlier. No point in it now; we'd be on his doorstep in ten minutes. I thought.

In fact, it was closer to half an hour. The causeway was wet still, black and glistening as the sea was on either side, a scary drive to a lad unsober and barely three months past his test; and when we did come to the island, while I'm sure Jarrold's instructions were clear and precise, we were anything but. We got muddled, we got lost, we found the wrong cottage twice before we found the right one.

Brutally late and brutally drunk, I suppose we shouldn't have been surprised at the chill of our greeting, but we were. The young are selfish anyway, and drink can make that worse; I was looking for open arms and a beaming smile, a gesture of dismissal to any casual apology we might have offered, perhaps a "pooh-pooh" and no more.

Which shows just exactly how wrong you can be. Uncle Jarrold was fatter than ever, but no jolly green giant, wrapped though he was in a jade silk dressing-gown with a purring ginger cat in his arms. It was sheer temper that made him throw the door open so wide, no welcome in the world; it was temper too that kept him silent as we staggered cheerfully in with our arms full of rucksacks and carrier-bags. We hadn't given a thought to a gift for our host, flowers or wine or whatever. Hell, we were kids; it showed.

When he did finally speak, after he'd closed the door behind us and thrown the bolts across, it was like a tubby kettle hissing steam.

"Don't begin to apologise," he said, which we hadn't thought of doing. We still hadn't even registered our offence: late, drunk, so what? Who wasn't? "If you don't have the decency to arrive when arranged"—his arrangement, not ours, though we were neither of us in a fit state to point that out—"or to phone through that you'll be delayed, there's no point pretending to have decent instincts of any sort. I hope you're not hungry," though his twitching nostrils told us what our breath was telling him, that we'd filled up on rather more than a couple of halves of ale, "your dinner will be inedible. Perhaps it would be best if you went straight to bed, and we all started again in the morning."

Which we did: up steep twisting stairs to a small room off the half-landing, where a queen-sized bed was squeezed in with chest-of-drawers and bedside table, washstand: all good pieces, he told us, with a watchful frown. Measuring, I thought, to see if we were too drunk to be allowed his guest-room. I almost told him that we were. We had sleeping-bags in the car, and there was plenty enough floor for two downstairs. Far be it from us to trespass where we were unwelcome, among pieces that outranked us.

But he said nothing more, he passed us, if barely; and I was too young or too chicken to force a confrontation. So much easier just to let it go, to listen to his heavy feet climb higher and exchange a speaking glance with Frankie, all apology on my side and longsuffering on his.

Too pissed to suffer long, we slithered in between the sheets and whispered comforts to each other: how we wouldn't stay even as long as we'd meant to, how we'd stick it for a day or two for manners' sake then go on up to Scotland, just the twain, the two of us and let the world go hang, we needed none of it...

SHAGGING on Uncle Jarrold's fine white sheets wasn't even an option; we'd come in hot but his icewater welcome had chilled us, and we were unconscious too soon to think about restoking what was quenched. We just snuggled up and drifted off on each other's beer breath and stubble, and I thought my life complete in spite of crosspatch uncles.

BUT cometh the hour, cometh the man; every hero finds his moment. Uncle Jarrold's came next morning, and he seized it gleefully.

We woke, of course, to monumental grief, two of those hangovers that only the young endure, thank God, because only the young could survive them. Again no question of a good-morning shag: moving was too difficult, moving *hurt*. Lying still was better, huddled against the warmth of Frankie's weight. When I cracked my eyes open, a bar of hard light lay across the lacy counterpane. I winced. We were going to be as late to rise as we'd been to arrive. I could hear movement down below, and foresaw stormy weather.

Nothing to do but endure it when it came. I was in no condition to play the diplomat, too sore of head and sick of stomach to drag myself out of bed. I closed my eyes, and maybe groaned a little. Frankie's hand squeezed my thigh gently, as much as either one of us could manage and as good I thought as anything was going to get.

Until the stairs creaked, too loud, too soon; the door banged open much too loud and much too soon, and there stood Uncle Jarrold.

With a tray in his hands, two steaming beakers and a pot, real fresh coffee: just the smell of it made my dry mouth ache with yearning.

"Up, you idle creatures, get you up!" He set the tray down carefully on the bedside table, with dire warnings against spilling a single drop on his precious linen; added that breakfast awaited us in the kitchen, which was far more than we deserved but that he was in the forgiving vein today; and swept majestically out.

As ever, coffee was sovereign. We sat up with exaggerated caution, cradled hot mugs possessively and sipped, gulped, poured and gulped again. No way would either one of us have let a drop spill, we needed it more than the bedclothes did.

Coffee does more than ale can, to justify man's ways to man. Inside twenty minutes we were up and washed, shaved—at my insistence: Frankie tried to claim holiday privilege, but Uncle Jarrold had earned so much, at least—and relatively sweet of breath and groping our way unsteadily down the stairs.

To be met by another magnificent scent arising, the mingled odours of bacon and something herby, backed by more elixir, essence of coffee. My uncle was at the stove with an apron around his midriff and a wooden spatula in his hand; he waved it at us with an appalling bonhomie and cried, "Sit, sit! Breakfast is immediate!"

Breakfast was. He set plates before us and heaped them with crisp bacon and slices of black pudding, with sausage and fried egg, with tomatoes and mushrooms too. He set a rack of toast between us and said, "Eat, enjoy…"

So we did that. After a minute—or perhaps a couple of minutes—I managed to remember manners enough to mumble, "What about you, Uncle Jarrold, aren't you joining us?"

"Don't speak with your mouth full, Tom. And no, I had my breakfast hours ago. We don't all sleep the best part of the day away. It's nearly lunchtime. I thought I'd take you to the Queen's Head for lunch. Don't talk, eat. You'll need to line your stomachs. Unless your disgusting behaviour of last night has left you unable to face the sight of a few noggins of ale this splendid day?"

To be honest, I at least was still young enough that the thought of more beer could make me queasy; but I was young enough too to deny it fervently, "Hair of the dog, Uncle, it's the best thing," as I reached for another slice of toast. "After food, I mean. These sausages are amazing, I've never eaten anything like them. What's in 'em, do you know?"

"They are good, aren't they? They're pork, of course, with onion and leek. Sage and thyme are the herbs, I believe, though there's another flavour that continues to elude me. Slow cooking is the secret, though. You can't cook a sausage too slowly. These have been on for an hour or more…"

AS he chivvied us out of the house, he raised a mute but expressive eyebrow at the car, and then said, "I must apologize, boys, for the unwelcome I gave you last night. Your behaviour was atrocious, but that doesn't excuse mine. You struck me in a tender spot, though; I am particularly sensitive to unpunctuality. Pray that you do not, but if ever you spend half the night waiting for someone who never comes home, then perhaps you will understand my reaction a little better."

"Oh, please, don't worry about it, Uncle," I said awkwardly. "It was our fault, we got cut off by the tide and never thought to phone."

"I agree, your fault entirely. Unfortunately, it played upon my most fragile sensibilities, and so I lost control. When you know me better, I think you will understand."

And his eyes turned to the wide sea, where it battered and sucked at a shelving shoreline.

THE island was a rocky promontory, inhabited first by monks and monastery servants. Gradually a secular community had grown up around the religious; now the monastery was a ruin, and the locals lived by fishing and tourism. Pubs at both ends of the causeway pretty much depended on the tides for their trade; we had hardly been the first idiots to find the road awash, and ourselves suddenly with hours to kill before we could cross.

The causeway itself, Uncle Jarrold said, had been laid barely a century before, atop the safest of the several known pathways. Before that you took a boat to the island's fishing-harbor, or else you risked your life on foot across the sands.

"The tide comes in at a sprint, boys, so don't you go tempting fate," he said, with solemn tone and meaningful looks from me to Frankie and back to me again. "Nor is the tide the only danger. There is quicksand out there, quicksand that will draw you down and never give you up…"

And he stared out across the flat sands and the rock pools, and I was astonished to see tears in his eyes.

HE took us to the pub—a ten-minute walk from the cottage, but that was universal: nothing on the island was more than ten minutes from anywhere else—and outmatched us pint for pint, and on what was for him an empty stomach too. It was impressive. We tried to pretend we were just slowed down by a heavy night and a heavy breakfast, but truth was he could have drunk us under the table, any night he chose.

That lunchtime, it seemed to me that drinking made him maudlin; later experience suggested that maudlin was his natural frame of mind, or else the state he chose to dwell in. He settled his eyes on us, two young lads sitting closer than we needed to, side by side on a settle, and he sighed mightily. Took a pull on his glass, and turned his eyes to the window, the inevitable view of glistening sand and mud and sea; and said, "You won't know this of me, Tom, your parents won't have told you, but I had a terrible thing happen to me here. A tragedy. A family tragedy, really, only your mother could never see it that way. I lost the one true love of my life, out there on the sands. That's why I keep the house here, why I can never truly leave. This place haunts me so…"

"Unh…" I didn't know what I was supposed to say to that, *do tell?* or what; but it didn't seem to matter. A grunt was enough.

"I wasn't a young man, even then," he went on, "and he was only a few years my junior, but it was a young love that we had; we'd been together barely a year. We both knew that this was the real thing, though, a lifetime commitment. Not like you two, we weren't playing at being men."

I felt Frankie shift in protest, and stilled him with a hand below the table. I wanted to hear this.

"We had arguments, of course, as lovers do. When you've been alone a long time, it's hard to make compromises, and we were both of us stubborn. I have a temper, too—well, that you've seen.

"We had a dreadful disagreement one night; it started from nothing, as these things do, and escalated into savagery on both sides. In the end he stormed out, as he often did. I was too upset to go to bed, so I just pottered around the house and waited for him to return. I knew where he'd be, walking on the sands, cooling off.

"It came on to rain, and I thought he'd come back then, he didn't have a coat. So I fetched a towel for his hair, and waited.

"He didn't come, though. I waited an hour, longer, and still he didn't come. He couldn't have been walking so long, in such weather; I wondered if he'd taken shelter with a neighbor, though it was terribly late. I put on my waterproofs and went out to see. There were no lights burning anywhere, so I went on down to the shore. The tide was coming in strongly, the causeway was entirely underwater already—and there was simply no sign of him anywhere.

"I walked, I shouted his name, I woke all my neighbors and organized a search, but we never found him. Then, or later: his body never turned up. He must have gone out too far in his fury and been caught in the quicksand, or else been outraced by the tide. It was dark, overcast, he might simply not have seen the water coming until it was too late. It was a terrible death, though, either way; and more terrible for me, I think, having to live on with the memories. Such a love only ever comes once in a lifetime, I can't look for so much luck again."

"SO what d'you reckon, then?" Frankie murmured later, as we lagged behind Uncle Jarrold on our way up to the island's height, where he was going to show us the monastery ruins.

"What? Sad story."

"If it's true."

"Frankie…"

"Oh, come on! It's the old 'I have suffered' routine, every faded drama queen has got one. Ask me, if this guy ever existed at all, he just lit out. Hitched a lift off before the tide came in."

"And then what? They were living together…"

"I dunno, do I? Changed his name, dropped out. Emigrated, maybe. Went straight, got married and he's raising kids in Arizona. Wouldn't you? With that to come home to?"

"Frankie, you're a bastard."

"Yeah, right. That's why you love me. But honestly, Tom, it's a fairytale. It's got to be. Christ, he didn't even tell us his true love's *name,* didn't you notice?"

I grinned, and slipped my hand into his back pocket. "We're not worthy."

LATER still, a lot later, long after the sun had sunk in glory behind the mainland, Frankie pleaded exhaustion and took himself off to bed, leaving me alone with my sad uncle and a bottle of malt. Looking for an excuse to follow, thinking that tonight we might just sully Jarrold's pure linen sheets, I slugged back my shallow share of the whisky and said, "Well, Uncle? Do you approve?"

"Approve? Of what?"

"Frankie. Frankie and me. God, I don't half love that boy…"

And that was when he ripped into me.

"Love? Love, do you call it? Don't insult me, Tom. Don't parade your adolescent conquest and call it by a holy name. You greedy, mocking apes—oh yes, I know you've been laughing at me behind my back, I'm neither blind nor deaf—you animals, what do you know of love? You sit there straining your jeans, your mind's already up there with him, you can't wait, you're almost drooling with impatience to get your hands on his body—and you dare, you *dare* to call that love? Immature lust, physical obsession—it's nothing, do you hear me? Nothing! A tissue paper tango, and it'll burn out as fast as tissue paper burns and it won't even leave ashes on your tongue. Don't talk to me of love till you at least know what the word means, even if you haven't braved its touch…"

And so on and on, a tirade—fuelled by whisky, loss and loneliness perhaps, but a tirade none the less—that shrivelled me, that shredded all my certainties. When the brutal run of his words finally ebbed to silence, to a scornful gesture of dismissal, I slunk upstairs and found Frankie genuinely out for the count; and didn't wake him, only laid my cold body next to his and prayed for warmth.

In the morning we left, we went north and west to the wild Scottish coast, and found no comfort in it. So we went our separate ways instead, to our separate homes for what was left of the long vac; and Uncle Jarrold proved to be absolutely right, rot him. Whether he'd sowed the seed of it or not, Frankie and I reaped a fiery harvest the following term, and wrote ourselves into college legend with the force of our mutual destruction.

And no, with hindsight, I no longer called it love, that frail, flickering thing we'd had, that pale light that had seemed to burn between us. St. Elmo's fire, perhaps, fool's gold but no true flame.

IN the years that followed I had other passions and many of them, other flames that seemed to me to burn hot and pure and true. Some of them I took to show to Uncle Jarrold after we'd made our peace, after family feeling and some need in me, in both of us had overcome my pride and his. But I never spoke of love, unless he asked me; and even then I was tentative, uncertain, and ultimately right to be so.

BUT now he was dead, my uncle, and I was his inheritor: of this house, and all that it contained. Which was more and a great deal more than furniture and books and bric-à-brac. *He is gone, he is gone, I cannot find him:* but standing there in Jarrold's absence with Quin shakily at my side it seemed to me as though that *cri de coeur* had cruelly reversed itself. Jarrold was dead, and yet his spirit still pervaded this place and hence my life, I might never be free of him now; and Quin was altogether there, slender fingers clinging to my arm for support, and yet I thought that he was all but gone already. I could almost taste the loss of him, and how that too would be a thing of which I could never be free.

"Come on, love," I said softly, "let's get you settled before I bring the stuff in from the car."

No question of the stairs, he didn't have the leg-power for a shallow flight of steps any longer, let alone that steep climb up. We'd brought a camp bed with us just in case, but memory said there was a luxurious sofa in the living-room, and Quin was very used to nesting.

The sofa was there still, little more worn than when I'd last seen it. I turned it to face the windows and saw Quin comfortable upon it, packed him about with cushions and left him with the radio on and a kiss for company while I hauled in all the gear that we had to travel with, clothes and medicines, food and drink, towels and toiletries and chamber-pot. I could carry Quin up to the bathroom when he needed it, but not at night; no room for two on that sofa, and he wouldn't let me sleep on the floor. Not yet, not while he still had the will to resist. *Later* was a promise I'd made to myself, that I hadn't yet shared with him.

When the gear was all fetched in and distributed, upstairs and downstairs and in my lover's chamber, I asked him, "Are you hungry?"

"No," he said easily, almost cheerfully, recognizing the gambit of a familiar game.

"Well, but will you eat?"

"Some soup? Perhaps?"

"Perhaps so."

So I heated soup from our great supply, added plenty of pepper because he tried sometimes to use the blandness of his diet as an excuse not to eat, and added a wallop of yogurt also in hopes of getting protein inside him somehow. Served it up in one of Jarrold's pretty porcelain bowls—one of my bowls, I supposed, now—and stood over him while he ate.

"What about you?" he asked, dipping his spoon and tasting slowly, every mouthful only a taster and a very long way from a full mouth, using almost more energy to get the food there than he could possibly gain from swallowing it.

"Sick of soup," I said lightly, truthfully. "I'll fix myself a sandwich later."

"You've got to eat," he told me, frowning; and oh, that sounded so good coming from him, I could have cried. Instead I went back to the kitchen, sliced bread and beef and pickles, searched out the horseradish and assembled all into a massive bellyfiller. This was how we lived, largely; he could barely eat solids and I wouldn't cook properly for myself alone, so we got through a small reservoir of soup and I snacked on the side. I'd roasted and brought up a joint of beef big enough to last me a week; I had no plans to stay longer than that. We were really only here to sort through my late uncle's things, to decide what to keep, what to sell and what to burn or throw away. If Quin felt up to it, then I'd take advantage of the chance to show him the island and the coast: to try to show him a little of my uncle's life and what it had meant to me, why I really wanted to keep the house. *Expensive memento*, his first comment had been; and it was true, and I felt a great need to justify it to him.

I hadn't expected to find us both plunged immediately into the sad and sorry heart of Jarrold's obsessive grieving; but it fitted, actually, it was apt. This was how Jarrold was in life, he left no margins, no neutral ground. In death, why should he be different?

I ate with Quin for witness, as he had with me, for me. We both needed that kind of watching. It should have been ironic somehow, but to me at least it only felt right. Of course I forgot my own body and my own needs, in caring for Quin's; of course he took care to remind me. How else should we live?

Reminded, I left him to doze while I went upstairs to get my own room sorted. On the way, inevitably, my eye was jagged by the graffito on the wall. I paused, and touched my finger lightly to one of the gouged letters. There was an immediate fall of plaster-dust onto the carpet. The floor should have been filthy with it already, and was not. There was a light film of regular dust everywhere in the house; I didn't believe that anyone had been in to clean since my uncle's death.

Well. It was another task for me before we left, and a little lighter than it might have been; no more than that. I trotted up to the old guest-room and made the bed quickly, unpacked a few clothes and necessities, hurried back down to Quin.

Found him lightly asleep, as I'd expected. He did little else but drift these days. I'd never told him so, but I hated to watch him sleeping, lying still and silent with his drawn face slack and empty. It was too potent a fore-telling, a premature taste of that time to come when I'd find him emptied indeed, comatose or dead already, and what would I do then...?

The sun was setting vividly outside the window. To save myself sitting and watching him, anticipating a vigil worse to come, I moved quietly about the room setting candles to burn in all the corners; strong lights hurt his eyes, so we lived our long nights out among guttering shadows. It seemed appropriate.

I left the curtains open; moon and stars and distant glows delighted him as much as candle flames and firelight. There was an open fire here, coal and logs and kindling all set ready by my uncle's foresight the last time he left, never foreseeing that he would never return. Quin would enjoy a blaze; I turned to attend to that, and saw his eyes open.

I was caught, trapped, as so often at these moments: bereft of movement or intent, free only to be ensnared. We gazed at each other, and my breath was shallower and more tremulous even than his.

He smiled, before I could; and said, "Well. Here we are, then."

"Yes. At last." I'd had reasons in plenty, not to introduce him to my uncle while Jarrold was alive. Chief among them—or perhaps the sum of all of them—was that simple snare that seized me, choked me time and again in Quin's company. Put it bluntly, say it straight, I was in love; and this love I had never been prepared to expose to my uncle's scathing. Jarrold had been important to me once, his approval had mattered; and for that memory's sake I could never bear to see him so belittle himself.

I sank down against the sofa, propped my elbow beside Quin's shoulder and rested my chin on it. "What shall we do? We could nip to the pub later, if you're up for it."

"No. Not tonight, Tom. It's been a long day."

It had. Too long for him, perhaps, though he'd slept through most of the drive up. "I'm sorry," I murmured, "but I couldn't leave you for a whole week."

"Yes, you could. I've got friends enough, you know that. You just didn't want to come alone."

True, and not true. The whole truth was that practicalities aside, I couldn't bear to leave him for a week; individual days I found hard enough, not knowing what kind of Quin I'd come back to, sharp or dozy, asleep or sick or dead already.

"If you didn't want to come…"

"If I hadn't wanted to come, you'd have sulked and stormed and threatened to stay yourself, to sell the house by proxy, anything to make me change my mind. You know you would. Luckily I did want to come, and I'm glad I'm here. I just can't face company tonight, that's all. Other company than yours, I mean. And that's all the comfort you're getting, and more than you deserve. Get my pills and a glass of water, before you get too comfy; get a drink for yourself and talk to me, okay?"

Better than okay, when such instructions were seasoned with a kiss, as they were. I did all of that and settled down again; and the first thing he said was, "Do you believe in ghosts, Tom?"

Ouch. I didn't want this conversation, not here and emphatically not now; but I never could say no to Quin. Specifically, this time, I couldn't say *no*. "I believe in being haunted," I said slowly. "By the living or the dead, or some dream that was never properly either one of those."

"What, you mean we make our own ghosts?" His voice was a whistle and a whisper, as reedy as any ghost's, a ghost itself of what it used to be. I closed my eyes, and was haunted yet.

"Well, Uncle Jarrold did. All the time I knew him, his lost love was at his heels." And now Jarrold was haunting me, and that wasn't fair, it wasn't right. I was haunted already, I'd brought my own ghost with me, still barely clothed in failing flesh and blood. My own lost love, and that I hadn't lost him yet was only a confusion of the timeline, or else it was God's little joke.

NESTING was one thing for Quin, any convenient sofa, now that he was too weak to manage stairs but still too social to keep to his own bed at home like a good invalid should. Sleeping through the night, now, that was another thing altogether. Another of those little jokes, the ironies of illness: he could sleep at any time of day, all day often, but come the night he was always wakeful. Sometimes I thought that he was frightened of the dark, scared to close his eyes against it, for fear of that greater dark to come when he would close his eyes and never open them again. I never taxed him with it, though, only stayed with him, kept him company as long as I could manage.

That night I fought off my own exhaustion for a while, for a long time, till we'd burned all the fuel on the hearth and watched the fire die to a sullen glow, barely any life left in it. At last he said, "Get yourself to bed, for God's sake. Christ, I can hear your jaw creak every time you swallow a yawn. You think it does me any good, watching your eyes sink to pits while you mumble like a moron? Christ…"

I smiled, kissed his cheek, put out all the candles for safety's sake except for one wee nightlight on a table, and took myself to bed.

And lay wide awake and fretful despite my weariness and the comfort of the bed; and so was still awake when something cracked in the quiet night. A sharp, destructive sound: I was up in a moment and running downstairs naked as I was, confused and anxious, frightened almost.

Stood in the living-room doorway staring in, and saw Quin's head turn to find me. Sobbed one breath in relief, the first I think since I'd heard that sound; and took another, far more calmly, as his acid voice said, "Sorry, sweets, you look nice as anything I've seen for months, but I'd be no use to you tonight."

Nor any night now, not that way, but never mind. "What was it? That noise?"

"I don't know. It was outside, in the street. I'd say someone had put a window out, except I didn't hear footsteps. It wasn't me, at any rate, I haven't broken yet. I haven't broken anything. Go to bed. And sleep this time, will you? Or you'll be no use to me in the morning."

OBEDIENT as ever, I went to bed, I went to sleep. And woke in the late morning, and found Quin dozy but demanding, no change there. I fetched him pills and the coffee he was not allowed to drink, in exchange for his promise to essay a little porridge, which I made. It was an hour or more before I could go outside.

It only took a second to spot what had cracked in the night. The car's windscreen was starred in one corner, as though someone had flung a pebble at it; but out of the crazed glass ran lines of fracture, and those lines spelled out a run of words, *he is gone.*

I stood there looking for a time, for a short time that seemed longer than it should. Then I got into the car and with my elbow I knocked out all the glass in the windscreen, before I went back indoors to phone the RAC.

THAT afternoon I took Quin for a drive around the island, stopping wherever I thought I might be able to beg some empty cardboard boxes: the few shops, the tourist information office, even the parish church. We finished the tour at the pub, which did us proud with crisp-boxes; it seemed only good manners to have a drink while we were there. Quin had a Bloody Mary, the evil of the alcohol—which he was absolutely not allowed to drink—offset, we decided, by the virtues of tomato-juice. I had a pint of my uncle's favorite ale, for old times' sake, and a quiet chat with the landlord. He'd known Jarrold since my uncle first arrived on the island, and offered a tradesman's conventional sympathy for my loss; said he was pleased that I was keeping the house on, and hoped to see plenty of me in the years to come. Plenty of me and my friend, he said. I didn't disillusion him. Instead, I asked the question that had been burning in the back of my head for years, ever since Frankie had set it to smoulder, the question I had never quite dared to ask while Jarrold was around; and yes, he remembered well the night that my uncle's lover had disappeared. Remembered the morning after, at least, the search: had joined in, indeed, as many locals had. Such a sad story, he said, and Mr. Farnon had never really got over it, had he?

No, I agreed quietly, he never really had.

BACK at the house, I piled my booty of boxes wherever I could and set about packing up Uncle Jarrold's things, under Quin's acerbic eye. The books he approved of, at least in theory, though some of the titles justified their existence by drawing a dry chuckle or a snort of amused contempt. The ornaments earned nothing but scorn, even where they were porcelain figurines that carried the stamp of Meissen or Worcester. Quin had no patience with prettiness for its own sake, nor for the sake of market value. I was less precious, except about the packing; all this was money in the bank for me, and Quin was expensive.

I'd meant to leave my uncle's bedroom for the following day, but the work went faster than I'd expected, and having built up a head of steam it seemed a shame to waste it. Besides, that was the one room in the house into which I'd never ventured yet. Curiosity drove me up the stairs, reluctance held me only a moment with my hand on the door before I pushed it open.

It was a dark room, even after I'd flicked the light on: heavy oak furnishings that must have been a trial to manoeuvre up the stairs, faded brown velvet curtains, bare boards with a scattering of rugs. A tester bed, a massive wardrobe—*his clothes, what to do about his clothes? Leave them for now, that's what. Sort them later, give them to Oxfam, whatever*—and another case of books, a dresser with more pretty things on doilies to arouse Quin's happy contempt.

The dresser had a mirror. I saw myself reflected, and thought it likely that I was the first young man to be so framed since Uncle Jarrold's tragedy. I'd been feeling glad, in a strange and not very comfortable way, that the story had proved true, at least in so far as there had been a young man and he had indeed disappeared. It seemed almost to validate my uncle's obsessive sorrow, to justify the emptiness of his life. Ghosts need to be real, to take the bathos away from a haunting.

But now, as I stood there thinking those charitable thoughts—and thinking too, thinking inevitably of Quin and my own haunting to come, which could itself prove lifelong—I saw words form slowly in the mirror, letter by letter, as if an invisible finger moved between the glass and the silvering.

He is gone, he is gone, I cannot find him.

And suddenly I had no sympathy and no pity in me, nor any trace of fear, only a blazing anger. I remembered how Jarrold had hacked at me in my own first gripping passion and I turned it all back on him, on whatever was left of him in this empty house.

"Oh, you shit," I whispered, "you sad, sorry little shit. You had your love and you lost him, yes, to the sea or to a pathetic argument, whatever; and you huddled around that little light and kept it feebly burning, you used that as your excuse against the world for all the rest of your life; and now you dare, you *dare* to shove it in my face, when all you had and all you lost can't hold a candle, not a bloody *candle* to what I've got waiting for me...?"

Tears stung my eyes, but I dashed them away in fury; and snatched up a shepherdess who might very well have been Dresden, only that I didn't stop to examine the base of her, I only flung her full force at the mirror.

More than the glass and the ornament was shattered, in that moment. More than shards of glass and porcelain fell crashing to the dresser, to the floor. I stood breathing heavily amid the silence until I'd stopped shaking, until I had some kind of weak control.

Then I turned and walked out of there, walked softly down the stairs, down all the stairs and into the living-room, that Uncle Jarrold had called his parlour and I would not.

Quin was sleeping, his face turned away from the light. Briefly—as so often at these moments, as ever—I thought he was gone already, I thought I'd never find him again.

STORY NOTES

T O BEGIN WITH, A WORD ABOUT the title: I did in fact write a short story called "Everything, In All The Wrong Order", but it didn't quite make the cut for this collection. I asked if we could still use the title anyway, and Bill Schafer blessedly said yes. (It had been his idea in the first place, before we knew that the story wasn't going to make it in.) So there you have it: this book clearly does not contain everything I've ever written, and we have worked quite hard—with a lot of help from Bill Sheehan—to put the contents into the actually right order, and nevertheless. "That title from a better man I stole," if we assume that past-me was an improvement on current-me; I always liked it, for it is the story of my life. (I have a truly terrible sense of timing: as witness, my first face-to-face with a major publisher, I was summoned to London so that she could explain to me that five years earlier they'd have bought my book with delight, but that particular genre was now dead, so no thanks. Forty-some years later, this is still true. If I'm not behind the wave, I'm ahead of it, alas and hey-ho.)

Uncanny Valley:

I moved to California—indeed, to Silicon Valley—eight years ago at the time of writing, and this is the first story I wrote about it, so it seems appropriate to start here. This is one of the stories written by invitation, for a themed anthology; my abiding thanks are due to Jaym Gates, first for asking and then for some hands-on editing. As sometimes happens, it's a much better story the second time around.

Like many of my stories, it started with the title, which I'd had in my head for some time already, as a notional non-fiction book about the utter strangeness of this place and what it's like to live here. That was to be a partner to my other unwritten non-fiction book, STATE OF GRACE, about the Vatican and its own utter strangeness. Apparently I am interested in small places that are quite unlike any other.

It's not uncommon hereabouts for an unattached title to transmute into another kind of thing altogether, and I knew that I was never actually going to write that book, so...

In Skander, For a Boy:

It may be that I spent my teenage years reading Lawrence Durrell and C P Cavafy, *inter alia*. There may be no finer preparation for manhood—so long as one is prepared to hoard a lifelong obsession with Alexandria.

Quite when I conflated Alexandria with exile, I'm not so certain. Its being a Greek city on an Arab shore may have helped the notion along, especially since the successive collapses of its various imperial overlords, to leave it uncontestably Egyptian and yet still so very Greek. It may have been a simpler transposition, between Cavafy so very much at home there and Durrell so very expatriate. However it came about, the connection is solidly in my head and in my heart together.

Also in my head is a whole bookful of stories about Alexandria under many different names and identities, in many different worlds but still itself. "In Skander, For a Boy" is the first of them. Vikings in the Med!—except not actually Vikings, and not actually the Med, and very much actual Alexandria except that I made it up, except that I didn't.

The Burial of Sir John Mawe at Cassini:

Moving to Silicon Valley was a revelation in many ways; one of the most obvious and easiest to accommodate is the local, almost the vernacular nature of world-leading scientific research and discovery. Our house sits beneath the flightpath to Moffett Field, a bare mile or two from our door; there's a NASA base there, alongside one of the largest freestanding structures in the world (Hangar One, since you ask: eight acres'-worth of building, with its own microclimate and everything). SETI is equally close, walking-distance, and they used to have a weekly symposium where physicists and astronomers and planetary scientists would talk about their latest projects. I attended more often than not, revelling in the way there were occasionally more Nobel-prizewinners in the audience than on the platform, or how two neighbours in my row would be murmuring together about the experiments they had on the next probe to Venus. One happy week the talk was about a new theory of entropy, which if true was clearly a Nobel prize in waiting, and the speaker closed by saying "Right now, there are only two people in the world who believe I'm right, and they're both in this room right now." That was adorable.

This was the time when the Mars Curiosity rover was constantly in the news, so my mind was abuzz with planetary science and exploration; and at the same time there was a conversation going on in the steampunk community, about how the default setting for the genre seemed to be the British Empire under Victoria, and it really didn't have to be that way. Writers were pushing at that particular envelope in all manner of interesting directions—but the further I travel from England, the more English my writing becomes. My mother was the classic child of empire, father in the Scots Guards and stationed out east between the wars, so that Mum was born in Rangoon and grew up in Kuala Lumpur and Singapore, till she was sent home to school as a teenager and never saw her parents for years after. I've always been intrigued by the experience of empire, and I began to interrogate the idea of space travel within that context: if Mars were a province of the British Empire, say, how would that actually have affected its history, both internally and internationally? If George III lost America, but won Mars in lieu? If Victoria had a whole planet in her back pocket...?

I've been asking and seeking to answer some of these questions for a number of years now, and I expect to go on to the end of my days. "The Burial of Sir John Mawe at Cassini" was the first short story to grow out of this project; there have been other stories since, there are novels finished and ongoing, there's a Patreon and a cookbook and a whole lot more besides, but this is where it started, more or less.

The Keys to D'Espérance:

This is one of the fairly rare stories that I wrote purely for its own sake, because it was in my head and I'd rather have it out in the world. I knew it would be an awkward length, and I had no market in mind. What I did have in mind before I finished it was a sequence of stories, all set in the same great house, depicting those changes that had overtaken British society through the twentieth century in a context that didn't change at all.

As it turned out, the story was first sent to press as a chapbook by the then-nascent Subterranean Press, publisher of this very collection and a company I've been proud and delighted to work with at various times in the twenty-some years since.

I didn't pursue the idea of a story-sequence at the time, but ideas like that tend to stay with me, and keep themselves fresh in the back of my mind, waiting for their time. Ten or twelve years later, an editor-friend asked if I'd like to write her some novel-length ghost stories, and of course my thoughts turned immediately to D'Espérance. *House of Doors* and *House of Bells* followed in fairly short order. [For the record, no: these are not haunted-house stories. D'Espérance harbours no ghosts of its own. People bring their own ghosts with them; the house is merely an enabler.]

White Tea for the Tillerman:

Farah Mendlesohn asked me to write something for a chapbook published to coincide with the 2006 Eastercon, the UK's national SFF convention. What the brief was, beyond "short", I do not now recall. But I'd recently been in Lincoln, and climbed Steep Hill, and found a purveyor of teas halfway up;

and as it happened I was curious to learn when tea had first come down the Silk Road from China to Istanbul—or Stamboul, or Constantinople—and if anyone was to know that, surely it should be the proprietor of a shop called Imperial Teas? So I'd gone in, and spent a lovely half-hour talking with him, and came out more than half persuaded that he was actually an elf (long tumbling hair that might very well be hiding pointed ears, an ageless face, and a general impression of walking more lightly on the earth than the rest of us). Also, of course, I came out with some tea: specifically, the first white tea I'd ever encountered. It's been my favourite ever since. And I'd also recently learned of the Chinese habit of calling it "white tea" when in fact they were drinking only boiled water; and hence, this story.

Ashes to Ashes:

David Bowie should have been immortal. It just…seems only right and fair, y'know? None of us should be obliged to live without him in the world.

Still, there he is, gone. With all the grace that he could muster, natch. And in the mourning after, I was contacted by someone wanting to produce a charity SFF anthology, where each story would carry the title of a Bowie song. I said hell yes, I was in, and had anyone claimed "Ashes to Ashes" yet, and if not could I have it?

They hadn't, so I could, and I did, and I ran with it, and this story is the result. To nobody's surprise, it's the first in a sequence. I love bar stories, and I rarely get to write pure science fiction, and it turns out that when I do I want to write space bar stories.

Sadly the anthology never appeared, because reasons, so this is actually the first appearance of the first story about Parry's. It's here because I still really like it, which is all the reason that it needs.

I Am Death's Brother:

This is the oldest story in the collection, by some distance. I wrote it when I was, what, twenty-three, twenty-four? Somewhere around then. I know it was already extant before Tynecon II in 1984, aka Mexicon, because

I let Geoff Ryman read it. Which actually puts him in a fairly small category of readers, for again it hasn't appeared in print before this. I kind of held it close, and never made any serious attempt to publish it. It wins its place here partly for nostalgic reasons and partly for historic ones, because there are threads to be seen here that can be picked out of many and many of my later stories. Fey boys a speciality. ("Fey boys and sensible girls" is how I usually say that, but the girls hadn't arrived yet, seemingly.)

The story was actually inspired by an image, which is rare for me: a poster I had from the Royal Shakespeare Company. To my shame I don't actually remember which play it advertised, never mind which production, but the graphic showed a woman overlaid by the form of a hawk. Oh, and it should also be noted that *Ladyhawke* is my favourite best-ever fantasy movie, but that must be consequent to this, because the movie didn't come out till '85.

Luke, Homeward Angel:

I glory in puns, they delight me. Especially this one, for all its grand impertinence. (Thomas Wolfe shares another small category with Geoff Ryman, viz writers-taller-than-I-am; he was so particularly tall that regular furniture didn't fit him, and he used to work standing up, using his refrigerator as a writing-desk.)

The titular character comes from a novel I wrote, *Dispossession,* back in the long-ago. I occasionally used to wonder about Luke, and his difficult path to redemption; then Kealan Patrick Burke asked me to submit a story to his anthology *Taverns of the Dead,* with an end-of-year deadline. Because procrastination is my prime attribute, I did nothing about it until it was almost too late. I wrote this story on Dec 31st, submitted it by email (was it my first such submission? Possibly; it was certainly among the first, for I remember rejoicing that it was finally possible to push a deadline quite so close, without needing to worry about printers and postage and allowing extra time for the mail to fail and so forth) and promptly went to a New Year's Eve party. From which I returned home in the not-very-early hours of the morning, to find

Kealan's acceptance in my inbox. For years after, that was my fastest-ever sale, and provided my new metric for how the business was changing.

Every Day a Little Death:

Back in the day, m'friend Dr Gail-Nina Anderson used to teach courses in art and literature at the adult-education wing of Newcastle University, and for a number of years I would attend, mostly for the fun of watching her expertise at work. For the literature courses, she fell into the habit of declaring the final session of the term an open-mic, where she and I and anyone else who cared to would read a piece we'd written, inspired by the subject of that term's course. One time, the subject was Terry Pratchett; and this is the story I wrote in response. No kind of pastiche, because no one does Terry but Terry himself; I merely meditated on the character of Death awhile, and remembered one of my favourite pre-Pratchett stories about him, and wrote my own variation.

Another Chart of the Silences:

So one time I was in the pub with m'friend the poet Sean O'Brien, and I'd been working for a while to lure him into writing prose too, and he said, "Y'know, what we should do, Chaz, we should write ghost stories for Christmas and give a reading." I think he had the M R James model in mind, a few selected friends invited for mulled wine and firelight; but the pub was just around the corner from my favourite place on the planet, which is the Lit and Phil: properly The Literary and Philosophical Society of Newcastle upon Tyne, it's a Georgian institution in a Regency building with a Victorian interior (thanks to a devastating fire in 1850), and essentially a private library. I practically lived there for twenty years or so, working in the Silence Room down in the basement, reading upstairs in the spectacular main room. Bringing in my lunch, buying coffee from the hatch, trying to persuade them they really needed a library cat...

Anyway, I asked the librarian if she'd like a Christmas reading of ghost stories, with me and Sean and maybe someone else; and she was all over the idea. So I walked up the hill rejoicing, for I had arranged a gig—and half-way up the hill I met two friends coming down, and one was a curator of art events, bringing funding and venues and creative folks together, and the other was among many things a small publisher. And I told them about the gig, and he said "New ghost stories? I'd be interested in publishing those," and she said, "What you need now is funding," and I turned around and we went back to the pub for a business meeting.

And that was the foundation of Phantoms at the Phil, a reading series which has been running now for more than fifteen years. The original team was Sean and Gail-Nina and me, for I think the first eight years, every Christmas and then at midsummer too. After I decamped for California they started bringing in guest writers, to triumphant acclaim. I'm not proud of much that I've left behind me, but I am inordinately proud of Phantoms.

This is the story I wrote for the inaugural session in December 2004—which sold out so quickly we repeated it after Christmas, played to another full house and could perfectly well have repeated it again.

Terminal:

I don't automatically look for series or sequence potential whenever I have the germ of an idea for a story; some are simply and inherently stand-alones. But my mind does seem to fall into that particular way of thinking, as often as not. I enjoy revisiting worlds or characters, in my own writing and in other people's; I read long series with relish, and I've always wanted one or more of my own. As it happens, I tend to be foreshortened by circumstance, rather than extended; I've published three two-book sequences that should have been trilogies, one trilogy that should have been four books. But the instinct, the sense that there are more stories than one to be told, that stays with me.

In this particular instance, I wrote "Terminal" as a stand-alone and then very strongly felt that I wanted to revisit not that world, and certainly not that character, but that society, the Upshot and the paranoia they invoke. As a result, I wrote the novella *Rotten Row,* and I might yet add a novel, wittily entitled *Germinal.* I know I have the first pages of it somewhere. Though I should probably reread the Zola first. (Now there's a man who could sustain a series: twenty volumes in *Les Rougons-Macquart*...)

"Terminal" was written for the themed anthology *disLocations*, edited by Ian Whates and published by NewCon Press, and was subsequently short-listed for the 2008 BSFA Award for Best Short Story. I am told by the people who count that it actually came in third, so I always feel I went home with a bronze medal, yay.

Keep the Aspidochelone Floating:

Heh. This I confess is a romp, and therefore by definition neither deep nor meaningful. That may be why it's a favourite of mine. It is also (surprise!) part of a sequence: Sailor Martin made his first appearance in "One For Every Year He's Away, She Said", and returned in "'Tis Pity He's Ashore", both of which are significantly darker. Sailor Martin is my Flying Dutchman, always there when I need him.

It will come as no surprise to anyone who has followed me down the years—or simply looked at either of my previous two collections, come to that—that I am obsessed by boats and water, from canals and rivers to the inevitability of the sea beyond. I was born and raised in Oxford, which is almost as far from the sea as you can come in Britain, but it is a city of water-ways and footpaths and punts and rowing boats and motor launches and more; and our grandparents had a beach-house in Essex with a garage beside which their car never penetrated, for it was full of Grandad's boats and fishing-gear. Which is to say that it was a magical cave to me, from the outboard motors to the wooden rollers to the shrimping-nets. I'm still working those treasures into fiction, fifty years and more down the line.

This particular story, though, is rather beyond my small-boat experience; I've only recently spent half a day on a tall ship, brailing up the spanker and so forth. (Best fun ever, if you ever have the chance.) I was invited to con-tribute to a volume of supernaturally-inclined sea-stories, and I was thinking sinister and foreboding thoughts when the editor phoned and said, "Chaz, write me an aspidochelone. I want one, and you're the man I'd trust."

So I did, and it turned into a romp. Because I used to be a serious teenager who read Orwell, I gave it the obvious title; and because I was kind of obsessed at the time by what should have been a much more popular song, I stole its final three words. (If you're curious, search YouTube for "gay pirates" and play the first result.)

From Alice to Everywhere, with Love:

From the longest story in the book to one of the shortest. Rhythm and pace—and changes in both—matter as much in prose as they do in music, and apparently in the ordering of a collection too.

"Alice" is the very definition of a story written for a particular market. *Nature* is a deeply serious journal, often cited in major news items about scientific breakthroughs or discoveries or threats; when I heard that they were publishing short science fiction on the final page of each issue, it wasn't so much a challenge to be attempted as a peak to be achieved. This was the first of three, each of which is collected in this volume, for I am proud of them all.

It's also the very definition of a story written directly to a title. I was walking home from town, thinking *science fiction,* thinking *short,* and I could still take you to the precise point where the title occurred to me. I can't now remember what other work it was echoing—the form, after all, is commonplace—but it came entire, and it embodied everything the story had to be about. So then all I needed do was write it, which was the work of a couple of hours. That's one to put down all the words, and another to take away as many as I could manage. I don't generally subscribe to the notion that less is more; I am a heretic in the classroom, telling students that sometimes less is just less. In this instance, though, there was much chipping-away before "Alice" could come in under 1000 words. Where I have chosen to leave her. Sometimes I restore edits made for some particular publication's particular requirements, but here I think her brevity is very much the point. It's what she would have wanted: no wastage, and pure focus.

Live at Maly's:

This may have been the first story I wrote after my move to California. Certainly it was very early, a commission from Deb Grabien for her Plus One Press. She'd published one anthology of music-based stories, including one by m'wife, and now she wanted to do a second volume. Karen would be in it too, the first time we'd shared a table of contents.

Tales from the House Band was the series title. Which inevitably reminded me of my favourite jazz album, *Live at Small's*. Small's is a legendary little club in New York, run largely as described in the story, if you will allow me a little leeway for fictional purposes. I'd already used it once in a novel—*Desdaemona,* since you ask, published as by Ben Macallan— but it was too good not to use again. The album gave me the title, the opening paragraph gave me the voice; I walked two characters down the stairs and in, and the rest of the story arose in due order from that beginning. Which is how I like my stories, the author going with the reader hand in hand and step by step, really not knowing what lies ahead. Any story is a journey, that the two of us take together. I don't much care about spoilers when I'm reading, but I really don't appreciate them when I'm writing. I like to be surprised.

Going the Jerusalem Mile:

This one's harsh. I don't remember how my life was going at the time, whether I was struggling with anything specific or just with the world in general; but then I'm rarely persuadable that depressed Chaz writes depressing stories, or indeed the reverse. Of course there's an intimate relationship between life-brain and story-brain—I have said it often and often, that every act of fiction is an act of autobiography; we give ourselves away with every word—but it's generally not that clear-cut, and retrospect is an unreliable tool.

The happiest part of this story was its consequence, not its cause. I was contacted after publication by Adriana Díaz Enciso at the Mexican Embassy; she wanted to add this story to a volume she was translating for publication in her home country, and would that be all right? Why yes, I said, that would be fine. Time went by, and funding disappeared, and other obstacles emerged, and I quietly assumed the project had missed its boat; but Adriana went quietly on working at it, dropping me an email every now and then to let me know that it was technically still alive, and then suddenly it really was happening, and the government was supporting it, and it would be launched at the international book fair in Mexico City, and there was funding to bring some of the authors down for the fair, and was I available…?

Why yes, I said, I was indeed. And I went, and a totally lovely week was had by all.

Dragon Kings Play Songs of Love:

Speaking of writerly travels to far-flung places, in the winter of 2000 I got to spend a number of weeks in Taiwan, courtesy of the Taipei City government. Arrangements were complicated, and the desiderata unclear—"a residency", they said, which might mean anything—and I arrived after a long journey grubby, nervous and exhausted. They picked me up in a limo, and told me cheerfully that I'd have five minutes to drop my bags at the hotel (the Ritz, as it turned out) before they took me to a press conference. Now I was really nervous, because I really didn't know what I was here for, only that I hadn't wanted to pass up the chance. Happily, there were a dozen other writers at the press conference, fetched in from all over the world, and it became rapidly clear that this wasn't a residency so much as a symposium, or more accurately a marketing exercise. They wanted photo opportunities while we were there, and then for us to go home and write nice things about Taiwan. Oookay, then…

Three months later I was back at my own expense, sleeping on my interpreter's floor and exploring the city by myself. Home again, I began to study the language and read a lot of books. Later there would be a trilogy of novels—*Dragon in Chains* et seq, published as by Daniel Fox—but first came "Dragon Kings".

For Kicks:

This short, hard story came about much earlier in my career, when I was still a crime novelist. I was having the strangest time of my life, by far: nursing a dying friend through his last difficult, painful year [see "Parting Shots" and "The Insolence of Candles Against the Light's Dying", and the Notes thereon], while at the same time doing an actual job, for the first time ever.

One morning, my phone had been unexpectedly hot with friends calling to say "Chaz, Chaz, have you seen the Guardian this morning? It says 'Chaz Brenchley wanted…'"

What it actually said was "Crime/Thriller writer wanted, for writer-in-residence on Sunderland sculpture project," but that was close enough. Ten miles, as the seagull flies. So I applied, and went through a day of interviews and such with my competitors, and got the job; and for the next year half my time was spent in a Portakabin on a building site, finding ways to combine two wholly different artforms into something that didn't constitute either my describing the sculptures or their illustrating my words.

One aspect of my brief was that I should produce a book while I was there. I took advantage of the opportunity to write a book's-worth of short stories, which wouldn't have been commercially viable else. They're all crime stories, and most of them take place more or less *in situ*. "For Kicks" even references some of the sculptures. [For more details about this, google "St Peter's Riverside Sculpture Project". Colin Wilbourn was the sculptor there, and his work is ongoingly fascinating.]

Parting Shots:

There used to be, and for all I know there still is, a monthly reading series in Newcastle. It took place upstairs in a pub, in a blue room, and it was called the Blue Room reading series. It was open to everyone, but only women were invited to read; that was the point and purpose, to extend opportunities for women.

The woman who organised the sessions was a friend of mine, and one day she collared me at some other event and said, "Chaz, Chaz: we'd like to invite you to come and read at the Blue Room."

I said, "I'd be delighted, Ellen, but, y'know. Isn't it just for women?"

"Mmm," she said, "we talked about that. We decided it should be for women and Chaz."

Then she laid out the requirements of the gig: I'd have to read something completely new, never before seen or heard in any context, and it could not possibly last longer than ten minutes.

Okey-doke, quoth I, and goeth off to think.

What came out of that was this, which is essentially the wake we held for Quin; I like to say that it's a true story, which is why I had to make it up. Also, if you want to see the silver dollar, I have it still. In my pocket, natch. It never leaves me.

A Fold in the Heart:

I've known Mark Morris for many a long year and oft. It's one of those friendships which I guess grow up in any community that covers both the professional and the social, as SFF does. At first we only ever came across each other in context, physically or otherwise: at conventions or book launches or parties, or else sharing a table of contents or a publisher. The advent of social media changed that, as it changed so much; I'm five thousand miles further away now, and much more in touch.

A few years back he got in touch to say that he'd been commissioned to edit the first in hopefully an annual series of new horror anthologies, and would I like to write him a story? Why yes, I said, indeed I would. There is some debate as to whether I was ever truly a horror writer (people used to enjoy telling me that my horror read like fantasy, my fantasy like crime, and my crime—of course!—like horror), but stories are no great respecter of genre classifications. Between the birds and the cliffs and the storm, I thought this probably qualified. Mark was happy to take it, at any rate, and I was delighted with the eventual book; few people know the genre—and its creators—as well as he does, and *New Fears* is a master-work of editorial craft.

At heart, this is a story about havens, and how very, very rarely they are safe.

Winter Journey:

One tries to be professional. One does try. Every now and then, though, a story overrides all sense of propriety or proper management.

I was invited to contribute a story to a forthcoming anthology. I turned in my copy months late and twice as long as it should have been, and the editor laughed at me and said "Chaz, Chaz, I can't take this. It's too late and too long and I just can't fit it in now."

I've shown it to a few people over the years since, and the general consensus has always been that it does belong somewhere, but not actually there.

With the encouragement of certain people hereabouts, it therefore makes its first appearance in this volume.

It owes an immeasurable debt to Kipling, of course, if only for the one line. To claim anything more would be impertinent.

Thermodynamics and/or The Remittance Men:

I did mention, I believe, that I am haunted by Alexandria?

So obviously are the men in this story, which is why they stay in Cairo.

'Tis often thus, I find, that you have to keep that distance if you want to keep that glow.

In Cairo—which is to say, of course, in *this* Cairo—glow is no more an issue than distance is. And to these men, distance comes by nature, by virtue of who they are. Exiles again, though they would say expatriates for the most part: I loved the breed, even before I joined them. I think it was always in my mind, at least in that romantic model that ends with death from consumption, that a writer should leave their homeland if only for the sake of perspective. I did move from the Oxford of my youth to the Newcastle of my adulthood, which is a kind of internal exile; but I needed to be middle-aged and in love and such before I found the courage to do it properly.

Some are born abroad; some achieve travel; some—in large part the men in this story—have exile thrust upon them. For all manner of reasons, with all manner of consequences. Of course they club together. This is another bar story underneath it all, except that instead of a bar it has a whole club.

Freecell:

Once again, this one's down to Farah Mendlesohn. In 2006, the British government introduced a law making it illegal to publish any statement that "glorified the commission or preparation (whether in the past, in the future or generally)" of acts of terrorism. Some of us felt this to be a major infringement of civil liberties and freedom of speech—to demonstrate which, Farah commissioned a couple of dozen of us to write something that deliberately and explicitly broke the law. The resulting pieces she collected into a book, *Glorifying Terrorism;* her introduction to the anthology begins, "The purpose of the stories and poems in this book is to glorify terrorism."

"Freecell" is my contribution to that anthology. It was also the occasion of one of my favourite mentions in a review: Tansy Rayner Roberts said, "it's kind of wrong that a story about suicide bombing should be this damn gorgeous, but that's Brenchley for you."

A Terrible Prospect of Bridges:

Here's another of the early crime stories. In fact, come to think, it may be the actually earliest, the first crime short story I ever wrote. I can't swear to that, but it does seem likely. When I sold my first novel (for values of "first" that include having my own name on the cover and an actual contract on file: it's complicated), I immediately joined the UK's Crime Writers' Association, a group with whom I kept up a mostly happy relationship for twenty-some years; and the best part of the CWA was the Northern Chapter, where I met many of my first writerly friends. We're a vigorous and independent set, we northerners, even we adopted northerners; in '92, under the editorial auspices of Martin Edwards, we published an anthology of our own stories, *Northern Blood*. This story was written for that collection.

It was also the occasion of a Ferocious Argument between m'self and Iain Banks, over a pint in a pub one time: he said "You totally stole my idea," and I said, "Did not, you totally stole mine." Ferocious, I tell you. We had to have another pint to recover.

White Skies:

This was written for another very specific anthology. In *When It Changed,* Geoff Ryman teamed established writers with cutting-edge scientists, to produce stories that took their ideas and ran with them, coupled with pieces by the scientists explaining the rationale and the likely consequences of the actual science.

Me, I got to talk about climate change, and various radical ways to counter it; and I started to wonder how things would fall out if one country went one way and another went in a completely different direction, because for sure there won't ever be a single global authority mandated to supervise international efforts. "White Skies" is the result of that thinking.

When Johnny Comes Marching Home:

This is another of the sub-thousand-word pieces for the back page of *Nature.* I've always been more fond of aftermath than action: what happens when the war is over, for good or ill, recovery or resistance or rebellion, occupation or restoration or retreat. I'm also fond of the mysteries of war, unknown causes and incomprehensible results. There seems to me to be no good reason to assume that an alien species would conduct a war on any recognisable grounds, or by any recognisable means, or...

Where it Roots, How it Fruits:

Another relatively early story, and another written not with a particular market in mind but very much with a proximate cause. I watched a TV documentary about Route 61, and then I couldn't get it out of my head. That's all.

2 Pi to Live:

...and again, this one's filed under "Stories written for the love of the thing", which might also be defined as "Stories which are the very devil to sell" (though this one did draw a very nice rejection letter from the *New Yorker,* which was very much a life goal for me). It's odd, how many of these turn out to be among my favourites. Unless maybe it isn't odd at all...?

Anyway: exploited child-wonder turns middle-aged, good. Traditional fictional travelling fair with sideshows, good. Geeky, fey and inseparable boys, good... Honestly, this just punches so many of my buttons. It felt indulgent to write it; it feels indulgent to include it. I don't care. Indulge me.

[Also, m'wife points out that we live in a slightly pi-obsessed household hereabouts. I always make pies on Pi Day, in a pi dish. Hell, we even have a pi shower curtain...]

Ch-Ch-Changes:

We're back at Parry's for this second Bowie-titled story. The editors—Michael Bailey and Darren Speegle—knew nothing of the first; they simply asked me for a story about the next evolutionary step for humankind, for their themed anthology *Adam's Ladder,* and I couldn't resist it, my mind went straight back to the space bar.

In a moment of self-doubt during the writing process, I did ask Darren if I dared call my story "Ch-Ch-Changes" (I don't believe I explained the Bowie connection even then, just asked without context), and he sent me back a charmingly laconic "Dare." So I did.

He and Michael ended up using this story to open the anthology, which is something of a place of honour. I was deeply chuffed.

Quinquereme of Nineveh:

The third and last of the *Nature* shorts, though in fact I think it was the second to be written and published. More to the point, it's the first story I ever wrote in California, which means in this house. We had arrived. I had jetlag. It was three-thirty in the morning and I was wide awake, and also tolerably uncomfortable because I was sleeping on the sofa and I didn't really fit; so I got up and made coffee and opened the laptop and, um, wrote a story. Which I thought was marginally impertinent, because Karen had only moved in a couple of days earlier and she should really have had the privilege of breaking the house's duck, as it were, penning the first story of her occupation. Still, this happened, and she doesn't seem to mind.

There is some truth in the opening of this story. My childhood home in Oxford, if you walked up the hill to Shotover (a major local landmark, once part of Wychwood Royal Forest, and once boasting a carven giant hill figure, but that was lost before the Civil War, alas), you crossed the ring road by means of a flyover (that's an overpass, I think, in US terms?). I loved that bridge, and some of my best memories of those days are of peering over the railing, watching the cars and lorries rumble this way and that, wondering about all their individual errands. Traffic: I was fascinated by it, then and now. (And there's a similar flyover a very short walk here from our door, which may well have been what put it in my laggy overstimulated mind.)

The Astrakhan, the Homburg and the Red Red Coal:

To start with the title (as I did, as I always try to do): when I was a young man, there was a political theatre group from Scotland called 7:84 (because 7% of the people owned 84% percent of the wealth; that figure would be… different now, for values of "different" that generally mean "worse"). Their most famous work was called "The Cheviot, The Stag and The Black Black Oil", and the rhythm of that title has stayed with me for forty-some years. Obviously, I stole it for this piece.

This is another of my Mars stories. The elevator-pitch rubric for these states that if Mars were a province of the British Empire, then [So-and-so] would absolutely have gone there—where [So-and-so] is a well-known figure generally from the early 20th century with a need or a tendency to travel. It might be T E Lawrence, when he was reinventing himself under other names after the war; camels and deserts, of course he'd go to Mars. It might be A E Housman, who developed a passion for flying in his age and could hardly have resisted another kind of flight altogether. It might be Rudyard Kipling, who simply went everywhere.

In this instance, of course, it's Oscar Wilde. After prison, after Paris— he would so very much have gone to Mars. Under, again, a *nom de guerre*. His wife might have changed his children's names; I saw no reason why he shouldn't do the same, to the same name, for he was a very loving father.

And it was sheer pleasure for me to offer him some kind of redemption, some purpose, once he got there.

The Insolence of Candles Against the Light's Dying:

For the record: I never had an Uncle Jarrold, no. Nor a place on Holy Island, that I could call my own. When we took Quin up there for a week's break—was it a break for him, or for us? or not even a break in routine for either party, only a different view out of the window?—there were half a dozen of us (it was never only me, in his home or in his heart) and the house was a rental, and we hot-bedded: eight hours on shift with Quin and your shift-mate, eight hours to relax or play or explore, eight hours in bed and not a moment more, and strip your own sheets off the bed and make it up for the next in line. It was fun, of course, in a deckhands-at-sea kind of way; and we were incredibly courteous to each other, because we could afford nothing other; and the off-shift team always made sure that there was food and drink and so forth, hot water and a fire against the chill of it. And then we came back to Newcastle, triumphant in a downbeat kind of way, and reinstalled Quin in his own flat and handed over to another shift of carers and scattered to our various abodes and took a real break, saw nothing of each other for a while. Until it was our turn back on duty. That was the strangest year of my life, and the most powerful, and I do still miss it in all its awful attributes, the abrupt horrors and the grim relentlessness of slow decay and the indomitable sense of something done, an ongoing achievement, honour satisfied. And love, I suppose, measured out in dressings and needles and the like. In being there.

I've been writing about it ever since. And avoiding the novel, too, for almost as long. Sometimes, short stories can be enough. Sometimes, they have to be.

COPYRIGHT INFORMATION